Ready for Anything, Anywhere!

BEVERLY BARTON

MERLINE LOVELACE

CATHERINE MANN

MILLS & BOON

First published in Great Britain 2011
by Mills & Boon, an imprint of Harlequin (UK) Limited,
Eton House, 18-24 Paradise Road, Richmond, Surrey TW9 1SR

READY FOR ANYTHING, ANYWHERE!
© by Harlequin Enterprises II B.V./S.à.r.l 2011

His Only Obsession, Stranded with a Spy and *Awaken to Danger* were first published in Great Britain by Harlequin (UK) Limited in separate, single volumes.

His Only Obsession © Beverly Beaver 2007
Stranded with a Spy © Merline Lovelace 2007
Awaken to Danger © Catherine Mann 2006

ISBN: 978 0 263 88344 2

05-0411

Printed and bound in Spain
by Blackprint CPI, Barcelona

HIS ONLY OBSESSION

BY
BEVERLY BARTON

Beverly Barton has been in love with romance since her grandfather gave her an illustrated book of *Beauty and the Beast*. An avid reader since childhood, Beverly wrote her first book at the age of nine. After marriage to her own "hero" and the births of her daughter and son, Beverly chose to be a full-time homemaker, aka wife, mother, friend and volunteer. The author of Romance Writers of America and helped found the Heart of Dixie chapter in Alabama. She has won numerous awards and has made *USA TODAY* bestseller lists.

To the members of my Alabama RWA
chapter, Heart of Dixie, past and present.
Thank you for all the good times we have
shared during the past twenty years.

Prologue

My dearest daughter,

I have asked your mother to give you this letter on your eighteenth birthday. It is my hope that after reading this, you will understand why I have been an absentee father all these years, why I have let you and your mother down, why I feel that I have no choice but to leave both of you in order to continue pursuing a dream that will consume me to my dying day.

Let me try to explain. It all began for me many years ago, long before I met your mother.

There is an ancient legend that tells of a mystical island located somewhere between what is known today as Bermuda and the West Indies. The story has been handed down, from father to son, for generations since before the time of Christopher Columbus. The tales of this island and the unique people who inhabit

it vary. Some say the natives of this island share the same
ancestry as the Mayans and the Incas, others claim they
were the first Europeans to arrive in the New World,
before Columbus. A few even claim that these unique
people originally came from ancient Egypt.

Most people believe the legend is nothing more than
a tale told by dotty old men to awed young children and
gullible adventurers. But a precious few swear the island
exists—out there somewhere, perhaps in the Devil's
Triangle. Some say it has streets paved with gold, while
others claim it is a tropical paradise with crystal-clear
waterfalls and lush vegetation. Although the stories
themselves vary in many aspects, there is one detail on
which all agree. The people of this mysterious, uncharted island—an island with no name—possess an
enviable quality, one the outside world would kill to
obtain: the average lifespan is two hundred years.

The first time I went to the Indies and sailed the Caribbean Sea with my parents and brother, I was a young
man of twenty. I had already chosen my college major—
botany. Nothing fascinated me more than the world of
plants. During our family trip, I collected specimens on
every island, from the Bahamas, Cuba, Jamaica, Barba-
dos, Puerto Rico and even as far north as Bermuda. My
father, a banker, a conservative thinker and a strict disci-
plinarian, did not understand me, and I think, perhaps,
did not approve of the profession I had chosen. But my
mother, sweet, doe-eyed Gwendolyn, who loved Elizabeth Barrett Browning's poetry and adored taking my
brother, Elliott, and me to the movies at least twice a
week, thought I could do no wrong. So, I suppose that
my father and mother balanced each other out.

I shall never forget that special summer…the last summer the four of us were together. Even then, I was amazed that my father actually took an entire month away from his successful, highly demanding job to give his family a once-in-a-lifetime vacation. Looking back, I can see all three of them in my mind's eye. Daddy with his sunburned face and thick, dark mustache. Mama with her straw hat and sunglasses. And Elliott, who had just turned fifteen, with his golden, tanned skin and sun-streaked brown hair.

We heard the legends of the mystic island at every port, each version slightly different, but each equally captivating. Being a realist, with both feet planted firmly on the ground, Daddy said it was superstitious native nonsense. Mama, on the other hand, ever the romantic dreamer, commented on how marvelous it would be to find the island and gain the Fountain of Youth secret.

I was then and am now my mother's son.

Late in June that summer, with less than a week left on our month-long vacation, we boarded the small rental yacht and sailed off from Bermuda, heading south, our destination the Bahamas. It was a warm, balmy day, with only a few fluffy white clouds in the sky. My father had checked weather conditions before leaving port and we expected only blue skies and sunshine for the entire trip. But less than two hours out to sea, we encountered sudden high winds, followed by dark, swirling clouds and an unexpected storm that tossed our yacht about with frightening force. My mother huddled with us belowdecks and prayed without ceasing for what seemed like hours. And then it happened. The yacht caught fire as if repeatedly struck by lightning. My father lowered the single lifeboat and my mother insisted that her two boys go first, which we did with great reluctance.

Everything happened so quickly that to this day, I'm not sure of the details. All I know is that once Elliott and I were in the lifeboat, our parents didn't join us, and the burning yacht sank with unbelievable speed. The choppy waters made it impossible for us to do any good with rowing, so we had little choice but to hunker down and allow the water and wind to take us where it would.

I don't know how long we drifted, how many endless days we went without food or water, but long enough for both of us to become delusional. Eventually we did little but sleep, both of us certain that death was imminent.

And then, on the very day salvation came, I awoke from a deathlike sleep to discover my brother missing. Sometime while I had slept, he had either fallen overboard or deliberately jumped into the ocean.

There I was alone, mourning the deaths of my parents and my only sibling and anticipating my own demise at any moment, when I saw the island. At first, gazing at it through the mist that surrounded it, I thought I had imagined seeing land, that it couldn't be real. I had no idea where I was or if I had possibly drifted south, southeast or southwest; or maybe simply east, out into the vastness of the Atlantic Ocean. Barely able to do more than sit up, I somehow managed to row the small lifeboat toward the island, and with each beat of my heart, I prayed that it was no cruel illusion. Could this be the Bahamas? I wondered. Or had I somehow bypassed the easternmost islands and was now approaching Trinidad? What did it matter? I saw land. I wasn't going to die.

What happened next, in the days and weeks that followed, no one would ever believe. But I ask you, my dear little Gwen, to suspend your disbelief, to open up your heart and mind to the possibility that there are indeed more things on earth than we have ever dreamed possible. There are miracles and magic and wonders to behold. I know these things exist for I have seen the mystical land of legends, met the men and women who live to be two hundred years old, who never suffer the cruelty of illness or deal with the ravages of time. You see, my child, I found the island. I was rescued by its people. And I discovered the secret of their illness-free lives and longevity.

Even then, as a youth of twenty, I longed to bring that miracle back to the rest of the world, but I was denied the privilege. These people do not welcome outsiders and would never willingly have contact with us. And they will kill to protect their secret.

They *have* killed to protect it.

After only three weeks on the island, I was forced to leave. They gave me food and water, then set me out to sea in my little lifeboat. I couldn't understand why they would save my life only to send me back to certain death. But oddly enough, the very next day I was picked up by a fishing vessel off the coast of Cuba. When I told others what had happened to me, about my weeks on the island and how I wanted to head an expedition and return to the island as soon as possible, people laughed in my face. Even the kindest and most caring thought that the legendary island where I'd stayed had been nothing more than a mirage, a figment of my feverish imagination. But I swear to you, it was real. It does exist!

This happened over twenty-five years ago and I have

spent most of those years on a quest to rediscover this uncharted island that lies somewhere between Bermuda and the West Indies. I have spent a great deal of my salary as a botany professor and most of my inheritance from my parents in pursuit of this dream…some may even say obsession. But hear me, daughter, on this island, there is a plant that exists nowhere else on earth that can give us mortals prolonged youth and protect us from illness.

When you read this, I pray you understand and forgive me for abandoning you. I love you and your mother very much, but your mother does not understand me, cannot accept my desperate need to bring this great gift to the world. She, like so many others, has decided that I am mentally unbalanced. Do not believe them.

My hope is that I will have found the island again and brought long life and health to the world's people before you turn eighteen and read this letter. But if not, then I pray that you will believe me and come to me to join me on my quest.

Your loving father,
Emery

Gwen Arnell read the letter, then folded it neatly and returned it to the yellowed envelope. Her father had written this letter eight years ago, shortly after her mother divorced him. Gwen had been ten, and despite the fact that her father had spent most of his time at work or in the Caribbean, she had adored him and treasured those infrequent but precious moments she spent with him. After the divorce, she hadn't seen him again for nearly two years. Sometimes he remembered to send her a birthday present, but often as not he would forget her birthday and Christmas. Every so often, sometimes after a year or longer, he would call for a brief conversation. She had seen him a total of three times since the divorce.

"You seem all right," her mother said. "The letter didn't upset you?"

"No."

"I had no idea what he wrote and wasn't sure how the letter would affect you. But I swore to him that I would give it to you when you turned eighteen."

"Weren't you ever tempted to open it and read it?"

Jean Arnell nodded. "I will admit that the thought crossed my mind, but it wouldn't have been right. It's the only thing your father has ever given you, the only thing he will probably ever give you, so I thought of it as your legacy from him."

Gwen sighed. "Do you truly believe he's crazy, the way all his colleagues believe he is? I realize everyone who knows Daddy thinks he's a fool."

Jean didn't respond immediately, then said quietly, solemnly, "Your father isn't certifiably insane."

"That's not what I asked."

"A tragic incident in his youth affected your father mentally and emotionally. Losing his entire family the way he did…" Jean reached out and took Gwen's hands in hers. "Emery loved me. He loved you. He still loves you, but he can never be the father you want him to be, and I really don't think he can help himself. He has allowed his obsession with finding that nonexistent island and that miraculous eternal-youth plant to consume his entire life."

"But what if the island is real? What if there really is such a plant? It is possible, isn't it?" Gwen wanted to believe in her father's dream, wanted to share it with him.

"I don't think so. There are no known islands anywhere on earth where your father claims this island was. And if it did exist, why has no one else found it in all these years? Why is it nothing more than a legend?"

"I don't know. Maybe Daddy is special, that it was meant for him to be the one to rediscover this place, to—"

Jean grasped Gwen's shoulders and gave her a gentle shake. "No. Do you hear me—no. The island does not exist. The plant doesn't exist."

Gwen looked her mother directly in the eyes. "I want to get in touch with Daddy and ask him if I can go to the West Indies with him this summer and help him in his search."

"Oh, Gwen, sweetie, no. Please, don't allow your father to suck you into his delusional world."

"Don't worry, Mother, the only obsession I have is to get to know my father. He's practically a stranger to me. Sharing a summer with him on his quest could be good for him and for me. Please, try to understand."

Jean squeezed Gwen's shoulders, then released her and said sadly, "You do what you must, but I'm afraid that in the end, he'll break your heart. Do not for one minute believe that you can ever be more important to him than his great obsession."

Chapter 1

Fifteen years later…

As Gwen unlocked her back door, she replayed the message left on her cell phone. "I'm in Puerto Nuevo. You must come here at once. I want you to be with me when I rediscover my island." Her father's voice had vibrated with excitement, the same elated tone she'd heard so many times over the years. "I have people who are interested in backing this expedition, people who believe in me, in my island."

Gwen sighed heavily as she entered her home in Madison, a short drive from the Botanical Gardens in Huntsville, Alabama, where she worked as CEO. Exhausted from trying to put a day and a half's work into one day while worrying about her father, she dropped her keys, shoulder bag, cell phone and briefcase down on the kitchen counter and headed straight to the refrigerator. Whenever a crisis confronted her, she turned to food, especially something sweet. She had spent a lifetime—all of her thirty-three years—fighting to keep her body in shape.

Of course, eating a salad would be the wise choice, but the leftover piece of cake from a recent retirement dinner for a colleague looked mighty tempting. Chocolate. Her favorite.

Grabbing the cellophane-wrapped concoction, Gwen tried to dismiss thoughts of her father's recent phone message from her mind. She seldom heard from him, but when she did, their conversations wreaked havoc on her life for weeks afterward. If only she could accept the fact that her father would never change, that he would forever chase a phantom island and be considered a lunatic by his fellow scientists. A brilliant lunatic, but a lunatic all the same. Gwen had learned years ago, after joining her father on two quests in the West Indies, that she could no more change her father than she could stop the sun from rising in the east.

Before her death ten years ago, her mother, Jean, had exacted a promise from Gwen to keep her distance from Dr. Emery Arnell and his insanity. Gwen had kept that promise, seeing her father rarely and never again joining him on one of his fruitless expeditions. But every year or so he'd call, breathless with anticipation, begging her to be a part of his great discovery, to share in the glory that was soon to be his.

Gwen removed the plastic wrap from the cake, retrieved a fork from a kitchen drawer and headed to the table. Before sitting, she kicked off her two-inch heels and wiggled her toes. Until she'd taken over as CEO of the botanical gardens, she'd worn jeans and walking shoes to work, but now she had to dress more appropriately, something suitable for her position.

Just as she finished the last bite of cake, the phone rang. Bone weary, she decided to let the answering machine take the call. It might be a solicitor. And if it was something about work, she could easily return the call later, after she'd taken a shower and put on her pj's.

The answering machine picked up. "This is Dr. Gwen Arnell. Please leave your name, number and a brief message at the sound of the beep and I will return your call as soon as possible."

"Gwen, darling girl, if you're there, please pick up the phone," Emery said, his voice quivering with emotion. "Everything is coming together for this expedition. My backers are eager for us to begin the journey. I want you with me, daughter, when I sail into the history books as the man who discovered the Fountain of Youth."

Oh, Daddy. Poor Daddy.

"Gwen…please."

She left the crumb-dotted plate on the table, shoved back her chair and stood.

"We'll set sail soon, very soon."

When Gwen reached the phone on the kitchen counter, her hand hesitated, hovering over the base.

"I…I've cashed in my life insurance policy to use as part of the investment, to subsidize this final expedition," Emery said. "But once I bring back the plant and offer it to the world, we will be rich beyond our wildest dreams."

Gwen grabbed the phone. "Daddy, I'm here."

"Gwen, how soon can you get to Puerto Nuevo? My backers are eager to set sail, as are Jordan and I."

"Who is Jordan?"

"Surely you know… Well, perhaps you don't. Jordan Elders is my research assistant. He was one of my students, a very bright boy. He has great faith in me and my plans to find the island. You see, we've come up with a theory as to why I've been unable to rediscover my island all these years."

"Oh, Daddy…"

"No, listen to this. Jordan and I believe that the island isn't visible all the time, only at specific intervals. Perhaps only certain months or even certain years. Maybe only once a year."

"Daddy, I can't come to Puerto Nuevo. I'm sorry, but my job is here in Huntsville. My life is here."

"Are you upset with me for cashing in my life insurance policy? You were my beneficiary, you know."

Gwen groaned silently, her mind reeling off a few well-chosen curse words. "No, Daddy, I'm not upset about that." But she was concerned that her father was practically penniless, that as a retired botany professor his income was enough to live on but not enough to fund repeated trips off into the vast unknown, searching for his Utopia.

"You have vacation time, I'm sure," he said. "Take two weeks. That's all I'm asking. Two weeks."

"Daddy—"

"Gwendolyn Arnell, I swear to you that this trip is the last trip, that this time I will not fail."

"I wish you all the luck in the world. I hope and pray you find your island and fulfill all your dreams, but… I can't—"

"Don't say you can't. Say you'll think about it."

Hesitantly, she agreed. "All right. I'll think about it."

"You've become your mother's daughter, haven't you?" Emery told her, sadness in his voice. "Come to Puerto Nuevo and join me, and open yourself up to possibilities beyond your wildest imagination."

"Where are you staying?" she asked, sighing in frustration. "Say if I were to join you, where would I meet you?"

"We're staying at the Pasada El Paso. It's in downtown Puerto Nuevo. Nothing fancy, but clean and safe. I'll reserve a room for you and—"

"No, don't do that. I'll make reservations, *if* I decide to join you."

"I love you, daughter."

"And I love you, Daddy."

The dial tone sounded. Apparently her father believed he had convinced her to join him. Damn him! How dare he assume she would rearrange her life to suit his needs? When had he ever done that for her? She couldn't remember sharing one birthday with him and not one Christmas since her parents had divorced.

The crazy old fool had cashed in his life insurance policy to help fund this one final folly. What would he do when this adventure turned into yet another failure? And what about these new backers he mentioned? Who in his right mind would invest money in the hare-brained scheme of a seventy-year-old botany professor notorious for having become a laughingstock to his colleagues?

What if these backers were unscrupulous people intent upon taking advantage of her father? What if they intended to rob him of his insurance money and leave him to fend for himself?

Damn it! Why couldn't her father be normal? And why, after the way he had neglected her all her life, did she feel obligated to look after him, to take care of him?

Because he's your father, she reminded herself. And he has no one else.

Gwen spent the next hour getting airline tickets to

Puerto Nuevo, making arrangements to take a week's vacation and packing her suitcase. First thing in the morning, she'd be on a flight to Mexico City, then change planes and fly directly into Puerto Nuevo.

She had no intention of joining her father on yet another quest for glory, fame and riches, but she had to do what she could to protect him from himself and anyone who might harm him.

Will Pierce arrived at Dundee headquarters on the sixth floor of the downtown Atlanta office building at precisely seven-thirty in the morning. The office manager, Daisy Holbrook, had telephoned him an hour ago while he was drinking his first cup of coffee.

"Sawyer wants you in his office immediately," Daisy had said. "He has two new cases and he wants to get agents out into the field ASAP."

When Will exited the elevator, he noted the peculiar quiet and vast emptiness on the floor. He remembered Daisy didn't arrive until eight, and the other office staff didn't usually come in until nine. As he approached Sawyer's office, the sound of voices shattered the early morning silence. He couldn't quite make out the conversation, but he paused at the closed door. Just as he lifted his hand to knock, he heard a loud crash.

"Damn it, Lucie, that was Waterford crystal," Sawyer McNamara said. "That paperweight was a gift."

"So dock my paycheck," Lucie Evans said. "For the paperweight and the glass shelves. I don't care. I'm sick and tired of you foisting off every cheesy assignment on me."

"If you don't like working at Dundee's, then—"

"I'm not quitting," she told him in no uncertain terms.

"You couldn't run me off with a stick. Not even a stick of dynamite."

"Then don't complain, accept your assignment and stop throwing temper tantrums. I'd thought that by now you would have learned to control that hair-trigger temper of yours."

"And I thought that by now you would have stopped punishing me for something that wasn't my fault."

Silence.

Strong, unnerving silence.

The door flew open. Sawyer stood in the doorway, obviously inviting Lucie to leave. When he saw Will, his gaze hardened for a split second.

"You made it here sooner than I'd expected," Sawyer said.

"If you two need more time, I can wait outside." Will wasn't sure what he'd walked in on and didn't want to know. During the year he'd worked at Dundee's, he had learned there was some sort of personal feud between the Dundee CEO and one of his agents, Lucie Evans. Why he didn't fire her or she didn't resign, no one knew. And even more puzzling was why the two seemed to despise each other so vehemently. Taken separately, each was a nice, normal person. Lucie was warm and friendly. If she had one flaw, it was that she allowed her emotions to rule her. On the other hand, Sawyer was aloof, an introvert who didn't socialize with his employees. He often seemed to have no emotions, his actions dictated only by cold logic.

"I was just leaving." Lucie zoomed past Sawyer, not bothering to even give him one of her infamous withering glares. "I'm on my way to Wyoming to investigate cattle rustling."

"Huh?" Had Will heard her correctly?

As if casually dismissing Lucie and the fact that she'd

smashed his Waterford paperweight into the glass shelves along the wall, Sawyer motioned for Will to enter.

"I'm going to need for you to go home, pack a bag and take the Dundee jet straight to Puerto Nuevo this morning." Sawyer tapped the slim file folder lying on his desk. "I just have the basic info right now, but as soon as Daisy comes in this morning, I'll have her compile a more comprehensive file on the case and e-mail it to you."

"Okay. What can you tell me now?"

"Sit."

Will took the chair in front of Sawyer's desk. Sawyer leaned against the edge of the desk and crossed his arms over his chest. Not for the first time, Will thought his boss resembled a model from the pages of *GQ*. One of the older, more sophisticated men who fell just short of being a pretty boy.

"Archer Kress contacted me at six this morning," Sawyer said. "You know who Archer Kress is, don't you?"

"CEO and major stockholder in Kress Petroleum."

Sawyer nodded. "Mr. Kress has a twenty-year-old daughter who went on vacation with some college friends to Puerto Nuevo. The Kress family has a villa there."

"Does he need a bodyguard for his daughter?"

"No, not now." Sawyer grunted. "It seems his daughter, Cheryl, and her friend—" Sawyer paused and opened the folder, glancing at the top file "—Tori Boyd are missing."

"How long have they been missing?"

"Since last night. The girls went out to a local bar yesterday evening and didn't return home this morning. Neither girl is answering her cell phone and Cheryl's car is still parked near the pier where the bar is located."

"Does the family suspect kidnapping?"

"No, not at this point," Sawyer replied. "If they did, Mr. Kress would have contacted the FBI, not Dundee's."

"Does his daughter make a habit of staying out all night? If so—"

"I have no idea what's going on in Mr. Kress's head. All I know is that he's paying Dundee's a small fortune to find his daughter and her friend ASAP. That's all we need to know, so if you fly to Mexico and discover Cheryl and her friend spent the night with a couple of local guys, then that's what I'll report to her father. But if foul play is involved, we don't want to be accused of downplaying any danger to Miss Kress."

"I understand."

"Good. So go home, get packed, pull out your passport and by the time you get to the airport, the Dundee jet will be fueled and ready for takeoff."

Will shook hands with Sawyer, picked up the file folder and headed for the elevator. Just as he punched the down button, the elevator doors opened and Daisy Holbrook emerged.

Daisy was pretty and plump and everyone who worked at Dundee's adored her. Her nickname was Ms. Efficiency.

"Good morning," Daisy said. "I hear you're off to Puerto Nuevo."

"If only I was heading down there for a vacation."

"Mmm…" When Daisy smiled, deep dimples formed in her cheeks. "I'll e-mail you all the info I can dig up on your case. You should have everything by the time you land."

"Hold the fort down while I'm gone."

"I'll try." She moved closer to Will and lowered her voice. "I met Lucie downstairs in the lobby. I hear there's a cleanup needed in Sawyer's office."

Will grinned. "Could be."

"Did you get here in time to see the fireworks?"

"I came in right as they went off."

"One of these days, those two are going to kill each other."

"Oil and water," Will said.

"More like dynamite and a lit match."

Will arrived at the Kress villa by midafternoon, armed with a healthy dossier on the Kress family and Cheryl in particular, as well as info on her friend, Tori Boyd. No matter what people said, the rich were different from everybody else. The villa was located in an exclusive area overlooking the water, an area lined with multimillion-dollar homes owned by wealthy foreigners. Mexico's Yucatán Peninsula had long been a favorite with tourists, even now when some areas were just beginning to recover from the devastation of recent hurricanes. But who could resist white sands and aqua water? Puerto Nuevo was a tropical paradise.

A maid met him at the door, asked his name and business, then escorted him into a massive living room with a twelve-foot ceiling and a wall of glass doors opening up to the terrace overlooking the Caribbean Sea.

"Señor Pierce, from the Dundee Agency," the maid announced.

Two bikini-clad young women, whom he surmised to be in their late teens or early twenties, stared at him with curiosity.

"Wow, you're the private investigator," the willowy blonde said. "Did anyone ever tell you that you look like Matthew McConaughey?"

"Can't say that they have." Will put on his serious I'm-in-charge face. "Cheryl's father is concerned about her. He believes that since she didn't come home last night, she and her friend Tori are missing."

"If he hadn't called to check up on her, he wouldn't have known." The brunette sauntered over to Will and smiled at him. "I'm Courtney and she's Kerry." She indicated the other girl with a nod in her direction. "And you're Will, huh?"

Obviously being rich didn't make you smart, Will thought.

"Yeah, right," he replied. "So, do you two think Mr. Kress overreacted? Don't you think Cheryl and Tori are missing?"

Kerry spread out on the sofa, lounging there as if she was preparing for a photo shoot. Will knew when a woman was trying to get his attention.

"Tori could have hooked up with that guy she's so hot about," Courtney said.

"What guy?"

"Oh, some geek with glasses and an Einstein IQ or something. Tori likes the brainy types."

"Were she and Cheryl meeting up with this guy last night?" Will asked.

"We don't know for sure," Kerry told him. "Courtney and I had dates last night. So Cheryl and Tori headed into town to a local bar where this guy Tori likes hangs out."

"What's the name?"

"Of the bar or the guy?" Courtney asked.

"Both."

"It's actually a bar and a restaurant," Courtney told him. "It's the Fiesta. We don't know what the guy's last name is, but his first name is Jordan and he works for some nutty old man he calls The Professor."

Will finished questioning the two young women as quickly as he could. The longer he was with them, the more he felt like a piece of meat they were thinking about devouring.

"I assume neither of you plans on leaving Puerto Nuevo anytime soon," Will said.

Courtney shook her head. Kerry responded, "We came here for a month-long vacation. We're staying. Anyway, I figure Cheryl and Tori will show up by tomorrow."

By the time Gwen arrived outside the Pasada El Paso in downtown Puerto Nuevo, she was hot and tired and longed for a shower and a soft bed. She'd flown out of Huntsville at six o'clock that morning, made a connection in Atlanta for Mexico City, had a two-hour layover there and finally boarded a plane south. It was now a little after five, local time.

Hoisting the straps of her purse higher on her shoulder and gripping the handle on her small suitcase, Gwen took a deep breath and reminded herself that she would not confront her father first thing. She'd take him out for dinner, and during dessert she'd explain that she wanted to meet his investors. If they turned out to be legitimate, possibly a couple of rich loony-tunes, then she'd return home and let her father have his new adventure. But if she felt the least bit suspicious, she'd put a stop to things immediately, even threaten the would-be investors with the police, if necessary.

The first thing she noticed when she entered the lobby was that it was air-conditioned. Thank goodness. Now, if only the rooms were.

The second thing she noticed was that the lobby was empty. Not a single soul in sight, except the man behind the registration counter. This hotel probably wasn't a tourist favorite.

She walked over to the lone man, smiled and said, "Do

you speak English?" She knew a few words and phrases in Spanish, but didn't know enough to carry on a decent conversation.

"*Sí,* señorita, I speak English," the man replied, his accent heavy.

"I'm Dr. Emery Arnell's daughter. I'm here to join my father. Would you please telephone his room and tell him that I've arrived."

The man smiled. "It will do no good to telephone his room."

"And why is that?" Gwen asked.

"He will not answer the telephone."

"He won't? Why not?"

"Because he is not here. Dr. Arnell left this afternoon."

"He left? Are you saying he checked out of the hotel?"

"*Sí,* señorita. Dr. Arnell and Mr. Elders are gone."

"Where did they go?"

The man shrugged. "I do not know."

"Does anyone here at the hotel have any idea where my father and his assistant went?"

"Perhaps, but I am the only one here now. Ria may know, but she works in the mornings, cleaning the rooms. I saw her speaking to Mr. Elders several times. Very friendly."

Knowing temporary defeat when it slapped her in the face, Gwen nodded, then asked, "Do you have a room available for tonight?"

"*Sí, sí.* You may have your father's room. It is nice and clean and faces the street and not the alley."

"I'll take it," Gwen said. "By the way, is there a restaurant nearby?"

"*Sí.* The Fiesta, down the street." He pointed in the direction. "They serve good *pescado frito* and cold beer. Very cheap."

Gwen thanked him, signed the register and took the key he offered. After dinner she would get some rest, then tomorrow she'd question the day staff and begin searching for her father. God only knew where he'd gone or what kind of trouble he would get into before she found him.

Chapter 2

The Fiesta turned out to be a bar and grill located a block from the hotel and on the opposite side of the street. Loud laughter and the roar of conversation almost drowned out the live band. Although seemingly clean, the place reeked of smoke from cigarettes and cigars. Apparently there wasn't a hostess, so Gwen found a small empty table in the middle of the room, feeling rather conspicuous as a lone American woman among so many locals. But within minutes the waitress who handed her a menu put her at ease.

"Our speciality is *pescado frito,* but I recommend the *empanadas* and a cold beer." The middle-aged redhead spoke with a definite Yankee accent.

"You're an American." The comment popped out of Gwen's mouth.

The waitress grinned. "Sure am. Born and raised in New York. Outside Buffalo to be exact. What about you?"

"I'm from Alabama."

"A Southern belle, huh?"

"Southern, yes. A belle, no."

"You know, you look familiar." The waitress studied Gwen, giving her a once-over, from head to toe. "Have you been in here before tonight? I swear I've seen you somewhere. I never forget a face."

"This is my first night here at the Fiesta and my first trip to Puerto Nuevo."

The waitress grimaced. "It'll come to me. I'll figure out how I know you." She glanced at the menu she'd handed Gwen. "So, what will it be?"

"Oh, the *empanadas* and a cold beer sounds fine."

"Coming right up."

By the time the waitress returned with her meal, Gwen had already declined two invitations, one from a gentleman who wanted her to join him at the bar and the other from a man who had asked if he could join her.

"Here you go." The waitress placed the dish in front of Gwen. "Need a refill on that beer?"

"No, thanks."

"I noticed you've had to deal with a few of our local Romeos. If you wind up with one you can't handle, just let me know."

"Thank you, Ms….?"

"Tammy Peloso, but just call me Tam."

Gwen held out her hand. "It's nice to meet you, Tam, I'm Gwen. Gwen Arnell."

Tam shook her hand, then stepped back, stared at her and laughed as she clicked her fingers together. "Damn, no wonder you looked familiar. You're The Professor's daughter, little Gwendolyn."

"You know my father?"

"Well, can't say that I know him all that well, but he's eaten lunch and dinner here every night for a week now. And he showed me a picture of his little girl once. His precious Gwendolyn." Tam studied Gwen's face. "It was an old picture. You couldn't have been more than sixteen. You were at a pier somewhere. There was a boat in the background."

"Oh, yes, I remember the photograph. It was taken when I was eighteen and went on an expedition with my father."

"Have you come to Puerto Nuevo to join your dad on his search for the lost island?" Tam asked, a hint of humor in her voice.

Gwen sighed. "I've come to find out who his backers are and if they're on the up and up."

"Taking care of the old man, huh? Good for you. He seems like a nice enough old guy, if a little odd. Sorry, but that's the truth."

"No apologies necessary. My father is a bit odd."

"Why didn't he come to dinner with you tonight?"

"I don't know where he is," Gwen admitted. "When I arrived at his hotel, he'd already checked out, and I have no idea where to start looking for him."

"Hmm…" Tam frowned. "Have you checked out the Yellow Parrot? I know The Professor's girlfriend especially likes that place."

Girlfriend? What girlfriend? "What's the Yellow Parrot, another bar and grill?"

Tam chuckled. "It's a bar all right, but they don't serve any food. Just loud music, liquor, street whores and your choice of drugs."

"This woman you refer to as my father's girlfriend—"

"He didn't tell you about her, did he? Can't say I blame

him. She's a lot younger than he is, and my guess is that she's after your old man for his money."

Her father's money? That was a laugh. "Do you think someone at this Yellow Parrot might know where my father is?"

"They might, but if you go there, be careful. It's no place for a lady."

Will checked into his hotel, a local Day's Inn, then set up his computer and contacted Sawyer McNamara with an update.

"There's a possibility the Kress girl and her friend aren't missing," Will said. "It seems the Boyd girl has been chasing after some young guy, and it could be the girls hooked up with him. If that's the case, then it's just a matter of tracking them down."

"I don't think I'll tell Mr. Kress that his daughter might be part of a *ménage à trois* and just lost track of time."

Will chuckled. "Cheryl Kress's friends staying at the villa don't seem concerned. They think her father over-reacted when he found out she wasn't there and they let it slip that she'd been gone all night."

"Kress is a wealthy man. His first thought was probably that someone kidnapped his only child, but when he didn't get a ransom note or call, he came up with other equally frightening scenarios."

"Kidnapping, rape or murder aren't necessarily illogical thoughts," Will said. "Look, Cheryl's friends told me that this guy hangs out at a place called the Fiesta Bar and Grill. I'm heading over there after I freshen up. Maybe someone saw Cheryl and Tori last night and can give me an idea where to find them."

Fifteen minutes later, after shaving, combing his hair and scrubbing his hands, Will headed out of the hotel. He asked the desk clerk for directions to the Fiesta Bar and Grill, which turned out to be less than a five-minute drive from where he was staying.

The exterior of the old building was painted brick red and the front door a bright turquoise. He could hear blaring music and loud voices coming from inside. He went in and headed straight for the bar. If anybody in a place like this knew something useful, it would be the bartender. After ordering a beer, Will flashed a hundred-dollar bill and recent photographs of Cheryl and Tori.

"Have you seen either of these girls recently? Like last night?"

The bartender snatched the hundred bucks from Will's hand, then turned and filled up a tankard of beer and set it on the bar in front of him. "Pretty American girls. The blonde was laughing and talking to a young guy last night and later both girls left with him."

"What time?"

"I do not know."

"Before or after midnight?"

"Before."

"Do you have any idea where they went when they left here?"

The bartender hesitated. Will took a fifty from his pocket. The bartender eyed the bill greedily. When he reached for it, Will jerked it back and shook his head.

"Information first," Will told him.

"I heard the guy say he needed to meet up with somebody at the Yellow Parrot."

"And where can I find this Yellow Parrot?"

"Four blocks from here, closer to the wharves, on the corner of Poc Na and Kukulcan."

Will handed the bartender the fifty, then took a hefty swig from the tankard and walked out of the bar and grill. If luck was on his side, he might have the case of the missing heiress wrapped up by the end of the night.

Gwen took a taxi to the Yellow Parrot. With each passing block, she grew more tense. It didn't take a rocket scientist to figure out that this dive was in the worst part of town. But living alone and occasionally working late hours, Gwen had learned to take care of herself. She'd attended several self-defense classes, but luckily had never faced a situation where she had needed to put any of the moves she'd learned into practice.

The minute she entered the bar, she realized that a smart woman would have brought a gun with her. The interior was hot, smelly and dirty. If that wasn't bad enough, the air was so smoky that it looked as if a pea soup fog had settled inside the building. In comparison, the Fiesta Bar and Grill was upscale. Before she had gone three feet, an old drunk came up to her and asked for money. Sidestepping him, she searched for someone who looked as if he or she might actually work here, someone other than the prostitutes who were trolling for customers.

After fending off a couple of grasping young men and ignoring several vulgar propositions—all spoken in an odd mixture of Spanish and English—Gwen found the bar. She ordered a beer from the burly, bearded bartender. When he set the beer in front of her, she took the opportunity to speak to him.

"I'm looking for a man. An older American man, in his

seventies. He was probably with a younger woman. This man is my father and—"

"*Yo no hablo Ingles.*"

"Oh." He didn't speak English and she didn't speak Spanish. Now what?

While she was considering her options, Gwen noticed a young man in skin-tight black pants and a black shirt open all the way down the front, easing closer and closer to her as he made his way past the other patrons at the bar.

Great! This was all she needed, some horny young guy mistaking her for a prostitute. Although she had dark hair and eyes, she certainly didn't look like one of the native girls, not with her distinct Anglo-Saxon facial features.

"Señorita." His voice was softly accented and slightly slurred. His breath smelled of liquor. "You are all alone, *sí?*"

"Please, go away," Gwen said. "I'm not interested."

He laughed as if he found her attitude amusing. "Then it is for me to make you interested. I am Marco. And you are…?"

"Leaving," Gwen said.

She realized it had been a mistake to come here alone tonight. She'd do better to come back tomorrow and try to speak to the owner. But when Gwen tried to move past her ardent young suitor, he reached out and grabbed her arm. She went rigid.

Looking him right in the eyes, she told him, "Let go of me. Right now."

"But you cannot leave." He got right up in her face. "The night is young."

Gwen tugged on her arm, trying to break free. He tightened his hold, his fingers biting into her flesh. With her heart beating rapidly as her basic fight or flight instinct kicked in, she glared at the man.

"I'm going to ask you one more time to let me go."

Grinning smugly, he grabbed her other arm, holding her in place.

Suddenly, seemingly from out of nowhere a big hand clamped down on Marco's shoulder, jerked him back and spun him around, freeing Gwen. She staggered slightly, but managed to hold her balance as the tall, lanky man in jeans and cowboy boots shoved her would-be suitor up against the bar.

"I believe the lady asked you real nice to let her go," the man said in a deep Texas drawl. "Where I come from, a gentleman respects a lady's wishes."

Marco grumbled something unintelligible in Spanish. Probably cursing, Gwen thought. Or maybe praying. If she were Marco, she'd be praying that the big, rugged American wouldn't beat her to a pulp.

When the Texan released Marco, the young man made a poor decision. He came at the other man, intending to fight him. Gwen's rescuer took Marco out with two swift punches, sending the younger man to the floor. Gwen glanced down at where Marco lay sprawled flat on his back.

Her hero turned to her. "Ma'am, are you all right?"

She nodded. This man was about six-two, with a sun-burned tan, sun-streaked brown hair and azure-blue eyes.

"What's a lady like you doing in a place like this?" he asked.

"Um…searching for my father," she managed to say.

"Come on, I'd better get you out of here. Our friend—" he hitched his thumb downward at Marco "—might have some buddies itching for a fight."

"Actually, I was just leaving. I just need to call a taxi."

When a rumble arose from several men nearby, her rescuer grasped Gwen's arm and led her through the filthy, smoky bar and out onto the sidewalk. Once in the fresh air, Gwen took a deep breath.

"My name is Will Pierce," he said. "I'm a private investigator for Dundee's in Atlanta, Georgia." He pulled out his wallet and showed her his driver's license and an ID card. "If you'll allow me, I'd be glad to take you back to your hotel."

"Thank you. I...I'd appreciate that." Gwen knew she was taking a chance by trusting this man, but instinct told her she was safe with him. "I'm Gwen Arnell." Only in business situations did she introduce herself as Dr. Arnell.

"Look, Gwen, would you mind waiting in my rental car?" he asked. "I'll give you the keys and you can lock yourself in. I really need to go back inside and speak to the bartender."

"He doesn't speak English."

"That's okay. I speak enough Spanish to get by."

"You said you're an investigator. Are you here in Puerto Nuevo on a case?"

"Yeah, it seems some rich man's spoiled daughter didn't come home to her papa's villa last night and he's worried about her. More than likely she spent the night with a guy, but I got a tip that they were headed here last night. I need to check it out."

Without conscious thought of what she was doing, Gwen grabbed Will's arm. "When you ask him about this girl and her boyfriend, would you also ask him if he's seen an elderly American man, around seventy, with a younger woman. The old man would have been talking about a great adventure he was going on."

"The old man, I assume he's your father?"

"Yes." Gwen nodded.

"By any chance do people refer to him as The Professor?"

Gwen gasped. "Yes, but how did you—"

"Your father has a young research assistant named Jordan?"

"Yes, Jordan Elders. He is one of my father's former students. My father was a botany professor before he retired a few years ago."

"Ms. Arnell, it would seem that your search and mine overlap," Will said. "The young man who my client's daughter might be with is your father's assistant, Jordan Elders."

Realizing she was holding fiercely to this stranger's arm, Gwen released him and leaned her body away from his. "I was told my father checked out of his hotel this afternoon, before I arrived, but I have no idea where he's gone."

"I'd say when we find Jordan Elders, I'll find my client's daughter and your father."

Thank you, God! Gwen said a hurried, silent prayer. Just when she thought it might be impossible to find her father and help him, a higher power had sent Will Pierce to her, an honest-to-goodness private detective.

"Where's your car?" she asked, suddenly feeling more confident. "I'll wait for you while you go inside and speak to the bartender."

Will grinned. Gwen's stomach flip-flopped. Not a good sign. She seldom reacted to a man's sexual charm. Burned once. Twice shy. A brief marriage that had ended in a heart-breaking divorce when she was twenty-two had taught her to steer clear of sexual entanglements. When she dated, which wasn't that often these days, she chose stable, reliable, boring men.

"It's the blue hatchback." He pointed to the small car parked on the street about forty yards from where they stood, then he tossed her the keys. "Lock yourself in. Put the keys in the ignition. I'll be back in a few minutes."

A few minutes turned into half an hour. After fifteen minutes she'd lowered the car's windows several inches to let in cooler air. After twenty minutes she started to worry. What was taking him so long? Was he all right?

Finally, just as she reached for the door handle intending to get out of the car and go back inside the Yellow Parrot to search for Will, he came out of the bar and straight to the car. She leaned across the driver's seat and unlocked the door. He got in, slid under the steering wheel and shut the door. Without saying a word, he started the engine.

"Are you okay?" she asked. "I was beginning to worry."

He turned to face her. She gasped. He had a cut on his cheek, a bloody mouth and bruised eye.

"What happened to you?"

"After I spoke to the bartender, I got in a little altercation with a couple of your buddy Marco's pals."

"Oh, I'm so sorry." Gwen lifted her hand, but stopped herself short of touching his face. "You fought off two men all by yourself?"

Will chuckled, then grunted. He wiped his bloody mouth with the back of his hand, then shifted gears and pulled the rental car out into the street. Gwen rummaged in her purse until she found her minibox of tissues. She pulled one out, reached over and wiped the blood from Will's mouth and then his hand. He tensed at her touch, but didn't withdraw.

"Do you need a doctor?" she asked.

"Nope."

"I'm so sorry about—"

"You've already said that once. Stop apologizing. It's not your fault."

Gwen sat quietly for a few minutes, then realized that he wasn't taking her back to her hotel. Oh, my God, she hadn't even told him where she was staying.

"I'm staying at the Pasada El Paso," Gwen told him.

"And I'm staying at the Puerto Nuevo Day's Inn. If you don't mind, we need to go by my hotel first so I can make some phone calls, send out a couple of e-mails and clean my cuts and bruises."

Gwen sat there silent and uncertain.

"Look, I'm not trying to pull anything," he said. "Before Marco's pals wanted to play rough, the bartender identified my client's daughter and her girlfriend from photos I showed him. They were there at the Yellow Parrot last night, with this Jordan Elders guy, or at least I'm pretty sure that's who he was. The bartender said that the young guy and the two girls kept calling this old guy The Professor."

"Then my father was there last night?"

"Yeah, and he was with a younger woman. The bartender said he knew her, that she'd been here in Puerto Nuevo for about six months and was a regular. Her name's Molly Esteban. It seems he thinks the woman's bad news."

"Poor Daddy. He's such a damn fool."

"The bartender overheard the young guy—Jordan— saying something about their heading out tomorrow, which is now today, leaving the island."

"Where were they going?"

"The bartender didn't know, didn't hear them mention where."

"Well, if it helps any, sooner or later, my father will have to charter a boat to take him where he wants to go. If he didn't charter a boat here, then—"

"When we get to my hotel, I'll call Dundee's and have them get us the info on all flights out of Puerto Nuevo today, plus any boat or yacht rentals today."

"Your agency can get all that information for us tonight?"

"They can probably get me the info on plane reservations tonight, but it could take a bit longer to check out all the boat and yacht rentals, because my guess is that there are a few dozen rental places."

"Mr. Pierce...Will?"

"Huh?"

"I know you're already assigned to a case, and I probably can't afford to hire you, but I was wondering if there might be some way I could persuade you to help me find my father and save him from himself. After all, there is a chance that your client's daughter went off with Jordan, and Jordan is with my father, and...well, what do you think?"

Will zoomed the rental car along, darting in and out of nighttime traffic, never taking his eyes off the road. "As far as I'm concerned, brown eyes, you and I are in this together all the way."

Chapter 3

Expect the unexpected. Be prepared for anything. Never take a person or a situation at face value. Trust no one. During his years as a CIA operative, Will had learned some valuable lessons. Some of them the hard way and others by observation.

After brewing a small pot of coffee for him and his guest, he settled her in a chair in the corner of his hotel room, then he went back into the bathroom, closed the door and washed the blood off his face. He checked his bruised eye and the cut on his cheek. Minor wounds. No big deal. He swiped the washcloth over his cheek, removing the dried blood, and tossed the cloth into the nearby shower stall.

Keeping the water running in the sink to mask his voice, he used his cell phone to call Sawyer's private number. With a few well-chosen words, he explained what was going on and asked that Dundee's run a quick check on a woman named Gwen Arnell.

"From her accent, I'd say she's from the South," Will said. "Deep South. Alabama, Georgia, Mississippi."

"She claims this man known as The Professor is her father and he's in some kind of trouble?" Sawyer asked. "And our client's daughter could be with this man's assistant, right?"

"Yeah, and my gut instinct says she's telling the truth, that she's on the up and up, but run a check on her and get me as much information on her as quickly as you can."

"Give me a physical description and an approximate age. We'll probably run across more than one Gwen Arnell when we start checking."

"Late twenties, early thirties," Will said. "About five-five, medium build, maybe a little on the plump side. Fairly nondescript. Dark brown hair and brown eyes." Not beautiful, but she has good features, Will thought, but kept that to himself. There was nothing fancy about Gwen Arnell, no jewelry other than a wristwatch, and she didn't appear to be wearing much makeup, just the bare minimum. The black slacks and gray linen jacket she wore were practical clothing for travel, nothing fashionable or trendy.

"I should have something for you in a couple of hours, on your Ms. Arnell and on the plane flights out of Puerto Nuevo today," Sawyer said. "Checking the boat and yacht rentals could take longer, maybe sometime tomorrow."

"One more thing…"

"What?"

"Ms. Arnell wants me to help her find her father. I think her search and ours could well turn out to be one and the same, so do you have any objections to—"

"Do whatever you need to do to find Cheryl Kress."

"Okay."

End of conversation. Will flipped his cell phone closed and hooked it to his belt.

When he emerged from the bathroom, Gwen rose to her feet and faced him. Neither smiling nor frowning, she met his gaze head-on, a combination of hope and fear in her coffee-brown eyes. The woman had the most expressive eyes he'd ever seen. She didn't need to speak for him to understand that she was, perhaps subconsciously, pleading with him for help.

Her long dark hair, pulled away from her face and twisted into a knot at the nape of her neck, looked disheveled, and her makeup-bare face showed signs of weariness. For the first time in a long time, Will felt a twinge of protectiveness stir to life inside him. It wasn't that he thought she was some weak, helpless female. On the contrary, it was the fact that she was putting herself at risk to find her father and that she hadn't cried or tried to use feminine wiles to persuade him to help her. He figured Gwen had never asked a man for help, that it went against her nature to think she might not be able to do the job—whatever that job might be—by herself.

"I spoke to my boss," Will said. "He should have some information for us in an hour or so."

Gwen nodded. "Thank you."

"Did you have dinner tonight? If you didn't, I can run out and get you—"

"I ate at the Fiesta, but thank you."

"I take it that you were following up a lead when you went to the Fiesta."

"Yes, how did you—"

"Me, too," he told her. When she eyed him inquiringly, he explained, "Our common denominator, Jordan Elders."

"Ah, yes, Jordan."

"What do you know about him?"

"Not much, just that he's one of Daddy's former students, that he's in his late twenties and he shares my father's belief in a mysterious, uncharted island that possesses a miraculous Fountain of Youth serum derived from a plant that grows nowhere else on earth."

"What?"

Gwen rubbed her hands together nervously. "It sounds preposterous, doesn't it? I know only too well just how outlandish my father's theory is. His insistence that he once visited this island when he was twenty and knows it exists made him a laughingstock among his colleagues. He's obsessed with finding this island again and in giving to the world this incredible plant that keeps people healthy and gives them a two-hundred-year lifespan."

"Are you telling me that your father actually believes this crap?"

When Gwen's cheeks flushed, he realized he'd hit a nerve.

"Yes, he believes it, with his whole heart and soul."

"It must have been tough growing up with a father everybody thought was nuts." Damn, Pierce. Open mouth, insert foot. "Sorry it came out that way. But you know what I mean."

"Yes, I do. But I didn't actually grow up with my father. He and my mother divorced when I was ten. He couldn't be bothered with a wife and a child, not when he had to fulfill his destiny and bring good health and longevity to the world."

"So, if he deserted you and your mom, why are you here now, trying to find him, wanting to help him?"

"Because he is my father, and he has no one else who really cares if he lives or dies."

Will shook his head. Not many adult kids would give a damn about a father who had deserted them, let alone go in search of that parent, hoping to save him from himself.

"You're a better person than I am," Will told her. "My old man was no prize, but he was there, working hard to support his wife and three sons. We didn't get along, didn't see eye to eye on a lot of things, but I respected him. If he had deserted us, I wouldn't have cared if he'd rotted in hell."

Gwen stared at Will, her eyes round with speculation. It was then that he realized he'd revealed a personal part of himself that he seldom shared with others. Seldom? Hell, make that never.

Will cleared his throat. "So, where does your father think this island is located?"

"Somewhere north of the Caribbean Sea, out in the Atlantic between Puerto Rico and Bermuda."

"In the Bermuda Triangle?" Will chuckled under his breath. "Get real. Every kook in the world believes some sort of supernatural nonsense about that area of the Atlantic Ocean."

"I know it sounds preposterous, but my father swears that when he was twenty, he lived for several weeks on this island. And he's spent the past fifty years searching for it."

"Damn!"

"He's an old man, seventy his last birthday, and he's spent every dime he has on this quest." Gwen sighed lightly, her expression one of sadness and concern. "He told me that he'd cashed in his life-insurance policy to help fund this latest expedition."

"Would he pay for everything by credit card or cash?" Will asked.

"Huh?"

"If he uses a credit card, we can trace—"

"I see. But I have no idea if he'd pay cash or use a credit card. I'm afraid I know very little about my father's personal life, other than his big dream, which seems to have consumed him completely."

"Why don't you sit down and relax?" Will said, indicating the single chair in the room. "I need to check my e-mail and send off a few while we wait."

She nodded and returned to the seat. Will went over to the desk and unzipped his carrying case. As he opened his laptop, he glanced over his shoulder at Gwen. She sat with her hands folded together in her lap, her head against the chair back and her eyes closed.

Why the hell did he feel so protective toward her? It wasn't that he was particularly attracted to her. She really wasn't his type, was she? A little too plain, a little on the plump side and his guess was that her IQ was higher than his. Plain, plump and brainy. Definitely not his type. Besides, he needed to stay focused on the job.

Gwen hadn't realized she had dozed off for over an hour until Will's cell phone rang. Startled awake by the distinct ring, she came to with a jolt. Searching the room for Will, she found him standing near the window, his back to her, his voice low as he mumbled yes and no and then hung up.

"Was that your boss?" she asked.

"Yeah, it was." Will turned to face her. "Sorry the call woke you. I should have put the thing on *vibrate* instead of *ring*."

"No, no, it's all right. I shouldn't have fallen asleep. It was rude of me."

"Hey, you're tired. No big deal."

"May I ask what information—"

His gaze locked with hers. "Look, you should know that I asked for Dundee's to run a check on you."

Her eyes widened and her mouth rounded in surprise.

"I don't take anyone or anything at face value," he said matter-of-factly.

"I see."

"If we're going to work together, Dr. Arnell, we need to be honest with each other. Agreed?"

She nodded. "Agreed." Why did she suspect that while he demanded honesty from her, he wouldn't necessarily always be totally honest with her?

"So you're the CEO of the Huntsville Botanical Gardens in Alabama, huh? You're a botanist, just like your father, the other Dr. Arnell."

"My father specialized in education, exploration and history," she said. "Whereas my interests are horticulture and breeding."

"Breeding?"

"Breeding involves the development of better types of plants. It also involves selecting and crossing plants with desirable traits, such as disease resistance."

"Interesting."

Gwen smiled, knowing full well that Will found the subject as dull as dishwater. "What else did you find out about me?"

"Just the basics. Date of birth, job, address, phone number, education background. Mother deceased. Father a genius crackpot. No siblings. And I know you were married at twenty-one, divorced at twenty-two and don't presently have a significant other. No children. No pets."

"If we're going to be partners, don't you think I should know the same things about you?" It seemed unfair that he knew the basic facts about her life when he remained a stranger to her.

Will sat down on the edge of the bed, across from the chair where she sat. "Just the basics, right? Okay, fair enough. I'm thirty-nine. Married and divorced in my late twenties. No children. My father's been dead five years. My mother remarried last year and moved to Louisiana with her new husband. My older brother still lives on the ranch where we grew up and my younger brother is a doctor in Ft. Worth. I have three nephews, ages two, five and eight."

"Hmm…all right, now we're on an equal footing. So, what about our investigation?"

"Our investigation?" Will chuckled. "Well, no one using the names Emery Arnell, Jordan Elders, Cheryl Kress or Tori Boyd were booked on flights out of Puerto Nuevo today and none are booked for tomorrow."

"Then they're either still here on the island or they left here by boat."

"So it would seem."

"When will you have a report about the boat and yacht rental companies?"

"Probably not until tomorrow sometime, hopefully by midmorning."

"Then I guess I should head back to my hotel." Gwen checked her watch. "Wow, it's past midnight."

"You're welcome to stay here." Will indicated one of the two single beds in the room.

"No, thank you." This offer was probably on the up-and-up, but she wasn't about to take any chances. "I left my suitcase back at the other hotel, and I want to speak to the day staff there and see if my father mentioned his travel plans to anyone."

"Okay. I'll drive you back to your hotel, then I'll come by in the morning and pick you up for breakfast."

"Thank you."

"No problem. Like I said, we're in this together. Right?"

Feelings of security and relief welled up inside Gwen. At an early age, she had learned to depend on no one, to take care of herself, so being grateful for having some big, strong man at her side in her search for her father was a new experience for her.

Just don't allow yourself to become too dependent on Will Pierce, said an inner voice. *He's a temporary fixture in your life. A means to an end.*

Will picked Gwen up at the Pasada El Paso at nine the next morning. She wore brown slacks and an oversize tan shirt, had pulled her hair up into a loose ponytail and had applied lipstick and a hint of blush. Apparently the woman didn't own anything colorful. He'd bet her underwear was plain white cotton.

"The desk clerk at my hotel recommended Pepe's for breakfast," Will told her once she was seated in his rental car.

"Anyplace you choose is fine with me."

He grunted, started the car and eased into downtown morning traffic.

"I spoke to the day staff at the hotel," Gwen told him. "And unfortunately none of them had any idea where my father intended to go when he left Puerto Nuevo. Ria, one of the maids, did say my father's lady friend said something about going to Jamaica."

"Do you know of any reason your father would go to Jamaica? Why not charter a boat here and sail up toward the Bahamas?"

"I have no idea." She shuffled in her seat. "I assume you haven't had any word from your boss about the rental—"

"Not yet, but anytime now, I'm sure."

"What will we do if they didn't rent a boat?"

"We'll assume they either traveled with someone who had a boat or that they're still here on the island."

An hour later, just as they were topping off their big breakfast with cups of a local speciality, *café de ola,* Will's cell phone rang.

"Will, we have confirmation that a Dr. Emery Arnell rented a 422 Sport Sedan cruiser, captained by a man named Mick McGuire. And before you ask, I'm running a check on McGuire as we speak," Daisy Holbrook said on the other end. "Arnell paid cash. And according to what I was able to find out, he rented the cruiser for a month."

"Any idea if the cruiser has left port?"

"I don't have that information, yet. But the cruiser either is or was docked at the Puerto Nuevo Marina."

"Hang on a minute," he said to Daisy, then spoke to Gwen. "Your father rented a cruiser, but we don't know whether or not he's left the country yet." Talking again to Daisy, Will asked, "Any info on Jordan Elders?"

"Not much more than you already know. He's twenty-eight. Was a student of Dr. Arnell's and later his assistant. He has no criminal record. As a matter of fact, he's squeaky clean."

"Hmm…"

"By the way, the cruiser the professor rented, the *Sun Dancer,* is equipped with upgraded cat diesel engines, with 435 horsepower each. That means speed. Why would he need a cruiser with that much horsepower?" Daisy asked. "What's the first thing that comes to mind?"

"Drug running."

"Bingo. And that fits right in with what I've found out about Molly Esteban. It seems the lady's got a record a mile long."

Will grunted. When his gaze met Gwen's, he forced a faltering smile. "Thanks, Daisy. Stay in touch with any updates."

"Will do."

He put away his phone and turned to Gwen. "Let me take care of the bill, then we should head off to the marina."

When Will stood, she stood, then reached over and grabbed his arm. "I heard you mention something about drug running."

Will hesitated, then told her, "The cruiser your father rented has a lot of horsepower, and fast boats are often associated with illegal activities. But that's not necessarily—"

"We're going to be honest with each other, remember? What aren't you telling me?"

Damn, why had he made a pact with her? "Your father's lady friend, Molly Esteban, has a criminal record. It's possible she's using your father and his quest to find his mythical island as a front."

"Oh, God!" Gwen rubbed her head and mumbled a few choice curse words that surprised Will, she being such a soft-spoken Southern lady. "Daddy, Daddy…what have you gotten yourself into this time?"

"Come on." Will motioned for them to get going. "If we're lucky, they haven't left yet."

"The *Sun Dancer* left late yesterday sometime," the charter office employee, a Mr. Calvino, told Will. "Dr. Arnell seemed eager to leave."

"Do you know where he was going?" Gwen asked, praying he knew the answer.

"Kingston, Jamaica," Calvino replied.

"Which means they're probably already there," Will said.

"More than likely. I believe Señora Esteban was eager to meet some friends there."

"What do you know about Mick McGuire?" Will asked. "I assume he works for your company."

"Actually, Dr. Arnell said he didn't need us to recommend anyone to captain the *Sun Dancer*. He said that he'd already hired Mr. McGuire."

Will groaned. "Anything else you can tell us? Ms. Arnell is quite concerned about her father. Uh, his health isn't good and she's afraid he's not up to making this journey."

Calvino shook his head. "I'm sorry, but that's all I know."

"One final question," Will said. "Other than McGuire and Señora Esteban, who else was with Dr. Arnell?"

"Just his assistant, a young man. I don't recall his name."

"You didn't see two young women with them? Girls about twenty?"

"No, no young girls."

Will shook hands with Calvino and thanked him, then led Gwen out of the office and down the wharf toward the parking area.

Assuming her partnership with Will had come to an end since the girls weren't with her father, Gwen said, "I'll get a reservation on the next flight to Kingston."

"You aren't going to Kingston alone. We're in this together, remember."

"What about your assignment? Mr. Calvino said there were no young women with my father and Jordan."

"Just because he didn't see them doesn't mean they

didn't board the cruiser and head off to Jamaica with Jordan Elders."

"Are you sure you aren't saying that just to reassure me that you're not abandoning your assignment to help me find my father?"

Will looked at her intensely. "Why would I do that?"

"I don't know. Maybe you feel sorry for me. If that's the case—"

He grabbed her shoulders, startling her enough that she gasped. "I do not feel sorry for you. Got that? And if I didn't think there's a damn good chance Cheryl and Tori are with Jordan Elders, I wouldn't fly to Jamaica with you. And if you think I'm going with you because I've got ideas about you and me, think again. I like you well enough, brown eyes, but you're hardly the stuff a wet-dream fantasy is made of."

Guess he put you in your place, an angry and hurt inner voice told Gwen. She blew out a huffing breath. "That's good to know, since you're not exactly my idea of Prince Charming."

"Are you looking for Prince Charming?"

"As a matter of fact, I'm not. I'm not interested in putting up with a man, any man, not even Prince Charming," Gwen told him, her voice quavering. "My father and my ex-husband proved to me that most men are incapable of putting the needs of the woman they profess to love above their own."

Will grinned. "Good. I'm glad we got that settled." He grasped her elbow and herded her along with him toward his rental car.

She kept up with his long-legged gait, but just barely. When they reached the car, Will released his hold on her and unlocked the passenger-side door. Just as she slid into the seat, his cell phone rang. Gwen held her breath until he answered.

"Pierce here."

She watched his facial expressions change rapidly, going from curiosity to dismay. "Look, you two stay put. I'm on my way."

Will didn't say anything to Gwen until he went around the car and got in on the driver's side. He slammed his big hands down against the steering wheel several times and cursed loudly.

"What is it? What's wrong?"

"The phone call was from a girl named Courtney Downey. She and another girl are staying at the Kress villa. They're friends of Cheryl and Tori. The Puerto Nuevo police just left the villa. It seems the body of a young blond woman was found on the beach not far from here early this morning. She had a set of keys in her pocket with a key ring that had a photo of the Kress villa on it. The police want the girls to come down to the morgue and see if they can identify the body."

"Is Cheryl Kress a blonde?" Gwen asked.

"No, but Tori Boyd is."

Chapter 4

Will and Gwen had accompanied Courtney and Kerry to the morgue. Gwen had insisted on being with him when the nervous girls viewed the body of the young blonde found on the beach. He sympathized with what the girls had to face, and was damn grateful there was an older woman around to oversee the emotional young females, a job he didn't like, didn't want and avoided at all costs. Not much scared Will, but women's emotions unnerved him in a way little else did.

"Oh, God, it's Tori!" Kerry had cried, then turned around and fallen into Will's arms. Crying her eyes out, she'd clung to him.

Courtney had taken one look at the corpse, went white as a sheet and threw up. Gwen had put her arm around the girl and led her to the nearest restroom.

After their visit to the morgue, Gwen waited in the car

with the girls, playing mother hen, which apparently came naturally to her. Will went inside the police station alone and spoke to the officer in charge of the case.

"Now that the girl has been identified, we will contact her family in the United States," a middle-aged, slightly balding Detective Sanchez said.

"Tori Boyd was last seen with her friend, Cheryl Kress. I'm a P.I., working for Cheryl's father. I'd appreciate any information you can give me about Ms. Boyd's death. That info might somehow help me find Ms. Kress."

"We can't say for sure until an autopsy has been performed, but we believe the girl was strangled, so we are treating this case as a homicide."

"Any suspects?" Will asked.

"No, none at this time."

Will handed Sanchez his business card. "I'm leaving later today for Jamaica to follow a lead on Ms. Kress's whereabouts. I'd appreciate your contacting me if you get a break in this case." The only real lead Will had was knowing Cheryl had last been seen with Jordan Elders. If the girl was still alive, there was a good possibility she was with this guy.

Sanchez nodded, then asked, "Does Señorita Kress's family wish to report their daughter as missing?"

"No, not yet. They prefer for my agency to handle the search for the time being."

Will finished his conversation with Sanchez as quickly as possible, knowing he had two badly shaken and frightened young women waiting in his car. Thank goodness for Gwen. Although he'd noticed her discomfort while they'd been at the morgue, she had been a rock for Courtney and Kerry, saving him from having to deal with them.

Comfort and understanding weren't his strong suits. As his old man had often said, "That's women stuff. Leave it to them."

When he returned to his rental car, he found Gwen in the backseat between the two girls. Courtney rested her head on Gwen's shoulder, while Kerry, her eyes glazed, held tightly to Gwen's hand.

The minute Will got in the car, Gwen said, "We're taking the girls back to the villa to pack, and then we're personally putting them on the first available flight back home."

"We are?" He locked gazes with Gwen. Obstinate determination glinted in her dark eyes. "Okay, we are."

Two hours later, with Kerry and Courtney safely aboard a flight back to the United States and Gwen checked out of her hotel, Will drove the two of them back to his hotel. While they had waited at the airport with the girls, Will had contacted Sawyer and filled him in on the situation.

Will unlocked the door to his room, motioned for Gwen to enter first, then suggested she take a seat.

"I need to contact my boss and see if he's spoken to Mr. Kress before I get my stuff together," Will said. "It could be that with this new development, he'll want the police involved in his daughter's disappearance and Sawyer will pull me in off the case."

"If that happens, then you'll go back to Atlanta today, won't you?" Gwen looked at him, a silent plea in her big brown eyes.

"If I'm called off this case, I'll get you to Jamaica today and help you try to find your father before I fly back to Atlanta."

Gwen released a deep sigh. "Thank you. You don't have to, you know. You aren't obligated to—"

"All I'm promising is to take you to Kingston and make some inquires." He held up his hand in a "stop" gesture when she started to speak. "If your father's not there or already gone by the time we arrive, then you're on your own. Understand?"

"I understand."

Will sat on the edge of the bed and called Dundee headquarters. Daisy put him through to Sawyer immediately.

"I just got off the phone with Mr. Kress," Sawyer said. "For the second time today. Since learning about Tori Boyd's death, that she was possibly murdered, he's understandably upset. He's concerned about his daughter's safety, so he's flying to Puerto Nuevo later today, with Tori Boyd's parents, and they plan to speak personally to the local authorities."

"Then I'm off the case?"

"No, not at all. Mr. Kress wants you to follow any and all leads. He wants Dundee's on the case until his daughter is found."

"Okay, that means taking the Dundee jet to Jamaica today. And it's possible I may need to rent a cruiser."

"Buy or rent whatever you need. Money is no object to Mr. Kress. He wants his daughter found."

"Okay. I'll check in later, if and when I know something."

His conversation finished, Will glanced over his shoulder at Gwen. "I'm still on the case, and I've been given a blank check for expenses. Is there anything you need to do in Puerto Nuevo before we go?"

She shook her head.

"Then come on. I'll call the pilot and tell him to have the jet ready for us when we arrive at the private airstrip. We're going to Jamaica."

* * *

Gwen had never flown in a private jet before and had to admit she was more than a little impressed. She sat on the large sofa in the luxurious lounge and tried to relax. Since she hadn't gotten much sleep last night, it would easy for her to fall asleep. Maybe she should take a nap while Will was in the cockpit with the pilot. Leaning back, letting her head rest comfortably on the cushioned leather, she closed her eyes and concentrated on erasing everything from her mind.

Gwen realized blocking out the events of the past two days was impossible. Here she was flying from Puerto Nuevo to Jamaica on a private jet with a man she'd met only last night. A man she instinctively knew had seen more than his share of trouble. He had shown her his credentials. He was a licensed private investigator. The problem wasn't that she didn't trust him, at least on some level. No, the problem was that she found him attractive, and not just his rugged good looks, but the way he seemed comfortable taking charge, making decisions, helping both her and the young women who had been forced to identify the body of their murdered friend. Will was one of those guys people depended on because he got the job done.

Gwen tried to shake off the feelings that Will stirred to life inside her. He was the opposite of her father in so many ways and definitely nothing like her ex-husband. She had chosen Jeremy Charles because she'd thought they had a great deal in common. He had been a botany major at Auburn, where they'd attended college together, and he'd been the most logical-thinking, down-to-earth young man she'd ever met. After being deserted by a father who kept his head in the clouds, she had wanted a husband who had both feet firmly planted on the ground.

"Gwen?"

She opened her eyes and stared up at Will, who was smiling down at her.

"You weren't asleep, were you?" he asked.

"No, just relaxing a little," she lied.

"I was wondering if you're hungry. We have a fully stocked galley."

"I'm not very hungry."

"Come on, you need to eat something. I'm going to make myself a big, thick sandwich and eat half a bag of chips and maybe some chocolate ice cream, too. What do you say?"

Chocolate ice cream? Was he kidding? She could eat chocolate ice cream every day and never tire of it. It was one of her comfort foods. "I'll take a sandwich, no chips and just a little ice cream."

"Give me five minutes."

When he turned and headed toward the galley, she called to him. "I'd be glad to help."

"You stay put, kick off your shoes and relax again. I can put together a couple of sandwiches."

Half an hour later, with their meal eaten, Gwen curled up on the sofa, her shoes on the floor, while Will sat across from her in one of the swivel lounge chairs.

"What do we do when we arrive in Kingston?" Gwen asked. "I suppose we should check with all the marinas and—"

"That's being done," he said.

"It's being done? How's that possible?" Then realization dawned on her. "Oh, right. I forgot that you work for some high-powered investigation agency. I suppose they're running a check right now."

"They're going through the usual channels to get what

information they can. But Dundee's has contacts in various places around the world, so when we need certain information, we use locals whenever possible."

"Are you telling me that Dundee's has a contact in Kingston?"

"Yes, we do. And at this very moment, he's doing some of the leg work, saving us time when we land." Will checked his wristwatch. "In about twenty minutes."

"That soon?" Gwen sat up straight, lifted her foot and extended it enough to grab one shoe with her toe.

"It's a short flight, less than two hours."

"So, what do we do when we land, meet the Dundee contact?"

"That's the second thing we'll do. The first thing we'll do is talk to a member of the JCM, a Lieutenant Seabert."

"The JCM?" Gwen asked.

"Jamaica Constabulary Force."

"Oh. So, why are we going to the police?"

"Dundee's has notified the Kingston authorities that we're investigating a missing person's case and gave them the names of the people who might be involved."

"Including my father's name." Had her father's misadventures led to this—to him somehow being involved with one girl's murder and another's disappearance? *Please, God, don't let Daddy have had anything to do with what happened to Tori Boyd.*

"Yes, including your father's name."

"You don't know for sure that Cheryl Kress is with Jordan Elders and my father."

"You're right, I don't know it for a fact. But both Cheryl and Tori were last seen with Jordan. And Jordan left Puerto Nuevo with your father, a woman named Molly Esteban, who we know has a criminal record, and a guy named Mick McGuire, who's captaining the cruiser your father rented."

"I'm surprised Dundee's hasn't come up with information about this Captain McGuire." She noted the odd expression on Will's face. "Oh, they have, haven't they?"

"McGuire's an alias. One of many this guy has used, if he's the same Mick McGuire. He's been in the Caribbean area for years, in and out of trouble. He's been suspected of smuggling, gunrunning and drug trafficking. He's served time in prison, but mostly for petty stuff, just like Molly."

"Wonderful. Just wonderful. This McGuire man and the Esteban woman are the investors my father was so excited about. And they're criminals. Somehow, in my gut, I sensed something wasn't right about people with enough money to help my father finance his latest expedition. Not unless they were as crazy as he is."

"If we're lucky, we'll catch up with them in Kingston."

"And if we're not that lucky?"

"Then we'll find out where they went and catch them at the next port."

"That might not be possible, not if they head out to sea, straight toward Bermuda, directly into the Devil's Triangle."

Lieutenant Seabert had done nothing to allay Gwen's fears that her father had gotten himself involved with a couple of dangerous criminals. Instead, Will realized grimly, the lieutenant had only frightened her more when he told them that Mick McGuire, alias Michael Smith, Mike Willis, Micah Muir, was suspected of murder. Several murders to be exact.

If Will thought it would do any good, he'd suggest that she let him handle things with their contact, while she waited like a good little girl in the car. But being a realist Will knew that wasn't about to happen. Gwen was the kind of woman who would resent a man trying to keep her safely in the background. And that's the reason he included her in his meeting with their Dundee contact, a wiry, brown-skinned Jamaican named Webster. Webster was a good operative. Dundee's had used his expertise in the past. So had the CIA.

"Where are we meeting him?" Gwen asked, as Will drove the rental car they'd picked up at the airport straight toward their destination.

"The Caribbean Marina," Will replied.

"Do you think that's where my father's rental boat is docked?"

"Webster didn't say."

"Well, what exactly did he say?"

"He said to meet him at the marina, that he had information for us."

"Why didn't you—"

"Gwen, stop asking me so many questions. You'll know what I know when Webster tells me. Got it?"

"Yes, I've got it!" she snapped at him, obviously aggravated.

He could explain that Webster didn't deliver messages over the phone, that he was a look-you-in-the-eye kind of guy. But he damn well didn't feel like explaining every move he made to her. After all, he was doing her a favor by letting her tag along. She should be grateful and just keep her mouth shut. But since she was a woman, that might prove impossible.

Ten minutes later they arrived at the marina. The piers were lined with docked sea craft, everything from huge yachts to small fishing boats. If the *Sun Dancer* was here, Webster would know and could take them directly to it.

"He said he'd meet us at the entrance," Will told Gwen as he opened the passenger door for her.

She got out of the car but didn't say a word, just followed along beside him as he headed for the entrance. Webster, wearing white slacks, sandals and a colorful floral shirt, emerged from where he'd been waiting just inside the stone pillar entrance.

"Who is she?" Webster asked, appraising Gwen as if she were a priceless jewel he wanted to purchase.

"She's mine," Will replied, not giving any thought to his answer.

Webster lifted his eyebrows. "Not your usual, is she, mon? This one, she is a lady."

"Thank you, Mr. Webster." Gwen smiled at the Dundee contact.

"Just Webster, pretty lady."

"Back to business," Will said.

"They are not here." Webster looked directly at Will.

"They're not here at this marina or they're not here in Kingston?" Will asked.

"They were in Kingston. Molly Esteban delivered a package. They were gone, back to sea, in three hours' time."

"Gone where?" Gwen asked.

"What about the package?" Will wanted to know.

Webster glanced at Gwen. "Gone to the next drop-off. San Juan, Puerto Rico." He looked back at Will. "We think the package contained cocaine. Molly and Mick are not major players, but they wish to be."

"Have the San Juan authorities been contacted?" Will asked.

"No, mon. The time is not right."

"What do you mean—" Gwen said.

"Now, don't you worry about things that are none of your business, honey." Will hurriedly draped his arm around her shoulders and dragged her up against his side.

Webster chuckled. Gwen bristled, but thankfully kept her mouth shut.

"Who's our contact in San Juan?" Will asked.

"Jose. He's new in the business, but you can trust him."

Five minutes later Will and Gwen were back in the rental car heading for the airport. Gwen hadn't spoken to him since they left the marina. He knew she was mad as hell.

"Okay, let me have it." He hazarded a glance at her stern face.

"Is all this cloak-and-dagger nonsense really necessary?" she asked. "And what was that 'she's mine' business all about, anyway?"

"Look, if you don't like the way I do things, then when we get back to the airport, we can go our separate ways. But I can be in San Juan in less than two hours and have a good chance of catching up with Jordan Elders. Don't forget that my only interest is finding Cheryl Kress."

Gwen fumed. Will could almost see smoke coming out her ears.

She didn't say another word all the way to the airport.

The Dundee contact in San Juan met them at the airport. Jose was short, stocky and remarkably good looking, with curly black hair and huge black eyes. He was pleasant to Gwen but for the most part ignored her.

He spoke rapidly in Spanish as he zipped along in late-evening traffic. Gwen, who was squeezed between the two men, kept her hands in her lap and listened, hoping that sooner or later, Will would translate at least part of the conversation.

He didn't. Jerk.

Glancing out the windshield, she watched the scenery flash by as they sped along. Gwen thought that under different circumstances she would enjoy doing some sight-seeing. She'd never been to Puerto Rico before. Usually on vacation trips she visited botanical gardens, explored nature trails and loved collecting information about the local flora.

It was almost twilight when they pulled up in the parking area of a small marina. Jose parked the car, got out and disappeared. Gwen crossed her arms over her chest and looked straight ahead, determined not to be the first one who spoke.

"Jose is checking to see if our cruiser is ready," Will said.

Snapping around to face him, Gwen stared at him, puzzled and speechless.

"The *Sun Dancer* is one step ahead of us," Will told her. "They left here about three hours ago, after Molly made a delivery."

"Why are we renting a cruiser instead of flying to the next destination?"

"Because the next destination is the Atlantic Ocean, somewhere between here and Bermuda."

"Crap! They're actually letting Daddy go on his adventure, aren't they? But if they're smuggling drugs, why would they?"

"Your father's mad adventure is a good front for Molly and Mick. They could be headed anywhere, maybe the Bahamas, maybe Bermuda. What harm would it do to let your father think they were helping him search for his mythical island?"

"You and Jose were doing a great deal of talking. Is that all he told you?"

"No, that wasn't all. It seems five people were seen aboard the *Sun Dancer* as it headed out to sea."

"Five people?"

"Mick and Molly, an old man fitting your father's description, a young man, whom we assume was Jordan Elders and a young redhead."

"Cheryl Kress?"

"That's my guess."

"You think she didn't go with Jordan willingly, don't you?"

"I don't know and I'm not making any assumptions about why she might be with your father and his assistant."

"And with two dangerous criminals."

"Remember that it's highly unlikely your father and Jordan know Molly and Mick are criminals."

"But if they killed Tori Boyd, then surely—"

"If Mick killed Tori, he would hardly have done it in front of witnesses," Will said.

"Then my father and Jordan really might not know the kind of people they've hooked up with."

"Let's hope they don't. As long as they believe Mick and Molly are investors, people who've simply bought into your father's crazy dream, then your father, Jordan and Cheryl should be safe."

"And if they learn the truth?"

"Let's hope we find them before that happens."

Chapter 5

"What do you mean we'll have to stay the night aboard the yacht and not leave until morning?" With her hands planted on her hips, Gwen glowered at Will.

"No vessels are being allowed to leave tonight," Will explained. "There's a storm just north of Puerto Rico, one that any sane sailor would try to avoid."

"What about Daddy and the others aboard the *Sun Dancer?* They set sail a few hours ago. Why were they allowed to leave?"

"Three hours ago the storm warning had not been issued." Will paused in their trek down the pier to where their rental boat, which Will referred to as a yacht, was anchored. With his vinyl bag hooked over one shoulder and carrying her small suitcase, Will turned and faced Gwen, then he laid his free hand on her shoulder. "This Mick fellow isn't going to risk his life. Once he learned of the storm warning, he probably dropped anchor at the nearest port, probably the Dominican Republic or possibly one of the Turks and Caicos islands."

"Then why can't we take the jet and—"

"And go where? We don't know for sure where they might have docked."

The wind whipped around them, a warm, moist tropical wind, a precursor of the approaching storm. The pressure of Will's strong hand on her shoulder felt reassuring, and yet the simple contact slightly unnerved her.

"How will we ever find them, chasing after them in a boat, when we have no idea where they are?"

"Look, I'll fill you in on details later." He looked skyward. "The bottom's going to drop out any minute now, and I'd prefer not to get drenched." He grabbed her arm. "Let's get on board the *Footloose* and I promise I'll do my best to answer all your questions."

They stood there on the pier for a locked-horns moment. Gwen was growing more and more frustrated with Will's reluctance to share important information about their search for her father and his shipmates. A flash of lightning lit up the evening sky. When a loud rumble of thunder followed the light show, Gwen quickly nodded in agreement and raced alongside Will, hoping to stay one step ahead of the approaching rain.

"There she is," Will said. "She's a Sea Ray 580 Super Sport. This little yacht is a compact beauty, with two staterooms."

Gwen stopped just long enough to size up the *Footloose,* and knowing very little about seacraft of any kind, her appraisal consisted of noting it was white, clean and apparently quite new.

"It must be expensive to rent," she said.

"Yeah, probably is. But that's not our concern. Dundee's is picking up the tab."

"Of course."

"The fold-out steps are hidden in the coaming," Will told her as he tossed their bags aboard and revealed the steps within the frame around a hatchway in the deck.

After boarding, Will helped her onto the yacht. Another streak of lightning lit up the twilight sky. Gwen barely had time to notice that the aft-deck layout included a large U-shaped seating area, high-low tables and what she thought was a wet bar before Will shoved her bag into her arms.

Hoisting his own bag over his shoulder, Will led Gwen to an acrylic door and hatch, flipped a switch to turn on an overhead light, then led her down the companionway. The first thing she noticed was the abundance of lacquered wood. Beautiful. Simply beautiful. Sleek and modern in design, the galley boasted abundant storage and molded black granite countertops. A large curved leather settee was nestled against the wall opposite the galley in the neat and compact salon.

"The galley's fully equipped," Will said. "I believe the master stateroom and bath are aft, and the guest stateroom and bath are forward. You can take your pick."

"I'll take the guest room," she told him. "As long as there's a bed and bathroom with a shower, I'll be fine."

"Why don't you go check it out, and if you don't like it, we can swap. If you'd like to take a shower and change clothes, go ahead and I'll whip up some supper for us. We're supposed to have enough supplies for a couple of weeks."

"I'll put my bag in the stateroom and be right back." She

looked directly at him. "But before either of us does anything else, I want us to have the discussion you promised me."

Will grunted. "What happened to the good old days when women just did what men told them to do?"

"Remind me just what century that was."

"Okay, okay. You made your point," Will told her. "I'm going to get a beer. Want one?"

"No, thank you."

"Suit yourself."

Aggravating, macho, bossy… Gwen silently grumbled to herself as she opened the door to the forward state-room; at least, she believed it was forward. She felt along the wall for a light switch and found one. The room was tiny, the bed taking up almost all the space. But like the rest of the small yacht, the room was clean and neat. She laid her bag at the foot of the bed, then opened the door and checked out the bathroom. Will would probably refer to it as the head. Wasn't that what bathrooms on ships were called? The head was finished in Fiberglass and what she thought was Corian. White and dark blue. Nautical-print blue towels hung on the bar across the front edge of the sink.

When she returned to the lounge area, she found Will sprawled out on the large settee, one leg crossed over the other and a bottle of beer in his hand. Her stomach did a stupid flip-flop as she stared at him. It was totally illogical, not to mention stupid, of her to be attracted to him. First of all, he didn't seem the least bit attracted to her. And second, he was just a little too "me Tarzan, you Jane" to suit Gwen.

"It's raining," he said. "If the winds get rough, we'll probably be rocking most of the night."

Completely ignoring his comment, Gwen asked, "How can you be certain we'll be able to follow the *Sun Dancer*'s path?"

"Straight to the point." He saluted her with the bottle, then downed a hefty swig, emptying half the contents.

"It's not that I'm ungrateful for your help, it's just that I feel as if we're on a wild-goose chase and are accomplishing nothing."

"If any of our operatives had gotten lucky enough to find the *Sun Dancer* while it was still in port, they might have been able to put a tracking device on board." Will paused. "No questions?"

She shook her head. "Go on."

"It's possible that might still happen."

She nodded.

"You're wondering how come if an operative could board the *Sun Dancer,* why wouldn't one of our guys simply detain the ship and all aboard." He waited for her comment, but when she said nothing, he continued. "My contacts—Dundee's contacts—are independent operatives. They work outside the law, and neither they nor I have any authority in these various countries, so our guys have to be careful not to get caught doing something blatantly illegal."

"Are you telling me that you—that the Dundee Agency has contacts everywhere, on every little island in the Caribbean?"

"No, I'm not saying that. We have contacts on several major islands, but our contacts have contacts who have contacts everywhere on earth."

A tight knot formed in the pit of Gwen's stomach. "When you said your contacts, you meant just that, didn't you? These contacts, these operatives aren't all Dundee's." She knew before she posed the question to him, but she had to ask, needed to hear him say it. "What did you do before you became a private investigator for the Dundee Agency?"

Will finished off his beer. "I worked for the government."

"Doing what?"

"I worked in the field," he said vaguely.

"Like the CIA or something?"

"There's another reason none of our contacts would try to detain the *Sun Dancer*," Will said as if she hadn't asked about his former line of work. "We don't know what Mick McGuire and Molly Esteban might do. They could easily fight back, and one of the other passengers could get hurt. Or they could take the others hostage. It's better for your father, Jordan Elders and Cheryl Kress if we can separate them from Mick and Molly before taking any kind of action."

"How do we know that my father and Jordan and Cheryl aren't already hostages?"

"We don't."

"In any case, their lives are in danger."

"Yeah, I'm afraid so."

The door lock clicked. Cheryl Kress backed up against the headboard of the bed in her small stateroom, a room in which she was kept confined whenever the yacht came into port. Only when the *Sun Dancer* was out at sea was she allowed any freedom.

"I've brought your dinner." Jordan Elders entered the room, a cloth-covered tray in his hands.

"I'm not hungry." She glared at him, hating him almost as much as she hated Tori for getting her into this situation. Here she was trapped aboard this boat with a crazy old coot, his assistant and his sleazy investors, while Tori was back in Puerto Nuevo safe and sound. Tori should be the one here, because it was Tori who had a thing for Jordan Elders, Tori who had planned to stow away on the boat and surprise Jordan.

"Come on, Cheryl, don't pout. You have to eat something."

"I'm not pouting. I'm pissed. I'm angry. I'm outraged."

Jordan placed the tray at the foot of the bed. "Look, I'm sorry we can't put you ashore so you can go home, but it's like Captain McGuire pointed out, we can't take any chance that you'll involve the police, maybe even claim we kidnapped you. If that happened, it would put an end to our voyage to find The Professor's island."

"I've sworn a thousand times over that I won't tell a soul, that I won't go to the police. Besides, who would believe me? I think you're all as crazy as that nut-job you call The Professor. Whoever heard of such nonsense as an island where people live to be two hundred and are never sick?" Cheryl laughed sarcastically.

"If you knew Dr. Arnell the way I know him, you'd believe," Jordan said. "He's seen this island. He's been there. When he was twenty, he spent three weeks with these people."

"Yeah, sure he did. And when I was a baby, my parents put me in a rocket ship and sent me to earth before our home planet exploded." Cheryl lifted her arms and wiggled her fingers at Jordan. "That's why I have supernatural powers."

"Laugh all you want, but when we rediscover The Professor's island and are able to bring back a miracle plant to the world, you'll understand why this trip is so important, far more important than any personal concerns you might have."

Cheryl screamed. "I'm on a boat to Hell with a bunch of psychos! Get out and leave me alone." Swinging her right hand across the foot of the bed, she knocked the tray onto the floor. Food splattered across the carpet as the plate overturned, and the open can of cola sprayed over the hem of the bedspread.

"Damn it, Cheryl, look what you've done." Jordan stared at the mess she'd made. "Why can't you look at this trip as a great adventure, one you can tell your children and grandchildren about? You realize that we could be famous, right along with The Professor, once we give the world—"

"Oh, shut up. You're an idiot, you know that, don't you?"

Cheryl eased off the side of the bed and stepped around the toppled tray and scattered food. Jordan Elders glared at her as if she were a disobedient child and he her stern parent. She marched right up to him and stared him in the face. What Tori ever saw in this geek was beyond her. He was tall, thin and gangly, with a mop of curly brown hair and a pair of— she studied him more closely—a pair of green eyes hidden behind his nerdy glasses. He wasn't exactly heartthrob material, but then, Tori always did go for the brainy types. Her last boyfriend had been majoring in chemical engineering.

"If you want to get rich, you don't have to try to find some nonexistent youth-serum plant," Cheryl said. "Get me off this boat and back to Puerto Nuevo or the States and my dad will give you any amount of money you want. A million dollars!"

He stared at her as she'd been speaking a language foreign to him. "You think I'm interested in getting rich? I want to make history, to be part of a group that will give the entire world this marvelous gift—a long, healthy life for every man, woman and child."

Frowning, uncertain if she could believe he was on the up-and-up, Cheryl shook her head and grunted. "Good grief. Are you for real?"

"Look, I'll help you clean up this mess." He knelt on the floor. "Then I'll bring you a sandwich later. But you have to promise you'll behave yourself. You can't keep causing so much trouble. I don't have time to babysit you."

Gritting her teeth, Cheryl balled her hands into fists and groaned. "You don't have to babysit me. Just let me go."

He turned the tray upright, set the plate on the tray and took the napkin and wiped the food from the carpet. "If you hadn't sneaked aboard the *Sun Dancer* before we left Puerto Nuevo, you wouldn't be here now. So you have no one to blame but yourself."

"Oh, I have someone to blame all right—Tori and you."

"How am I to blame? It's not my fault that Tori misunderstood our relationship and thought I was serious about her. You should have talked her out of following us to the marina and trying to stow away."

"No, what I should have done was let her follow you by herself, instead of tagging along and trying to keep her out of trouble." Cheryl went into the bathroom, got a towel and then dropped down on her knees to mop up the spilled cola. Her gaze connected with Jordan's. "If I'd gone back to the villa and let her chase after you all by herself, then she'd be the one stuck here with you now and not me."

Jordan lifted the tray as he stood. Cheryl got up, dumped the damp hand towel on the tray and huffed.

"Do you still not remember what happened after you and Tori boarded the *Sun Dancer?*" Jordan asked.

Cheryl shook her head. "We followed you and The Professor to the marina and saw you two go aboard the *Sun*

Dancer. We boarded the yacht so that Tori could ask you
to take her with you. I knew you'd say no, and that's why
I was with her, to be there when you broke her heart."

"You told me that you remembered hearing voices and
Tori telling you to hide. Do you remember anything else?"

"I remember hiding in a large storage compartment on
the cockpit and waiting and waiting. I'm not sure if I fell
asleep or passed out. The next thing I remember was that
the yacht was leaving the marina. When I came out of the
storage bin, Captain McGuire saw me and dragged me to
my feet. Then I screamed, and the next thing I knew, you
and The Professor and Molly were all there and I fainted
dead away."

"Why do you think Tori went back to shore and left you?"

"I don't know, but when I see her again, we're going to
have it out."

A long, drawn-out moment of silence vibrated between them as Cheryl and Jordan gazed at each other. She
didn't think she'd ever seen such green eyes, a blue green,
almost turquoise.

Snap out of it, she told herself. This guy is not only
a nerd, but he's crazy. Don't start thinking of him as a
nice guy, as someone you could actually like. But she
could pretend to like him, couldn't she? There weren't
many guys she couldn't wrap around her little finger
and make them do whatever she wanted. Why should
Jordan be any different? She could play nice, and maybe,
just maybe, he'd help her get off this damn boat and
back to civilization.

"I'll bring you a sandwich later." Jordan opened the
door and walked into the salon.

"Jordan?"

He glanced over his shoulder. "Yes?"

"I'm sorry I've been such a brat. And if you bring me a sandwich later, I promise I'll eat it."

When he smiled, he was almost cute.

After she'd eaten a bite of supper, Gwen excused herself and went into the small guest stateroom. She took a shower and donned her cotton sleep shirt with Huntsville Botanical Gardens imprinted across the front and a screen-printed photo of the rose garden on the back. Then she settled into the surprisingly comfortable bed and meditated for a good ten minutes until she felt relaxed and drowsy. She had begun meditating years ago, learning the technique from a friend who, like she, had difficulty winding down at the end of the day.

The wind moaned, almost like a woman weeping, as it bombarded the yacht, rocking it none too gently. Think of yourself in a big cradle, being rocked to sleep.

Just then, lightning danced in the sky outside the porthole and booming thunder announced the storm had hit. Rain poured down, the sound blending with the wind, becoming an unnerving roar.

Gwen shot up in bed. There was no way she could sleep. She could go into the salon and fix herself a drink, just as Will had after dinner. Maybe that would help her sleep.

After easing open her stateroom door, she crept into the salon, tiptoeing on bare feet across the carpet. The room lay in semidarkness, lit only by the light from her stateroom and the dim light Will had left on over the sink. As she made her way across the salon, she thought she heard a noise.

"Can't sleep?" Will asked, his voice coming from the curved settee on the opposite side of the salon.

Gwen gasped and jumped. "You scared me half to death."

"Sorry."

"What are you doing sitting in here in the dark? I thought you went to bed."

"I did, but I couldn't sleep."

"All that wind and rain and thunder are pretty noisy," Gwen said.

"Hmm… Why don't you come over here and sit down. We can pass the time by swapping old war stories."

Gwen turned on more lights. Will grunted.

"Turn those off," he told her.

She looked at him and noticed he was sitting there bare-chested and barefoot, wearing only his jeans. His chest was as richly tanned as his face and arms, and quite muscular. He hadn't shaved since they'd left Puerto Nuevo, so a light-brown beard stubble gave him a rough, rakish quality that unsettled her.

She turned off the lights and walked across the salon. When she stood over him, he patted the large leather settee. She sat beside him but made sure there was several feet between them.

"When I was a kid, I used to sit on our back porch at night, after everybody else was asleep," he said. "I liked the dark, the solitude. I had to share a room with my brothers, so there was never any privacy and hardly ever any quiet. If Mama wasn't fussing at us for fighting and roughhousing all the time, the old man was issuing orders and reprimanding us for not being tough enough."

"I had my own room," Gwen said. "And my mother was a very quiet, easygoing person. We were very close. And being an only child living with a single parent, there were times when I longed for a brother or a sister."

"I guess it's only human to want what you don't have."

"My father lost his entire family the summer he was twenty. His parents and younger brother. They had rented a yacht and were sailing the Caribbean when a freak storm came up. Everyone was lost, except Daddy."

"Was that when he discovered his mythical island?"

"Yes. My mother always said that losing his family that way did something to him, sort of warped him, so he invented this outrageous tale of an island where people live to be two hundred and are never sick."

"Did you ever think there might be some truth to his tale?" Will turned sideways and faced her in the semidarkness.

"Sure. When I was a little girl, I believed everything my father told me. And then when I was older, I actually went with him on two of his quests to rediscover his island. I was eighteen the first time and nineteen the second time. Even though I didn't believe in his island, I wanted to. It was during those summer voyages with him that I learned how truly obsessed he was with finding this island. My mother had tried to warn me that nothing and no one meant more to him than his totally irrational dream of finding the island and bringing the Fountain of Youth plant to the world."

Will stretched out his arm behind her head and leaned toward her. Gwen's breath caught in her throat. He was too close. She could feel the heat coming off his partially naked body.

"Is that why you hide behind your brains and your baggy clothes and your clean-scrubbed face and—" he lifted a thick strand of hair from her shoulder and slipped his fingers through it as he let it drift back into place "—frumpy hairdo? Because you don't ever want to get involved with a man and have him disappoint you the way your father disappointed your mother and you?"

Gwen felt trapped by the gentle touch of his hand on her shoulder. "I'm not hiding behind anything. I'm just not the frilly, girly type whose main objective in life is to attract men."

Will ran his hand down her arm, over her waist and settled on her hip. She sucked in a deep, concerned breath.

"I got a glimpse of your nightshirt," he told her. "Don't you own anything the least bit sexy and feminine?"

"I dress for comfort, especially what I sleep in."

"I made a bet with myself not long after we met that you probably wear white cotton panties and bras. Am I right?"

Gwen's heartbeat accelerated alarmingly. He had no right to ask her something so personal, so private. But the very thought of him being curious about her underwear sent quivers through her body.

"That's none of your business," she finally managed to tell him.

He inched her nightshirt up her leg enough so that he could slip his hand beneath and caress her hip. She should protest, but somehow she couldn't move, couldn't speak, could barely breathe.

"I don't know what color they are," Will said, rubbing his hand from her hip to her belly. "But they're definitely cotton."

When he chuckled, she lifted her hand, intending to slap him. She had never slapped a man, not even her ex-husband, and he had broken her young and foolish heart. But she wanted to hurt Will Pierce, wanted to make him stop laughing at her. He caught her by the wrist just as her hand neared his cheek.

Before she realized what was happening, he yanked her

forward until she toppled onto his lap. Startled and gasping for air, she didn't expect what happened next. He kissed her. A long, slow, tongue-thrusting kiss that ignited a fire in her belly. He didn't touch her while he ravaged her mouth, except for his hand, manacled tightly around her wrist. Unable to stop herself, she responded, kissing him back with equal passion.

Finally, when they came up for air, Will released his hold on her wrist and gazed deeply into her eyes.

"You kiss pretty damn good for a brainy, frumpy, no-frills gal," Will said.

She eased away from him and stood. "I do a lot of things pretty damn good."

Will chuckled. "Anything else you'd care to demonstrate."

"Not for you, Mr. Pierce, now or ever."

When she tromped across the salon and into her state-room, she heard his low, rumbling chuckle. Arrogant bastard!

Chapter 6

Gwen lay on the silk sheets, which were smooth and cool to the touch. As if captured inside a transparent bubble, Will and she touched and kissed and explored each other until every nerve in her body screamed for release. Will lifted himself up and over her, then took her with gentle force. Whimpering with pure pleasure, she grasped hold of his shoulders and gave herself over to the uncontrollable hunger she could not deny.

She climaxed with earth-shattering intensity.

Still quivering with the aftershocks of her release, Gwen opened her eyes and realized that she was alone in the round-edged bunk bed nestled inside the belly of the *Footloose*. Not fully awake, she ran her hand over the cotton sheets and felt terribly alone.

Will had not shared her bed. He hadn't made love to her. It had all been a dream. A sensual dream. An erotic dream.

Dear Lord, she'd never dreamed about making love with a man, any man. And she'd certainly never had an orgasm while she was dreaming.

This was bad, really bad. She kicked back the covers, hopped out of bed and went straight into the tiny bathroom. She couldn't allow herself to get hung up on Will Pierce. The very idea was totally ridiculous. She didn't like his type—swaggering macho he-man. Even though she understood that gentle, intellectual dreamers like her father, and sweet, nonthreatening types like her ex-husband, were not necessarily loyal, caring and steadfast, she would never sink so low as to jump in the sack with the first horny Neanderthal who asked her what kind of underwear she was wearing.

He hadn't just asked. He'd found out for himself. Remembering the feel of Will's big hand caressing her hip and belly sent shivers through Gwen.

No. Absolutely, positively no! She was not going to have sex with Will. She didn't have brief, meaningless flings. It wasn't her style—not in her nature.

By the time she finished showering and had dressed for the day, Gwen felt much better, confident that she could handle her silly attraction to Will. *For heaven's sake, I don't even like him!*

When she emerged from her stateroom, she found the salon empty. Was Will still asleep? Suddenly she realized the cruiser was moving. Had she been so preoccupied with her sex dream that she'd missed that all-important fact?

She climbed the steps leading up to the deck and emerged into bright sunlight and the smell of the salty ocean. Will sat on the bench seat at the helm, shaded by the arched hardtop. She sat down beside him. He glanced at her, smiled and nodded.

"Good morning, sleepyhead."

"How long have you been up?" she asked grumpily. "And how long have we been out at sea?" Looking all around her, she saw nothing but the turquoise blue of the sea and the azure of the sky, the two meeting and melding on the horizon.

"I've been up a couple of hours and we set sail about thirty minutes ago."

"Why didn't you wake me?"

"I thought you needed your beauty sleep," he said in a teasing voice.

"Ha-ha. Very funny."

"Ah, come on, brown eyes, don't you have a sense of humor?"

"Maybe women who wear white cotton bras and panties don't have senses of humor. Ever think of that?"

"Nah, can't say that I have, but then, I don't know many of those women. The gals I know usually wear the black-and-red and hot-pink silky stuff. Either that or they don't bother with underwear at all."

"I walked right into that one, didn't I?" Gwen looked pointedly ahead, determined not to make eye contact with Will. "Exactly where are we going?"

"St. Mallon." He nodded toward his covered metal mug perched in the cup holder. "If you want to do something to help, how about making a fresh pot of coffee and refilling that for me."

"Why are we going to St. Mallon?" she asked, ignoring his request.

"I was in radio contact with Dundee's this morning. An

operative on St. Mallon said that the *Sun Dancer* dropped anchor there late yesterday."

"They'll be gone by the time we get there."

"Probably, but my contact said he'll try to find out where they're headed. It'll help if we know whether they're heading straight for Bermuda or if they have another stop or two on the way. If we hear something before we get to St. Mallon, we can keep going to their next destination and possibly catch up with them."

Gwen removed his mug from the cup holder and stood. "I'll make fresh coffee." As she crossed the cockpit, she paused and asked, "Any other womanly duties you'd like for me to do? Cook breakfast maybe?"

"Are you offering to cook something for me?"

"I'm hungry. You're hungry. I don't see why not."

"Thanks."

"You're welcome." *Okay,* Gwen told herself, *maybe if you're pleasant to Will, he'll be pleasant to you. There's no need to argue. We can be friendly without being friends. Or lovers.*

An hour later, after sharing a breakfast of coffee, scrambled eggs and banana muffins, they docked at St. Mallon. Will's contact, whom she suspected was a freelance operative he'd known during his years as a government agent, met them at the marina.

"Molly Esteban made a drop this morning, then they headed out." The man—whose name, she suspected, even Will didn't know—spoke with a British accent. "They're probably going to Baccara next."

"Why Baccara?" Gwen asked.

Will gave her a withering glare, silently reminding her that he'd told her to keep quiet, to let him do all the talking.

Ignoring Gwen's question, Will asked, "Did you see anyone on board, other than the Esteban woman and Captain McGuire?"

"An old man with snowy white hair and a curly-haired boy."

"You didn't see a young redheaded woman?"

"No. The only woman I saw was Molly Esteban."

"Thanks."

As soon as Will's contact left them, Will grabbed Gwen's arm, turned her around forcefully and marched her toward the *Footloose*.

"Why hasn't someone arrested Molly Esteban?" Gwen asked, keeping in step with Will as she tugged to free her manacled arm. "Or at the very least, why haven't the authorities detained her?"

Will released his tenacious hold on her but didn't slow his pace as he responded in an aggravated tone. "The contacts that Dundee's uses often work on both sides of the law. They're not in a position to report crimes, even if they're eyewitnesses to them."

"Then why doesn't Dundee's—"

Will groaned. "You ask too many damn questions."

"So Dundee's uses unscrupulous people for undercover work when it's necessary. I might not approve, but I do understand. And as for asking questions, if I don't ask, how can I learn?"

When Will didn't respond, she kept quiet until they were halfway to the boat, then asked, "How do you know you can trust that man? How can you be sure the *Sun Dancer* is really headed to Baccara? He wouldn't even tell us why they'd go there."

"I trust him as much as I trust any Dundee contact. As

for him lying to us—he'd have no reason to lie. And Baccara is the last island north of here before you hit the wide expanse of the Atlantic on the way to Bermuda. If Molly and Mick are delivering drugs, they'd hit Baccara for sure."

"Oh, I see. So, I take it that we're off on our wild-goose chase again."

"Yeah, and the *Sun Dancer* has less than an hour's head start," Will said. "It sure would help if we knew exactly where they planned to dock."

"You mean your contact couldn't find out that small detail for you?"

"Stop being a pain in the ass, will you?" He urged her into motion.

She kept pace beside him, all the while wondering why on earth she didn't just give up on finding her father and go back to her safe, contented life in Huntsville.

Because her father's life was in danger and the old fool hasn't got sense enough to know it!

But definitely not because she wanted to stay near Will Pierce.

Molly Esteban looked at herself in the mirror. *Face it, you've got ten good years left, at most.* She needed to be socking away some money now, while she was still young enough to get by on her looks. God knew, she didn't have much else going for her. And she wasn't exactly getting rich hooking up with losers like Mick McGuire. But for now he'd have to do. Why couldn't The Professor have been a rich old codger instead of a certifiable kook? The guy was crazy about her. She'd seen to that. Lucky for her, he could still get it up. At least occasionally. If there was one thing Molly knew how to do, it was make a man happy in the sack.

If Emery was wealthy, she'd marry him. After all, at seventy, how long could he live, especially with her around to give his heart a workout on a regular basis?

"You look good enough to eat." Mick came up behind her, nuzzled her neck and groped her boobs.

Shrugging him off, she scolded, "You can't be doing stuff like that. Not now. What if Emery or Jordan came down here and saw you?"

"They're all on deck," Mick said, grinning suggestively. "How about a quickie, baby doll?"

"No! And I wish you'd stop asking. We've got a strictly business arrangement for now. I'm The Professor's girlfriend until we dump him and the other two in Bermuda." She straightened her low-cut, sleeveless shirt where Mick had messed it up, then ran her fingers through her short black hair and headed for the steps leading up to the deck.

Mick caught her halfway up, whirled her around and gave her a hungry once-over with his heated gaze. "After screwing around with that old goat, you'll be hot as a firecracker when you're finally with a real man."

"That old goat rented this boat for us," she reminded Mick. "And having him along as a front for us is working out just fine, isn't it?"

"So far, but what happens when we finish our deliveries? If it was just The Professor and his assistant, there wouldn't be a problem, but what about the little redhead?"

"I don't know, damn it, but you are not going to kill her—" Molly lowered her voice to a whisper "—not the way you killed that other girl."

"If I'd known there was another one hiding out on this boat, I'd have gotten rid of them both at the same time," Mick said.

"As long as she believes we're Emery's friends, just investors in his hare-brained scheme, she won't be a problem. We can just unload her in Bermuda with Emery and Jordan."

"Are you really that stupid?"

She glared at him. "Yeah, maybe I am, so why don't you explain it to me."

"Baby doll, the old man, the kid and the redhead—we're going to have to dump them overboard some night before we reach Bermuda."

Baccara was the capital city of the tiny island nation of Latille, a tropical paradise with a rotting underbelly of crime and corruption. Will had been here once before, nearly five years ago. Even before he and Gwen stepped ashore at the marina, his gut tightened. He possessed a sixth sense when it came to trouble. That's why he'd slipped the 9 mm Ruger under his lightweight jacket.

"Are we meeting someone here?" Gwen asked.

"Not here. I have to go into town to meet our guy."

"You mean *we* have to go into town."

"You're staying here at the marina. There's a halfway decent restaurant where you can eat lunch and—"

"I'm not staying here. I'm going with you."

He took her shoulders gently. "It's too dangerous for you to go with me. The part of town where I'm meeting my contact isn't safe, especially not for—"

"This guy is going to take you to where the *Sun Dancer* is anchored. If you go without me, what excuse will you use when you approach Mick McGuire? If I'm with you, I can tell him the truth, that I'm The Professor's daughter and tracked him down to make sure he's all right."

"I shouldn't have told you that the *Sun Dancer* is here."
Dropping his hands from her shoulders, Will huffed.
"There's a good chance McGuire killed Tori Boyd and that
she wasn't the first person he's killed. The guy's dangerous.
I know how to deal with dangerous people, but if you're
there, you'll be in the way. I'll have to take care of you."

"I can take care of myself."

"You *think* you can."

"If you try to leave me, I'll follow you."

"Yeah, yeah."

He could easily give Gwen the slip, but then she'd be
wandering Baccara alone. Because, no doubt, she'd try to
find the *Sun Dancer* on her own.

"Okay, you're going with me," he said, knowing a
no-win situation when it slapped him in the face. "But you
will do what I tell you to do without question. Understand?"

"No, I don't understand, but I'll do it. I'll do whatever
you tell me to do."

He eyed her skeptically.

"Cross my heart," she told him.

"Stay at my side, keep your mouth shut and don't do
anything unless I tell you to. Can you handle that this time?"

She stared daggers at him but kept silent. He took that
as a yes.

"Why did Mick say we were stopping again?" Jordan
Elders asked The Professor.

"He and Molly need to transfer some funds," Dr. Arnell
replied as he sipped leisurely on his rum and cola.

"I don't understand why they didn't take care of everything
before we left Puerto Nuevo. We're wasting a lot of time—"

"Actually, if my calculations are correct, we're right on time. These little delays have been no problem, because if we headed due north earlier, we would have been too soon. As of tomorrow, we should be able to find the island. It was precisely fifty years ago tomorrow that I washed ashore there."

"Professor, I know your theory about the island being hidden by some sort of cloaking device is as plausible as the belief in the plant that can produce longevity and good health to the people of the island, but it's totally illogical."

"I've spent the better part of the past forty-five years searching for the island," Dr. Arnell said. "I've borrowed money, acquired grants under false pretenses and used up all my own resources to fund expeditions into the vast unknown between the West Indies and Bermuda. If the island is visible at all times, then why haven't I been able to find it? Why has no one else been able to find it?"

Because the island doesn't exist. Jordan wanted to believe in the island, in the miracle plant that grew there, because he longed to be a part of the discovery that could help mankind. And because he not only respected Dr. Arnell, but he genuinely loved the old man. The Professor had taken him under his wing when he'd been his student, had become like a father to him. Without Dr. Arnell's help, he would never have gotten the scholarships to finish his studies and go on to graduate school. If nothing else, he owed the old man his loyalty on what could be his last great adventure.

"You aren't beginning to doubt me, are you, Jordan?"

"No, sir. I want you to find your island and I want to be at your side when that happens."

The Professor lifted his wrinkled hand and clasped Jordan's shoulder. "As soon as Molly and Mick return from their little errand, we will go back to sea, due north. I remember my father setting a course straight for Bermuda. If we retrace the journey I took with my parents and brother all those years ago, I'm certain we'll find my island again. Fifty years to the day."

Fifty years to the day. The Professor now believed that the mythical island was visible only a few weeks every fifty years. What nonsense!

Or was it?

Gwen had never ridden a motorcycle and she wasn't finding this experience something she'd ever want to repeat. Will had explained that they needed fast, reliable transportation to whip down back alleys, up on sidewalks and down dirt paths. Knowing absolutely nothing about motorcycles, she had no idea what make or model she was at present sitting astride behind Will, but her guess was that the monstrosity was far from new. It smelled awful, sounded awful and resembled a rebuilt piece of junk.

Downtown Baccara looked a great deal like most Caribbean cities, and once again, she was missing everything of any interest because they were continuing their frantic wild-goose chase. Only this time, if luck was on their side, they'd make it to the *Sun Dancer* before she set sail again. They whizzed by groves of banana trees and fields of sugar cane.

When the scenery changed dramatically from what she'd seen at their other ports of call, a sense of foreboding crept up her spine. Shacks and dilapidated shanties dotted the roadside.

Gwen hung on tightly around Will's waist, her heartbeat accelerating as Will slowed the cycle, exited the street and crept up a back alley. She felt open and exposed, knowing there was no protection between them and the sinister ugliness around them. They weren't even wearing helmets. A mixture of odors assaulted her when Will stopped and parked the cycle behind a ramshackle house. Rotting garbage. Stagnant water. Human waste.

God, she was going to be sick.

"Wish you'd stayed back at the marina?" Will got off the motorcycle, then turned and helped her dismount.

She couldn't speak, afraid that if she opened her mouth she'd vomit on the spot.

"You look green around the gills," Will said. "If you're going to throw up, do it now and get it over with."

Unsympathetic bastard! At that precise moment, Gwen hated him for being so smugly superior, for not being nauseated himself and for not giving a damn that she was.

Okay, Gwen, stop feeling sorry for yourself. You're a big girl. Deal with it. You can't blame Will. He did advise you to stay at the marina.

Being here in this godforsaken, rancid alleyway was her own damn fault. And the fact that she was on the verge of upchucking was something Will could do nothing about one way or the other.

"I'll be fine," she said, before covering her nose and mouth to shield them from the stench.

"Shh…" he cautioned her.

A slender, ragged figure appeared as if from out of nowhere. He spoke English with a hint of an accent, his voice low and gruff.

"You got the money?" he asked, his gaze darting in every direction.

Will pulled a couple of hundred dollar bills from his pants pocket and offered it to the man. He grabbed the cash, inspected it and stuffed it into his shirt pocket.

"I'll show you where the *Sun Dancer* is docked. That's all your money buys you."

Will nodded. "That's good enough."

Gwen's heartbeat quickened, and uneasiness shivered through her. The man, the place, the tension radiating from Will combined to issue her a warning. She was in the middle of something she knew nothing about, something dangerous.

The dirty little man eyed Gwen. "You should not bring your woman with you. For another hundred dollars, I can take her back to town and guard her for you."

"My woman goes where I go," Will said in a voice that allowed no argument.

They followed their Baccara contact, the first one that had to be paid in cash, as he turned the corner and led them along a back street. Will rolled the motorcycle along with them as they left the alley, until their guide mounted a black Moped. When Will got on the cycle, Gwen positioned herself behind him and wrapped her arms around his waist. Will's two-hundred-dollar contact led them along a dirt path, through a weed-infested area of high grass and down to the backwaters from the nearby lagoon. The guy made a U-turn, pointed northeast and zoomed back in the direction from which they had come, leaving Will and Gwen alone. Will parked the motorcycle behind a stand of tall trees, then helped her off.

"Where are we going?" she whispered.

"Northeast," Will told her in an equally low voice. "My guess is that there's a small harbor nearby, probably one used by smugglers and other unsavory characters."

Gwen groaned silently, wondering if, in her own way, she wasn't as crazy as her father. After all, here she was, in way over her head, and all because she was trying to save her father from his own madness. What was she doing here, with someone who seemed perfectly at home playing spy games in the wilds of a lawless little island?

When they had gone about a quarter of a mile, Will stopped abruptly, shoved her behind him and listened intently. Voices! But she couldn't understand the conversation, was unable to distinguish what language the men were speaking.

Following Will's lead, she crept alongside a chainlink fence that separated the wooded area they'd just come through from what appeared to be a small marina. In the distance she could see four docked boats. As they made their way closer, she caught a glimpse of two burly men deep in conversation.

Will turned to her, put his finger to his lips warning her to be silent, then reached inside his jacket and drew a gun from the back waistband of his jeans. Gwen gasped. He glared at her.

"Hold up there," a deep, threatening voice called to them.

Will whipped around, one hand holding his weapon, the other nudging her behind him, and faced the two approaching strangers. Gwen thought her heart would beat right out of her chest. Cold sweat popped out on her face and moistened her hands.

"What do you want?" one of the men asked.

"I'm looking for a fellow named McGuire," Will said.

"What do you want with him?"

"Personal business," Will said.

"This is a private marina," the taller of the two dark-haired, bronze-skinned men told him in English with no accent. "How did you get here? Who brought you?" Both men eyed the gun in Will's hand.

"I don't want any trouble. If McGuire's here, I want to talk to him. That's all."

"You going to shoot one of us?" the shorter man asked. "Bad idea. You shoot one of us, the other will kill you and take your woman."

Both men came toward them. Gwen clung to Will's arm, shivering, trying to think what she could do to help get them out of this situation. But before she had a glimmer of an idea, all hell broke loose. Will shot one man in the head. He dropped instantly. Gwen's mouth flew open, but she stopped herself just short of screaming. The other man lunged forward, barreling into Will. The two struggled, rolling around on the ground, fighting for the weapon.

While Gwen stood by, feeling helpless, not knowing what to do to help Will, the gun positioned between the two fighters went off.

Oh, God. Will. Will!

Chapter 7

Gwen held her breath for a split second, then rushed forward to where Will lay beneath the burly guard. She needed to find something to use to knock this guy in the head. If he'd shot Will—

Suddenly, only seconds after the first shot, another exploded between the two prone men. Gwen hollered, an involuntary reaction. Before she had a chance to search for a weapon of some kind, the man on top of Will lurched upward, then fell sideways and rolled over onto his back. She stared down at Will, at his bloody hand clutching his gun. Huge red spots covered his tan shirt, from belly to shoulder. Splatters of crimson dotted his jeans, his arms and his face.

Grunting, Will lifted himself into a sitting position. The men they had heard talking when they first arrived began shouting.

Gwen leaned down over Will. "Are you hurt?" Had he

been shot? Or did all that blood belong to the dead man lying beside Will?

Will came to his feet, wincing as he tensed his left shoulder. Then he grabbed her arm and said, "We have to get out of here, now!"

As they backtracked their steps, Gwen could barely keep up with Will. Twice he had to slow down until she caught up. When they reached the parked motorcycle, Gwen jumped on behind him as he revved the motor. Holding on for dear life, she glanced over her shoulder as they sped through the underbrush. She caught glimpses of two men chasing them on foot, but by the time the cycle hit the dirt path, she could no longer see anyone behind them.

"We've lost them," she shouted over the roar of the cycle's noisy engine.

"Not hardly," Will shouted back at her.

That's when she heard a vehicle bearing down on them. When she looked back, she saw a tattered old Jeep tear through the woods and onto the dirt road.

"Hang on," Will told her.

She clung to him, all the while praying like she'd never prayed in her life. Their pursuers fired at them, bullets sailing all around them, one hitting the cycle's back bumper. Will zig-zagged the motorcycle back and forth, then suddenly formed the figure eight by back tracking, swirling around, crisscrossing, and then, when the Jeep finally turned and headed toward them, he went in the opposite direction. By the time the Jeep caught up with them, they had reached the main paved road into Baccara.

Although their hunters ceased firing when they reached civilization, the Jeep continued following them, all the way into downtown Baccara. Once among the traffic and the congested streets, Will managed to maneuver them in and out, around and about, until Gwen had no idea in which direction they were headed. But she didn't care because she hadn't caught even a glimpse of the Jeep for the past few blocks.

Will pulled into an alley behind a hotel, parked the cycle and got off. Gwen didn't wait for his assistance. By the time he held out his hand, she was already on her feet.

"I need you to go into the hotel and ask them to call a taxi for you," Will told her. "I'll wait outside until the taxi arrives, then I'll get into the backseat right after you."

"You want me to get a taxi?" Her voice quivered.

He grasped her chin with his thumb and forefinger. "Take a deep breath."

She did.

"Listen carefully," he told her. "We're safe for now. I lost those guys. But we need to leave Baccara as soon as possible. If anyone sees me looking like this—" he glanced at his bloody clothes and skin "—they might call the local police. We don't want that happening."

"Because you…you killed two men."

"Yeah, because I killed two men."

Gwen nodded. "I'll get us a taxi."

He squeezed her chin, then released her. "Good girl."

Breathing in and out slowly, taking deep, calming breaths, Gwen walked out of the alley and onto the street in front of the hotel. Fixing her loosened ponytail, she straightened her shoulders, walked into the hotel lobby and went directly toward the desk clerk.

What language did they speak in Baccara? Spanish? French? English. Think, Gwen, think…. English. They speak English.

She marched up to the desk clerk, forced a cautious smile and said, "I need a taxi, please."

"Yes, ma'am," the clerk replied and made a quick phone call before informing her that the taxi would arrive shortly.

Barely keeping her smile in place, she nodded, said thank-you and walked outside where she waited in front of the hotel until the taxi arrived, approximately five minutes later. While she waited, she glanced toward the alley once, but didn't see Will.

He's there, she told herself. *He's just staying out of sight.*

When the cabby got out, he stared at Gwen, then asked, "You do not have luggage?"

"No. No luggage."

He opened the taxi door for her. She paused, glanced over her shoulder, didn't see Will and hesitated.

"Is something wrong?" the driver asked.

"No, I'm fine."

She slid into the backseat. The driver rounded the trunk. By the time he slid into the front seat, the back door flew open and Will scooted into the seat beside Gwen.

The driver swiveled around, stared at Will and asked, "Is this man with you?"

"Yes." Gwen barely managed to gulp out the word.

Will issued the driver orders, telling him where to take them—back to the marina where the *Footloose* was docked.

Gwen reached over and grabbed Will's hand. He squeezed her hand tightly.

The driver started the taxi and moved into afternoon traffic. On the drive to the marina, he kept glancing in his rearview mirror, no doubt wondering why Will's clothes were soaked in blood.

When they reached the marina, Will got out and all but

yanked Gwen from the taxi. While she waited, he pulled out several bills that she suspected were hundreds and handed them to the driver.

"You haven't seen us," Will said to the driver.

"No, sir, I have not seen an American woman with a man covered in blood."

Will gave the man a another bill. The driver grinned, then got in his taxi and drove off down the road.

Will clutched Gwen's elbow. "We need to leave Baccara as quickly as possible."

"And go where?"

"Out to sea. We'll drop anchor once we're out far enough, and then I'll plot our course for tomorrow."

"What about the *Sun Dancer?*"

"My guess is they'll head for Bermuda first thing in the morning."

"What were all those gunshots about?" Jordan asked Mick McGuire the minute he and Molly returned from their trip ashore.

"Nothing for us to worry about," Mick said. "It seems they caught a couple of people trying to rob one of the boats anchored here."

"They caught them and called the police," Molly added, a wide smile deepening the wrinkles around her eyes.

"See, Jordan, I told you it was nothing that concerned us." Dr. Arnell patted Jordan on the back, then opened his arms to welcome Molly.

Hugging The Professor, she stood on tiptoe and kissed his wrinkled cheek. "Did you miss me, darling?"

"I always miss you when you're away from me, but I know you and Mick had business to attend to." He glanced at Mick. "Are we all set now? Do we have everything we need for our trip?"

"We're all set." Mick winked at Jordan. "Are you ready to head into the Triangle and rediscover The Professor's island?"

Jordan didn't especially like Mick and sometimes got the feeling the guy was making fun of him and The Professor, but Mick was a seasoned captain and seemed perfectly willing to take them into the Devil's Triangle, in search of the mythical island. Besides that, Mick and Molly had put up part of the capital to fund this expedition.

As giddy as a child on Christmas morning, The Professor beamed with happiness. "If we leave in the morning, then tomorrow we can sail directly into the Triangle, straight to my island."

Mick grinned. "That's what we're hoping for, but it's a big ocean out there and there are no guarantees. We could wind up with no choice but to go on to Bermuda."

"No, no, that won't happen." Dr. Arnell slipped his arm around Molly's slender shoulders. "You're going to be so proud of me, my darling, when I rediscover the island and am able to bring long life and good health to the entire world."

"Emery, you must know that I hope we find your island," Molly said. "I can't bear the thought of your being disappointed."

"I won't be disappointed. Tomorrow we will find my island, exactly fifty years to the day of my first arrival there."

"You seem so certain." Molly gazed lovingly into The Professor's eyes.

Jordan wondered if the woman actually cared about Dr. Arnell or if she was simply infatuated with the thought of being married to man who might soon be famous and possibly rich.

"I have never been more certain of anything in my life," The Professor said. "The island will be visible tomorrow. It's out there...waiting for me." He looked from Molly to Mick and then to Jordan. "It's waiting for all of us."

When they boarded the *Footloose*, Will went below to change out of his bloody clothes, asking Gwen to stay topside until he returned.

Curious as to why he'd made that request, she waited a few minutes, then rushed headlong down the stairs to the salon. The door to the master stateroom stood wide open, but she didn't see Will. Walking quietly, barely breathing, she entered the stateroom and found it empty. She gazed at the partially closed bathroom door.

What is he doing? she asked herself. He probably just wants a little privacy to strip out of his soiled clothes, take a shower and put on a clean shirt and pants.

Suddenly Will came out of the bathroom and stopped dead when he saw Gwen. Gasping, unable to remove her gaze from his totally nude body, she stammered, "I'm sorry. I didn't...I'll leave."

With heat warming her face, she forced her gaze from his impressive sex and up to his muscular chest. As she inspected his broad shoulders, she noticed blood trickling from a shallow wound and realized that all the stains on Will's shirt were not from the other man's blood.

"You were shot!" Without thinking, she moved toward him.

"Don't go all female on me, brown eyes," Will told her. "The bullet just grazed my shoulder. A little alcohol and a bandage and I'll be fine."

"How much blood have you lost? Are you feeling faint?

What can I do to help you? Oh, God, Will, why didn't you tell me you'd been shot?"

"I didn't tell you for this very reason. I didn't want you to get hysterical."

"I am not hysterical."

"Do you want to help me?"

"Yes, of course I do." She gazed into his gorgeous blue eyes, and all she could think about was how much she wanted to take care of this man. Well, that and the fact he was naked and absolutely drop-dead gorgeous.

"Get me some briefs, a shirt, a pair of jeans and socks out of my duffel bag over there—" he indicated the counter space built into the wall "—while I take a shower."

"Of course." She shooed him back into the bathroom. "I'll lay everything out on the bed."

"Thanks."

As he walked into the bathroom, she couldn't stop herself from looking and was rewarded with the sight of his firm round buttocks. *What a body!*

Oh, Gwen, get your mind out of the gutter.

She picked up his vinyl bag, set it on the bed and rummaged through his possessions until she found the items he had requested. She laid out a pair of plain white briefs, a faded pair of jeans, blue cotton socks and a light-blue cotton pullover shirt.

"Hey, Gwen," Will called.

"Yes?"

"I hate to ask, but would you mind giving me a hand?"

"What?"

"Toss me my briefs and then come in here. My shoulder's gotten pretty stiff and I'm probably going to need a little help cleaning this wound and dressing it."

"Okay." She carried the briefs with her, cracked open the door and tossed the underwear to Will.

A minute later he said, "You can come in now."

She opened the door and found him sitting on the commode. There was just enough room in the tight area for her to stand directly in front of him.

"There's a first-aid kit under the sink," he said.

She nodded, turned around and bent over to retrieve the kit, but before she could open the cabinet under the sink, her backside hit Will's knees. She jumped.

He laughed, then slapped her on the butt.

"Stop that!" she told him.

"Sorry. I couldn't resist. You've got a nice ass, Dr. Arnell."

So do you. "You must be delirious."

He chuckled again.

She bent back over, being careful not to rub against his knees, opened the cabinet door and pulled out the first-aid kit. When she turned around, she discovered that Will had stood and they were now face-to-face. Actually, they would have been face-to-face if they were the same height. As it was, with him barefoot and her in tennis shoes, her head hit him at chin level.

"Maybe we should go into the bedroom to do this," Gwen suggested.

"Whatever you say."

He followed her into the stateroom, sat at the foot of the bed and waited for her to doctor him. She flipped open the kit, removed a small bottle of rubbing alcohol and searched for some cotton balls.

"Just pour it on the wound."

"It'll burn."

"I've endured worse."

A lot worse. Although unspoken, she heard those words inside her head. She unscrewed the lid on the bottle, lifted a piece of cotton gauze to catch the overflow and poured the alcohol directly over the gaping wound on his shoulder. He winced slightly. She blew on his shoulder. She laid the wet gauze aside and retrieved another piece, then placed it over his wound. Holding the dressing by the top edge, she used her other hand to pick up the roll of tape. Luckily, the tape tore easily, so she managed to rip off four strips and secure the bandage in place.

"I think you need stitches in that shoulder," she said.

"Probably."

"Otherwise, it's going to leave a nasty scar."

"It won't be my first scar, or hadn't you noticed?"

She really hadn't noticed, but now that he mentioned it, she ran her gaze over his chest and saw two separate scars, both faded to a creamy white. One slashed across his abdomen. A knife wound? The other was smaller and almost round, located on his right side. A bullet wound?

He turned sideways so she could see his back. Another scar. Ragged and pink. A more recent wound?

"Compared to the others, this is just a scratch," he told her.

She stepped back, away from him, and their gazes met. "Do you need me to help you get dressed?"

He shook his head. "I think I can manage."

"It's been years since I was on a boat, but if you gave me some pointers, I might be able to—"

"I can handle things. And we'll leave just as soon as I get dressed. Why don't you rustle us up something to eat and bring it topside?"

"All right. I'll see what I can dig up in the kitchen. I mean the galley."

When she turned to leave, he said, "Gwen, everything's going to be all right. If we don't encounter the *Sun Dancer* out at sea, we'll catch up with them in Bermuda."

"I hope you're right, but after what happened on Baccara—"

"I won't tell you not to worry about your father. He's gotten hooked up with a couple of really bad characters. But as long as he's useful to them…"

"And when my father's no longer useful to them, they'll kill him, won't they? Daddy and Jordan and the Kress girl, if they haven't already killed her."

"I'm not going to lie to you—Yes, there's a good chance they'll kill them."

"Before they reach Bermuda?"

"I don't know. Possibly not, unless Bermuda is their final destination."

Gwen stood frozen to the spot, feeling as if she might burst into tears at any moment and knowing she'd hate herself if she shed one single tear. At least, not in front of Will. She figured he was the type who not only wasn't affected by a woman's tears, but would consider her weak and foolish to waste energy crying.

She turned and walked out, choking back unshed tears.

Will sat in the cockpit, drinking a beer and staring up at the night sky encrusted with countless glittering stars. Gwen sat beside him, her legs against her chest, her arms draped around her knees. The balmy, tropical breeze blew softly through her long dark hair, which fell loose about her shoulders.

Figuring the *Sun Dancer* wouldn't head out to sea before morning, Will felt safe dropping anchor for the

night. At first light he would take the *Footloose* directly into
the Bermuda Triangle, and hope for a miracle—that they
would encounter the *Sun Dancer* at sea. His job was to
rescue Cheryl Kress. His last report from Daisy had been
that Cheryl's parents were probably worried out of their
minds because she was still missing. He knew if his
daughter was in the situation Cheryl was… *His daughter?
Yeah, like he would ever have children.* He was the kind of
man who thought kids should be born to a married mother
and father, so the odds were against his ever having a
family of his own. After all, he was nearly forty, and since
his first marriage had ended—a mutual decision that they
were wrong for each other—Will hadn't loved another
woman. There had been a couple of long-term relationships, if you can call eight or nine months long-term, and
he'd dated dozens of women, some dates ending in bed,
others ending with a kiss good-night.

"You're awfully quiet," Gwen said. "Penny for your
thoughts."

"You wouldn't believe what I was thinking about if I
told you."

"Try me."

"I was thinking about how worried I'd be if I had a
daughter in Cheryl's situation."

"Why did you think I wouldn't believe you?"

Will shrugged. "I figured you didn't see me as the
family-man type."

Gwen lowered her legs and turned sideways so she could
look at Will. "Do you want to get married and have a family?"

"What woman would want a beat-up old warhorse like
me?"

Gwen laughed. "You're kidding me, right? Will Pierce,

I've seen you stark naked and I'm here to tell you that you may be slightly beaten-up and scarred, but you're not old by a long shot. And only about half the women in the world would be interested in taking on the job of taming you."

"Taming me?" Will grinned. "Do you think I'm such a wild beast that I need taming?"

"Most definitely. Taming you wouldn't be a job for the faint-hearted. You won't succumb without putting up a fight."

"Do you think I'd be worth the effort?"

"That depends."

"On what?"

"On how much she loves you." Gwen's voice became whisper soft. "And how much she knew you loved her."

As naturally as taking his next breath, Will slid his right arm around Gwen's waist and drew her close, until they were eye to eye, a hair's breadth between them. "Dr. Arnell, I believe you're a romantic."

"The only reason you're flirting with me is because you're the kind of man who can't help hitting on an available female."

"Are you available?" His breath mingled with hers, their lips almost touching.

"I'm not your type, remember. I'm plain and plump and frumpy."

He lifted his head, putting a couple of feet between them. "I didn't say you were plump." He ran his hand down over her hip. "A little hippy, maybe, but not plump."

Realizing he was kidding her, she socked him playfully on the chest. "I've had my heart broken twice. I'm not looking to make it three times."

"What makes you think I'd break your heart? Wouldn't

you have to care about me for me to have that kind of
power over you?"

"I'm not a one-night stand type of woman," she told him
truthfully. "If we had sex, I'd probably rationalize things
by telling myself I was in love with you. And neither of us
wants that, right?"

She had him there. Gwen *wasn't* his type. Under different circumstances, he doubted he'd give her a second
glance. In the past he'd gone for flashier women, usually
tall, leggy blondes, with an occasional voluptuous brunette
thrown into the mix.

Gwen wasn't tall and leggy, wasn't voluptuous and definitely wasn't flashy.

So why was he sitting here with his arm around her,
thinking about how much he'd like to make love to her?

"No, neither of us wants that," he said firmly.

Chapter 8

What was the matter with her? It wasn't as if she'd never been propositioned before or felt the stirring of sexual attraction. She hadn't become a born-again virgin after her divorce, although there hadn't been many men in her life, and she certainly didn't think of herself as some rare gift for one lucky man. So, why was she fighting her desire to jump into bed with Will Pierce? She might not be his type or he hers, but there was an undeniable chemistry between them.

She had to be honest with herself. She wanted Will. But what if they had sex and it was great? What if after sleeping with him, she realized she'd fallen hard and fast for the big lug? That's what frightened her and what had made her put on the brakes before Will drove them both over an emotional cliff.

"So, if we aren't going to fool around, do you have any suggestions for whiling away the next couple of hours?"

Will asked, easing his arm from around her waist and sitting back on the U-shaped lounger.

"We could indulge in a dying art form," she told him.

He eyed her questioningly.

She smiled. "I'm referring to the art of conversation. You know, idle chit-chat. Or meaningful discussion. I'll tell you about mine, you'll tell me about yours."

"That last part about yours and mine sounds promising." Will scooted closer and draped his arm across the lounge's backrest, directly behind Gwen.

She looked at him pointedly. "The 'yours and mine' I was referring to is your life and my life. Remember trading war stories?"

Will sighed dramatically. "Yeah, I was afraid of that."

"So?"

"So?" he shot the one-word question back at her.

"So, why don't we spend a little time becoming better acquainted?"

"What is it with you women? Why do you want to know what a man is thinking, what he's feeling, about the previous women in his life? Men are simple creatures. I'm usually wondering how I can persuade the woman to have sex with me. And as for feeling things—I think I'd feel good if I had sex. And as for the women in my past—that's where they are, in the past, even if that past is only a week or two ago."

"Okay, so we won't talk about what you're thinking or feeling," Gwen said. "And I couldn't care less about the women in your past, even if that past was only a few days ago." She leaned her head back and rested it against his shoulder. Staring up the beautiful night sky, she thought how perfect this moment would be if she weren't concerned about her father and if Will and she were truly romantically involved. "Did you have a dog when you were a kid?"

"Huh?"

"Did you?"

"Yeah, I had a dog, my brothers and I. An old mix-breed hound. I hadn't thought about Sooner in ages. He was a damn good hunting dog."

"Sooner?" She giggled. "You're kidding?"

"Nope. The old man named him."

"You said you went hunting as a kid, right?"

"Honey, I was born and raised in Texas. I was toting a rifle when I was in diapers." He chuckled. She nudged him in the ribs. "Okay, that's a slight exaggeration, but not much. My old man loved to hunt, and he made sure my brothers and I learned how to use a rifle at a young age. By the time I was twelve, I'd made my first kill. I don't think Dad was ever as proud of me as he was then."

"I don't understand the pleasure in hunting, in stalking an animal and killing it."

"And I don't understand the pleasure somebody gets out of having a flower garden." Will leaned his head against hers.

"How did you know I have a flower garden?" Pivoting her head slightly, she glanced up at him.

"It was just a guess. It wasn't a giant leap from frumpy botanist to flower garden." He grunted when she jabbed him in the ribs again. "You don't happen to have a cat, too, do you?"

"No, I don't, but I did. Periwinkle died last year, and I haven't had the heart to get another cat to replace her."

"Periwinkle?" Will kissed Gwen's temple. "Brown eyes, you amuse me. You really do. I've never met a woman like you."

And I've never met a man like you, all macho cocky swagger and yet kind and understanding and...

"I'm not all that unique," she told him.

He ran his fingers along her shoulder in a caressing tap. "Yeah, I think maybe you are." He squeezed her shoulder. "Hey, you do know I was kidding about the frumpy part, don't you?"

"Were you kidding?"

He maneuvered her so that he could see her face. She looked right at him.

"You deliberately downplay your physical assets, don't you? You wear your hair in a bun or a ponytail, don't use much if any makeup, wear loose, colorless clothes and white cotton underwear." The corners of his mouth lifted into an amused smile. "It's almost as if you're saying don't look at me, don't notice me."

"Life is easier if you don't expect too much, if you don't long to be noticed, if you don't need someone's undivided attention, if you—" Realizing she had already revealed too much of her private self, she stopped talking.

Silence. Soft, gentle silence. The hum of the ocean, the beating of two hearts, their rhythmic breathing. Will slipped his hand between them and took her hand in his, then entwined their fingers.

"How old did you say you were you when your parents divorced?" he asked.

"Ten."

"That's a very impressionable age."

"Don't try to psychoanalyze me, okay?"

He lifted her hand to his lips and kissed it. "How much did your husband remind you of your father?"

"That's a very personal question."

"Yeah, it is."

Gwen turned her head and closed her eyes. "Jeremy Charles was a botanist, like my father. He was brilliant, just as Daddy is. Physically they resembled each other a bit. Tall, slender, distinguished. But Jeremy wasn't a dreamer. He had both feet firmly planted on the ground. He was steady and reliable, and I thought he was loyal and trustworthy."

"You married a guy you thought was an improved version of your dad," Will said. "So what happened? Did Mr. Loyal and Trustworthy cheat on you with some hot little blonde?"

"As a matter of fact, Ryan was a hot little blonde."

"Ryan?"

"Uh-huh. You see Jeremy wasn't quite the man I had thought he was."

"Damn!"

"I was shocked at first, then as time passed I realized I should have figured it out sooner. Poor Jeremy."

"Poor Jeremy, my ass!"

"No, really. We had an amicable divorce and we've remained friends," Gwen said. "He and Ryan still live in Huntsville. They're very happy together and I'm happy for them."

Will slid his arm down and around her waist, pulled her close to him and kissed her. A gentle, nonthreatening kiss. A sweet kiss.

"I've never had my heart broken," Will admitted in a quiet voice.

"Never? Not even by your ex-wife?"

"Marla and I loved each other, but it was no grand passion or anything. After a couple of years together, we realized getting married had been a mistake. Once the red-hot sex fizzled out, we didn't have anything left."

"You both needed more."

"Yeah, I guess we did. Unless I find that something more, I don't plan to get married again."

"I want something I can never have." Gwen wasn't sure why she was actually considering admitting her deepest desire to him. After all, why should he care what she wanted?

"What's that, this something you think you can never have?"

"I want a man to love me the way my father loves his dream of that damn mythical island and the miracle plant. I want to be someone's obsession, the only thing that matters to him, above all else."

"Whew, honey, you don't want much, do you?"

"I said it was something I know I can never have. It's just a silly, romantic notion."

"I don't know. I think you deserve to get what you want. Maybe someday—"

Gwen pressed her index finger against Will's lips. "I think all this fresh sea air has drugged me. I don't usually open up and confess my heart's desire to…to just anybody."

She pulled out of his arms and stood.

"Gwen?"

"I'm going below deck. We'll want to start out early in the morning, so maybe we'd both better try to get some sleep."

She escaped as quickly as she could, all the while calling herself a fool. What had possessed her to tell Will that she longed for a man to love her to the point of obsession? He probably thought she wasn't the type of woman that could inspire that kind of passion in any man. Let alone him.

Jordan Elders had unlocked the door to Cheryl's tiny stateroom and escorted her into the galley an hour ago, while the cruiser was leaving port. Now, she was sitting topside with Jordan, drinking a diet cola and finally breathing in some fresh sea air. They had kept her locked up most of yesterday and all night last night. Apparently, the others had appointed Jordan as her caretaker because he was the one who brought her food and checked on her.

"So where are we going now?" Cheryl asked, gazing to the east, at the rising sun. "North somewhere, I guess."

"Into the North Atlantic, directly into the Bermuda Triangle, in search of The Professor's island," Jordan replied.

"Does he really think he'll be able to find one little island out here in the Atlantic Ocean? Doesn't the Triangle cover thousands of miles?"

"The Bermuda Triangle, also known as the Devil's Triangle, covers over four hundred thousand square miles, and since 1854 more than fifty ships and aircraft have vanished inside the Triangle."

"Well, that's reassuring," she said sarcastically.

"The Professor found the island once or, rather, it found him. He believes the island will come to him again."

"You sound as crazy as he does." Cheryl finished off her canned cola, crushed the can and threw it overboard.

"Did anyone ever tell you that you're a whiny pain in the butt?"

"Did anyone ever tell you that kidnapping is illegal?"

"No one kidnapped you." He glowered at her, as if he had a right to be critical and condemning. "You sneaked aboard the *Sun Dancer* and hid. You were trespassing."

"I was trying to protect a friend, to be there when she got her heart broken. Tori was determined to follow you, and that's the only reason I boarded this damn boat."

"Tori had sense enough to leave before she got caught.

You stowed away, so don't even think about accusing anyone of kidnapping you."

"Maybe I wasn't kidnapped in the beginning, but I'm being held here against my will."

"Yap, yap, yap. How many times do I have to tell you that once we complete our expedition, you'll be free to go home to your rich daddy."

"You may believe that, but I don't. If your noble professor's cohorts find out who my father is, do you honestly think they won't at least consider demanding a ransom for my safe return?"

"No one else knows who your father is. Only I know, and I have no reason to share that information with anyone else. And besides, The Professor trusts Captain McGuire, and he's asked Molly to marry him. He has promised them a percentage of any material gain from the sale of the miracle plant we find on the island."

Cheryl rolled her eyes heavenward. "Are you really as naive and gullible as The Professor?"

"What do you mean by that?"

"Take a look up there at Captain McGuire." She surveyed the middle-aged man sitting at the helm. Overly long salt-and-pepper hair. A scruffy dark beard. Leathery tanned skin. A cigarette dangled from his lips. "Doesn't your gut instincts tell you the guy is a sleaze?"

"I don't judge a man by the way he looks."

"What about judging a woman by the way she looks?" Cheryl nodded upward toward the flying bridge where Dr. Arnell and Molly stood looking out at the vast ocean, searching for sight of the nonexistent island. "Does Molly look like the type of woman who'd be interested in a dotty old professor?"

"She admires and respects Dr. Arnell, just as I do," Jordan said. "Any woman should be honored to have him interested in her."

"Get your head out of your ass, will you? There is no mythical island, no miracle plant. Captain McGuire is a sleaze and probably a crook. And Molly is a whore if I ever saw one. She's probably bedded half the men in the Caribbean."

"What made you so cynical?" Jordan asked.

"What made you so stupid?" she countered.

Grunting disgustedly, Jordan grasped her upper arm. "Look, Cheryl, you got yourself in this situation and you're doing nothing to make it easier on yourself. I get it that you want to go home. I understand you're upset and frustrated, but you're stuck here with us until we either find Dr. Arnell's island or we land in Bermuda. So, grow up, will you, and stop acting like a spoiled brat!"

She jerked away from him, so angry she could spit nails. "If I ever do get home, I'm going to have my daddy make sure you're all put in jail for the rest of your lives!"

She whirled around and ran down the steps to the salon below deck. Not only would she make sure everyone aboard the *Sun Dancer* went to jail, she had a score to settle with someone else. Once she got her hands on Tori, she was going to wring her best friend's neck for getting her into this mess!

Gwen sat at the helm with Will as they headed farther out to sea on a rather bright, sunny, balmy morning. They'd been up since daylight, both of them anxious to set sail. The odds of their finding the *Sun Dancer* in the vastness of the Bermuda Triangle were probably nil, but Gwen knew they had to try. Both the *Sun Dancer* and the *Footloose* had left Baccara and were headed into the Triangle, with Bermuda as the final destination. Will had pointed out that logic dictated a northeasterly route.

"I think we should try to make radio contact with the *Sun Dancer* on and off all day today." Will took a sip from the mug of fresh coffee Gwen had brought him.

"What?" She whipped around and glared at him.

"I said—"

"I heard what you said, but I don't understand. Do you mean we could have made radio contact with them before now and didn't?"

"I did try," he admitted, a sheepish expression on his face. "More than once."

"And?" Gwen held her breath.

"I didn't get a response. My guess is that Mick McGuire has ordered radio silence. He doesn't want anyone aboard giving away their location or—"

"When I first woke this morning, I thought I heard you talking to someone and you said you were just getting a weather report. Are you lying to me? Did you speak to someone aboard the *Sun Dancer?*"

Will placed his mug in the cup holder, clamped his hands around the wheel and stared straight ahead. "I did get a weather report."

"But that's not all, is it?"

"I tried to contact your father's ship," Will told her. "But I didn't get a response. After that, I contacted several other vessels that are traveling into the Triangle today, to ask them to be on the lookout for the *Sun Dancer*. My boss, Sawyer McNamara, was able to get me the information about the other ships in the area."

"So, we do have a chance, no matter how slim, of actually finding the *Sun Dancer?*"

"Yeah, we have a chance."

She picked up on something in his voice, but couldn't quite put her finger on it. "If we don't catch up with them at sea, we'll catch up with them in Bermuda, right? That's what you said."

"Yeah, honey, that's what I said."

Suddenly she knew why she'd heard just a hint of desperation in his voice. "You're pretty sure that Mick and Molly are going to kill my father and Jordan and Cheryl Kress before they reach Bermuda, aren't you?"

Will didn't respond.

Gwen sat beside him, not saying anything else, just breathing, listening to the cruiser's motors and the steady ocean rhythm. They remained silent for quite a while, then a call on the ship's radio shattered the silence with earsplitting intensity.

The call came from a fishing vessel, the *Sea Hunt*. They had spotted the *Sun Dancer*, due east of them. While Will repeated the coordinates, Gwen memorized them.

"They're approximately an hour ahead of us," Will told her. "But I think we can catch up with them in a few hours, as long as they don't change course. There will be no reason for them to increase their speed since they have no idea that we're following them or that we know their coordinates."

Overcome with relief, Gwen threw her arms around Will's neck and kissed him.

"I like seeing you happy," he told her. "But don't get your hopes too high. We haven't caught up with them yet and when we do, there could be trouble."

An hour ago they had entered the waters known worldwide as the Bermuda Triangle. Jordan kept watch with The

Professor and Molly atop the cruiser on the flying bridge. The farther they sailed into the ocean, the more tense Dr. Arnell became, his eyes glued to the horizon, searching, silently praying that this time would be The Time.

Mile after mile of endless sea stretched before them, lay behind them and surrounded them. Although a part of Jordan wanted desperately to believe they would find this mysterious vanishing island, with each passing minute, he grew more uncertain and wondered if Dr. Arnell could endure another failure.

"Tell me again about your island," Molly said, clinging to The Professor's arm.

"You must be weary of listening to my old tales," Dr. Arnell said.

"Don't be silly, darling, I never tire of hearing you talk about something that means so much to you."

"I wish my wife had felt as you do, my dear Molly. She thought me a fool."

"She should have believed in you, and so should your daughter."

"Sweet little Gwendolyn. She did believe in me once. She even went on two expeditions with me, but as she grew older, she became cynical."

"She'll change her tune once you rediscover your island." Molly patted The Professor's hand.

Jordan watched the display of affection between Molly and Dr. Arnell and hoped that the woman's feelings were genuine, that she was on the up-and-up. But ever since Cheryl had put doubts in his mind—about Captain McGuire and Molly—he hadn't been able to shake the uneasy feeling that something was wrong, that they were in trouble. Big trouble.

"Look at those dark clouds." Molly pointed due north. "I thought the weather was supposed to be perfect today."

Jordan looked to the north. The gray clouds swirled and thickened, rapidly growing darker. Suddenly the wind picked up, and within minutes whipped around them with amazing speed.

"We'd better go below," Jordan said.

He and Molly assisted Dr. Arnell, whose arthritic knees hindered him going up and down steps easily. By the time they reached the salon, the dark clouds surrounded them on all sides and streaks of lightning broke through like giant spears of fire. The winds grew in intensity, churning the ocean, sending huge waves up, over, and onto the deck. The choppy waters tumbled the *Sun Dancer* about as if it were a toy ship.

Jordan went to Cheryl's room and unlocked it.

"What's going on? I swear I'm getting seasick," Cheryl said, jumping off her bed.

"We've run into a storm," Jordan told her. "Put on your life jacket and stay in the salon with the others. I'm going back up to find out from McGuire what the hell is going on."

When Jordan returned topside, the wind almost knocked him down and giant waves washed over him, drenching him to the skin. He tried to make his way to the helm, but barely made it on deck before he realized that this was no ordinary storm. It was as if the ocean beneath the *Sun Dancer* was whirling around and around, forming a watery vortex, and the force of the downward current would soon rip the cruiser apart and take it to the bottom of the sea.

Chapter 9

The rough winds and high waves pounded the *Sun Dancer,* tossing the cruiser about with damaging force. Captain McGuire came below, wearing a life jacket and aiming a gun at Jordan and the others who were huddled in the cabin.

"Molly, you're coming with me. We can use the life raft and provisions and have a chance to survive," McGuire shouted at her.

"We can't leave the others!" Molly screamed.

"Come with me or stay here and die with them."

Jordan wasn't sure what The Professor was thinking when he suddenly rushed McGuire, who aimed his weapon and fired. Molly put herself in front of Dr. Arnell and took the bullet meant for him.

McGuire cursed, then raced up the companionway. Jordan followed, knowing if McGuire took the lifeboat, they were all goners. Without warning, a wave crashed over the boat, sweeping McGuire overboard.

Knowing he mustn't waste time, Jordan yelled for the others to come up. Then he helped The Professor, Cheryl and an injured Molly climb into the life raft.

Once aboard, Jordan noted that Cheryl seemed to be in a state of shock. There wasn't much he could do for her right now as they rocked violently in the treacherous waters. He had other things to concern him.

"We need to make sure there's nothing on us or in the raft that could puncture it," Jordan told The Professor.

"What?" Dr. Arnell asked, his gaze focused on Molly. "We have to do something for her. Mick shot her. Why did he shoot her?"

"To hell with Mick McGuire!" Jordan shouted, totally frustrated and scared half out of his mind.

"I've managed to stop the bleeding, but…" The Professor mumbled. "She needs a doctor."

Jordan grabbed The Professor by the shoulders and shook him. "Snap out of it. If you don't help me, we're all in trouble."

"Yes, yes, my boy. What must I do?"

"Help!" a man's voice echoed through the torrent of wind, rain and roaring sea.

"Did you hear that?" Dr. Arnell asked.

Jordan scanned the area around the raft, searching for the source of the voice. He knew, even before he caught sight of him, that the voice belonged to Captain McGuire.

"Let him drown," Molly told them, her trembling hand grasping hold of Dr. Arnell's arm. "Let the son of a bitch drown."

"My dear, we can't do that. Despite what he did, he is a human being," Dr. Arnell told her.

Within minutes, Mick McGuire swam up to the lifeboat and hoisted himself aboard. Short of knocking him back into the water, Jordan had little choice but to allow him to join them on the raft.

Gwen sat beside Will at the helm as they sailed along in search of the *Sun Dancer*. The balmy wind and smooth waters added to the perfection of the warm, sunny day, barely a cloud in the clear blue sky. Despite the odds against them, Gwen felt moderately confident that they would somehow be able to rescue her father, Jordan and Cheryl Kress. That confidence came from knowing that if anyone could accomplish the impossible, it was Will.

"Did you put on more sunscreen?" he asked her.

"Not yet." She extended her arms, flipped them over and back, looking at her skin. "I'm not even pink. That SPF 50 sun blocker I brought with me really works."

Will reached over and tapped her on the head. "Keep that cap on. It'll partially shade your face."

She studied him for a few minutes. "For a blond, you sure do tan easily."

"Blond? Who me?" Will chuckled.

"Sandy brown, maybe. But I bet you were a cotton top as a kid."

"Yeah, me and both of my brothers. Our hair was so light, it was almost white. Our mother was a blue-eyed blonde. The old man had Indian blood in him. Cherokee I think. His folks were from Oklahoma. My dad stayed brown as gingerbread from working out in the sun."

"Would you believe that I was bald when I was born and now I have this thick mop?" Moving her head back and forth, Gwen flipped her loose ponytail. "My mother said

I looked like a beautiful little boy with my big brown eyes, round little face and no hair."

"I can't imagine you ever looking like a boy."

When he glanced at her, Gwen smiled and they exchanged a meaningful look.

"By the time I was one, I had wispy brown curls and was an absolute doll. Mama dressed me in the frilliest little outfits, ruffled panties and—"

"No white cotton underwear for little Gwen, huh?"

She groaned, then laughed. "You'll never let me forget about my plain, prim underwear, will you?"

"I tell you what, brown eyes, once we get back to civilization, you go buy yourself some red-hot silk undies, show them to me, and I'll never bring up the subject of your white unmentionables ever again."

"You've got a deal."

When he offered her his hand, they shook on the deal. Gwen's heart fluttered and her stomach quivered. Did he realize he had implied that they would be seeing each other again after this wild adventure ended?

He doesn't mean it. He's just making conversation, passing the time, joking around. She shouldn't make too much of their little flirtation. After all, Will was a man who liked women, and she just happened to be the only available female. Once he had his pick of women, he'd forget she even existed.

"You got awfully quiet," Will said. "Are you thinking about that red silk underwear?"

"Why red? Why not some other color?" she asked.

He kept his gaze focused straight ahead. "I think you'd look great in red. I can just imagine how red would look on you, with your dark hair and eyes and peaches-and-cream complexion. You'd be a knockout."

"Oh, I didn't know our deal included your seeing me in the red underwear. I thought I just had to buy it and show it to you."

"No way. You have to model it for me or the deal is off."

Gwen laughed. "You're crazy, you know that, don't you? Once you've found Cheryl Kress and taken her home to her father, you'll go back to Atlanta and forget you ever met me."

He turned and looked at her, a sly grin curving his lips and a twinkle in his eye. "Something tells me that you're not going to be so easy to forget."

His comment rendered her speechless.

"What, no comeback?" he asked.

"It must have taken years of practice to become so adept at telling a woman what she wants to hear." What woman didn't want to be unforgettable?

"I can be Mr. Smooth when the occasion and the woman call for some sweet-talking, but in your case…"

"In my case, what? And don't you dare think I'd believe you if you told me I'm unforgettable. I'm not that naive."

Will shrugged. "You really don't know your own potential as a femme fatale, do you?"

Before she had a chance to react, Will cursed under his breath, then said, "Look up ahead. It's the damnedest thing I've ever seen."

"What?" She followed his line of vision, toward the vast blue sky-meets-the-sea horizon. "Oh, my God!"

"Something's not right here. I need to get another weather update right now."

Gwen couldn't manage to look away, as if the mesmerizing occurrence miles in front of them had hypnotized her. The swirling dark clouds appeared to be rising from the water, from inside the spinning ocean waves. Silent bolts of lightning danced about, shooting not from the heavens to earth, but from the sea into the sky.

Will tried to radio for a weather update, then muttered a few choice obscenities.

"What's wrong?" Gwen asked.

"Our radio is dead."

When Mick McGuire scrambled toward Molly, The Professor blocked his move.

"Stay away from her. Don't you think you've caused her enough harm?"

"I didn't mean to shoot her," Mick said. "If the stupid bitch hadn't been trying to save your sorry ass—"

"Shut up and sit back," Jordan told Mick, his tone deadly serious.

Chuckling, Mick glanced over his shoulder and looked at Jordan. "What makes you think you're giving the orders?"

"You're one man," Jordan told him. "Dr. Arnell and I make it two against one."

"Make that three against one," Cheryl said, her voice unnaturally calm.

All eyes turned to her. Jordan noted how pale she was, but her dazed expression was gone, replaced with a look of anger and determination.

"You're not so brave without your gun are you, Captain McGuire?" Cheryl made her way around Mick and went directly to where Molly lay huddled semiconscious in The Professor's lap. Cheryl looked at him and asked, "What can I do to help her?"

"I'm not sure there is anything we can do," Dr. Arnell said. "I grabbed the first-aid kit before we abandoned ship, but I'm afraid I lost it when I climbed into the raft." He caressed Molly's cheek. "She's lost quite a bit of blood. Unfortunately, the bullet lodged in her side. It needs to be removed, but without the proper equipment…" Tears welled up in The Professor's dark eyes.

Cheryl turned on Mick. "This is your fault. All of it. You shot her. You were the captain and you took us right into the middle of a storm."

Mick snarled. "I'm not going to listen to your bellyaching, you little—"

Cheryl reached out and slapped Mick. Reacting instinctively, he grabbed her wrist and yanked her toward him. Screeching, she hit and kicked him repeatedly.

The raft undulated, tossing about on the waves as if it might go under at any moment. Jordan grabbed Cheryl away from Mick and pulled her against him, her back to his chest, then held her down, all the while talking quietly to her.

"Calm down. You're rocking the raft. If you keep kicking, you could capsize us. You don't want to do that, do you?"

With each passing second, Cheryl's frantic movements slowed, her screeching died away, and finally she went limp in Jordan's arms.

Holding her, he spoke to everyone on the raft. "We all need to sit low and distribute our weight. No one should sit on the sides and we can't be moving about or try to stand up."

"What difference does it make?" McGuire glared at Jordan. "We're all going to die, either now or later. We'll wind up as fish food."

Jordan knew the odds were against them. The vicious storm had taken them completely by surprise. Only by sheer luck had he managed to get everyone into the raft.

He hadn't had time to bring water or food on board. Unless by some miracle they were rescued in the next twenty-four hours, Mick's prediction of them becoming fish food would probably come true.

"The radio is dead," Will repeated, as if he couldn't believe his own words. "I don't understand. It was working perfectly."

"What can we do?" Gwen asked. "We can't sail into that storm."

"I'm going to try to outrun it. We'll turn around and head toward Nassau. It should be the closest landmass."

While Will maneuvered the cruiser, Gwen stared at the approaching storm, puzzled by the unusual clouds and lightning, both seeming to come from the water, as if the ocean and the sky somehow had switched places. Streaks of broad white light shot up from below the ocean's surface as if dozens of enormous spotlights on the ocean floor had been turned on and were shooting thousand-megawatt beams into the atmosphere.

"Will, I don't know anything about ocean travel, but is that—" she pointed to the far horizon "—the way storms look out here at sea?"

"No way," he told her. "I've never seen anything like this. It's freaky."

"Do you really think we can outrun it?"

"I don't know, but I'm damn well going to try." He turned to her. "Get the life jackets. We need to put them on now, just in case. And once we do that, go below and put together some supplies—water, nonperishable food, the first-aid kit and—"

"You don't think we can outrun the storm, do you?"

Their gazes met and locked. "Pray, brown eyes. Pray like you've never prayed before."

With her head resting in Dr. Arnell's lap, Molly had lapsed into unconsciousness. Jordan noticed Dr. Arnell caressing her face, brushing stray tendrils of damp hair from her cheeks. The rest of them sat quietly. Tense, frightened and praying for help. Hoping to live. The sudden violent storm that had sunk the *Sun Dancer* died down as quickly as it had sprung to life, leaving them floating along on a calm, tranquil sea. Gradually the dark clouds surrounding them disappeared, leaving behind an azure-blue sky and shimmering sunlight.

Cheryl sat beside Jordan, her hands resting in her lap.

"I'm sorry," she said in a quiet voice.

"Huh?" Jordan glanced at her.

"I'm sorry I got hysterical and nearly capsized us."

Jordan nodded.

"Is Captain McGuire right— Are we going to die?"

"No, my dear young lady, we are not going to die," Dr. Arnell told her. "We survived, all five of us. It's only a matter of time before we come upon my island. And when we do, the natives will provide us with all that we need." He laid his withered old hand over Molly's bloody wound. "They will be able to save my Molly. You wait and see. This is just as it was fifty years ago when I lost my parents, right before I discovered the island."

"I wish you'd shut the hell up, old man," Mick said. "I'm sick to death of hearing about that island."

"You never believed in my island, did you?" The Professor looked at Mick quizzically. "I don't understand why you agreed to back this expedition, why you—"

Mick laughed gruffly. "You're a gullible old fool. All we had to do was play along with your foolish idea of a scientific exploration and we had the perfect front."

"A front for what?" Cheryl asked.

"For our drop-offs," Mick said. "In Kingston and San Juan and St. Mallon and Baccara."

"Illegal drugs." Jordan didn't know why he hadn't figured it out sooner. Because he'd had his head in the clouds, just as Dr. Arnell had.

"Yeah." Mick snorted. "You and the old man aren't so smart, are you? Book smart maybe, but dumb as dirt out in the real world."

"You said *we*." Dr. Arnell stared at Mick. "Who do you mean by *we*?"

"Who do you think I mean? Molly and me. As soon as she met up with you at the Yellow Parrot back in Puerto Nuevo, she came up with the idea of our pretending to believe in your theory about that stupid island."

"I don't believe you. Molly cares for me. I care for her. We're going to be married after I bring the miracle plant back to the world."

Mick laughed and laughed.

Cheryl reached over and patted Dr. Arnell's hand. "Don't listen to him. Whatever her original motives were, isn't it obvious that Molly does care about you? She took a bullet for you, didn't she?"

With tears streaming down his face, Dr. Arnell stroked his bony fingers through Molly's short, dark hair and cupped her head tenderly.

"Oh, my God!" Cheryl shouted.

"What is it?" Jordan's gaze followed hers. He couldn't believe his eyes.

"Land," Cheryl cried out gleefully. "I see land."

"There is no land out here," Mick said. "We're in the middle of the Triangle. There's nothing out here but ocean and more ocean."

"No, you're wrong." The Professor gazed at the horizon, a smile of pure bliss on his tired, old face. "It's my island. I knew it would come to me again. Fifty years to the day that I landed here as a young man."

"What's wrong?" Gwen asked when she realized the *Footloose* wasn't moving, that the engines were quiet.

"The engines just died," Will told her.

"What? How is that possible?"

"Hell if I know. First the radio goes out, now the engines die."

Gwen glanced over her shoulder at the approaching storm, the storm rising from the ocean's depth. "Oh... Will...Will...it's nearly on us."

"Son of a bitch!"

Within seconds, dark, menacing clouds surrounded them. High waves attacked the cruiser, tossing it about, as rain pelted them and lightning struck the starboard side of the boat.

Gwen screamed. Will grabbed her and held her.

We're going to die. Dear God, we're going to die.

Chapter 10

Gwen had no idea how much time had passed—if it had been minutes or hours—since the *Footloose* had been engulfed by a raging storm. She had clung to hope, had prayed with every breath she took, had tried to prepare herself for death. And as suddenly as the bizarre storm had descended upon them, it disappeared, as if it had been a merciless mirage, leaving behind utter calm and deadly quiet.

Will grasped her shoulders and shook her. "Gwen? Gwen, snap out of it."

"Huh? What?" From where she huddled on the double seat behind the helm, she gazed up into Will's blue eyes. Suddenly she realized that his knees straddled either side of her legs, that he hovered over her, concern in his stern expression.

He helped her into a sitting position, then rested beside her. "Are you all right?"

"Yes, I think so. What about you?"

"I'm okay."

"What happened?"

Will rose to his feet, held out his hand and, when she accepted it, dragged her up alongside him. The deck of the *Footloose* appeared undamaged, just thoroughly soaked, with water standing a couple of inches deep beneath their feet. Overhead, white fluffy clouds floated along dreamily in the clear blue sky. Beneath the cruiser, the ocean lulled softly, but within seconds she sensed something odd was happening. Will sensed it, too. With her hand in his, she felt him tense.

"We're moving," he told her.

Gwen glanced in every direction. "We're drifting due north."

"No, we're not drifting. We're being pulled."

"How is that possible? There's nothing out there to pull us."

"I don't know. It's some kind of current in the ocean and it's dragging us slowly along with it."

"Is that normal?"

He looked right at her, and what she saw in his eyes unnerved her. Not exactly fear, but apprehension. If a man like Will was concerned about their situation…

"What is it?" she asked. "Tell me."

"There was nothing normal about that freak storm we encountered. There's nothing normal about a late-model cruiser in tip-top shape having sudden engine trouble and losing radio function. Nothing works. None of the navigation instruments, compasses, our cell phones. Not a damn thing."

"Do you think what happened is because we're in the Bermuda Triangle?"

He grunted. "I don't believe in superstitious nonsense, but it's possible some type of magnetic field is wreaking havoc on the engines and the radio and other equipment. Whatever caused the storm and the cruiser's problems is what's probably creating the current that is pulling us along."

"If it continues moving us due north, it could take us closer to Bermuda."

"Or it could simply take us farther into the Atlantic and leave us stranded."

"If that happens…"

"We have water and supplies to last a few weeks, but without being able to radio for help—"

"I'm not ready for the we're-going-to-die scenario," she told him. "Not quite yet. Give me a best-case scenario."

"We're spotted by another vessel and rescued. Or better yet, the engines become operational again or maybe the radio."

"And the odds are?"

He shrugged. "I'm going to check the engines and see if I can discover anything wrong. Same for the radio."

"I wonder if my father and the others aboard the *Sun Dancer* encountered the same storm we did."

"If they took the same route we did, then the storm hit them, too, before it hit us."

"Then my father and the others could be alive and stranded just like us. Or they could be—"

Will grasped her face, cradling her chin between his thumb and forefinger. "Don't think about the alternative. Remember, no death scenarios."

Half an hour later, Will joined Gwen at the helm where she'd been sitting while he checked out the engines. Both were in perfect condition. Both should be working, but they weren't. He couldn't figure out why. Same with the radio and the ship's instruments. Although he didn't believe in the supernatural or the paranormal, he'd seen enough of the world and its mysteries to keep an open mind. Almost every strange occurrence had a basis in scientific fact, so that meant whatever had happened to the *Footloose* could eventually be explained. No voodoo-hoodoo involved.

When he approached the helm, Gwen jumped to her to feet and came to meet him. "What did you find wrong with the engines?" she asked, a hopeful note in her voice.

He shook his head. "The engines are fine. So's the radio."

Hope died instantly. "We're still gliding along, due north. I don't need a compass to tell me that."

He nodded. "Uh-huh."

"How long did that storm last?" she asked.

"What?"

"I've been trying to figure out how long the storm lasted, but for the life of me, I'm not sure if it was only a few minutes or if it was hours. Our watches don't work." She tapped her wristwatch. "Nor do the clocks. The sun is in the west now and it was in the east when the storm hit, so that must mean the storm lasted for hours, right?"

"Right." Like Gwen, when the storm had ended, he'd had no sense of time, of the actual duration of the event.

"Why can't I get a grip on time? I feel as if I've lost hours."

Will huffed. "Yeah, I know what you mean."

"You feel the same way?"

"Yeah. Everything that happened during the storm was weird, as if time stopped, as stupid as that sounds."

"No, no." Gwen grabbed his arm. "That's exactly how I felt. As if time stopped. But that's not possible, is it?"

Will shook his head. "No, it's not possible." He searched the sky, noting that the sun was deep into the western horizon, which meant it was late afternoon. "We both must have passed out for hours. That's the only explanation."

She squeezed his arm. "Do you remember passing out? I don't. I remember clinging to you, of being afraid, of thinking we were going to die. I heard the horrible noise of the wind and the waves. But from the minute lightning struck the boat until the sea calmed and the wind died away, it seemed like only minutes passed."

Will tensed. That was another thing he couldn't explain. The *Footloose* had taken a direct hit from the lightning bolt. He'd bet his life on it. But there was absolutely no sign that the cruiser had been struck by lightning.

"What is it?" Gwen's gaze bolted to his.

"Lightning didn't strike the *Footloose.*"

"Yes, of course it did. We saw it hit. We felt it."

"Yeah, we thought we did." He clasped both of her arms, just above the elbow. "There's no damage to the cruiser, not even a scratch, nothing to indicate we were hit by lightning."

Gwen's big brown eyes widened. Wonder? Fear? Disbelief? He couldn't tell for sure.

"What's going on?" she asked. "I don't understand any of this and I don't like it."

"You think I do? But there has to be a logical explanation of some kind for what's going on."

"Why?"

"Why what?"

"Why does there have to be a logical explanation? After all, we are in the Bermuda Triangle, a place that's known for the unexpected, the strange, the illogical."

Hating her train of thought, he released her, his gaze narrowing as he glared at her. "The next thing I know, you'll be telling me you believe your father's mystical island is out here somewhere and we're drifting straight toward it."

Her cheeks flushed. Her eyes sparkled. She smiled.

"Damn it, Gwen, I wasn't serious. Don't you know a damn joke when you hear it?"

"You're not sure what's happened to us, and it scares you. You don't like being taken by surprise and not being able to get a handle on things."

"I'm not scared. I'm pissed. There's a big difference."

"Well, I'm scared. We're lost in the middle of the Atlantic, in the Devil's Triangle, with hours of our lives missing, a boat with inoperable motors, useless instruments and we're being pulled slowly but surely toward some unknown destination." She glowered at Will. "You're a damn fool to not be scared."

"Then I'm a damn fool." He turned his back on her and stared out at the sea surrounding them. The big wide ocean. Calm, peaceful, tranquil. Then he glanced up at the sunny, blue sky.

"Will?"

"Just leave me alone for a while, okay? I'm going below again, so stay put."

Needing to get away from her and her fanciful ideas, Will left her alone topside as he went below to the salon. He had to think, had to consider his options, few as they might be. They either stayed aboard the *Footloose* and waited to see how long the mysterious current carried them and where it carried them to, or they boarded the seven-man life raft and tried to row free of the current. Either could be a death warrant.

If he didn't report in soon, Dundee's would know he was in trouble. But since he had no idea how far off course the storm had taken them or where the current was dragging them, it could take weeks for a rescue team to find them, if ever.

Will opened the minifridge, retrieved a beer, removed the cap and took a hefty swig. After wiping his mouth with the back of his hand, he flopped down on the sofa and closed his eyes. If they stayed aboard the cruiser, they had food and water that would last for weeks, but the current could guide them into the middle of nowhere, if it hadn't already done so. If they took the life raft— No, that would be a last resort.

Damn! He hated feeling helpless. He wasn't accustomed to having no options. But then again, he'd gotten out of some deadly situations, a few that had seemed hopeless. It wasn't as if, when he'd been on assignments, he hadn't known the risks involved, that he could as easily die as live. One of the reasons he'd left government work and signed on with Dundee's was because, at almost forty, he'd wanted a little more security, to work on cases that didn't always put him one step away from the Grim Reaper's grasp.

"Will!"

Gwen's scream startled him. He dropped the beer bottle in his haste to stand, then ran up the steps and onto the deck. She came running toward him, waving her arms, gasping for breath. What the hell?

She grabbed his arm and tugged. Her eyes were bright, her lips curved into a wide smile. "Come on. Hurry. You've got to see this."

"What is it?" He allowed her to escort him to the helm.

"Look," she said, pointing straight ahead. "See for yourself."

Will looked, blinked, shook his head, closed his eyes, and then looked again. He wasn't seeing things. It was really there, wasn't it? He scoured the horizon. A greenish tint colored the sky, which in the tropics usually meant reflected sunlight from shallow lagoons or shelves of coral reefs. He checked the sky, focusing his gaze on the fixed cumulus cloud hovering over the distant land mass, while clouds all around the cruiser moved ever so slowly.

"My God, it's an island."

"Yes, it's an island," Gwen said.

Land? How was that possible? "We must have gotten blown way off course, maybe back toward the Turks and Caicos or—"

"That's not possible. We're drifting due north. All those islands are south of us."

Damn, she was right.

"It's an island out here in the Bermuda Triangle," Gwen said, a wistful expression on her face and a hopeful tone in her voice.

"It's not what you're thinking," he told her. "It's not your father's mythical island."

"We can't be sure."

"Yeah, I'm sure. And I can prove it to you, once we set foot on the island. It's probably a tiny, uninhabited landmass that's uncharted."

"We are going ashore, aren't we?"

"Yes, we're going ashore. I'll drop anchor and we'll take the raft. The raft doesn't have a keel, so we can't sail it into the wind, but we can sail downwind."

"What if the island is inhabited?" Gwen asked. "What if—"

"What if up is down and down is up? What if the

world is flat and we just sailed off the edge? What if this is your father's mystical island and you've discovered it instead of him?"

Gwen's smile vanished. "You don't have to be hateful."

"And you don't have to be stupid."

Gwen gritted her teeth.

She was right. He didn't have to be downright mean, but if she knew him better, she'd know getting angry was the way he handled frustration. Angry with himself, angry with circumstances, angry that he couldn't fix things.

He was on the verge of apologizing when he noted the stunned and hurt expression on her face had altered. She stared at him with an ambivalent look as if she were torn between hating him and needing him. What was it about Gwen Arnell that had him tied in knots, that made him act out of character? It wasn't his style to care so much about another person. But he cared that he'd hurt her. Cared so damn much that he'd been about to apologize—something he never did!

"Okay, so I'm hateful and you're stupid," he said. "Does that make us even?"

She stared at him, her nose crinkled and her eyes squinched as if she were studying him, trying to figure out what made him tick.

"Round up some water bottles and packets of nonperishable food," he told her when she didn't reply to his question. "I'll anchor the boat and get the raft in the water. Then we'll go explore the island."

"Is it safe?"

He grunted. "Safe? Probably not, but we're no safer on this boat."

* * *

Twenty minutes later Will spotted a point of land jutting out into the ocean and decided that if at all possible, that was the place to bring the raft ashore. Hopefully, safely ashore. Knowing they'd go through the surf to reach shore, Will removed the mast from the raft, then inflated Gwen's life jacket and his own. He lowered the raft's anchor over the stern, extending all the line he had. Using the paddles, he constantly adjusted the sea anchor to keep a strain on the line, knowing his actions would keep the raft pointed toward shore. Anticipating the next wave in the medium surf and feeling no offshore wind, he tried his best to keep the raft from passing over the wave too quickly and capsizing them. When the raft neared the beach, they rode it in on the crest of a large wave. Will rowed as hard as he could, bringing them as close to the beach as possible.

"Don't jump out!" he yelled to Gwen. "Wait until the raft has grounded, then get out as quickly as you can when I tell you to."

She nodded and then waited for his orders. When he told her to jump, she jumped. *Good girl.* He jumped out, grabbed the raft and pulled it ashore, securing it for their return trip to the *Footloose*.

Once ashore and drenched from the ocean waves, they lay in the sand, breathing heavily. Will came to his feet first, then offered Gwen his hand. She took it, if somewhat reluctantly. Together, they scanned every direction. A sandy beach spread out from left to right, seeming to go on endlessly. Behind them, and equally as endless, lay an island jungle, the trees and brush appearing untouched by man.

"It's so quiet," Gwen said.

"What did you expect, a party of two-hundred-year-old natives to greet us?" Damn, why had he said that? There was no way she'd think the comment was funny.

Gwen glared at him. "Are we going to just stand here or are we going to explore the island?"

Will glanced at the sun hanging low over the western horizon. "It's too late in the day to do much exploring. It'll be nightfall within a couple hours. I suggest we stay on the beach, maybe hike a mile or so down one end. Then we can sleep here on the beach and get an early start in the morning to explore inland."

"We're going to stay on the island tonight?"

"Sure. It's not a good idea to take the raft back to the cruiser tonight. Besides, if we can gather enough drift-wood, I'll build a fire."

"A fire that can be seen if a plane flies over."

"Maybe. But it could get chilly and I wouldn't want you to be too uncomfortable sleeping on the beach."

Gwen had some difficulty keeping up with Will as they trekked down the beach. She wasn't totally out of shape, but then again, she wasn't into running marathons, either. It didn't help that Will was taller, had long, slim legs and apparently had the lungs of a long-distance runner.

They had traveled at least a mile in both directions and found nothing more than pristine beach. Not a trace of humans or animals. But they did figure out after their long walk that the island was probably no tiny speck, despite apparently being an uncharted landmass in the Atlantic. At one point, they had spotted what appeared to be hills, each progressively higher as they faded into the distance, their tops shrouded in a foggy mist that hid them from view.

They returned to the raft, their arms loaded with drift-wood, which they piled high away from the water's edge and near the abundant thicket behind them. She watched in fascination as Will started the fire and fanned it to life.

"Hungry?" he asked.

"Thirsty."

He'd carried the supplies in a waterproof backpack and had left the pack hidden beneath the raft. When he lifted the raft and felt underneath, Gwen held her breath, halfway expecting the pack to be gone, thinking perhaps the natives had discovered it. Will pulled out the pack, laid it on the ground, unzipped it and retrieved two bottles of water. When he tossed one to her, their gazes met.

"You look disappointed," he said. "What's wrong? Had you expected our food to be gone?"

She didn't reply. He already thought she was teetering on the edge. No need to give him more proof.

He chuckled. "You did, didn't you? You thought maybe the natives had come out of the woods and—"

"Oh, shut up! I'm in no mood to be made fun of. I'm tired, thirsty, hungry and confused."

"And touchy."

She growled. "You're acting as if this is all some sort of game. It isn't, you know. We're stranded—either on this island or on a boat that isn't going anywhere. This is a life-or-death situation and all you can do is poke fun at my foolish hope that maybe my father isn't as crazy as everyone thinks he is."

Will gave her a heavy-lidded glare. "Do you honest to God think we've landed on some mythical island?"

"Yes." She shook her head. "No." Sighing deeply, she

turned away from him. "I don't know. I told you that I'm tired and confused."

She felt the heat of his body as he approached, coming up directly behind her but not touching her. Closing her eyes, she wrapped her arms around herself in a protective hug.

"Gwen?"

She didn't reply. She couldn't. Emotion tightened her throat.

His big hands clamped down on her shoulders. She tensed. "I don't deal well with frustration. I tend to take it out on whoever happens to be around, and this time, that's you."

"Maybe it is stupid to think this is the island my father found fifty years ago."

Will drew her closer until her back rested squarely against his chest, then he engulfed her in his big strong arms. Holding her breath, needing his comfort and understanding, but afraid to expect it, she relaxed against him.

He brushed the side of her forehead with his lips and said in a soft whisper, "I think you love your father."

She did love her father, despite his having abandoned her for a hopeless dream, an obsession that had not only ruined his life, but had brought her here, to the ends of the earth, to the very brink of death.

Cheryl Kress's stomach growled. She hadn't had anything to eat since breakfast that morning on the boat and now she wished she'd eaten every bite instead of picking at her food the way she had. Standing over the driftwood fire that Jordan Elders had built, Cheryl glanced around at the others. Captain Mick McGuire sat apart from everyone else, a good hundred feet down the beach. The Professor rested against the ruptured life raft that Jordan had managed to salvage after their disastrous landing. The raft had capsized, toppling them all into the ocean. She and Jordan had managed to get The Professor and Molly ashore, neither of them concerned in the least about Mick. Her father would have said that his type was too damn mean to die.

Poor Dr. Arnell looked ninety. A tired, haggard ninety. She wondered just how long he could last if they weren't rescued soon. And Molly. She had not regained consciousness. It would be a miracle if she lasted the night.

Cheryl's gaze rested on Jordan, who sat on the other side of the fire, his back to her as he faced the dark ocean. She would never again look at him and see a nerd. From the moment the storm had hit the *Sun Dancer,* Jordan Elders had transformed from a brainy geek into a rugged hero. In one way or another, he had saved all of them, even the nefarious Mick. Odd how taking charge, issuing orders, doing what needed to be done had come so naturally to Jordan.

Walking around the fire that she hoped could be seen from the sky, Cheryl approached Jordan. Without saying a word, she sat down beside him. He neither moved nor spoke, just kept gazing at the waves as they hit the shore.

"Jordan, dear boy," Dr. Arnell's weak, almost inaudible voice called out.

"Yes, sir?" Jordan replied without turning around.

"I'm too tired to try to find help, but you must seek out the natives tonight. If you don't, I'm afraid we'll lose Molly."

Cheryl sensed the tension in Jordan and understood his situation.

"I'm sorry, but I can't go inland tonight," Jordan replied. "We lost what few supplies we had when the lifeboat capsized. I have no compass, no flashlight and I have no idea where to go. We don't have a choice but to wait until morning."

"If you won't go, then I must," The Professor said.

Jordan groaned softly. Cheryl reached over and squeezed his hand.

Their gazes met, the three-quarter moon shimmering over them as the blaze from the fire behind them added extra illumination to the black night.

She leaned closer and whispered, "Tell him we'll go now and search for the natives, then you and I can walk up the beach and out of his sight. I give him fifteen minutes, twenty at most, before he falls asleep from sheer exhaustion."

Jordan nodded, then rose to his feet and extended his hand to help her. He turned to his old professor. "Cheryl and I will see if we can find someone. You stay here with Molly. We'll be back as soon as possible."

Smiling faintly, Dr. Arnell sighed. "Thank you. Thank you, my boy."

They walked up the beach, remaining silent until they were out of earshot, then Cheryl said, "I wish this had been The Professor's island. I wish he could have his dream before he dies."

Jordan paused, looked at her and then continued walking. "We don't know for sure that this isn't his island."

"What?" Cheryl stopped dead still.

Jordan stopped and turned to face her. "We lost our boat in a freak storm, then our lifeboat seemed to drift on a current that led us straight to this island. An uncharted island in the middle of the Devil's Triangle. Fifty years to the day that Dr. Arnell discovered his island when he was twenty."

"You can't seriously think that this is—"

"Why do you think it's not possible?"

"Well, for one thing, this island seems to be uninhabited. There are no two-hundred-year-old natives bringing us food and water and a healing plant to save Molly's life."

"They might not know that we're here."

"Okay, you're spooking me out with talk like that."

"That wasn't my intention," he told her. "And it's quite possible that this is nothing more than an uncharted, uninhabited island. But come morning, I'm going inland…in search of Dr. Arnell's Utopia."

And then she said something that she wouldn't have thought, not in a million years, that she'd ever say. "I'm going with you. And I hope we find it. The people, the plant, everything the old man believes in."

Jordan stared at her. "Either you've changed a great deal or I didn't have any idea who you really are. There's a lot more to you than just a spoiled, bratty heiress."

"Was that a compliment?" She smiled at him.

"Just an observation."

"Well, I've observed something, too," she told him.

"What?"

"That you're quite a man, Jordan Elders. And I trust you to keep me safe."

Chapter 11

Gwen sat in front of the blazing fire, her back propped against a huge piece of driftwood, her gaze focused on the dark ocean. Was there anyone out there? A ship? A plane? Someone who would come to their rescue? Or were they trapped here on this supposedly nonexistent island, doomed to die here together? Nothing seemed real. Not this island, not her journey in search of her father, not even her relationship with Will Pierce. It was as if she had stepped outside her life—her real life—and had fallen headlong into a parallel universe. Was this how her father had felt most of his life, as if he were a part of two different worlds?

"I return bearing gifts," Will said as he came back from his short visit into the wooded area directly behind them.

Gwen glanced over her shoulder. Will carried an armful of palm fronds. She watched while he arranged the huge leaves in a large rectangle atop the sand. When he finished, he bowed to her.

"My lady's bed awaits."

"Where are you going to sleep?" she asked.

He eyed the makeshift pallet. "I thought surely you'd share with me since there's plenty of room. Besides, if it gets chilly, you might need a little body heat."

"You take the bed. I don't think I can possibly sleep tonight."

Will came over and sat down beside her. "Why's that?"

"I'd think it would be obvious. We're lost in the middle of the Atlantic. No one knows exactly where we are. We have no means of escape."

"Yeah, well, there is that." He chuckled.

She glared at him. "How can you find this amusing? We could die here."

Will shrugged. "The way I look at it, given our circumstances, we're damn lucky."

"You're going to have to explain that one to me. How can you say we're lucky?"

"We have several weeks of food, water and supplies on the *Footloose*. We've landed on a tropical island. Fish will be plentiful. Plus my guess is that there are all kinds of fruit trees and more than likely a lagoon of fresh water somewhere around. We could easily live here indefinitely."

"So you think the possibility of living here indefinitely makes us lucky?"

"It sure as hell beats the alternative."

Gwen groaned. "Well, when you put it that way…"

"And there's one other plus to our being marooned together."

"That would be?"

He grinned sheepishly. "The obvious. You're a woman. I'm a man."

"Which to you equates sex, right?"

"Right."

"I think you're being awfully presumptuous."

"I'm being realistic. Even if we're stuck here for only a few weeks, we're both going to get horny. It's just a matter of time before we—"

"Speak for yourself!" How dare he assume that because of their predicament, she'd be eager to have sex with him.

"I am speaking for myself." He ran the tips of his fingers down her spine, from shoulder blades to buttocks. "I'm all for celebrating being alive. What better way to do that than to make love?"

"It would hardly be making love," she told him, wishing he'd move his hand from where he'd spread his open palm across her lower back. "It would just be sex."

"What's wrong with just sex?" He eased his palm up, then underneath the waist of her pants and slipped inside, his flesh firm and rough against her soft buttocks. She tensed.

She couldn't go all mushy female, despite the decidedly sexual sensations clutching and releasing in her nether regions. It would be a mistake to allow what she was feeling right now to override her common sense. Will didn't want her, Gwen Arnell. He wanted a woman, and she was the only one available. If he had another choice, she seriously doubted he'd choose her. She was certainly no man's fantasy, and she hated the thought of being just a warm body in the night.

"There's nothing wrong with just sex," she told him. "As long as that's what both parties want."

"And you don't want sex? You aren't the least bit interested? You can go the rest of your life without it?" He caressed the top curve of her buttocks, then moved from one hip to the other. "Don't lie to me. I can feel you trembling. You need it as badly as I do. Admit the truth."

Was she trembling?

Yes, damn it, she *was* trembling. And it was all because of Will, because he was touching her.

Maybe he was right. It had been quite some time since she'd been with a man. The problem was that she wasn't the type for meaningless affairs, and committed relationships didn't happen all that often for her. Besides, even in the few relationships she'd had since her divorce, she had never felt completely fulfilled, either physically or emotionally. Men said "I love you" as easily as they breathed if they thought it would get them what they wanted. But no matter how sincere those three little words might be, they were just words. Without the action to back them up, they were meaningless. A woman wanted to hear those words, needed to hear them, but in the long run, actions speak louder than words. And not once had any man ever proven to her by his actions that she was the most important thing in the world to him.

"You can't give me what I want." Gwen pulled away from Will and jumped to her feet.

With one swift leap, he came up beside her and cradled his hand over her shoulder. "What makes you so sure that I can't give you exactly what you want?"

She jerked away from him. "Damn it, I'm not talking about sex. I'm sure sex with you would be great. It would be mind-boggling. Unforgettable. But I'd regret it later."

"Why would you regret it? I'm not married. You're not married. We're both adults, and I can promise you that I'm disease free and I'd bet my bottom dollar you are, too. So—"

"So what about contraception? You don't happen to have a box of condoms on you, do you?"

Raking his fingers through his thick wavy hair, Will cursed under his breath. "Yeah, that could be a problem."

"As much as I'd like to be a mother someday, I'd like to be married before I have a baby."

As if some brilliant idea had suddenly popped into his head, Will grinned. "There's more than one way to have sex."

Gritting her teeth, Gwen groaned. "You just won't give up, will you?"

"Not when I really want something."

"You don't want me."

"Oh, yes, I do."

"You want sex, and I just happen to be the only available woman." Gwen glared at him. "Thanks, but no thanks."

When he reached for her, she sidestepped his grasp and turned her back to him.

"Between your father and your ex-husband, they did quite a number on your self-esteem, didn't they?" Will made no move to touch her again.

His comment hit home, hurting her as if he'd plunged a knife into her back. But only because there was an element of truth in what he'd said. "My self-esteem is just fine, thank you."

"Maybe your self-esteem as a botanist is just fine, but not your self-esteem as a desirable woman." Will's deep, soft voice wrapped around her in the darkness, its power as potent as if he'd actually caressed her. "Just because your father didn't treasure you the way a man should treasure his little girl doesn't mean you aren't worth more than all the mythical islands and youth-serum plants that might or might not exist. And just because your husband was incapable of loving and appreciating you the way a man should doesn't mean you can't inspire complete devotion from another man."

Stop talking! Don't say these things to me. I can't bear to hear you tell me what my heart longs to hear.

With emotion lodged in her throat and on the brink of tears, Gwen walked hurriedly away from Will. The farther she moved away, the faster she walked, until she broke into a slow run as she fled along the beach into the warm, shadowy night. Only the moonlight shimmering on the ocean waves and glimmering against the crystal-white sand saved her from being lost in total darkness.

Twilight had faded into night so slowly that Cheryl's sight adjusted easily to the soft moonlight that cast a golden shadow over the waves and set the sand beneath her feet sparkling like a zillion tiny diamonds. Under different circumstances, she would have found this place beautiful, a truly unspoiled tropical paradise. But knowing she was a castaway with no means of communicating with the outside world tarnished the Eden-like atmosphere. She was certainly out of her element. Being the daughter of a billionaire, she wasn't used to roughing it.

"What's the matter?" she asked Jordan when he simply stared wide-eyed at her after she'd told him that he was quite a man. "Can't you take a compliment?"

"I, er, yes, thank you. I think. But I'm afraid I don't understand why you'd say such a thing. I thought you despised me." Jordan began walking again, moving up the beach at a leisurely pace.

Cheryl followed alongside him. "I did despise you, but I despise Tori even more for getting me into this situation. I swear I couldn't understand what she saw in you, even though she tended to always go for the brainy nerds." Cheryl laughed. "Sorry. I guess being called a brainy nerd is sort of a backhanded compliment, isn't it?"

Jordan grunted. "Yeah, I guess it is."

"I think maybe she saw something in you that I see now. I guess you really can't judge a book by its cover. I'd have never thought you'd wind up being the big, strong hero."

"Me?" he asked, honestly puzzled that she'd referred to him as a hero.

"Yes, you. You do realize that without you, the rest of us would probably be dead. In one way or another, you saved all of us today."

Jordan paused and looked out at the ocean. "I just did what had to be done."

"Yes, I know. And that's what makes you a real hero."

"You've been pretty heroic yourself. Instead of falling apart on me, you've helped me with Dr. Arnell and Molly. I appreciate that."

A long, lingering silence vibrated between them. Cheryl wasn't sure what to say or do next. If she did what her instincts told her to do, she'd go up behind Jordan and wrap her arms around him. She would tell him that she wasn't heroic at all, that she was on the verge of panic, that she was scared out of her mind. If not for trying her best to follow his example, she would already have crumbled to pieces.

"Jordan?"

"Huh?"

"Is there any chance that we'll be rescued?"

"I don't know."

"If we're not…"

Jordan faced her and pulled her into his arms. "I'm scared, too. I have no idea what's going to happen to us. I'm just hoping that we can find a freshwater stream somewhere on the island and maybe fruit trees and wild berries."

Cheryl laid her head on his chest and clung to him.

"I'm pretty much useless, you know," she told him. "I've never done anything in my entire life. I've never made a bed or fixed toast or—" She burst into tears.

Jordan cupped her face in his hands and lowered his lips to hers. His kiss took her breath away.

He skimmed his hands over her shoulders, across her back and downward to cup her buttocks. She stood on tiptoe to participate fully in the kiss. Hot, hard, tongue thrusting. Wow!

They were so absorbed in the kiss that neither of them heard the odd noise; not at first. But as Jordan lifted his head and they stared dreamily into each other's eyes, Cheryl froze.

"Do you hear that?"

He clutched her shoulders. "Be still and quiet."

She did as he ordered, not moving, not speaking, barely breathing.

In her peripheral vision, she saw a dark shadow approaching.

Could it be Mick McGuire? Had the man come after them? If so, that could only mean trouble.

Oh, God, now there was another shadow approaching and another and another.

"Jordan?" she whimpered his name.

"Shh."

"What is it?"

"I don't know."

Whoever or whatever created those dark shadows, they now surrounded Jordan and her. Circled them.

Suddenly a loud, frightened scream rent the night air. *Who was screaming?* she wondered, then realized that she was.

Stopping to catch her breath, Gwen sucked in huge gulps of air to refresh her aching lungs. Doubled over and panting, she could not hold back the tears. She cried so hard that the tears streamed down her cheeks, over her nose and off her chin. Had her entire life, all thirty-three years, led to this moment, to being deserted on an uncharted island in the middle of nowhere, with a man she barely knew? Was there no chance of their being rescued, of her having the opportunity to return to her safe and secure home in Alabama? She wanted to go back to the real world, to escape from this bizarre fantasy. Had she, in the end, become her father's daughter simply by chasing after him, hoping for the impossible just as he had? When all was said and done, was there really any difference between his improbable dream and hers? He hoped to find a mythical island where a magical plant grew, while she longed for a loving, nurturing, normal relationship with her father.

Lifting her head, Gwen stared out at the dark, endless ocean. A sense of hopelessness overwhelmed her. More than likely her father and his shipmates had encountered the same freak storm that Will and she had. But if her father and those with him had survived, where were they now? An inner voice of doom whispered one word: *Dead*. Had the Devil's Triangle, that vast section of the Atlantic that had obsessed her father, finally destroyed him?

Daddy. Daddy, where are you?

She had been so absorbed in her thoughts that she hadn't heard Will approach, hadn't realized that he had followed her, until she felt his strong arms reach around her and pull her back against his chest. And it wasn't until that moment, wrapped securely in his embrace, that Gwen knew how much she needed Will. How much she wanted him.

In another place, at another time, where the world was right-side up and life had a logical order, she would not allow herself to succumb to purely physical attraction. But here, now, reality blurred with illusion, and left her vulnerable to the fear that her life had amounted to nothing, that she would die before having ever really lived.

Absorbing Will's warmth and strength, sensing that he had the power to make her feel alive in a way she so desperately needed, Gwen leaned her head back against his chest and crossed her arms over his where they held her at the waist. With her heartbeat drumming inside her head and her body pulsing with life, she sighed deeply. Will lowered his head and brushed his lips against her neck. She shivered. He nipped at her neck, then licked a moist trail up to her ear.

"Say yes," he whispered.

"Yes." That one word reverberated inside her like an echo that had no ending.

While kissing her ear, her neck, her jaw, Will eased his hands downward, over her belly, across the top of her thighs, then delved between her legs, his fingers rubbing and petting. She moaned when he cupped her mound.

When he moved his hands up to her blouse and slowly but efficiently undid each button, she simply leaned back against him and enjoyed the sexual tension steadily building inside her. He covered her breasts with the palms of his hands and lifted them just enough so that he could flick the nipples with his thumbs. Hot, shivering sensation shot through her.

He adeptly undid the front snap of her bra and freed her breasts. When his hands touched her naked breasts, her rational mind tried to interfere with the pleasure, but she shoved aside cautious thoughts and allowed what she felt to dictate her actions.

Will kneaded her breasts gently, his thumbs and fore-fingers working magic on her nipples, which tightened and extended, sending shards of excitement shooting through her whole body. While one hand remained on her right breast, he lowered the other to her slacks and worked hurriedly to unsnap and unzip the sensible tan pants.

Within seconds, he had maneuvered the garment down her hips and over her legs. When they fell to her ankles, Gwen lifted her feet out of the slacks and kicked them aside. Wasting no time, Will slipped his hand inside her white cotton panties. As his hand inched steadily lower, she held her breath, tingling with anticipation.

As his fingers slid through the curls, Will pinched one nipple and gave her neck a sucking kiss. She whimpered, the sound a plea for him to touch her more intimately, to give her what her body yearned for. He slipped between her feminine lips and inserted two fingers inside her. She closed her thighs around his hand, trapping him. Her body shivered as his rough fingertips eased out of her and then over her highly sensitive nub. With his mouth pressed against her neck and his other hand tormenting one nipple, he increased the pressure and the tempo of his caresses between her legs, bringing her to the brink, then stopping momentarily to prolong the pleasure.

"No, please, don't stop," she cried softly.

He took her to the brink hurriedly, then paused again.

"No…no…" She whimpered.

"You're so hot…so wet…so ready."

He ended her torture, taking her over the edge with several frantic strokes. She shook and shivered and moaned, her body gushing with release. Gasping air as the aftershocks of her climax spiraled through her, Gwen's knees turned to rubber. With one hand still between her thighs and the other wrapped around her waist, Will kept her on her feet.

Giving her all the time she needed, he held her, kissed her temple, and whispered softly into her ear, "I loved the way you came for me, brown eyes."

Able to stand without assistance once again, she turned in his arms. He cupped her face and brought his lips down on hers. She smelled her own musky scent on his fingers. They kissed with raw passion as Gwen ran her hands over him, ripping open his shirt and spreading her fingertips across his hard, lean chest. Oh, how she loved the feel of him.

When she undid his jeans and tugged them downward, he immediately divested himself of the jeans, taking his briefs with them. He stood there, barefoot and naked except for his gaping blue chambray shirt. Gwen kissed a trail from nipple to nipple and was rewarded with Will's deep groans. She made her way down across his belly to the thatch of brown hair surrounding his bulging sex. When she dropped to her knees in the sand, he speared his fingers through her hair and held her head, urging her to take him into her mouth.

She had never wanted to taste a man this way, to capture him with her mouth, to pleasure him so primitively. She licked him from root to tip and loved that the action made him tremble. The heady sense of power thrilled her. She licked and teased and took the tip between her lips and sucked. She repeated these movements again and again until Will captured her head and growled.

"Take all of me," he ordered, his voice a rough rumble.

She opened her mouth and enveloped him, taking him as fully as possible. The strong masculine scent of him, the feel of his tight, muscular legs, the vital energy of his pulsing sex excited her almost beyond reason. She made passionate love to him with her mouth, giving him release. As he shook and groaned, she savored the moment of complete control, knowing that she had rendered this big, strong man temporarily helpless.

After gently easing her mouth from him, she licked her lips, capturing his taste. Will dropped to his knees in front of her, yanked her to him and kissed her until they were both breathless.

Chapter 12

Will wasn't surprised by the awkwardness between Gwen and him the following morning. What did surprise him was his own reaction to what they had shared during the night. After making love that first time, they had strolled back up the beach to the bonfire and the bed of palm fronds. They had shared the makeshift bed, Gwen wrapped in his arms. And they had made love again several times, with their mouths and hands, although he had wanted to be inside her more than anything he'd ever wanted in his life. In the warm darkness, they had explored each other's bodies and had become intimately acquainted. Gwen had a lush, womanly body, with round hips and round breasts and skin as smooth as silk.

Even though love had not been involved in what they had shared, Will couldn't deny there was something more than sex involved. Just looking at her made him hard, made him want her again. He suspected even Gwen hadn't realized that beneath her cool, controlled exterior, she possessed the passion of a wild woman.

But only with me.

That thought both tormented him and pleased him. Of course he had only his instincts to guide him—and possibly his sizable ego—but he'd bet his last dime that Gwen had never let go with another man the way she had with him last night. The very fact that her actions had not possessed the expertise that came from repeated practice had excited him unbearably.

And now, this morning, watching her as she dabbled in the ocean, cleaning herself, totally unashamed of her partial nudity, a sense of possessiveness engulfed Will. On some purely primeval level, he had claimed her as his woman.

When she emerged from the ocean, she shook her head, flipping the strands of her long, dark hair around her shoulders, spraying a circle of water droplets in every direction. Her tight nipples pressed against the thin barrier of her white cotton bra, and a dark triangle was visible through her white cotton panties. One thing for sure—he'd never look at white cotton underwear in the same way, ever again.

"What's for breakfast?" she asked as she shimmied into her wrinkled slacks.

He eyed the two apples, two granola bars and two bottles of water he'd laid out atop the knapsack. "A gourmet delight," he told her.

She offered him a hesitant smile, her gaze not quite connecting with his as she picked up her blouse from their palm-frond bed and slipped into it. "I'd kill for a cup of coffee."

And I'd kill to be buried deep inside you. "If we can find a freshwater spring or maybe even a lagoon, we can have coffee later."

"I'm glad I put coffee and tea in your knapsack." As she buttoned her blouse, she came toward him.

"I didn't want to waste our few bottles of water making coffee, but if we can find fresh water on the island, then we're set."

Gwen nodded, her gaze focused on his unbuttoned shirt instead of his face. He glanced down at where the top three buttons were missing. Her cheeks flamed hot pink. He chuckled. Apparently she'd just realized that she had ripped open his shirt last night, popping off several buttons.

When he reached out to grasp her arm, she tensed. "Come on. Let's sit down and eat. After that, we'll explore the island."

Relaxing, she nodded and allowed him to help her down onto their makeshift bed. He tossed an apple and granola bar into her lap, then handed her a bottle of water before he sat beside her.

"I wonder how big this island is," Gwen said, then unwrapped the granola bar and took a bite.

"I have no idea. But it can't be all that big since no one has ever charted its existence." He unscrewed the cap on his water bottle and took a hefty swig. "Then again, it can't be all that small because the shoreline seems to go on endlessly in both directions."

"What do you think we'll find when we go into the jungle?" Gwen alternated between bites of the granola bar and bites of the apple.

"Trees."

She swatted his arm playfully. "Very funny."

"I figure we'll find fruit trees, maybe coconut at the very least. And possibly some small wild animals."

"Wild animals?"

"Small wild animals, which I can trap and we can roast and—"

"Yuck."

"I figure there's a freshwater source somewhere, which means we won't die of thirst and we can bathe in salt-free water."

They ate in relative silence, each devouring the meager fare. After Will put on his shoes and strapped the knapsack to his back, Gwen slipped into her shoes. Preparing for their trek into the wooded area, he studied her already pink face.

"You're going to blister in this hot sun," he told her. "But it can't be helped. No cap—" he tapped her bare head "—and no sunscreen." He ran his fingertips across her cheek.

She drew in a deep breath when he touched her. "I'll manage."

"Yeah, honey, I know you will." *I'll make sure you do.*

In the early morning hours, the sun low in the eastern horizon, they entered the jungle not far from the beach. Will tore away vines that clogged their path, but the underbrush grew so heavily in places that they simply waded through it, scraping their legs and arms on briars and low branches. The deeper into the jungle they went, the more certain Will became that he had underestimated the island's size. Approximately an hour into their trek, when they emerged into a clearing, Will paused, then slowly turned in a circle. When he faced due east, he did a double take. There in the distance a mountain rose high and wide into the blue sky. How was that possible? Was he hallucinating?

"I see it, too," Gwen said, as if reading his mind.

"This doesn't make any sense." Will stared at the unbelievable. "This island is much larger than I thought, which means it can't be an uncharted island."

"What if it is? What if... Oh, God, Will, what if this really is my father's island?"

"This isn't some mythical island. It can't be. There has to be another explanation." *But what?*

"I know it's difficult to believe that this might be—"

"I don't know what's going on," he admitted. "But our main concern is survival. That means finding fresh water."

Gwen stood, riveted to the spot, staring dreamily at the mist-shrouded mountain.

"Come on." He gave her a gentle shove. "Let's get going."

He chose east, directly toward the mountain, although he surmised it would take days to reach the distant foothills.

By the time the sun shone directly overhead, Will sensed that Gwen needed to rest, but suddenly and unexpectedly, before he mentioned stopping, they came upon another clearing, this one wide and vast, as if it had been cleared recently. Not a clearing created by nature but by man. A shiver of uncertainty hit him square in the gut, instinct telling him that he and Gwen were not alone on this island. In the distance, toward the east, he thought he saw a path.

"I'm tired, Will. I need to rest," Gwen told him.

"Not yet. In a minute." He grabbed her arm and all but dragged her toward the path.

She grumbled but went with him. A few minutes later they stopped dead still, at the edge of a winding stone pathway. Standing immobile, silent and unmoving, Will heard the sound of rushing water.

"I hear water," Gwen said.

He nodded.

"Will?"

"Shh."

He listened closely, halfway expecting to hear human voices. All he heard was the water.

"Follow me," he told her. "But stay behind me. And if I issue you an order, just do what I tell you to do without question. Do you understand?"

"Yes."

They followed the stone path, a path not made by Mother Nature, until they reached a thirty-foot waterfall that flowed into a small, rocky lagoon. The water was clear, the surface shimmery with golden sunlight. Thick, lush vegetation grew in abundance around the pond.

"It's beautiful," Gwen said.

"Yeah, but the main thing is that it's freshwater."

"Can we rest now?" she asked. "Is it safe?"

"We can rest. But I'm not sure how safe this place is. I'm not sure of anything right about now."

"There are—" she cleared her throat "—or there were at one time, people on this island. Human beings made that stone path."

"Yeah, you're right. That clearing and the stone path were man-made."

"Don't you think that there's a chance, even if just a slight chance, that this is the island my father discovered when he was twenty?"

Puzzled, confused and uneasy, Will didn't respond. He found a boulder near the lagoon's edge, removed the backpack, dropped it on the boulder and then sat. Gwen followed his lead and sat beside him. While they stared at the cascading waterfall, Will tried to put his thoughts in order, to make some sense of their surroundings. A landmass large enough to hold an enormous mountain range would hardly have gone uncharted. Something this huge couldn't hide, not even in four hundred thousand miles of ocean. So that meant that either the cruiser had veered into a charted island and they simply hadn't reached civilization yet or they were on some mysterious island, perhaps even the one Emery Arnell claimed he had discovered fifty years ago.

"Did your father ever tell you any details about the island he claims to have discovered?" Will asked.

"Then you do believe it's possible—"

"Just answer my question, will you?"

"He talked about this place—this fabulous island—with a mixture of awe and excitement in his voice," Gwen said. "But I don't remember him talking about details, other than the fact that a magical youth plant grew here, one that somehow enabled the people of the island to live, free of illness for two hundred years."

"Do you remember him mentioning a mountain range?"

"No."

"Waterfalls? Rock pathways?"

Gwen shook her head. "No. His only real interest seemed to be in the plant and its effect on the people."

"What about the people? What did he tell you about them?"

"Not much, only that they lived, on average, to be two hundred, that they were never sick and…well, that's about it."

"Did he say what they looked like, if they were dark or fair or—"

"He referred to them as natives, so I assumed they were

dark-skinned, dark-eyed, but he never actually described their physical appearance."

"Didn't you think that odd, along with the fact that this island of his had no name? You'd have thought the natives would have told him where he was and the name of their country. You'd have thought he would ask. I would, wouldn't you?"

"Yes, I suppose I would. But you have to remember that my father was only twenty, he'd just lost his entire family and he'd been near death when he washed ashore here."

Will gripped her hand tightly and squeezed. "Maybe this island is where your father landed fifty years ago, but he could easily have hallucinated about the natives and their magical plant. If he ran a high fever, if he was ill."

"You're saying it's all right to believe the island exists, that we may actually be on my father's island, but that I shouldn't believe there's magic involved, because you don't believe it's possible."

He released her hand. "There's only one way to find out. We get back on the rock path and follow it to its conclusion."

"You're right." She stood. "I'm ready when you are."

Will stood, picked up the knapsack and strapped it to his back. Then, taking the lead, he returned to the stone path. Gwen kept up with him, but only because he adjusted his gait to hers.

Less than fifteen minutes later they came to a junction. The stone path formed a cross in the middle of the jungle. The north and south sections remained narrow, while the east and west sections broadened to the width of a one-lane road.

"It's a road," Gwen said.

"So it is."

"There are people on this island. You can't deny that fact."

He nodded. "There *were* people here. The stones in the path are worn deep into the earth and are smooth on top, which means the path and that road—" he pointed to the east "—have been here for a very long time, perhaps hundreds of years."

"These people could be the natives my father talked about. And don't tell me that it's not possible."

Will grunted. How could he tell her that her father's mad, rambling stories were not possible? He couldn't. Not when he stood on an ancient path, obviously man-made, on an enormous, uncharted island.

Judging from where the sun rested in the middle of the western sky, Gwen surmised that it was early afternoon, probably around two o'clock, give or take. It seemed to her that they had been following the stone road for days instead of a couple of hours. Will had stopped twice to let her take a breather and drink some water. It irritated her no end that she was worn to a frazzle, while their long trek seemed to have had no effect on him.

As they rounded a bend in the road, Will stopped abruptly and yanked her with him as he dove into the thick jungle that lined either side of the road. Dragging her behind a tree and down on her haunches, Will put his finger to his lips. Widening her eyes, she silently questioned his actions.

And then she heard what Will had apparently heard. Voices!

Although the sound came from too far away for her to understand what was being said, she recognized human voices when she heard them.

"It's—"

Will clamped his hand over her mouth and glowered at her.

Gritting her teeth, she grabbed his hand and removed it, but she remained quiet.

He motioned for her to stay put, then rose to his feet. She came up beside him. He frowned and motioned for her to get back down behind the tree. She shook her head. After grabbing her by the shoulders, he placed his mouth on her ear and whispered, "Stay here."

She shook her head.

Then he did something totally unexpected. He caressed her cheek as he mouthed the words, "Please, stay here."

How did a woman refuse a man whose motive was to protect her, even if she neither wanted nor needed his protection. *Oh, get real, Gwen, you do need his protection.*

She nodded. The corners of Will's lips lifted ever so slightly. He caressed her cheek again, then kissed her forehead. Before she could respond, he shoved her behind the tree and urged her to squat, then he disappeared into the dense brush surrounding them.

Gwen stayed put. Waiting. Wondering. And praying a little. As the minutes ticked by, she prayed a little harder, a little longer.

Reminding herself that Will hadn't been gone all that long, so there was no reason for her to panic, not yet, Gwen did her best to be patient. Her legs ached from squatting. Sweat dotted her face and trickled between her breasts.

Just when she'd given up hope of Will returning and had decided to try to find him, he came through the jungle, silent and deadly, surprising her. The moment she saw him, she leaped to her feet and rushed to him. Throwing her arms around him, she clung to him.

"It's okay, brown eyes," he told her in a soft, low voice. "I'm back."

She smothered his face in kisses, then when he grasped her upper arms, she stilled and stared right at him.

"What did you find?" she asked.

"I could tell you, but I think it's better if you see for yourself," Will said.

"All right. Show me."

When he led her back onto the stone road, she halted and stared at him questioningly.

"We can follow the road most of the way there, then veer off into the jungle."

Trusting Will, she nodded and then followed him along the road. When the voices grew louder, easily heard, he led her off into a heavily wooded area.

"What language are they speaking?" Gwen whispered.

"I have no idea," Will replied. "It's nothing I've ever heard before, and I'm familiar with a lot of languages."

He led her through the thicket, clearing the way for her, then he stopped, pulled her around in front of him and held her shoulders while he pointed her in the direction of the voices and the laughter.

Will yanked back a veil of plush vines to give Gwen an unobstructed view. She gasped, barely managing to stifle the sound.

There before her, like something from a history book or a movie screen, lay a large village of well-constructed mud huts with thatched roofs. Tall, slender, deeply tanned natives stirred about in the village square. Men, women and children. Not a white-haired person in the cluster of people. No one looked older than forty. The men wore only simple loincloths of some creamy white material, leaving their smooth, muscular legs and chests bare. The women wore short dresses, made of the same thin off-white material, their arms and legs bare. The smaller children ran around laughing and playing, all of them totally naked. Both men and women had long, black hair, the men's knotted in one long braid and the women's plaited in three separate lengths.

"They're not the same race as the natives in Central or South America," Will whispered in her ear. "Their skin is not as dark. And their features are—"

"Egyptian," Gwen said.

Chapter 13

Egyptian wasn't the first word that came to mind, at least not for Will, but he could see where Gwen might make that assumption. His first thought had been that these natives looked Middle Eastern, possibly Arabic. But he supposed Egyptian was close enough to his assessment that he and Gwen were in agreement. The fact that this island was inhabited, and by people who bore no resemblance to the natives of Central and South America, puzzled him. Although dark-skinned, neither were they descendants of the African slaves that populated so many of the Caribbean islands.

"You know what this means, don't you?" Gwen snapped around to face him, a look of astonished joy on her face.

"Don't jump to conclusions."

"It's not much of a jump to assume that this is the island my father discovered fifty years ago and these are the people who live to be two hundred years old."

"We don't know where we are or who these people are, so—"

"So there's one way to find out. We go meet them and find out if anyone speaks English."

When she turned around and took a step forward, Will grabbed her. "Not so fast. We have no idea if these people are friendly. For all we know they could be cannibals." Okay, so that notion might be a little farfetched, but his concern about their friendliness was perfectly logical.

Gwen grinned at him. "Cannibals? Look at them." She pointed toward the village. "Do they look uncivilized to you?"

"We can't just go walking into their camp," Will told her. "First we need to observe them and get some idea what's what."

"Aren't you being overly cautious?"

"It pays to be cautious. Let's get out of sight and discuss this. Okay?"

She hesitated, then replied, "Okay. I yield to your superior knowledge and experience in situations like this."

He drew her farther into the jungle, away from the village. When they were far enough away to be neither seen nor heard by anything other than the colorful birds dotting the trees, Will paused.

"No matter who these people are, we know nothing about their culture, their laws, their religious beliefs. Their culture could be radically different from anything we know. We can't walk into their camp and automatically know what is and is not acceptable to them. Do you understand?"

She nodded. "Yes, of course. It's as if we've landed on another planet, isn't it?"

"Sort of. And that's all the more reason to be cautious, to take our time making contact."

"How long should we wait?"

"At least another day. I want to observe them, get as close as possible without them noticing me. Once I determine a few things, I'll approach a single person and use sign language."

"You mean, *we* will approach—"

"No, I mean I will. Once I determine there's no danger, I'll come back for you."

She shook her head.

"For God's sake, Gwen, now is not the time to be stubborn."

"And now is not the time for you to go all macho protective on me," she told him. "If something happens to you, just how long do you suppose I could survive on my own?"

"I think you're a lot more resourceful than you think you are."

"Maybe, but it would be only a matter of time before I encountered the natives or had to go to them for help, right?"

Will knew this was a losing battle. "All right. I'll observe these people today, then we'll camp in the jungle, and tomorrow morning we'll go into the village and let the chips fall where they may."

"I have a good feeling about this. If we're friendly and courteous, I truly believe they will not see us as their enemy."

"I hope you're right." Without more knowledge of these people, Will wasn't going to assume anything. "Let's set up a campsite and get you situated, then I'll go—"

"I'm going back with you," she interrupted him again. "I'll be quiet and I'll follow your orders, but I want to observe them, too."

Will groaned. "Whatever you do, stay out of sight and don't leave my side."

By late afternoon they had been watching the village for several hours and had seen nothing suspicious, simply the daily activities of a people who apparently had no modern conveniences. They baked in huge central ovens and roasted meat over central open fire pits.

Staying on the outskirts, Gwen and Will were able to ascertain that the village was comprised of maybe thirty-five well-constructed huts, the exterior walls whitewashed. In the center of the village was what Will assumed might be a meeting house. Not far from the village, huge fields of grain grew profusely, along with several large gardens filled with a variety of vegetables. In another area, there was a grove of trees, all heavily laden with ripening fruit.

Gwen quickly studied the fields, gardens and the fruit trees, trying to identify the various plants. Without closer inspection, she could only guess, and although some appeared nothing out of the ordinary, typical tropical vegetation, others were unfamiliar, perhaps hybrids of some type.

While they watched what appeared to be a daily routine of men coming in from the fields and being met by their wives and children, a sudden disturbance caught their attention. Escorted by two guards, both carrying spears, a man whose appearance set him apart from the others walked into the village. Although obviously of the same race, he wore a tunic of deep scarlet and carried a case fashioned out of some type of leather. The man Will had picked out as the village leader met the visitor, greeted him with a hand signal that was probably the equivalent of a handshake, then led him inside one of the large huts.

Whispering, Gwen said, "Who do you suppose that is?"

"Someone important. A ruler from another village or a tax collector or a witch doctor. Your guess is as good as mine."

"I wish we understood their language."

"Yeah, that would help."

"If we knew what they were saying, it would help us to know how they might feel about us being here."

"We'll just have to hope that when the time comes, we can communicate by using some sort of sign language, and if we're stuck here indefinitely, we should be able to learn their language."

Gwen looked right at him. "In the excitement of discovering that this island is inhabited, I'd almost forgotten that we're all but marooned here."

"There's no 'all but' to it, honey, we are marooned here."

She sighed. "If this turns out to be my father's island, it won't be fair that we found it, not unless he somehow can make his way here, too. He's the one who should be rediscovering this place, not me."

Will admired her devotion to her father, even if he felt it was somehow misguided and certainly not earned. No matter what great deeds a person might perform in a lifetime, if a person failed as a father, they failed at their most important job. If he ever had a child, he'd try his damnedest to be a good parent. Better than his old man had been and for sure better than Dr. Emery Arnell had been.

"Look, someone's coming out of the house where that man went in." Gwen's attention focused on that single hut.

Will narrowed his gaze when he saw a young man—a slim, brown-haired, fair-skinned man in his late twenties, emerge from the hut. Definitely not a native. He wore tattered jeans, a dirty shirt and had heavy beard stubble.

"Look." Gwen grabbed Will's arm.

Before Will could reply, a young woman followed the man from the hut. He put his arm around the redheaded girl, who placed her head on his shoulder as she cried. Will recognized her immediately from her photograph.

"Oh, my God! That's Cheryl Kress, isn't it?" Gwen tightened her hold on Will's arm.

"Yes, I believe it is. And my guess is that the man with her is Jordan Elders."

"Then that means my father—"

As if on cue, a tall, distinguished white-haired man, his shoulders slumped and tears glistening in his eyes, emerged from the hut.

"Daddy," Gwen cried loudly.

Will cursed through clenched teeth.

Gwen released his arm and shoved aside the foliage hiding them from view. Will reached for her, but she managed to escape before he grabbed her. *Damn! Why couldn't she think with her head instead of her heart?* She was heading straight into the village.

Will rushed after her, catching up with her only after they were spotted by Gwen's father's shipmates, as well as numerous natives. Coming up behind her, Will clasped her hand. She paused and smiled at him.

"It's my father. He's alive. He's all right."

Dr. Arnell's head jerked up, his gaze scanning the area. When he saw Gwen, he did a double take, then cried out her name.

"It's my little Gwendolyn!"

He broke away from the others and hurried toward her. Despite the man's age and the weariness that etched his features, Will saw a strong resemblance between the old man and his daughter. Same dark eyes, same square jaw and prominent cheekbones, same high forehead.

Gwen broke into a run, rushing headlong into her

father's open arms. Will stood back a few feet, his gaze darting from them to The Professor's shipmates to the large group of natives collecting around them. He didn't see any weapons, other than the spears held by the two escorts who waited outside the hut where the scarlet-robed man had entered. But considering the odds, unless he had a machine gun, he wouldn't be able to take out more than a few natives before their sheer number overcame him. Maybe, just maybe, these people were friendly and not hostile. The Professor, Jordan Elders and Cheryl Kress seemed unharmed, even if they all looked tattered, worn and upset about something.

Gwen's father pushed his daughter back, clutched her shoulders and stared at her, apparently happy to see her. "It's another miracle, your being here. But it was meant to be, wasn't it? It is only fitting that you're here to share this magnificent discovery with me."

"Then this *is* your island," Gwen said. "The one you've been searching for all these years?"

"Oh, yes, this is my island. And it has a name, you know. It's Umi. It's an Egyptian word meaning *life*."

"Egyptian?"

"Yes. The village elder, Sebak, has been very kind to us. He is trying to help us. He even sent to another village for a healer for Molly."

"Molly Esteban is with you?" Gwen glanced at the guarded hut.

"She was…injured…and there seems to be nothing that can be done for her. It's too late."

"Daddy, how did you communicate with this man named Sebak?"

The Professor turned and motioned to the tall, broad-shouldered man with a dark, lean body and thick black hair braided to one side. "Please, come and meet my daughter and—" He glanced at Will.

"My friend Will," Gwen said. "He and I have been one step behind you all the way from Puerto Nuevo."

"If only I had known you would actually come to Puerto Nuevo, I would have waited," Dr. Arnell said. "But you were so adamant about not joining me."

The man called Sebak approached, his eyes alert and inquisitive as he surveyed first Gwen and then Will. "You are welcome to Oseye and to the great land of Umi." His English was excellent, spoken with only a slight accent.

Startled, Gwen said, "You speak English."

"Sebak speaks English and French and Spanish," Emery Arnell explained. "As do one or two of the other villagers. But most do not."

"The scholars of Umi are fluent in many languages," Sebak added.

"Are you one of these scholars?" Will asked as he moved protectively to Gwen's side. Although he sensed that Sebak didn't pose a threat, at least not right now, Will did pick up on something negative, some odd gut-instinct type of warning.

Sebak smiled. "No, I am simply a village elder. But my eldest son, Darius, is a scholar."

"Look, I don't mean to be rude," Will said. "But exactly where are we? Where is Umi located? I don't think I've ever seen it on any map. Why is that?"

"Please, the questions can wait until later." Dr. Arnell took Gwen's hand. "Come with me and let me introduce you to my assistant, Jordan Elders, and to—"

"No, I don't think the questions can wait." Will looked

directly at Sebak. "I've asked a simple, uncomplicated question. Where are we?"

Sebak's facial expression didn't alter, not by a twitch or a nod. He met Will's determined stare and replied, "Your question is simple, but the answer is very complicated and best left until later, until we have dealt with the woman's death." He glanced toward the guarded hut. "My people are unaccustomed to one so young dying. It will be difficult for them to understand, and I must explain to them that she and all of you who are visitors from outside Umi, are people who do not share our gift of longevity."

Gwen's gaze connected with Will's for a split second, silently communicating. He could almost hear Gwen saying, "This is my father's island and everything he has told us about it is true." And although he was pretty damn sure she was picking up on his doubts and concerns, he was certain that she thought he was overreacting, that he had no reason to distrust Sebak.

But he wasn't overreacting. Something wasn't quite right here. And it was a lot more than the weird factor, more than his when-did-we-enter-the-Twilight-Zone reaction to this entire situation.

"Sebak is right," Dr. Arnell said. "There will be time enough to ask questions, to study the island, to explore the wonders of Umi, once we've tended to my dear Molly." Tears glazed the old man's dark eyes as he squeezed Gwen's hand. "I didn't tell you about Molly because I wanted you two to meet in person and for our engagement to be a surprise for you. I haven't cared for a woman as deeply as I do Molly since your mother."

The curious natives who surrounded them began whispering in their unique language, but they quieted the moment Sebak's dark gaze circled the crowd. He spoke to them in their native language, his voice loud and authoritative, his words dispersing them, sending them back to their evening routines.

"Emery, please bring your daughter and her—" Sebak looked to Will. "Emery's daughter is your woman, is she not?"

Without giving his answer a moment's thought, Will replied, "Yes, she's my woman."

Sebak nodded. Dr. Arnell smiled faintly and sighed, as if greatly relieved that Will had given Sebak the correct answer. Another red warning flag popped up in Will's mind.

"Come along. We will prepare a place for you," Sebak said. "If you wish to stay with Emery until his woman's earthly life ends, you may do so. I will send someone with food and water." He then spoke to The Professor. "I will make preparations for your woman's farewell."

"Thank you," Dr. Arnell said.

After Sebak left them, Gwen stopped her father before he returned to the guarded hut. "What was that all about, that business of my being Will's woman?"

"Apparently, it is the custom with these people," Jordan Elders said, as he and Cheryl approached. "A woman's identity and status is based upon the man to whom she belongs."

"You're kidding?"

"No, he's not kidding," Cheryl said. "We found out pretty quickly that around here, if a woman doesn't already belong to a man, they will give her to someone. Otherwise she has no identity and quickly becomes an outcast."

"Don't go all Women's Lib on me," Dr. Arnell told

Gwen. "Please don't judge these people until we get to know them and understand them."

"I don't want to get to know them much more," Cheryl said. "They've been nice enough, but I swear, they creep me out."

"You're Cheryl Kress," Will said.

"Yes, I am. How did you know?"

"I'm Will Pierce, a private detective. Your father hired my agency to track you down and bring you home."

Cheryl's eyes widened. She smiled warmly, and fresh tears sprang into her eyes.

"You can't imagine how ready I am to go home." She glanced from Gwen to Will and back again. "How did you two hook up?"

"We met in Puerto Nuevo and quickly realized we were on the same quest," Will told her. "Once we found out that both the girl I'd been sent to find and Gwen's father were connected to Jordan Elders, we simply followed Mr. Elders's path."

"I wish you'd found us sooner," Jordan said. "I'm afraid we got ourselves hooked up with a criminal and then hit a freak storm and wound up on Dr. Arnell's island."

"I assume you came by boat," Dr. Arnell said. "Dare I hope it survived the storm?"

"It survived," Will replied. "But unfortunately the engines aren't working and neither is the radio or anything else."

Dr. Arnell waved his hand, as if brushing off any worry. "It doesn't matter. I'm sure Sebak will provide us with a boat when the time comes for us to leave."

Will noticed Cheryl rolling her eyes heavenward. Apparently, the young woman was as skeptical as he was about this island being some kind of magical paradise. On the other hand, Gwen and Jordan Elders were probably so devoted to Emery Arnell that, despite any misgivings they might have, they both wanted to share his enthusiasm over finally rediscovering his Utopia.

Utopia by any other name…

Umi. An Egyptian word meaning *life.* Isn't that what The Professor had said?

The Egyptian connection puzzled Will as much as anything else, adding to his list of questions. Questions that Sebak seemed very reluctant to answer.

Gwen had stayed with her father in the hut where an unconscious Molly Esteban had been cared for by a healer. In those quiet, somber hours before Molly died, Gwen's father had explained not only how Molly had been shot saving his life, but also about the abilities of the man he referred to as the *adom,* meaning *one* who receives help from God.

"The people of Umi are never sick, and all live to at least two hundred," her father had told her. "But they are not completely immune to accidents, to bodily injuries, and therefore they require a healer. The *adom* is somewhat like one of our doctors, only these men have a combination of medical and spiritual knowledge."

"Witch doctors," Gwen had said before thinking. "Sorry, Father."

"No, no. It's quite all right. In a way, that's what the *adom* is. But unfortunately, since Molly had never been given the Eshe plant before, giving it to her now would do little to help her. One dose doesn't heal. Only repeated doses over several years achieves the desired effect."

"The Eshe plant? Is that the youth-serum plant?"

Emery nodded. "Just as *umi* means *life* in Egyptian, so

does *eshe*. The island provides life for the people and the plant prolongs that life."

Molly Esteban died shortly after nightfall and was taken by the natives out of the hut and through the village. When Gwen questioned her father, he shook his head, requesting her silence. Then he walked away from her and went with Sebak, the two men walking slowly behind the small procession carrying Molly's body away from the village.

How at home her father seemed here, how easily and quickly he had adapted to these people and their customs. Had he, all those years ago, learned more about them than he'd ever told anyone?

A young native woman came up beside Gwen, touched her arm and motioned to her. When she spoke, Gwen did not understand a word she said, but followed the girl to a small hut on the far side of the village. When she drew closer, she saw Will, Jordan, Cheryl and another man standing outside near an open fire pit that gave off heat and light. Odd how soon after sunset the temperature had begun dropping. Not that it was cold by any means, but with each passing hour, it became chillier.

"Where's Dr. Arnell?" Jordan asked.

"Molly Esteban is dead." Gwen went straight to Will, who slipped his arm around her waist.

"Molly's dead?" the scraggly middle-aged man asked.

"Yes, and you killed her," Cheryl told him.

"He's Mick McGuire." Gwen spoke her thoughts aloud.

"And you're The Professor's little girl, huh?" Mick moved in closer to the others and gave Gwen a once-over. "You're not so little, are you? You're all grown-up and filled out pretty good."

Mick McGuire made her skin crawl. Not only did he look sleazy and dirty, his attitude gave away his white-trash background.

Will stepped between Gwen and Mick. She thought she heard Will growl, a sound deep and low in his throat.

"Don't get bent out of shape, buddy," Mick said. "I get it that she's yours. Besides, I've got my eye on one of the native girls. One of the young ones. You know, one with a firm little ass and a pair of big tits."

"Why don't you shut up, McGuire. You're disgusting," Cheryl said.

"You'll be sleeping out under the stars on a pallet again tonight," Jordan told Mick. "You're not sharing a hut with either of us." He hitched his thumb toward himself, then toward Will. "Only couples have their own huts. Single men who have been ostracized are expected to sleep outside, and since Dr. Arnell explained to Sebak that Molly's injuries were caused by McGuire here, he's persona non grata."

Mick glared at Jordan. "I'll find a corner for myself, but you just remember that when it comes time to go for the gold, I expect to get my share." Mick turned around and walked off.

"What's he talking about, what gold?" Gwen asked.

"He's talking about the Eshe plant," Jordan said. "It seems there is a special plant that grows on this island, the one The Professor told us about, and Mick wants his share of the money when we take the plant back to the rest of the world."

A tight knot of apprehension formed in Will's gut. "Does Sebak know about Dr. Arnell's plans to take the plant off the island and share it with the world?" Will asked.

Jordan shook his head. "We've been on the island about

twenty-four hours, and in that time Dr. Arnell's main concern has been saving Molly. He thought certain the Eshe plant could be used to heal her."

"What have you found out about this place, this island? And about Sebak and these people?" Will asked.

"Not a great deal." Jordan nodded to Cheryl. "As you already know, a woman has no status unless she belongs to a man. First to her father or eldest male relative and then to her mate. Every woman is placed with a man as quickly as possible. That's the reason I claimed Cheryl."

"I understand," Will told him.

"As far as I know, only Sebak and a couple of other men in the village speak English. The others speak some ancient tongue that not even The Professor is familiar with."

"Have you been able to figure out exactly where we are and why this island has never been charted, why it's not located on any map?"

"We're in the Atlantic Ocean, inside the Bermuda Triangle. This island has never been charted and isn't on any map because—" Jordan paused "—because it isn't visible to the outside world."

Will squinted as he glared at Jordan. "Run that one by me again. If it's not visible, how come Gwen and I were able to see it? Why were you—"

"I'm not sure, but I believe that Dr. Arnell's theory that the island is only visible once every so many years, maybe every fifty years, might be correct. And that means people can land on the island and depart only during a specific time frame."

"Which would be how long?" Will asked.

"When he was twenty, The Professor stayed here three weeks, then he was sent away. My guess is that the window of opportunity to arrive and depart is connected to that three-week time frame."

"If Dr. Arnell's theory is correct, that means if we don't leave this island within a specific time frame, be it three weeks or four, then we'll be trapped here for years, maybe for the rest of our lives."

Chapter 14

Gwen had wanted to speak to her father again tonight, but Sebak had forbidden it. When a loved one dies on Umi, the deceased person's mate is expected to stay with the body that night, until at midnight, when the body is cremated. Then at dawn the mate takes the ashes and distributes them over a place called the Fields of Eshe.

"Isn't Eshe the name of the plant that keeps everyone healthy and gives you a long life span?" Gwen had asked Sebak.

Sebak had nodded, but said nothing, then departed hurriedly with a group of men that Will had said he believed to be Sebak's guards. Although the natives had carried no weapons, all six of the men with Sebak had been very young, quite tall and muscular.

Since watches didn't work here on Umi, there was no way to tell the exact time. But not long after Sebak departed, natives went around and extinguished all the central outdoor fires. Two men motioned for Gwen, Will, Jordan and Cheryl to enter their huts.

"Let's do as we're told, for now," Will said. "No need to create a problem until we figure out what's what around here."

Although she and Will dreaded the thought of telling Cheryl about her friend Tori's death, they felt she had a right to know, so they invited the other couple to join them in their hut.

"Tori's dead? How…? I don't understand." Cheryl's eyes filled with tears.

"She was strangled and left on the beach in Puerto Nuevo," Will told her. "There's a good possibility that Mick McGuire murdered her."

While Jordan held a weeping Cheryl, he looked directly at Will. "What can we do? We can't let the guy get away with killing Tori and Molly Esteban, too."

"There's nothing we can do now," Will said. "But once we get off this island, we'll turn him over to the proper authorities."

Jordan took a grieving Cheryl back to their hut, leaving Will and Gwen alone to settle in for the night. For the first time since entering the hut, Gwen took a really good look. She wasn't sure what she'd been expecting, but definitely not the neat, well-maintained contents that, although certainly not modern, were not crudely constructed. There was a wooden table and four chairs in an area near a fireplace in which a roaring fire blazed. A large black kettle hung over the fire, its contents smelling of stew. A bowl of fresh fruit and a large, oval loaf of bread, surrounded by thick, fat, glowing candles, graced the center of the

smooth, polished tabletop. On the other side of the room
was a glossy wooden bed framed by sheer fabric that
created a canopy. The bed itself boasted a thick cotton
mattress and was covered with creamy white bed linens,
in a cloth similar to the clothing the natives wore, and
topped with a thick white quilt. The walls were a mellow
cream, as if once white and now yellowed slightly by age.
There was no indoor bathroom. Cheryl and Jordan had explained that the natives bathed in the nearby lagoon and
that four centrally located outhouses were spread about
the village.

"You're awfully quiet." Gwen placed her hand on
Will's shoulder.

Sitting in front of the fireplace, his chair sideways to
give him a view of the door, he glanced up at her. "There's
something not right about this place."

She smiled. "You mean other than the fact that its very
existence is an incredible mystery and that if the Eshe plant
really can prolong life, my father will become very famous."

"And very rich."

"I don't think the money matters to him."

"Probably not," Will said. "But it will matter to others."

"You mean once we're off the island and my father
takes the plant back to the world."

"Yeah, if that ever happens."

"What are you trying to tell me?"

Will's shoulders heaved, then relaxed as he took a deep
breath. "There is no logical explanation for why this island
even exists, yet here we are. And for all intents and
purposes, we're trapped here, with no way to leave."

"Don't you think Sebak will help us leave, just as
someone once helped my father leave all those years ago?"

"Possibly. We can hope they will. But something tells me that they're not going to be too keen on the idea of your father taking samples of the Eshe plant with him."

"But why would they object?" Gwen knew the answer the moment she asked the question. "Oh. They don't really want anyone else to know about the existence of Umi, do they?"

"Which doesn't make sense if your father's theory is correct that this island is visible only every fifty years." Will rose to his feet, rubbed the back of his neck and cursed under his breath. "Do you realize how crazy that sounds? An island the size of Umi going undetected just isn't possible."

"We're like *Alice Through the Looking Glass,* aren't we? We've entered another world."

"You said it, honey. That and then some." Will paced back and forth, then paused and looked right at her. "If this island is invisible, then these natives or maybe the scholars of Umi that Sebak mentioned know a way of cloaking the island or it happens naturally somehow. Then for some reason, every so often, maybe every fifty years, or twenty or whatever, it becomes visible to the outside world. If it's every five or ten years, then once this place is known to the world, and the Eshe plant is proven to provide longevity—"

"The world will come calling and the island will be overrun by outsiders."

"Exactly."

"My father won't leave here without the Eshe plant," Gwen said.

"We need to talk to Sebak tomorrow and get some things settled." Will grasped her shoulders. "You have to convince your father that our only chance of leaving this place alive may depend upon him."

Gwen glowered at Will. "How can you ask me to persuade my father to give up his lifetime dream of bringing back this miracle plant to the world?"

Will tightened his hold on her shoulders. "What's more important, your father trying to take the Eshe plant with him or our living long enough to leave this island?"

Gwen jerked away from him. "What makes you so sure that it's an either-or situation?"

"Gut instinct," he told her. "And if you'll think with your head instead of your heart, you'll know I'm right."

Dr. Emery Arnell observed the beautiful sight as dawn light shimmered pale-gold over the Fields of Eshe, a valley located four miles from the village of Oseye. Emery and Sebak had been taken from the crematorium to the fields by a rickshaw-type conveyance pulled by two strong young men from Sebak's village.

Emery stood on a knoll overlooking the endless fields where the tall, willowy Eshe plants grew in profusion. Their yellow-green leaves glistened with dewdrops in the faint illumination. The early morning air was crisp and clean.

"Come," Sebak said. "I will walk with you as you distribute your woman's ashes."

Emery held the silver urn in which Molly's ashes had been placed. He had known her for such a short time, but had come to adore her, perhaps only in a way a doddering old fool can love a beautiful, young woman. Even knowing that she had played him for a fool did not lessen his fondness for her. After all, in the end, she had given her life to save his.

As they entered the fields where the knee-high plants grew, Sebak pointed to the urn. "Turn the cap and it will open partially, enough to allow a small amount of ashes to come out, a little at a time."

Emery nodded, turned the urn's round cap and then followed Sebak as he led him along the narrow paths, up and down the rows of Eshe plants. It took no more than five minutes to empty the urn, which Sebak took from him, laid on the ground and stomped on it with his foot. The silver urn, apparently made of some porous and easily broken material, smashed into tiny shards no bigger than a child's fingernails.

Sebak then turned to Emery and said, "We will walk to the end of this row and then offer our prayers for the afterlife of your woman before we return to Oseye."

Sebak's prayers were in his native tongue, one Emery suspected was unknown anywhere else on earth, perhaps a dialect spoken thousands of years ago.

They were taken to within a mile of Oseye by the rickshaw-type buggies, then were put on foot to continue their journey.

"I have many questions," Emery said.

Sebak nodded.

"I told you that I washed ashore on this island fifty years ago, when I was only twenty. I have been searching for Umi all these years without any success. Why was I never able to find this island again?"

"I recall when I was a youth of forty, a young boy from the outside world arrived on Umi, in the nearby village of Niut. I have a cousin who lives there who told me about this boy." Sebak walked slowly, keeping in step with Emery. "You were helped by the people of his village, and once you were recovered, you were sent back to your world."

"Why did your people send me away? Why wasn't I allowed to stay and—"

"You were sent away to save your life, just as you and the others must leave very soon. You cannot stay in Oseye. It is not safe for outsiders to remain on Umi."

"I'm afraid I don't understand."

Sebak was silent for several minutes, then he paused and faced Emery. "Here on Umi, we live a long, healthy life filled with peace and contentment. We have good food, sweet music, happy days of work and nights of pleasant sleep."

"You live in paradise," Emery said.

"Yes, paradise." Sebak's brow wrinkled. "There are several villages spread out over the island, all similar to Oseye, but the high priest and his scholars, along with their elite brigade and their families, live in the center of the island, atop Mount Kaphiri."

Emery's heartbeat accelerated as excitement flushed through his body. A high priest. An elite brigade. Brilliant scholars.

"I must meet with your high priest," Emery said. "I must see everything here on Umi. Meet everyone—"

"No!" Sebak clamped his hand over Emery's shoulder. "The only contact we have with the priestly tribe is when the Eshe is distributed every year to the villagers."

"I don't understand, if you grow the Eshe, why is it not available to you—"

"The Eshe does not belong to us. It belongs to our high priest. He and he alone harvests the crop each year. We are given enough Eshe for the entire village…." Sebak paused, then his gaze locked with Emery's. "We exchange the life of one villager for the Eshe. Usually the oldest person in the village volunteers to go with the elite brigade."

At first Emery was uncertain that he had understood correctly what Sebak had told him. Surely he did not mean that a villager's life was given in exchange for the Eshe. Perhaps the person simply went into some type of servitude.

"What happens to the person who is taken?"

Sebak said quietly, "This person is sacrificed by the high priest to appease the gods." Sighing heavily, Sebak released his hold on Emery's shoulder.

The truth hit Emery hard. This incredible paradise, this magical island that he had spent his life pursuing was ruled by an order of priests who demanded human sacrifice in exchange for giving the villagers long life and good health.

"Outsiders do not understand the ways of our world," Sebak told him.

"Have very many outsiders found Umi?"

Sebak nodded. "Many? Over thousands of years, quite a few have been brought to Umi. When the island is visible for one month every ten years, the sea brings visitors to our shores. In the past, long ago, the high priest ordered their deaths, fearing the world would learn of Umi. But we are not killers. We do not wish harm to anyone. We, the people of Umi's villages, send our unwanted visitors away whenever we can, before the elite guard learns of their existence and takes them to the high priest. This is what was done for you fifty years ago."

Emery grabbed Sebak's arm. "Can you help us leave Umi as soon as possible?"

"Yes, of course. The elite brigade will not make their rounds to Oseye for three weeks. We are the last village on their route."

Clutching Sebak's arm tightly, Emery asked, "And you will give me some samples of the Eshe plant to take with me, won't you?"

Sebak flung Emery's hand from his arm. "No, you cannot take any of the Eshe plants with you. It is forbidden for anyone to cut the Eshe plants except members of the elite brigade. We are allowed only to scatter the ashes of our loved ones in the fields to nourish the roots of the Eshe plants."

"But how would the elite brigade know if I took only a few plants."

"The Fields of Eshe are guarded day and night by the power of the high priest. If one plant is removed, Lord Baruti would know."

"I don't believe this. It's simply something you've been told to prevent you from harvesting the Eshe yourselves."

"The high priest does not lie to his people. It is blasphemy for you to say such a thing."

Realizing he must reassure his host, the man in whose hands his fate and the fate of his party rested, Emery said, "Then I apologize. I meant no offense. I will, of course, abide by your laws." Yes, he would apologize. He would try to make things right. He would say whatever was necessary to reassure Sebak. But in the end, no matter what, he would not leave this island without a sample of the Eshe plant.

Gwen woke warm and safe in Will's strong arms. When had he come to bed? What time was it? Why was she in his arms? Coming out of a restless sleep, she opened her eyelids, then closed them when Will's lips pressed against her neck. She shouldn't be lying here enjoying this moment. She should still be angry with Will. They had argued last night. She had been so furious with him that she had walked away from him, to end an argument neither of them could win. She had gone to bed, fully clothed, leaving him standing by the fireplace. She had lain there for hours, waiting for him to come to her, to apologize, to tell her that he understood her need to support her father, that he would stand by her, come what may.

But she had fallen asleep waiting.

Will nuzzled Gwen's ear. She shivered. All he had to do was touch her and she unraveled. She hadn't meant to fall in love with Will. After all, she knew only too well that he wasn't in love with her.

"Still mad at me, brown eyes?" he whispered as he eased his hand down over her belly and slipped it between her thighs.

Her femininity clenched and unclenched, longing for the feel of his fingertips without the restriction of her slacks and panties.

"I might still be a little upset with you," she told him.

"Tell me what I have to do to make things right." He nipped her neck as his thumb stroked her through the barrier of her clothing.

"Mmm-mmm. Please don't do that. I can't think when you touch me."

He flipped her over onto her back and straddled her hips. Gazing down at her, he smiled. "It's not necessary for you to think. Just feel."

He kissed her throat, then nudged his way to the V-neckline of her blouse. She quivered as his hot breath fanned over her skin. And when he opened his mouth and brought it down on one breast, she gasped. He suckled her through her blouse and bra, making a damp mark on the material.

She bucked up, bringing her mound against his hard sex.

"We've got on too many clothes," he told her, then lifted himself up and off and quickly removed all his clothes.

She unbuttoned her blouse and removed it, then discarded her bra, slacks and panties. When he came back to her, they were both naked and aroused. She held open her arms to him.

"Do you have any idea how much I want to be inside you?" He rubbed himself intimately against her.

She grasped his shoulders and lifted herself against him, joining him in the undulating dance. "I want that, too, but we can't."

"Yeah, I know."

When he kissed her and his big, hard body covered her, she longed for any excuse to succumb to temptation. They were trapped on an island that wasn't supposed to exist, in a world that neither of them understood. Weren't the odds against their ever escaping from Umi? If they were forced to remain here, she would continue to be Will's woman, wouldn't she?

As his hands caressed her, aroused her, and his mouth tormented first one breast and then the other, all rational thought ceased to exist for Gwen. She was ruled by her needs, by the primitive longings urging her to mate with Will.

As her hands covered his body with enticing caresses, her desire grew stronger. "Make love to me."

"That's what I'm doing," he mumbled against her breast.

She circled his erection and urged him between her thighs, opening herself for him, inviting him in.

"Are you sure?" he asked, his voice a husky groan.

"I'm sure."

He didn't wait for her to have second thoughts. He slipped his hands beneath her, cupped her buttocks and lifted her up to meet his downward lunge. He shoved into her; she expanded to take him completely. Nothing had ever felt so good, so right. She wanted to shout, "I love you." She wanted to hear him say that he loved her, too. But as soon as he began moving inside her, in and out, increasing the tempo ever so gradually, she didn't need words any more than he did. All she needed was Will. Buried inside her. Making passionate love to her. Filling her world so completely that nothing and no one else existed.

Her release came first, in a frenzy of sensation. And then, as if her climax triggered it, his came seconds later. They moaned and shivered with pleasure. And when Will collapsed on top of her, she wrapped her arms around him, capturing him, keeping them joined as the aftershocks of release rippled through them. Minutes later, he rolled over and off her, then pulled her to his side and kissed her.

Neither of them spoke for a good while afterward. They just lay together enjoying those lethargic, sated moments after sex.

Will caressed her naked hip. "Are you okay, brown eyes?"

"I'm fine," she said. "No, I'm better than fine. I'm wonderful."

Will chuckled. "We're good together. You know that, don't you?"

"Yes, I know."

"When we get off this damn island, I'm buying you some red panties and a red bra and we're going to spend a week in bed at some swanky hotel, doing nothing but making love."

"A whole week, huh?"

"Yeah, at least a week, then we'll—"

A loud banging on the hut's single wooden door interrupted Will midsentence.

"What the hell?" he grumbled.

"Will. Gwen. It's Cheryl. Jordan sent me to get you two. The Professor is back and he's talking crazy, saying all kinds of wild things about high priests and human sacrifices."

"We'll be there in a minute," Will said.

"Hurry, will you? Jordan's trying to calm The Professor, but he's not having much luck."

Will and Gwen rummaged around on the floor and the foot of the bed searching for their rumpled clothes. After gathering up their garments, they took turns hurriedly washing up, using water from a clay pitcher sitting on the hearth. They dressed and left their hut, intending to go next door to the hut Jordan and Cheryl shared. But once outside, they heard Jordan and Emery Arnell arguing, then Gwen's father came storming out of Jordan's hut.

"Daddy!" Gwen called to him.

He stopped and stared at her.

"What's wrong?" She went to him, took his hands in hers and forced a smile, hoping to reassure him. "Please, tell me what's going on."

Jordan and Cheryl emerged from the hut, but didn't approach Emery. Will glanced at Jordan who shook his head.

"Jordan refuses to believe me. He thinks I've lost my mind," Emery said.

"I'm sure that's not true." Gwen glanced at Jordan. "Please, tell my father that you don't think he's crazy."

"I didn't say he was crazy," Jordan said. "I told him that he was talking crazy." Jordan focused on Emery. "Tell them what you told me. About the high priest and the human sacrifices and—"

"It's true," Emery said, his eyes wild. "Sebak told me. There are villages all over the island, but high atop the mountain is a city where the high priest lives, along with his scholars and an elite brigade. Although the *villagers* are kind to visitors from the outside world, the high priest orders outsiders to be killed. He will not let them leave the island."

They all listened as The Professor rambled on. His tale of the sacred Eshe plant, human sacrifice, a diabolical high priest and a murderous elite brigade seeming far-fetched. But the more Will listened, the more convinced he became that Emery Arnell was telling the truth, that Sebak had shared this crucial information with him.

When Emery finished talking, he leaned against the hut, obviously exhausted. Gwen put her arm around her father and hugged him.

"I believe him." Gwen glared at the others.

"So do I," Will said.

"Have you both lost your minds?" Jordan asked.

"There's one way to find out," Will told them. "I'm going to speak to Sebak. If what Dr. Arnell has told us is true, we need to get off this island as soon as possible. Today."

"No!" The Professor cried, "I will not leave without a sample of the Eshe plant."

"Then you stay here and risk your life," Will told him. "The rest of us are leaving today. We'd be better off floating around in the Atlantic, hoping to be rescued, than waiting here on this island, knowing we were going to wind up as human sacrifices."

"I agree with Will even though I wanted to find this island so desperately," Jordan said. "But if Sebak backs up The Professor's story, then we must leave the island today."

Will looked at Gwen. "Talk to your father. Make him see reason. I'm going to find Sebak."

Before the sun rose high overhead, Will returned and gathered everyone together, including Mick McGuire, inside his and Gwen's hut. His gaze went around the room, studying each person for a brief moment.

"Dr. Arnell was telling the truth," Will said. "Sebak thinks we will be safe here for a few days, possibly another week or two, but the longer we are on the island, the greater the odds that the high priests' elite brigade will discover that we're here. If there was only one of us, it would be easier for them to hide us. But there are six of us."

"Then I say we leave the island as soon as possible." Jordan glanced at Emery.

"Leaving here sounds good to me," Mick said. "But just how do you propose we do that? Our cruiser was destroyed in the storm and you said your boat's motors aren't working."

"Sebak told me that my boat will take us to safety. He explained that when the high priest lifts the cloaking spell from around Umi, that act creates freak storms and disrupts everything within a hundred miles around the island. It's some sort of weird magnetic field. Sebak feels certain that the *Footloose*'s engines will work now. I know it sounds crazy, but it's our only hope."

"And you believe this crap?" Cheryl asked.

"I'm going to take the lifeboat that Gwen and I left on shore, row back to the *Footloose* and check the engines myself," Will told them.

"Won't that be dangerous?" Gwen looked at him with great concern.

"How do we know you won't make it to the boat, find

out the engines are working and go off and leave us?" Mick got right up in Will's face.

Will tapped Mick in the chest, warning him to move back, which Mick did. "I'd like to leave your sorry ass here on Umi and let the high priest's elite brigade take care of you, but there's no way in hell I'd leave the others." Will looked directly at Gwen. "I'd die before I'd leave you behind. You know that, don't you?"

Gwen's heart lurched, tightened by a combination of joy and sorrow. How did she tell him that she couldn't leave her father, who would not leave Umi without a sample of the Eshe plant?

"I trust you," Jordan told Will. "Is there anything I can do to help you?"

"Just look after Gwen while I'm gone."

"I can take care of myself," she said.

"In our world, you probably can," Will told her. "But not on Umi. I've told Sebak where I'm going and that I'm leaving my woman under Jordan's protection. Do you understand?"

"Yes, I understand, and I'm sorry that I let my feminist instincts surface," Gwen said. "You have enough to worry about right now. I promise that while you're gone I'll behave myself and not get in any trouble."

"I won't leave here without samples of the Eshe plant." Dr. Arnell spoke up loud and clear, reiterating his intentions.

Gwen patted his hand. "Now is not the time to discuss this, Daddy. First, Will has to make sure the *Footloose*'s motors are working. Once he does that, we can make plans to leave."

"As long as you understand—all of you—that I must have samples of the plant to take with me," Dr. Arnell said.

Picking up his backpack, Will motioned to Gwen, who

followed him outside the hut. He cupped her chin between his thumb and forefinger, then kissed her. "While I'm gone, don't take any chances. And do your best to keep your father from going off half-cocked."

He kissed her again, then strapped his knapsack to his back and headed toward the road that would take him through the jungle back to the beach. Gwen stood and watched him until he disappeared from sight.

Cheryl came up beside her. "You're in love with him, aren't you?"

"Oh, yes. I'm most definitely in love with him."

"What are you going to do?"

"About what?"

"About choosing between your father and the man you love. The Professor won't leave this island without a sample of the Eshe plant, and Will Pierce won't leave this island without you."

Chapter 15

Will returned to Oseye before nightfall and gathered everyone together inside his hut, where Gwen was waiting with the others. During Will's absence, she had tried again and again—unsuccessfully—to make her father see reason.

"I will not leave Umi without samples of the Eshe plant," he had told her repeatedly.

No matter what tactic she took, no matter what she, Jordan or Cheryl said to him, he refused to change his mind. In the end, Gwen knew what she would do, what she had to do for her father.

When Will entered the hut at twilight, Gwen ran to him, relieved that he had made the journey and returned safely. If anything had happened to him…

He lifted her off her feet and hugged her fiercely, then set her in front of him and smiled. "Good news, brown eyes. I can't explain it, but the motors on the *Footloose* are working just fine. The radio is still out, but with the cruiser operational and the instruments online, we can leave this place first thing in the morning."

"Man, am I glad to hear that." Cheryl hugged Jordan. "I am so ready to leave this damn place."

"Why not get this show on the road and leave tonight?" Mick McGuire asked. "As soon as the old man gets his Eshe plants, I say we hightail it out of here before the goon squad finds out what's happened."

Will glowered at Mick. "We're leaving at dawn tomorrow morning. It will be safer traveling through the jungle and entering the ocean waters after daylight. And we will be leaving Umi without any Eshe plants."

"No way," Mick said. "The old man's going to get those plants. They'll be worth millions, maybe billions. And he's going to share equally with all of us. Isn't that right, Professor?"

"Quite right," Dr. Arnell said.

Will looked from person to person. "Trying to steal samples of that plant will be signing a death warrant for all of us."

"This is something Mick cooked up between him and The Professor," Jordan said. "Cheryl and I agree that we should leave as soon as possible, without the Eshe plant samples."

Gwen took Will's hand. "I need to speak to you alone." She nodded toward the door. "Outside. Okay?"

"Yeah, sure." He opened the door and went with her a few feet away from the hut. She took both of his hands in hers. "Daddy refuses to leave Umi without samples of the Eshe plant, and he's convinced Mick that he can make him a wealthy man if—"

"Then I'll just knock your father on his ass and carry

him with us to the *Footloose* tomorrow. And if McGuire gives us any trouble, I'll leave him here."

"No." Gwen swallowed hard. "My father is an old man. He has spent his entire life searching for this island, dreaming of the day that he could take the magical youth-serum plant back to the world as a gift. How can I ask him to leave here without the Eshe plant? It would kill him."

"And if he stays here, he'll die."

"I know. But there is one other solution."

"I'm already not liking the sound of this."

She squeezed his hands. "You take Jordan and Cheryl with you at first light in the morning, back to the shore where you left the lifeboat. I will go with Daddy and Mick before dawn to the Fields of Eshe and help them gather a few samples. Then we'll join y'all. If we don't make it, if we're captured or—"

Will grabbed her by the shoulders and shook her. "No way. No way in hell."

"Please, Will. I have to do this."

"No, Gwen, you don't."

She pulled free of his tenacious grip, then turned and walked farther away from the hut. He came up behind her, not touching her, not saying a word.

"Daddy and I have talked this through, and we've agreed that it's the only way. No matter what happens, you and the others will be safe." She couldn't face him, couldn't look him in the eye, knowing how angry he was.

"To hell with my being safe. If you think I'll leave you here, you'd better think again."

"Please, Will."

"No. And that settles it." He grasped her shoulders and yanked her back up against his chest.

"You can't knock all three of us out and drag us with y'all through the jungle," Gwen told him. "If you do this my way—"

"I'm not leaving you. Get that through your head." He encompassed her in a possessive embrace. "If you won't leave this godforsaken island without your father, and he won't leave without that damn plant, then I'll go to the Fields of Eshe at dawn and get the samples for him."

She whirled around in his arms. "I would never ask you to take such a risk." She caressed his cheek. "If anything happened to you, I couldn't bear it."

His eyes narrowed as his gaze locked with hers. "Then you know exactly how I feel."

"But you don't understand. I love you and—"

"Do you think you're the only one who's in love?"

She didn't dare believe her own ears.

He captured her face with his open palms. "Of everyone in our group, I'm the only one with the kind of training it will require to go into those fields, steal a sample of the plant and get away without being captured."

"You can't go in alone. I'll go with you."

"No. You will take your father, Cheryl and Mick back to the beach and wait. I'll take Jordan with me and we'll meet up with y'all as soon as we have samples of the Eshe plant."

A bittersweet feeling engulfed Gwen as she realized the depth of Will's love for her and knew that she couldn't allow him to risk his life to fulfill her father's dream.

"All right," she said, lying to him. "We will do this your way."

"That's my girl."

When he kissed her, she clung to him, wanting to hold on to him forever.

* * *

Will woke with a start, but had no idea what had roused him. After making love with Gwen, he had fallen asleep almost instantly. He turned over in bed and reached for her. The other side of the bed was empty. He shot straight up and surveyed the dark room, the only illumination coming from the dying embers of the fire in the fireplace and the moonlight shining through the open window.

"Gwen?"

No response. Completely naked, he got out of bed and searched the hut. Where the hell was she and why hadn't he heard her leave?

After putting on his clothes, he went outside. She was nowhere in sight. A sick, gut-tightening sensation gripped him. He made his way to the hut next door and knocked softly, calling Jordan's name.

Within minutes Jordan opened the door. "What's wrong?"

"Have you seen Gwen?"

"No. Why? What's happened?"

"She's gone."

Cheryl came up beside Jordan. "Maybe she went to see her father, to try to talk sense to him again."

"Why would she go in the middle of the night?"

"You think something's wrong, don't you?" Jordan asked.

"I know something's wrong."

Gwen hoped Will wouldn't wake up until it was too late to try to stop her. If he figured out where she'd gone, he would come after her and risk his own life. She couldn't let him do that. Not for her. Not for her father. She was Emery Arnell's only child. It was her duty to stand by her father, to do her best to care for him, to help him.

The small child that still existed inside Gwen believed that if she did this, if she enabled her father to fulfill his lifelong dream, he would be grateful to her. He would love her.

Before her father and Mick McGuire had left her hut last night, she had told her father that she would slip away from Will in the night and come to him.

"Tell Mick to stay with you and when I can get away, I'll come get you and we'll go to the Fields of Eshe and get the samples you want."

"But I thought Will was going to—"

"No, Will isn't going." She had told her father what she wanted him to believe. "Will was lying to you, to pacify you. He has no intention of getting the plants for you. If you want the plants, we have to get them ourselves, before dawn."

She, her father and Mick had made their way by moonlight to the Fields of Eshe. The knee-high stalks glowed softly in the predawn darkness, as if they were lit from within.

"There's not a guard in sight," Mick said, keeping his voice low. "This should be a piece of cake."

"Sebak said that Lord Baruti, the high priest, has a power that oversees these fields," Emery told them. "We can't be too careful. You two must let me gather the samples."

"Go to it, old man," Mick said. "Just make sure you get enough." He gazed at the acres of flourishing plants that gleamed like yellow-green gold in the moonlight. "And I'll carry them plants for you, Professor. They'll be safe with me."

"We will each carry a sample," Emery said. "That way at least one sample should survive."

"Good idea." Mick's smirking grin made Gwen's skin crawl. He was such a sleazy bastard.

"We'll stand guard while you retrieve the samples."

Gwen kissed her father's cheek. "I'm so proud of you, Daddy. You're going to be very famous."

"And rich as Donald Trump—like a billionaire," Mick added.

Her father smiled broadly. "This is the most exciting moment of my life. Nothing can compare to the knowledge that I will be able to give the world a precious gift and prove to my colleagues that I am no fool."

Gwen's heart beat loudly in her ears as she watched her father enter the fields. He walked slowly along the rows, inspecting the plants, taking his time as if there was no rush.

"What the hell is he doing?" Mick grumbled.

"He's savoring the moment," Gwen replied.

When her father had gone approximately twenty feet down the second row, he reached into his pants pocket and removed an old switchblade knife and a tattered handkerchief. He knelt down on his knees, spread the handkerchief out on the ground and grasped the tall, willowy Eshe plant, holding it with one hand while he used the knife to carefully dig around the roots. He unearthed one plant, laid the roots on the handkerchief and repeated the procedure with two other plants.

Gwen held her breath, waiting for an alarm to go off, for hidden guards to appear, for iron bars to come up out of the earth and surround the fields. But nothing happened. The only sound she heard was her own heavy breathing.

"Sebak was lying to the old man." Mick laughed. "These people are stupid to let some high and mighty leader scare them from taking these plants for themselves."

"Shh. Be quiet," she warned him.

"Why? It's not like the plants can hear us." He laughed louder.

Emery came to them carrying the Eshe in his arms, the plants' delicate roots wrapped in the handkerchief. "I will need to water the roots and keep them damp. But they are large and healthy and should survive the journey without any problem."

Mick slapped Emery on the back. "We're in the money now, huh, Professor."

Emery frowned. "Yes, yes, we're in the money."

Gwen realized her father was simply humoring Mick because he believed he could use the man's greed to his advantage.

"There's no point hanging around here," Mick said. "I say we get these million-dollar babies—" he eyed the plants in Emery's arms "—aboard the *Footloose* as soon as we can and set sail for the nearest port."

"Aren't you forgetting something?" Gwen asked.

"If you're talking about the others, forget them," Mick said. "The Eshe plants are ours. I prefer dividing up the billions three ways instead of six. Besides, I've got no intention of letting your boyfriend turn me over to the authorities when we get back to civilization."

Before either Gwen or her father could contradict Mick, beams of blinding white lights shot up from the earth, all around the Fields of Eshe.

Gwen gasped. Emery clutched his beloved plants to his chest. Mick's eyes bugged out in shock.

"What the hell?" Mick bellowed.

"We have to make a run for it," Gwen said. "Come on, Daddy. Hurry."

Mick fled, leaving Gwen and her father, who couldn't run. With her arm through his, Gwen hurried her father along, away from the fields and toward the jungle, intending to steer clear of the stone roadway. As they scurried for safety, Gwen heard a loud, thundering noise behind her, but realized turning back to see what pursued them would simply waste valuable time.

She caught glimpses of Mick as he rushed ahead of them. Suddenly a thin white light came flying through the air and hit Mick in the back. He dropped instantly, falling out of sight. Dear God, was he dead? Had their trackers killed him?

Suddenly her father grunted, then dropped to his knees. In her effort to keep him on his feet, Gwen went down with him. She wasn't strong enough to hold him, so all she could manage was to ease him to the ground as slowly as possible. His arms fell open and the Eshe plants tumbled freely onto the grass.

"Daddy? Daddy!" Gwen patted his cheek.

With his eyes wide open but dazed, he looked either dead or unconscious. She felt for a pulse. He was alive, but just barely.

Daring a glance over her shoulder, through the plush jungle greenery, Gwen saw what appeared to be ornately carved golden chariots off in the distance, just outside the fields. But before she could ascertain whether she was hallucinating or not, a thin beam of light struck her chest and the world went black.

Sebak led Will, Jordan and Cheryl to the Fields of Eshe. They arrived moments before dawn. Will realized what had happened as soon as he discovered that not only was Gwen missing from Oseye, but so was Dr. Arnell and Mick McGuire.

"They've gone to the Eshe fields," Will had told the others.

"But why? They knew you were— Damn!" Jordan shook his head. "Gwen did this, didn't she?"

"She didn't want you to risk your life," Cheryl said.

"Yeah. And I should have known what she'd do. Damn stupid woman!" His chest ached with emotion. He'd never been so angry with anyone and at the same time had never been so certain that a woman loved him beyond all reason.

"What can we do?" Cheryl had asked.

"What else? Go after them."

So, here they were approaching the fields, with Sebak in tow as their guide. But there was no sight of Gwen, her father or McGuire. The Fields of Eshe looked serene and undisturbed.

"Fan out and search for any sign of them, anything the least bit out of the ordinary," Will ordered. His gut told him that they were too late. "Cheryl, you search around the periphery while we enter the fields." He turned to Sebak. "If they aren't here—"

"You will not find them," Sebak said. "I tried to tell you that the elite brigade captured them and took them to Mount Kaphiri to be punished by Lord Baruti."

Glowering at Sebak, Will grabbed him. "If we don't find them, you will guide us to Mount Kaphiri and tell us how to find this Lord Baruti."

"No, I cannot. I am but a lowly village leader. I am unworthy to ascend to Mount Kaphiri."

Will shook Sebak, then circled his neck in a death grip. "Worthy or unworthy, you're going to show us the way. Either that or I will wipe out your entire village, starting with you."

"You cannot think you are capable of overpowering an entire village. You and Jordan are only two men."

"Two men with weapons. Guns. Do you know what a

gun is? I just happened to have picked up a couple of them when I went back to my boat yesterday, and they're safely tucked away in my backpack."

"If your guns are weapons that render people unconscious, then I know what they are. The elite brigade have such weapons."

"Do their weapons kill?" Will asked.

"Kill? No, they do not kill. There have been no murders on Umi in a thousand years."

"No murders, huh? What do you call human sacrifice?"

While Sebak stared at Will, a perplexed expression on his face, Cheryl cried out, "I've found something!"

Will forced Sebak forward. Cheryl, who had gone approximately thirty feet into the jungle, turned to face them, a dirty handkerchief in her hand. Jordan came running up behind them.

"It's The Professor's handkerchief," Cheryl told them.

"They were here," Jordan said.

"And now they are gone." Sebak shook his head sadly.

"We're going after them." Will didn't care what it took, didn't care if he had to move heaven and earth, he was going to find Gwen. "Sebak says the elite brigade took them to Mount Kaphiri."

"It will do no good to follow them," Sebak said. "You cannot rescue them. Their lives are now in the hands of Lord Baruti."

Will gave Sebak a hard shove. "And your life and the lives of your fellow villagers are now in my hands. Do you understand?"

"Yes, I understand. I…I will show you the way to the foothills of Mount Kaphiri, but I can go no farther. I would be of no help to you. I have never been up the mountain itself, but when my son, who is a scholar, has visited me, he has told me that there is a road that leads from the foothills straight to the high priest's palace. But the elite brigade guard the entrance to the palace, day and night."

Gwen regained consciousness slowly, at first not remembering what had happened, but the minute her eyes opened and she didn't recognize her surroundings, the events of their capture came back to her. When she sat straight up, her head pounded unmercifully, forcing her to lie back down on the soft pillow. Lying flat on her back while the throbbing ache in her head subsided, she glanced right and left, up and down. She lay in an intricately carved black bed. Ebony? The sheet beneath her felt like silk. The walls were decorated with murals, island scenes of waterfalls and villages and the Fields of Eshe.

When she tried sitting up again, more slowly this time, she realized that she was naked. Dear God, what had happened to her?

And where was her father? Where was Mick? For that matter, where was she?

She wrapped the silk sheet around her and tucked one end under the edge that crisscrossed over her breasts, then walked across the room to the gilded door. The handle was gold, encrusted with gems—rubies, diamonds and emeralds.

She tried the handle. The door opened to reveal a long, narrow hallway with stark white walls and a black marble floor. The moment she stepped into the hallway, four women came through a door at the end of the long corridor and rushed toward her.

She stopped and waited for them to come to her. Better to get this initial meeting over now, she told herself.

When the women came near, they paused and looked at her as if waiting for her to either say or do something. The four women looked like sisters, each dark-haired, tall, slender, doe-eyed and elegantly dressed in azure blue off-the-shoulder dresses tied with silver cords directly below their breasts.

"Where am I?" Gwen asked, hoping beyond hope that one of them could speak English. "How long have I been here?"

"You were brought to the palace of Lord Baruti yesterday," one of the women replied.

Yesterday? That meant she had been asleep—unconscious—for at least twenty-four hours. She vaguely recalled seeing a white light hit Mick and then her father. She had been the last struck with the weapon. A tranquilizer of some kind? If so, it certainly was powerful, to produce such a long-lasting effect.

"Lord Baruti is the high priest, isn't he?"

"Yes," another answered.

"I was brought here with two men. Where are they?"

"The men are in another area of the palace," a third woman responded. "You will join them for an audience with Lord Baruti."

"When?" Gwen asked.

"Before the sun reaches a midpoint in the heavens," the fourth woman told her. "We have come to prepare you for the ceremony."

"The ceremony?" Gwen's stomach tightened.

All four women smiled, but only the first one spoke, as if they had to take turns. "The Ceremony of Olumfemi. Those who are sacrificed are the beloved of the gods. Even those who have done great evil find redemption in death."

Chapter 16

On the trek to Mount Kaphiri, Will had given Jordan a minicourse in combat and survival. Despite his lack of experience, the guy had picked up on the essentials quickly and agreed without question that Will was in charge. When they had reached the foothills at daybreak and stopped in a village called Bahiti, Will had made the decision to leave Cheryl behind. There was no point putting her at risk, especially since she would only slow them down, and Jordan would be distracted by her presence because his first priority would be to protect her.

Will's gut told him he could trust Sebak not to give them away. After all, if he or the other villagers had wanted to turn them over to the elite brigade, they could have done that immediately after they arrived on Umi.

"I will take care of your woman," Sebak had told Jordan. "If you do not return, I will make sure she leaves

Umi safely. If you return, I trust you to do no harm to my village."

"Your village is safe from us," Jordan assured him, then looked to Will. "Isn't that right?"

"We will repay you for your help by not harming you or your people," Will said.

Jordan had thanked Sebak for all he'd done for them, then spent a few minutes alone with Cheryl to say goodbye. Will had led Sebak aside and questioned him, knowing that any knowledge the man possessed could help them when they reached Lord Baruti's palace.

"How long do we have?" Will had asked.

"I do not know for sure," Sebak had replied. "They will not perform the Ceremony of Olumfemi before the sun is at its highest point in the sky."

"This ceremony—"

"A ceremony of sacrifice. Emery and the others will be sacrificed to the gods, and in this way, they will be redeemed for having committed a grave sin."

Sebak's knowledge of the high priest's palace was limited to what his son, the scholar who lived atop Mount Kaphiri, had shared with him. But even that information was better than nothing.

During their climb up the mountain, Will and Jordan used the roadway that wound steadily upward like a slithering snake. At any hint of danger, Will led them off the main pathway, a twenty-foot-wide rock lane similar to the ones that ran through the jungles, only this road was wider. Twice on their journey, Will spied checkpoints that were guarded by two men he assumed were members of the elite brigade. Their physical appearance was similar to the other natives, but their attire differed. They wore dark-blue loincloths, silver breastplates and heavy sandals with straps that rose to midcalf. The two men stood at either side of the road and each held a spear, but the tips were rounded instead of pointed, which made Will wonder about their purpose.

Taking no breaks, they arrived outside the walls of the palace shortly before high noon. Will ascertained from their appearance that the walls were undoubtedly more for decorative purposes than protection. Rising no higher than eight feet, with sections of silver-and-gold metal stakes carved in intricate designs, the open fencing allowed a breathtaking view of the interior. Built a good twenty feet higher at the very apex of the mountain, the palace rested like a goddess on a cloud. Will guessed the palace covered at least an acre. It was a magnificent structure of stone, with numerous enormous columns and huge statues guarding the entrance.

Richly dressed people stirred about, each one apparently rushing to the same area of the palace. Rushing to witness the Ceremony of Olumfemi?

"We can't enter through those front gates," Will said. "There are too many guards. We'd be spotted in seconds. We'll have to find another way to get in."

"All those people are hurrying in one direction." Jordan's gaze focused on the palace. "Maybe that's the way to the temple where Sebak said the ceremony will be performed."

Will looked up at the noonday sun. "We don't have any time to waste. Just remember to follow my orders. And if anything happens to me, leave me behind. Save Gwen, then get her and Cheryl off this godforsaken island."

With an expression of somber acceptance on his face, Jordan nodded.

Obviously, those who lived high above the lowly natives on the island below had few worries about uninvited guests. Will found it far too easy to breach the security of the palace grounds and even the palace itself. If their physical appearance was not so vastly different from the people of Umi, Will would have secured native clothing for Jordan and himself.

"We watch and wait," Will said. "Once the coast is clear and everyone is assembled in the temple, we'll make our move."

Jordan nodded.

Suddenly a loud trumpet sounded. Jordan's gaze met Will's.

Will ventured a guess. "It's a signal that the ceremony is about to begin."

"Yeah, that's what I thought."

"You know how to use the Ruger I gave you, how to aim, fire and how to replace the clip. When the time comes to act, don't stop and think about what you're doing, just do it. If we get out of this alive, there will be plenty of time later to think about how many people you killed."

Jordan swallowed.

"If we can save all three of them, we'll do it," Will said. "But my main objective is to rescue Gwen. Understand?"

"Understood."

The four doe-eyed maidens had dressed Gwen in a diaphanous, single-strap, cream gown, then placed golden sandals on her feet and a heavy gold choker about her neck. They had braided her long hair into three layers and painted face with the type of makeup they wore. Although she had asked them numerous questions, they had responded to only a few, while keeping up a stream of idle chit-chat.

As they led her down the black-marble-floored corridor, one phrase the women had used often kept repeating itself in Gwen's mind. "A willing sacrifice will receive great honor in the afterlife."

A willing sacrifice? Not hardly. But until she saw her father, knew that he was alive, she planned to cooperate. Besides, what good would it do her to put up a fight? The maidens had informed her that resisting was useless, that if necessary the elite brigade could use the *sefu* of Baruti to subdue her. It had taken her several questions to get enough meaningful answers so that she could figure out that the round-tipped spears her abductors had used to shoot a powerful white light to render her, her father and Mick unconscious was what the maidens referred to as the *sefu* of Baruti.

The maidens led her along three different corridors, taking her from building to building within the palace grounds. She caught only glimpses of the exterior, slashes of palm trees in magnificent garden areas that boasted incredible greenery and an abundance of flowers. As a botanist, she could happily spend endless hours exploring the gardens.

When they reached a structure slightly apart from the main palace—a two-story, tan building decorated with bright emblems in reds, blues, yellows and greens—the maidens paused, as loud trumpets proclaimed the beginning of the ceremony. The massive silver doors swung open to reveal two long lines of the elite brigade flanking either side of the path that led to a dais where an elaborately clothed man of undeterminable age stood waiting. Gwen assumed he was the high priest, Lord Baruti.

At Lord Baruti's side stood Gwen's father. Her heart leaped with joy when she saw that he appeared to be not only alive, but well. Like she, he had been dressed in elaborate native attire.

While keeping her gaze focused directly on her father, Gwen caught flashes in her peripheral vision of people standing behind the elite brigade.

As she neared the dais, she hazarded a quick glimpse to her right, where a small group of robed men knelt, their heads bowed. She counted six men in all. Then she glanced to her left. Blazing fires flickered like freshly lit torches atop six twelve-foot pillars that lined the wall directly behind a large marble slab.

Gwen gasped.

A completely naked Mick McGuire lay atop the marble altar, his arms lifted over his head and secured with gold chains. Identical gold chains around his ankles held his legs in place.

Her survival instincts told her to run, to escape by any means necessary. Forcing down the salty bile that rose to her throat, Gwen focused once again on her father's face. Oddly enough, he appeared not only calm but serene. Had he been drugged?

When they reached the steps leading up to the altar, the maidens stopped. Her father held out his hand to her. She hesitated, then walked up the two marble steps and hurried to her father's side. He opened his arms and wrapped her in a trembling embrace.

"This is your daughter?" Lord Baruti asked. "Your only child?"

"Yes, Lord Baruti." Emery released Gwen and turned her so that she stood in front of him, facing the high priest.

"You have risked your life to aid your father," Lord Baruti said. "Such devotion and loyalty to a parent will be rewarded."

Gwen released a quivering breath, wondering if by some miracle this all-powerful ruler intended to spare their lives. After all, his attitude toward her father was far from hostile.

Nothing else was said before the high priest turned, leaving Gwen and her father on the raised podium. Drums beat rhythmically, a repetitive cadence, a musical announcement. With his sheer robes floating behind him like transparent, low-slung wings, Lord Baruti descended from the podium and walked directly to the altar. Gwen reached down and clasped her father's hand.

A member of the elite brigade, who carried a four-foot-long silver case, approached the high priest, knelt in front of Lord Baruti and lifted the case high above his head. The priest opened the case and removed a gleaming golden sword with a shimmering two-foot blade.

Gwen watched in mesmerized horror as Lord Baruti approached the altar where Mick McGuire squirmed, his voice ringing out with threat-filled obscenities. Lord Baruti stood over Mick and lifted the sword with both hands over his head. A robust shout erupted from the onlookers.

Squeezing her father's hand, Gwen stood on tiptoe and whispered, "Can't you do something to stop this?"

"The gods demand sacrifices," her father murmured. "McGuire will have a chance to redeem himself in the afterlife."

Releasing her death grip on her father's hand, Gwen stared at him, unable to believe that he could accept this inhuman act with such a cavalier attitude.

"Daddy?"

"Quiet, daughter." He hushed her. "Show this solemn moment the respect and reverence it deserves."

Oh, God! Why was her father acting this way? It wasn't possible, was it, that he had been brainwashed in less than twenty-four hours? Didn't he realize that once Mick McGuire was killed, they would probably be next?

Will and Jordan managed to sneak onto the narrow mezzanine area of the two-story central chamber inside the temple. The chamber was filled to capacity, but the upper level was vacant except for the carved stone dignitaries seated in silver pews. Will glanced at the silent, imposing figures and wondered who or what they represented. With no more time to waste musing about this strange place, Will motioned for Jordan to go left while he went right. They kept down, out of sight, and moved in absolute silence. Positioned on either side of the overhanging railing, which was fashioned out of pink marble and decked with heavy metallic ropes, Jordan and Will peered down at the ceremony taking place in the temple.

Will clenched his teeth when he saw the man he assumed was the high priest raise the glistening sword and slash open Mick McGuire, from neck to pubic area. Mick screamed in pain as the blade cut him open, effectively gutting him.

Will's gaze connected with Jordan's. Will issued him a silent warning—suck it up and sit tight. Well aware of the fact that Jordan had never been exposed to such deadly violence, Will hoped the young guy didn't fall apart on him.

While the priest's assistants caught McGuire's blood in a silver bowl, Will scanned the room and saw a pale-faced Gwen standing beside her father on a raised platform. She wore a sheer gown that revealed the ample curves of her body. A thick coating of heavy makeup had been applied to her face, and her long, dark hair had been plaited in three braids.

The soft, eerie music of flutes filled the temple, the sound unnerving and oddly out of place at a ceremony that glorified human sacrifice. The priest's underlings brought the bowl of blood to Lord Baruti, who carried it with him as he returned to the podium. He set the bowl on a marble stand, then turned to Dr. Arnell and Gwen.

"For the high crime of removing the life-giving Eshe plants from the holy fields, the first sacrifice has been made," the priest announced to his audience. A loud cheer rose from the crowd. "But the gods are not satisfied. They demand another sacrifice."

Gwen's heart caught in her throat when Lord Baruti looked directly at her father. What had he meant by another sacrifice? Had her father made a bargain of some kind with the priest, a bargain to save Gwen's life?

Lord Baruti motioned for them to come to him. Her father went without hesitation, all but dragging Gwen with him. The priest smiled.

"Emery Arnell, you came to Umi to steal the precious Eshe plant and take it back to your world. But it is forbidden for anyone other than my elite brigade, under my guidance, to harvest the Eshe plants. Do you understand the severity of your crime?"

"Yes, Lord Baruti," Emery replied.

"And do you understand that the penalty for stealing the Eshe plant is death?"

"Yes, my lord."

"But you still desire the Eshe plant, do you not? You treasure it above all else?"

Gwen's stomach knotted painfully.

"I do, Lord Baruti. I have spent my life searching for Umi, dreaming of the day I could return to my world with samples of the Eshe plant and give all people the gift of good health and long life."

"You are a benevolent seeker," the priest said. "I shall spare your life and allow you to return to your world with a sample of the Eshe plant, if you are willing to pay the ultimate price."

"I will give you anything you ask for," Emery said. "No price is too high."

Baruti's ring-adorned hand lifted. He pointed his index finger directly at Gwen. "I give you the choice—your life and a sample of the Eshe plant in exchange for your daughter's life."

Gwen held her breath.

Emery turned to her, grasped her hands and sighed heavily. "You know that I love you more dearly than anyone on earth."

"Yes, Daddy, I know."

"I wish it could be different," he said. "I wish I did not have to make such a terrible choice."

Every nerve in Gwen's body trembled with realization, every muscle constricted.

"It is with great regret that I give you my daughter as a sacrifice," Emery told Lord Baruti.

Despite hearing her father's declaration, Gwen did not fully comprehend that he had chosen his own life and the Eshe plant over saving her life. Before her brain absorbed the horrific truth, Gwen watched as the high priest motioned her father to him, then led him to the bowl filled with Mick McGuire's blood. He dipped his index finger into the blood, painted a slash across her father's forehead and across each cheekbone.

Another riotous roar rose from the assembled group. The elite brigade stomped their spears, the *sefu* of Baruti, against the marble floor.

It was at that moment, with the roar of the crowd thundering in her ears and the glazed look of madness shining in her father's eyes that Gwen realized he had finally lost his mind.

"You, Emery Arnell, are a fool to believe that anything, even the Eshe plant, has greater value than one who is blood of your blood, bone of your bone." The priest bowed his head for a moment, then shouted, "For such unforgivable foolishness, both you and your daughter will be sacrificed to the gods!"

"No, no!" Emery cried. "You can't do this. You promised me the Eshe plant. You swore to me—"

"Silence!" Lord Baruti motioned for two members of the elite brigade to come forward and take Emery.

Emery struggled against them, crying out to Gwen, who tried to go to him but was restrained by one strong, burly guard.

"Daddy!"

Lord Baruti followed the precession to the altar, where others of the elite brigade were unchaining Mick McGuire's mutilated body. The guard restraining Gwen dragged her off the podium while the drums began beating again. Loudly. Rhythmically. As if announcing the departure of one soul and the beginning of a new ritualistic sacrifice.

All eyes focused on the altar and the high priest as

Mick's body was carried away and maidens rushed forward to wash the bloody marble slab. Gwen's guard loosened his tenacious hold on her, enough so that after a few minutes, she managed to free herself without him noticing. She stayed at his side, not wanting to alert him that she was only biding her time until she could slip away from him.

While the drums pounded and the people chanted, Gwen searched the temple for any means of escape. As her gaze lifted to the mezzanine, she saw a flash of movement near the pink marble banisters. Her heart caught in her throat when she noticed a man cut through one of the metallic ropes draped across the banisters. With the crowd's attention focused on the ceremony, Will climbed down the metallic rope and dropped onto the floor, only a few feet behind a group of people absorbed in the gruesome spectacle. Gwen slowly moved away from her guard and managed to edge ever so gradually toward the back wall. By the time the guard realized she was missing, Gwen had escaped. Within minutes, she met up with Will, but not before they were spotted.

"We've got to get out of here," Will told her as several people in the crowd started moving toward them.

"But I can't leave my father."

"It's too late to save him." Will grabbed her arm.

She hesitated for half a second, then, knowing Will was right, she followed him. Before they could reach an escape route, Will stopped, shoved her behind him and pulled his pistol from the waistband of his pants. He aimed and fired repeatedly, sending half a dozen natives to the marble floor, their life's blood oozing from them.

Barely managing to escape the temple, Will would not allow Gwen to look back, to slow down for even a second.

They met up with Jordan outside the temple and the three of them fled down one exterior corridor after another, at least ten members of the elite brigade chasing them. The white light of one of the *sefu* spears grazed Jordan's shoulder. He staggered like a drunk, but somehow managed to stay on his feet. Will shoved Gwen behind a twenty-foot pillar and covered Jordan while he struggled to catch up with them, shooting several guards and halting their pursuit.

Will hurried to Jordan, circled his waist and dragged him behind the pillar with Gwen. He took the Ruger hanging in Jordan's limp hand and handed it to Gwen.

"Do you have any idea how to use this?" Will asked.

She shook her head. "Don't worry about hitting anything. Just aim and shoot. Got it?"

"Got it."

"Leave me," Jordan said, his speech slightly slurred. "You can't get away…with me holding you back."

Ignoring Jordan's pleas to leave him behind, Will and Gwen flanked him, lifted him under his arms and crept away from the pillared corridor. Will didn't understand why the elite brigade wasn't following them, but he didn't stop to check out the situation. They needed every advantage they could get. A five-minute head start might give them a fighting chance, especially if they could lose themselves in the jungle area of the mountain. How close he could take them to the village where they had left Cheryl and Sebak remained to be seen.

"Why aren't they coming after us?" Gwen asked, slightly winded, her face dotted with perspiration.

"I have no idea, unless they're trained to tend to their wounded immediately regardless of anything else," Will told her. "It's only a theory, but I don't give a rat's ass why they've stop chasing us, at least for now. We need to get moving while we have the chance."

Will led them along the fence until they reached a closed gate. When he tried to open the gate, he found it locked. Not hesitating, he aimed his gun, fired and blew off the lock. With no more than a nudge, the gate swung open, and they left the palace grounds. They emerged closer to the massive stone entrance than Will realized and were confronted by four members of the elite brigade. Shooting, he downed two guards in rapid succession. As the remaining two aimed their weapons, he shoved Gwen and Jordan to the ground, shouting for them to roll. He managed to sidestep an oncoming light ray, all the while firing his gun repeatedly. Another guard fell, but the fourth man stopped suddenly, dropped his spear and stared at his downed colleagues, a look of bewildered horror on his face.

It was in that moment, brief though it was, Will realized these men had never seen anyone killed in any other way except ritual sacrifice. They were stunned by the deadly force of Will's weapon.

Will eased over to the nearest dead guard, grabbed his spear, then stuck his gun into the waistband of his pants.

"Come on," he called to Gwen and Jordan, then helped them to their feet. "Let's get the hell out of here while we can."

"What's the matter with that guard?" Gwen asked. "He looks as if he's gone into a trance."

Will hurried her along, helping her with Jordan, who seemed to be sleepwalking. As they headed toward the stone roadway leading off the mountain, Will answered Gwen's question. "I think he was stunned to see his three comrades dead. I believe that's the reason the other soldiers stopped following us."

"Oh my God!" He saw the look of realization in Gwen's eyes. "The *sefu* only tranquilizes its victims. Here on Umi, death usually comes only to the very, very old and to the human sacrifices."

"We need to get off the road and into the jungle as soon as possible. We can't be sure that once they come out of their shock and regroup, they won't come after us."

They didn't reach the village of Bahiti until the following morning. Will could have managed to keep going all through the night, but neither Jordan nor Gwen would have made it without the half dozen brief rest stops. During every moment of their escape, Will had stayed constantly alert to any signs that they were being followed.

Despite her exhaustion, blistered feet and brush-scratched arms and legs, Gwen had not uttered one word of complaint, and thankfully, before dawn Jordan returned to normal, the effects of the tranquilizer having finally worn off.

The central fires in the village burned brightly, warming the chilly morning air. Men were already working in the fields and women were busying themselves in the village. Small, brown-skinned, naked children ran around laughing and playing. A tropical paradise, Will thought. So deceptive.

Cheryl saw them as they entered the village and came running, rushing straight into Jordan's arms. Sebak emerged from a nearby hut and waited for them to come to him.

"Did Lord Baruti allow you to leave Mount Kaphiri?" Sebak asked, his eyes wide with astonishment.

"Not exactly," Will said.

Sebak looked behind them, searching the pathway that led into the village. "Where is Dr. Arnell? And the other one?"

"They're dead," Jordan replied. "Both of them were sacrificed."

Cheryl cringed.

"It's only a matter of time before the elite brigade come after us. Not only did I save Gwen from being the third sacrifice, but we killed at least a dozen guards when we escaped," Will said. "We need to get to the beach on the other side of the island as fast as we can and leave Umi today."

"I understand. I will guide you back to Oseye," Sebak said. "From there, you must go on your own."

"What will the elite brigade do to you and the other villagers?" Gwen asked. "They'll know that you helped us, that you didn't report our presence on the island."

"Your weapons kill," Sebak said, as if that explained everything.

"We forced you and your village to help us. You did as we ordered you to do out of fear for your lives." Will knew that the elite brigade would believe Sebak's reason. Hadn't they panicked and become stunned to the point of terror when they realized that guns killed, not simply tranquilized?

Grasping Sebak's hand, Will said, "We owe you our lives, my friend."

Will, Gwen, Cheryl and Jordan reached the beach at twilight. Despite the dangers involved in taking the raft back to the *Footloose* in the dark, Will knew that other risks were far greater if they waited until the next day to leave.

While Will started the engines and manned the helm, Gwen stayed at his side. Cheryl and Jordan stood on the deck and gazed back at the mystical island of Umi. When they were several miles out to sea, Will handed Gwen the *sefu* of Baruti spear.

"You know what to do with this," he told her.

She nodded, stood, left the helm and joined Jordan and Cheryl on the starboard deck. Will knew what Gwen thought—that the spear was warm, as if alive, and as light as a feather. She lifted it over the railing and tossed it into the Atlantic.

When she rejoined Will at the helm, he slipped his arm around her waist. She rested her head on his shoulder. They remained that way for quite some time.

Finally Will broke the silence. "I'm sorry about your father."

"So am I."

"If I could have saved him—"

"No one could have saved him. He was lost long before he rediscovered Umi. His obsession destroyed him. In the end he was insane."

Will kissed her temple. As tears trickled from her eyes, Gwen clung to Will.

"I love you," he told her.

"I know," she said. "You've proven to me just how much you love me."

"More than anything or anyone on earth."

"You already know that I love you in the same way."

"When we get back to the States—"

"You're going to buy me some red silk undies."

"Yes, ma'am, I am. And you're going to wear them on our wedding night."

Gwen sighed deeply. "Was that a proposal?"

"Let's call it a trial run. Once we get home and we put our lives back together, I'm going to do it right. A diamond ring, flowers, music, me down on bended knee."

"Will we ever be able to put our lives back together?"

"Eventually. But the only way we can do that is if the four of us—" he nodded toward Cheryl and Jordan "—never reveal the truth about what happened to us, never breathe a word that your father's island and the magical youth plant exist."

"I think they'll agree, don't you?"

"Yeah, I think so. Something tells me that they want a future together, just as you and I do."

Gwen snuggled against Will as he took the *Footloose* due west, straight toward the Bahamas. In time the anger and pain and disappointment that she had experienced in the temple of the high priest's palace atop Mount Kaphiri would lessen, and perhaps someday vanish completely. Forgiving her father would not be easy, but with Will's love and support, Gwen knew that she could learn to release the past and happily face the future, knowing in her heart of hearts that she, and she alone, was Will Pierce's only obsession, just as he was hers.

Epilogue

Gwen stood over Will where he sat on an armless chair in their honeymoon hotel room, his gaze riveted to her body. She did a sexy little dance, shimmying her hips and swaying her breasts. The red bra she wore was sheer lace with underwired, pushup cups that made the very most of her B-cup breasts. The matching bikini panties were strips of silk holding the V-shaped lace that barely covered her. She had never worn anything so blatantly skimpy and alluring in her entire life. But loving Will brought out the vamp in her, and there was nothing she liked more than giving her man what he wanted.

This was the third set of matching red underwear that Will had bought for her, and each set had become progressively skimpier and sexier. The first set, which he'd bought a few weeks after their return to the United States, had been relatively tame, but she hadn't managed to keep them on long enough for him to appreciate them. One look at her in the satin bra and panties and Will had ripped them off her. The second pair had been red silk with black lace trim. He'd bought them at an exclusive lingerie shop in Atlanta before he moved to Huntsville a few months ago and opened his own P.I. agency. She had worn them for him on the night of their engagement party six weeks ago.

They had married this morning, seven months after meeting in Puerto Nuevo, in an afternoon wedding at the Huntsville Botanical Gardens. Cheryl Kress, newly engaged to Jordan Elders, had been Gwen's maid of honor, and Jordan had been Will's best man. Will's family had flown in from Texas—brothers, sisters-in-law and nephews, as well as his mother and stepfather from Louisiana—and several Dundee agents had driven over from Atlanta. Gwen's ex-husband and his partner, along with her friends and colleagues had attended the ceremony. The wedding had been perfect, and only once had Gwen allowed herself a moment of grief, giving that little girl inside her a chance to wish that her father was there to give her away. But she had walked down the aisle alone, knowing that once she became Will's wife, she would never be alone again.

Gwen slid downward slowly and seductively, then straddled Will, who was as naked as the day he was born. He reached up and unhooked the front snap of her bra, freeing her breasts.

After nuzzling each breast, he asked, "Is it my imagination or are these beauties getting bigger?"

She squirmed against his erection, eliciting a pleading groan from him.

"They may be just a tad bigger. I believe it's quite normal for a woman's breasts to enlarge throughout her pregnancy."

Will grabbed her hips to stop her from moving against him. "What did you say?"

"It's a good thing you made an honest woman out of me today," she told him. "I took a home pregnancy test this morning and I'm definitely pregnant. If my calculations are correct—"

Will let out a loud whoop, then wrapped his arms around Gwen, effectively trapping her against him as he took her mouth in a hot, hungry kiss. When they were both breathless, they broke apart and grinned at each other.

"It happened six weeks ago," he said proudly. "The night of our engagement party. Right?"

"Mmm-hmm. That would be my guess."

"You're happy about the baby, aren't you?" He caressed her shoulders.

"If I were any happier, I'm not sure I could stand it." She wrapped her arms around his neck. "What about you? Do you want to be a daddy?"

"You bet I do. I want a little girl who looks just like you, brown eyes."

"Well, I want a little boy who looks just like you."

Six months later, they both got their wishes, only in reverse order. Willard Hunter Pierce III, with his mother's brown eyes and dark hair, came howling into the world five minutes before his twin sister, Gwendolyn Jean Pierce, who was her daddy's spitting image.

* * * * *

STRANDED WITH
A SPY

BY
MERLINE LOVELACE

Merline Lovelace grew up on military bases all around the world. She spent twenty-three years in the United States Air Force herself, pulling tours in Taiwan, Vietnam and at the Pentagon before she hung up her uniform for good and decided to try her hand at writing. She now has more than sixty-five published novels under her belt, with more than nine million copies of her works in print.

Merline and her own handsome hero live in Oklahoma. When she's not glued to her keyboard, she loves travelling to exotic locations, chasing little white balls around the golf course and enjoying long, lazy dinners with family and friends. Check www.merlinelovelace. com for release dates of future books.

To my darling who loves to ramble and explore
as much as I do. Thanks for the castles of the
Loire Valley, picnicking under the arches of the
Pont du Gard, lunch at the Ritz Carlton in Cannes
and most of all—for Mont St. Michel

Prologue

With the threat of bombs being detonated in midair by fanatics heavy in their minds, the inspectors screening the baggage going aboard the nonstop flight from D.C.'s Dulles Airport to Paris took no chances.

Bomb dogs sniffed long rows of suitcases and other checked items before handlers slung the pieces onto the conveyor for X-ray screening. Additional handlers waited down line to remove the items from the conveyor and load them onto carts for transport to the Boeing 777 parked out on the ramp.

Certain pieces received additional scrutiny before hitting the cart. Specially trained inspectors pulled off luggage electronically tagged by ticket agents as having been checked by individuals who fit certain profiles, who looked nervous or whose body language was in some way suspicious. Each of these bags were opened and their contents closely examined.

The inspector pawing through one of those bags had worked security at the General Services Administration Headquarters before transferring to the Transportation Security Agency. Otherwise he might not have recognized the logo on the computer disk he found tucked inside a commercial CD case.

"Hey, Chief!"

The call jerked his supervisor's head around. "What have you got?"

"The case says it's a CD by a blues singer by the name of Corinne Bailey Rae, but the disk has no markings except this."

He pointed to a tiny blue square on the inner rim of the silver disk. Inside the square were the letters *GSA,* with a small star forming the crossbar of the *A.*

"That's the General Services Administration logo. The disk is government property."

"Wouldn't be the first time a civil servant ripped off government supplies for private use," his supervisor mused, "but let's see what's on it."

Careful to handle the disk by the rim with his gloved hands, the inspector slipped it into the computer at his boss's workstation and clicked on the single file that popped up. Seconds later the computer screen painted with line after line of names, addresses, birthdays and other identifying data.

Several names were highlighted in bold print. The one halfway down the first page elicited a startled *"Sonuvabitch"* from the inspector and drained all color from his supervisor's face.

Grabbing his phone, the supervisor punched a speed-dial number that connected him directly with the TSA Operations Center.

"This is Peterson. I've got a Code One!"

Chapter 1

A crisp September breeze rustled the leaves of the chestnut trees lining a quiet side street just off Massachusetts Avenue, in the heart of Washington, D.C.'s embassy district. When a taxi pulled up at an elegant townhouse halfway down the block, the driver frowned and shot a quick look in the rearview mirror.

"You sure you got the right address?"

"I'm sure." His passenger peeled off two bills. "Keep the change."

Despite the hefty tip, the driver's frown stayed in place as his fare hauled his beat-up leather carryall out of the cab.

No big surprise there, Cutter Smith thought sardonically. He hadn't slept in going on forty-eight hours and he hadn't shaved in twice that long. And not even four days' worth of raspy whiskers could disguise the scars on the right side of his chin and neck. When most people noticed the puckered skin, they quickly turned away. Others, like the cabbie, looked long and hard, as if memorizing the face that went with the scars in case they later had to pick him out of a police lineup.

As Cutter hefted his carryall and mounted the front steps, his gaze went to the discreet bronze plaque beside the door. The carefully polished lettering identified the townhouse as home to the offices of the Special Envoy to the President of the United States. Most Washingtonians familiar with the political spoils system knew the position of Special Envoy was one of those meaningless jobs handed out to wealthy campaign contributors with a yen for a fancy title and a Washington office. Only a very small, very select circle knew the Special Envoy also served as head of OMEGA, an agency so secret that its operatives were activated only in extreme situations.

Or, as in Cutter's case, reactivated. He'd returned from a month-long undercover operation in Central America only this morning, had conducted an exhaustive debrief and was headed home when a call from OMEGA control had turned him around.

Wondering what the hell was so urgent, he reached for the brass latch on the red-lacquered door. He knew it had to be something big for his boss to direct him to enter via the townhouse's front door instead of going through the labyrinthine maze that led from the secret entrance in an underground parking lot a half block away.

The receptionist who buzzed him in knew him by sight but still carefully checked his ID before passing him into the area ruled by the Special Envoy's executive assistant. The ornate Louis XV desk was normally occupied by Elizabeth Wells, a serene, silver-haired grandmother who regularly qualified at the expert level on the 9mm Sig Sauer nestled in a handy compartment in her desk.

But Elizabeth had fallen while doing a foxtrot with her latest beau on a Big Band Potomac Cruise. While she recovered from hip replacement surgery, a temp was handling her duties. An *extremely* well-qualified temp, with the necessary top-level security clearances, background and smarts to handle Elizabeth's extraordinarily sensitive duties.

Gillian Ridgeway was the daughter of two of OMEGA's most legendary operatives. She was also goddaughter to the man she referred to as Uncle Nick, OMEGA's current director. As luck would have it, she happened to be home on leave from her job at the American Embassy in Beijing when Elizabeth hit the deck. Nick Jensen had jumped on Gillian's offer to fill in for his temporarily disabled assistant.

Tall and slender, Gillian had inherited her mother's ready smile and her father's black hair and startlingly blue eyes. The twenty-six-year-old already had half the male operatives seriously in lust. That she'd also won the friendship and respect of OMEGA's female agents was testimony to her bright, engaging personality.

"Hi, Jilly." Depositing his carryall beside a leafy palm, Cutter crossed the parquet floor. "What's up?"

"Uncle Nick will explain all, Slash."

Gillian had assumed Cutter's code designation was a play on his first name. He hadn't disabused her.

"Go on in. He's waiting for you."

Nick Jensen, code name Lightning, didn't look like anyone's uncle, honorary or otherwise, when Cutter entered his office. Nor did he look like the owner of a string of outrageously expensive watering holes that catered to the rich and famous. He looked, Cutter thought with a lift of one brow, ready to chew nails and spit them out like shrapnel.

"Sorry, Slash." His jaw tight, Nick yanked at his Italian silk tie and popped the top button of his white shirt. "I know you haven't even changed your watch from jungle time yet, but I need to send you back into the field."

"No problem. What's the op?"

"I think we might finally have a lead on the Russian."

Cutter's pulse kicked up a half dozen notches. OMEGA had been trying to nail the shadowy figure known only as the Russian for more than a year.

"Mike Callahan will act as your controller." Nick shot back his cuff to check the sleek Swiss job on his wrist. "He's choppering up from Quantico. Should be about fifteen minutes out."

Cutter nodded, considerably reassured by the information. Whatever this mission entailed, it would go down a hell of a lot smoother with Mike Callahan, code name Hawkeye, handling things on this end. A former military cop, Hawk was a cool head and a dead shot.

"In the meantime," Nick said grimly, "we've got two hundred and thirty passengers cooling their heels at Dulles while maintenance works a small 'mechanical' problem on their aircraft. We suspect one of those passengers is on her way to connect with the Russian."

He slapped a file down on a mahogany conference table the size of a soccer field. Pinned to the front of the folder was a color photo of a tight-lipped blonde with most of her face hidden behind oversized sunglasses.

"A looker," Cutter commented, "but obviously not happy with the world. Who is she?"

"Mallory Dawes."

Nick said the name as if Cutter should know it, then gave an impatient shake of his head.

"Sorry. I forgot the crap hit the fan after you left for Central America. Dawes is…or was, until a few days ago…a staffer for Congressman Ashton Kent, Chairman of the House Banking and Trade Committee."

"The old goat knows how to pick 'em," Cutter commented, taking in the chiseled cheekbones and chin-length sweep of pale-gold hair.

"As a matter of fact, that's precisely what Dawes claimed in the sexual harassment complaint she filed. Said Kent admitted hiring the males in his office based on their brains and the females on their bra size. The comment came right after he reportedly groped her a second time and she allegedly whacked him with a copy of the *Congressional Record*."

"Reportedly. Allegedly. I'm getting the impression Dawes's complaint boiled down to a case of she said/he said."

"It did. An investigator dismissed it two days ago for lack of evidence, but the media had a field day with the charge."

Cutter eyed the angry blonde again. "Bet they made her life hell in the process."

"And then some. We suspect that may be why Dawes quit her job, cleaned out her desk and departed the House of Representatives with a disk containing the names, addresses, social security numbers and bank account numbers of more than twenty million government employees. Including," Nick drawled, "the President of the United States."

Cutter whistled, low and long. That explained the high pucker factor. All brisk business now, Nick filled him in on the background.

"Kent's Committee recently conducted a series of closed hearings on the vulnerability of U.S. banks to hacking. One of the witnesses demonstrated just how easy it was to obtain this kind of sensitive data. We suspect Dawes secretly made a copy of the information this guy extracted from various sources before the file was destroyed."

"And we think she plans to sell the data?"

"We think that's a distinct possibility. Mallory Dawes isn't a happy camper right now. After the arbitrator dismissed her claim, she spoke on camera. The woman sounded both bruised and angry. Talked about how the accuser had become the accused, and how she wasn't given the protection she was supposed to be afforded under the law. What better way to get back at the system that failed you than by selling personal data to the highest black-market bidder?"

"Which would most likely be the Russian," Cutter acknowledged grimly.

OMEGA suspected the nameless, faceless thug had masterminded at least two other massive identity thefts. Both had wreaked havoc on the international financial scene and had devastating effects on the lives of millions of individuals. One of those individuals had been Cutter's great-aunt May, who'd lost her entire life savings in a series of swift, incredibly complex and as yet untraceable wire transfers.

Cutter *really* wanted to nail this bastard.

"Do we have a specific link between Dawes and the Russian?"

"Intelligence picked up an e-mail indicating he expects a major delivery soon."

No small feat, both men knew, given the billions of electronic communications screened daily.

"We also have evidence suggesting he's on the move. Intel thinks he may be headed for Paris."

"Like our girl, Dawes," Cutter said softly.

"Exactly."

"We've got her under close surveillance at Dulles while we substitute a disk containing fake data for the one in her bag. We're also tagging the CD's case with a monitoring device so we can track its every move. I want you in Paris, waiting at the airport, when she and the bag come off the plane. With any luck, she'll lead you to the Russian."

Lightning checked his watch again.

"We have an air force jet standing by at Andrews. The chopper that delivers Mike will take you out to the base. You've got fifteen minutes to shower, shave and jump into clean clothes. Field Dress has everything you need upstairs. Mac's working your comm as we speak. Your cover is businessman on vacation."

At his operative's pained look, Lightning relaxed into a smile for the first time since the call had come from the White House less than a half hour ago. A former Army Ranger, Cutter still preferred boots and floppy-brimmed boonie hats to business suits.

"Sorry, Slash. It was the best Field Dress could do on short notice. Take the file on Dawes with you and read it on the chopper."

"Will do."

Cutter climbed aboard the chopper less than twenty minutes later. His hair was still damp from his ninety-second shower and his cheeks stung from the aftershave he'd splashed on after scraping off his whiskers. His boots and jeans were gone, traded for a suede sport coat and open-necked white shirt paired with black slacks and polished loafers.

Shutting out the whap-whap of the chopper's rotors, he slid the folder from the expensive Moroccan leather briefcase Field Dress had thrust at him on his way out the door and settled in to read the background dossier on Mallory Dawes.

Mallory sat quietly in a corner of the International Waiting Area. She'd had to slip out the back door of her apartment to evade the reporters camped out front. With escape so close, the last thing she wanted now was to draw attention to herself.

Shielded behind tinted glasses, her gaze roamed her increasingly impatient fellow passengers. Some paced, some checked the monitors for an update on their departure time, others flipped through magazines. A young mother kept twin toddlers on security leashes and walked them like frisky puppies, hoping to use up their store of energy. She'd taken a nearby seat a while ago and tried to strike up a conversation. Mallory had cut her off with the excuse of having to go to the ladies' room.

The past weeks had taught her to distrust *everyone*. Reporters had resorted to all kinds of ruses in their relentless pursuit of intimate details about her life and loves. One had disguised himself as a deliveryman and shown up at Mallory's apartment with a dozen roses. Others had donned overalls and sifted through the Dumpster behind her apartment. As voracious as scavengers feeding on rotting corpses, they'd dug up skeletons Mallory didn't know she had.

Like the junior-high-school "sweetheart" who couldn't wait to tell the world how hot she was. As best she could recall, she'd kissed the kid once, while playing spin the bottle at some eighth- or ninth-grade party.

Then there was the lobbyist she'd dated all of twice, yet he claimed they'd had a torrid affair after she picked him up in a bar. It was a *sushi* bar, for God's sake, and *he'd* picked her up, but that hadn't made for good copy. Her mouth twisting, Mallory folded her arms and stared out the plate-glass windows until an announcement came over the speakers.

"We apologize for the delay, ladies and gentlemen. Our minor maintenance issue has been resolved. Flight 17 nonstop to Charles De Gaulle Airport, Paris, is now ready for boarding."

Thank God!

Because of tightened security on international flights, Mallory had checked everything but a small wallet purse containing her passport, ID and the one credit card she hadn't maxed out. She'd drawn against the others for loans to pay the lawyers she'd had to hire to defend herself against Congressman Kent's counter-allegations.

Don't think about the legal bills waiting to be paid, she lectured herself sternly as she boarded the transport that would take the passengers out to the aircraft. Don't think about the ugliness or smut or vicious lies.

Think about France. Undulating vineyards. Fairytale castles. Crusty bread and melt-in-your-mouth pastries.

And anonymity. Blessed anonymity.

Ten whole days with no reporters hounding her, no microphones shoved in her face. She'd lose herself on back roads. Put the awful mess behind her.

Nine hours, she thought as she found her seat and buckled in. Nine hours flying through the night, then freedom.

As soon as the jumbo jet reached cruising altitude, she plugged in her earphones, slipped on the eye mask provided by the airline and reclined her seat.

Ms. Dawes was one cool customer, Cutter decided, watching from a few feet away at the baggage carousel.

He'd tracked her from the moment she exited the aircraft. She'd looked straight ahead as she stood in line at passport control, didn't so much as nod or speak to any of her fellow passengers. Same here at the baggage carousel. Below the shield of her sunglasses, her mouth was set in a line that warned off all comers.

With seeming nonchalance, Cutter pulled out a slim cell phone. Mackenzie Blair, Nick's wife and OMEGA's guru of all things electronic, had packed the slim case with enough gadgetry and software to make Bill Gates drool.

She'd replaced the built-in camera with one so powerful she swore it would capture a mosquito in flight a block away. With a flick of one button, Cutter could reverse the lens and activate an iris scanner. The digitized image identified him instantaneously to his controller at OMEGA headquarters. Voice-recognition software provided additional security, as did the satellite encryption transmissions. Not even the spooks at the National Intelligence Collection and Processing Center could intercept these calls.

What interested Cutter most at the moment was the embedded GPS transceiver that caused the phone to vibrate when the compact disk tucked into Mallory Dawes's suitcase moved so much as an inch.

It was moving now. The vibrations tickled Cutter's palm and had every one of his nerves jumping in response. Screwing in an earpiece, he flipped up the phone and made like the other half dozen or so passengers busy calling home or confirming reservations now that they'd landed.

"I've got movement."

He didn't bother to identify himself. The phone took care of that. Mike Callahan's reply came through the earpiece.

"Roger that, Slash. I'm tracking the case via the airport's security cameras. It's on a baggage cart, headed your way."

Cutter acknowledged the transmission and tucked the phone back in his pocket. As the vibrations grew stronger, his instincts went on full alert.

His gut told him the most likely spot for the Russian or one of his cohorts to make the pickup was right here at the airport. Odds were it would happen shortly after Dawes claimed her bag.

He was right on her tail when she exited through passport control, had the woman and her roller bag firmly in his sights when she strode through the terminal, felt the phone vibrating like hell in his shirt pocket as she marched up to a rental-car counter.

It was still vibrating when he tossed his briefcase and carryall in a rental car some minutes later and trailed her midget Peugeot out of Charles De Gaulle Airport.

Chapter 2

Mallory was amazed that she could still function with semiefficiency.

The long flight across the Atlantic should have wiped her out, especially coming on top of all the weeks of stress. Not to mention the sleepless nights wondering why she hadn't just quit after Congressman Kent had grabbed her ass the first time.

Dillon Porter, Kent's senior staffer and Mallory's closest friend on the Hill, had smoothed things over that first time. Dillon had agreed with her that their boss was a throwback, a total Neanderthal. He'd also warned that Kent was so slick, any charges Mallory brought against him would slide off his Teflon-coated back.

How right Dillon had been!

Only now, after two hours of ambling west along the two-lane road that led from Paris to Evreux, were Mallory's jagged nerves beginning to smooth out. The brisk sea breeze as she neared the coast of Normandy blew through the open windows of her pint-sized rental like the breath of life.

This wasn't the route she'd laid out when she'd planned this long-dreamed-of vacation in such meticulous detail. A history major in college, she'd intended to spend at least three days exploring Paris before heading south to visit the medieval walled city of Carcassonne and the Roman ruins at Nîmes.

With the miasma of the hearing hanging over her, however, Mallory had decided to reverse her itinerary. She needed calm and space and solitude, which she certainly wouldn't get in the bustle of Paris. She'd hit the city on her way back. Maybe. For now she'd just follow the coast and let the winds blow away the stink of the past weeks.

Her first stop was Caen, William the Conqueror's stronghold and the site of vicious battles during the Second World War invasion of Normandy. Mallory squeezed out of her rental car and treated herself to a flaky quiche and a sinfully rich napoleon eaten at an outdoor café in the shadow of the castle walls. After lunch she visited the museum housing the Bayeux Tapestry embroidered by William's wife, Matilda, after her husband had conquered England.

Musing at the vagaries of fate that had one nation invading another, only to be invaded itself centuries later by the nation it had once conquered, Mallory drank in the history that went into the hundred-and-sixty-eight-foot tapestry. The segment that dealt with William's visit to a nearby holy place spawned another spur-of-the-moment decision.

"Mont St. Michel," she murmured, her gaze fixed on the embroidered panel depicting mounted warriors pulling pilgrims from the treacherous waters surrounding the shrine. Mesmerized by the scene, she consulted her plastic-coated, foldaway tourist map.

The shrine was only a little over an hour from Caen. Not on her original route, but so what? She wasn't too jet-lagged yet. She could do another hour of driving easy. After she'd explored the ancient abbey, she'd find a nice little seaside pension and crash.

Bad decision, Mallory thought two and a half hours later.

Very bad.

The countryside of Lower Normandy was pretty enough. She'd left the sea behind at Caen to cut across a broad peninsula dotted with magnificent forests and tranquil streams flowing through rich farmlands. Apple orchards lined the road and hand-painted signs pointed to tasting stands for Camembert, Livarot and Pont l'Evêque cheese. Without intending to, Mallory had stumbled onto France's Wine and Cheese Road.

Which would have been fine except that the fall harvest was in full swing. Tractors hauling trailers mounded with apples competed for road space with busloads of tourists come to sample fresh-squeezed cider and pungent cheese. As Mallory inched through a picturesque village behind yet another tractor, she looked in vain for an inn or a pension. She was ready to call it a day *and* a night.

The tractor finally turned off at a crossroads. A tilted signpost pointed to villages with names Mallory couldn't pronounce. Below the signpost was a blue historical sign indicating that Mont St. Michel was five kilometers away.

"Finally!"

Surely there would be plenty of hotels at such a touristy spot. Aiming her tiny rental car in the direction of the sea once more, she soon left the forests and orchards behind. The topography flattened to marshy fields topped by feathery grass. The tangy scent of the ocean again flavored the air.

Then Mallory turned a bend in the road and there it was, rising out of the salt marsh. Stunned, she pulled to the side of the road and sat there, arms looped over the wheel.

Mont St. Michel was a small island, an outcropping of solid granite thrusting up from sand flats at the mouth of St. Malo Bay. A defensive wall bristling with turrets and a fourteenth-century barbican encircled the rock at its base. Above the battlements, a village of slate-roofed buildings stair-stepped up the steep slopes. A magnificent twelfth-century abbey crowned the island, overwhelming in its size, overpowering in its grandeur. Atop the abbey's tall spire was a gilded statue of Saint Michael that glinted in the afternoon sun.

According to Mallory's guidebook, the Archangel Michael had appeared on this spot in 708 AD. The glorious abbey was built to honor that visitation. All through the Middle Ages, pilgrims had risked the treacherous tides that rushed in, cutting the island off from the mainland, to worship at the site. Modern-day tourists were no less enthralled. Mesmerized by the magnificent sight, Mallory paid no attention to the tour bus that chugged by her, spewing diesel exhaust.

The driver of the vehicle some yards behind the lumbering bus cursed as he approached the car pulled onto the side of the road. Cutter had been swallowing exhaust for twenty minutes. He'd had to, to keep some distance between him and his target. God knew there wasn't any other cover on this stretch of flat salty marsh.

Now he had no choice but to drive right past the woman and onto the causeway leading to the island dead ahead. The causeway was elevated above the sand flats and wide enough to accommodate dozens of parked cars and buses. Cutter could turn around easily enough if the woman he was tailing didn't follow him onto the bridge.

"Come on, Dawes," he muttered, "put it in gear."

He kept her in the rearview mirror and was all set to make a turn when the cell phone in his pocket began to vibrate. The car behind him eased back onto the road.

"That's right. Come to Papa."

Dividing his attention between the vehicle behind and the battlements now looming before him, Cutter cruised the long bridge. The tide was out, baring the hard-packed sand below. Overflow traffic was being directed to park on the sand, but a minivan pulled out of a parking space atop the causeway as Cutter got close. Whipping into the space, he remained in his vehicle with the engine idling while his target neared the island.

He speared a quick glance at the walls looming above him. Was this where Dawes planned to make contact with the Russian or one of his henchmen? Or would she just diddle away a few hours, as she had in Caen? Or had she tipped to the fact that she was being followed and had decided to lead her tail away from a possible rendezvous point instead of toward it?

Cutter was ninety-nine-percent certain that wasn't the case. With the directional signal implanted in her suitcase to guide him, he'd stayed well out of her line of sight while on the road. He'd mounted a closer surveillance in Caen, waiting, watching, his instincts on full alert. But she hadn't removed the disk from the suitcase locked in the trunk of her rental car. He'd trailed her into the museum, keeping well back, knowing the signal device would alert him if someone *else* retrieved it. No one had.

Wondering if this pile of rock would be the rendezvous point, Cutter narrowed his eyes behind his aviator sunglasses and watched as Dawes drove along the causeway. The bridge was a quarter-mile long and raised some ten or twelve feet above the sand flats. Dawes drove the length of the causeway, searching for a parking space, before nosing down a ramp to the hard-packed sand.

When she exited her rental, Cutter held his breath. Would she unlock the trunk? Slip the disk into the wallet-type purse slung over her shoulder?

To his intense disappointment, she did neither. Instead she joined a throng of tourists decamping from a bus and trekked up the ramp toward the barbican. Muttering a curse, Cutter pulled out his cell phone.

"The target has exited her vehicle," he advised Mike Callahan after the iris scan and voice data print had verified his identity. "Again."

"Roger that. You want to confirm the location? GPS is showing her parked about ten yards off the causeway leading to the island of Mont St. Michel, in what should be about eight feet of water."

"The tide's out, Hawkeye, so it's high and dry. She's walking up to the island from her car, minus her suitcase."

"Could be intending to establish initial contact before making the drop."

"Could be," Cutter agreed, shouldering open his car door. "Check the tide tables for me, will you? I want to know how long we've got here."

"Will do."

He could have spared Mike the trouble, Cutter realized as he trailed his target toward the massive gates guarding the entrance to the walled town. Warning signs posted at several points along the causeway warned visitors in five different languages to stick to designated walkways to avoid dangerous quicksand. The signs also advised that high tide would occur at eighteen hundred hours that evening.

Three and a half hours, Cutter thought grimly. Plenty of time for Ms. Dawes to establish contact, return to her car and retrieve the disk.

As he had at Caen, he stayed out of her line of sight. Not hard to do, with so many tourists thronging the narrow, cobbled streets. Then again, Dawes made for an easy tail. She wasn't all that tall. Five-

six, according to the background dossier OMEGA
had hastily compiled on her. Yet her cap of shining
blond hair acted like a beacon amid the shadows
thrown by the tall, narrow buildings lining the streets
and alleys. The navy blazer she wore with a white
tank top and jeans also stood out among the post-
summer throng of primarily middle-aged tourists in
jogging suits and windbreakers.

Eyeing the trim rear and slender thighs encased
by those jeans, Cutter had to admire Congressman
Kent's taste, if not his morals. Ms. Dawes's behind
looked eminently gropeable. Her front looked
pretty good, too. Narrow waist. Full breasts. A determined chin softened by lips he suspected might
tempt a man to sin if she ever smiled. Cutter could
certainly understand why the clown she'd picked up
in a D.C. bar had described her to the press as a real
piece of eye candy.

But it was the way she moved that stirred unwelcome memories. Cutter had known a woman who
walked with that same hip-swinging grace once. He
still wore the scars she'd left on him.

Which was probably why he noticed when Ms.
Dawes began to move with considerably less elegance. Obviously, the climb up the winding streets
and steep stairs was taking its toll. Her pace got
slower and more deliberate. Her shoulders started to
sag. She paused more often to study shop windows

displaying fresh pastries, cheeses, handmade lace and the inevitable cheap souvenirs.

Cutter was thirty yards behind her when she veered toward a small café carved out of the rock below the walls of the cathedral. Potted geraniums added splashes of color to the tiny patio, which contained all of three tables. Dawes dropped into a chair at the only empty table. When she shoved her sunglasses to the top of her head to study the menu, lines of exhaustion were etched into her face.

Cutter continued his surveillance from a combination *boulangerie* and sandwich shop across the street. Surrounded by the seductive aroma of fresh-baked baguettes and twisted loaves of rye, he ordered a ham and Swiss and coffee. He carried both to a stand-up table in the window and had the crusty sandwich halfway to his mouth when he froze.

Eyes narrowing to slits behind his mirrored sunglasses, Cutter assessed the heavyset male who scooted his chair around to face Dawes. Early fifties. Dressed as a tourist in no-press khaki knit pants, a blue windbreaker and a baseball cap with some kind of a logo on it. Heavy jowls, flushed cheeks and a knowing smile that lifted the hairs on the back of Cutter's neck.

The guy knew Dawes. He'd recognized her, perhaps had been waiting for her. Whipping out his cell phone, Cutter zoomed in on the man's red face and took several quick shots with the instrument's built-in, jazzed-up camera. A click of a button transmitted the photos instantly to OMEGA. Cutter followed with a terse instruction to Mike Callahan.

"Give me an ID on this guy, and fast."

"Will do."

He needed to get closer for the sensitive receiver built into the phone to pick up the conversation between his target and the fleshy tourist. Abandoning his coffee and sandwich, Cutter exited the *boulangerie* and crossed the cobbles. He kept to the shadows thrown by the cathedral directly above. With each step closer, the receiver filtered out the background noise from the busy street until Dawes's voice came through sharp and angry.

"No, thank you."

"Ahhh, c'mon. We're both 'Mericans. Let me buy you a glass of wine. Jes' one glass."

From the sound of it, the supposed tourist had already downed several glasses. Or wanted to give that impression.

"Didn't you hear me? I said no."

Dawes's icy reply didn't deter the man. His heavy cheeks creasing into a smirk, he hooked his arm over the back of her chair.

"I heard you. From what Congressman Kent and those others said, though, your 'no' really means 'maybe.'"

With a sound of disgust, Dawes slipped her sunglasses back onto her nose and gathered her purse.

"Hey! Where y'going?"

Stumbling to his feet, the big man tossed some bills down on his table and followed her into the street. If this was an act, Cutter thought, it was a damned good one.

Dawes kept her face averted and marched stiffly ahead, but that didn't deter the persistent tourist.

"The papers said you like to pick up men in bars," he said, loud enough to turn the heads of several passersby. "I've got a couple hours to kill before I have to climb back onto that damned bus. Plenty of time for us to have some fun."

Shoulders rigid, Dawes turned into a narrow alley to escape her tormentor. The tourist followed, with Cutter some yards behind. Ingrained habit had him doing an instinctive sweep for obstacles, hostiles and possible escape routes. There didn't appear to be many of the latter.

Tall buildings with carved lintels and slate roofs leaned in on both sides, cutting off the sunlight and almost obscuring the flowers that decorated doorways and windowsills. A stone horse trough was set dead center in the middle of the cobbles, testimony to Mont St. Michel's main means of transportation for centuries.

"Wait up, sweet thing!" Dodging the watering

trough, the tourist grabbed his quarry's arm. "We kin…"

"Let go of me!" A mass of seething fury, Dawes whirled around and yanked her arm free of his hold. "Touch me again, you obnoxious ass, and I swear I'll…"

"You'll what?" He waggled his brows in an exaggerated leer. "Charge me with sexual harassment, like you did Congressman Kent?"

"I'll do what I *should* have done to Kent," she ground out through clenched teeth, "and knee you in your nut-sized brain."

The threat didn't faze her tormentor. If anything, it seemed to add spice to his sport.

"Whoo-ee. Aren't you a feisty one? That guy you dated in school said you liked it raunchy, even rough sometimes. That's fine with me."

Cutter kept to the shadows. He'd prefer not to break cover or show himself to his target, but the situation was starting to get ugly.

A few yards away, Mallory had come to the same conclusion. She knew damned well all she had to do was scream. They were only a few yards off a main street crowded with tourists. One panicked shriek, one piercing cry, and a dozen people would charge to her rescue.

Then the police would arrive on the scene. She'd have to deal with their questions, their carefully blank faces when this loudmouthed fool ranted about how she'd led him on, like she had all the others back in the States.

Better to handle the situation herself, utilizing one of the more effective moves she'd learned in the self-defense class she'd taken when she first got to D.C. Before the heel of her hand could connect with the bridge of the beefy tourist's nose, however, he jerked backward. A startled Mallory watched him lift off his feet. A second later, he landed butt-first in the stone horse trough.

"What the hell…?"

Cursing, he struggled to lever himself out of the narrow trough. The man who'd put him there planted a hand on his head, pushing him down and under.

As her attacker gurgled and flailed his arms and legs, Mallory's surprise gave way to fierce delight. The dunking went on a little too long, however. She was about to issue a curt order not to drown the bastard when the man holding him under relented.

The jerk who'd accosted her came up sputtering and ready to fight. When he shook the water from his eyes and got a good look at the individual looming above him, however, he plopped back down into the water.

"Smart move," his chastiser said in a voice as deep as it was cool and steady. "I suggest you listen next time a lady says no."

"Yeah, yeah, okay."

When the stranger straightened and stepped out
of the shadows, Mallory registered short-cropped
brown hair, wide shoulders and a well-cut sports
jacket paired with an open-necked shirt. Then she
saw the scars puckering one side of his neck and
swallowed a gulp. No wonder the loudmouthed
tourist had planted his butt back into the water.

"You okay?" the newcomer asked.

"I'm fine." Rattled by the incident and pissed at
having the first day of her precious vacation tainted
by the ugliness she'd come here to escape, Mallory's
response was somewhat less than gracious. "Thanks."

Her tone implied she could have handled the situation herself. She reinforced that impression by
sweeping past both men. The one still standing said
nothing, but the waterlogged tourist made the
mistake of muttering aloud, "Bitch."

The vicious epithet was followed by a yelp and
another splash. Mallory didn't slow or bother to look
around. For all she cared, the scarred stranger could
drown the moron.

Chapter 3

Mallory had never climbed so many steps in her life!

The stairs leading to the abbey were carved into the granite. In some places they climbed straight up. In others, they followed a zigzag pattern that shortened the rise but doubled the distance required to travel. She stopped several times along the way to shake the kinks out of her calves and was huffing long before she reached the small terrace that faced the abbey's magnificent vaulted doors.

If the steep climb and the wind whipping off the Bay of St. Malo hadn't stolen Mallory's breath, the view would have done the trick. Waiting for her heart to stop hammering, she leaned her elbows on the terrace wall. Far below, mud-brown flats stretched all the way to the sea. A storm was forming far out on the bay. Thunderclouds had piled up, forming a dramatic vista and no doubt accounting for the wind that whipped Mallory's hair.

She was surprised to see people walking across the flats. Signs posted all around Mont St. Michel warned about the dangers of quicksand. They also posted the time of the incoming tide.

Frowning, Mallory glanced at her watch. She'd wasted too much time in the village. She'd have to hurry her tour of the abbey to get back down to the parking lot before the water nipped at the rental's tires.

Adjusting her sunglasses, she eased into the stream of tourists entering the cathedral. She'd already decided not to join one of the guided tours that took visitors through the adjacent Benedictine monastery. After the nasty incident in the village, she was in no mood for the company of others. Instead, she slipped through the cathedral's massive doors and was immediately swallowed by the vastness of its nave.

Like most European churches, this one was laid out in the shape of a cross. The long main transept ended in a curved apse that faced to the east and the rising sun that symbolized Christ. The shorter, north-south transept bisected the main vestibule at the choir and led to richly decorated chapels.

Three tiers of soaring granite arches, all intricately carved and decorated, supported the vaulted ceiling high above Mallory's head. *Unlike* so many other European cathedrals, however, this one was filled with light. Gloriously white and shimmering, it poured in through the tiered windows and added a luminescent sheen to the gray granite walls.

Guidebook in hand, Mallory took in the richness of the altar and choir before exploring the side chapels. The musky scent of incense lingered in the alcoves and mixed with the smoke from hundreds of flickering votives. She stood for long moments before a bank of votives dominated by a stained-glass window depicting Saint Michael slaying a dragon.

Part of her ached to drop a franc in the slot, light a candle and pray for the strength to forgive Congressman Kent and everyone in the media who'd slandered her. The rest of her was still too bruised and hurt. She wasn't ready to forgive or forget, and she figured God would recognize a fake prayer quick enough.

Sighing, Mallory followed the signs pointing to the stairs that wound down to the crypts. There were two of these subterranean chambers, one under the north transept, one under the south. The first was big and ornate and contained the sarcophagi of previous bishops and abbots. The second was much smaller and plainer. Barrel-vaulted and constructed with Romanesque simplicity, it had the dank smell of centuries long past.

There, in the south crypt dedicated to Saint Martin, Mallory founded a semblance of the serenity that had eluded her upstairs. It was so quiet in the crypt, and so empty. The only objects in the round-roofed chamber were a plain altar topped by a wrought-iron cross and a narrow wooden prayer bench set alongside one wall.

Mallory eased onto the bench and leaned her shoulders against the granite wall. A chill seeped through her navy blazer, but she barely noticed it.

Why *couldn't* she forgive and forget? Why had she let Congressman Kent destroy her pride along with her reputation?

Her friend, Dillon Porter, had tried to warn her. In his serious, no-nonsense way, Kent's senior staffer had reminded his coworker how Jennifer Flowers and Monica Lewinsky had become the butt of so many vicious jokes. Yet Mallory had plowed ahead, convinced she had right on her side.

Yeah, sure.

With another long sigh, she tilted her head against the granite and closed her eyes. Maybe if she just sat here a while, the utter calm of this place would leach into her troubled soul.

What the hell was she doing?

Cutter lounged against a stone pillar, pretending

interest in a brochure he'd picked up at the entrance to the abbey. The brochure happened to be in Japanese, a fact that had escaped his attention until he'd been forced to hide behind the damned thing for going on twenty minutes now.

Was she waiting for someone? The Russian? The obnoxious tourist?

Or had the woman fallen asleep? Sure looked like it from where Cutter stood.

Her head rested against the granite wall. Her lashes feathered her cheek. The arms she'd hooked around her waist had loosened and sagged into her lap.

She'd stirred, blinking owlishly when the muted sound of an announcement drifted down the stairs. They were too deep in the bowels of the church to distinguish the words, and she was too lethargic to do more than turn her head toward the distant sound. Moments later, her lids had dropped and she was breathing deeply again. This time a small smile played at the corners of her lips.

Sweet dreams, Dawes?

Thinking about all the goodies you'll buy when and if you sell the data you stole?

Frowning, Cutter shot a quick look at his watch. The warning signs posted around the island were vivid in his head when the cell phone in his pocket began to vibrate. This motion had a different pattern from that of the GPS tracker attached to the disk in Dawes's suitcase.

That was Mike Callahan signaling him. He must have IDed the fleshy tourist. Keeping the entrance to the small crypt in sight, Cutter retreated into the dim recesses of the subterranean vault and screwed the phone's earpiece into his ear. A click of the receive button brought Callahan's face up on the screen.

"What have you got?"

His voice carried no more than a few feet in the dank, gloomy stillness. Callahan's came through the earpiece clearly.

"Your friend is Robert Walters."

A photo of the paunchy tourist replaced Mike's face. This shot showed him in a business suit, smiling for the camera as he gestured toward a warehouse with a sign announcing Walters Products.

"Age," Hawkeye reported succinctly, "fifty-three. Born, Sterling, Indiana. One hitch in the Navy. Made three trips to the altar, the same number to divorce court. Owns a siding-and-storm-door installation company in Indiana. He and two buddies are on a tour of the Normandy beaches, sponsored by their local American Legion."

"Doesn't sound like the profile of someone with ties to an international thug like the Russian."

"Didn't to me, either," Hawkeye agreed, "until I dug into his financials and discovered our boy Walters is six months behind in alimony to wife number two *and* wife number three. He also owes a cool hundred thou to his bookie. Seems he has a weakness for the ponies."

"Interesting."

"Yeah, it is. I'm working authorization to run his cell, home and business phones. Will get back to you as soon as… Hang on!"

The terse admonition came at precisely the same instant the instrument in Cutter's hand began to vibrate to a different pattern. Smothering a curse, he recognized the signal before Mike's voice cut back through his earpiece.

"We've got movement on the disk, Slash."

"Yeah, I'm receiving the signal."

"Is the target back at her vehicle?"

"No."

She hadn't moved, dammit! Not so much as an inch. She still dozed on that bench. Or pretended to. The perfect decoy.

Swearing viciously under his breath, Cutter took the stairs from the crypt two at a time. Tourists sent him startled looks as he raced through the cathedral, his footsteps echoing on the granite blocks.

Dodging a group of Chinese visitors, he burst through the abbey doors onto the small terrace. The western side looked to the sea. The south edge, he saw when he pushed through a gawking, pointing crowd, looked down over the causeway and what *used* to be the overflow parking lot.

The sand flats on either side of the causeway were empty now except for a single tour bus with its wheels awash in seawater…and Dawes's rented Peugeot, floating on the tide. As Cutter watched, tight-jawed, the little car bobbed farther and farther from the causeway.

Loudspeakers blared, slicing through the tourists' excited babble. An urgent message was broadcast first in French, then English, then in Japanese.

"Attention! Attention! The driver of Tour Bus Number Fifty-Seven must return to his vehicle immediately! The storm at sea has created a severe riptide. Your bus will soon be afloat."

So that was the muffled announcement that had failed to penetrate to the subterranean crypts! The off-shore winds had churned up a vicious riptide and sent it rushing in, well ahead of the posted times for normal high water.

Drivers alerted by the announcements had managed to clear most of the vehicles parked on the sand. Only two hadn't been rescued—the heavy tour bus with gray-green water now swirling up to its fender skirts and Mallory Dawes's lightweight Peugeot, at present floating on the outgoing current.

"Omigod!"

The shriek came from directly behind Cutter. He edged to the side to make room for the woman who elbowed her way through the crowd.

"That's my car!"

Her dismay spiraled into panic. Cupping her hands to her mouth, Dawes screamed at the ant-like figures on the causeway far below.

"Hey! You down there! That's my car floating away! *Do* something!"

Even she could see it was too late for anyone to save the little car. The fast-moving tide had already carried the vehicle a good half mile and it was starting to take on water. As she watched, horrified, the little car tipped to one side, rolled over and went wheels up. Like a puppy begging to have its stomach tickled, it floated a few more yards before slowly sinking into the sea.

Utter silence gripped the crowd. Cutter could swear he almost heard the gurgle of the bubbles that rose to the surface as the mini disappeared.

Sympathetic clucking noises from several of the Japanese tourists broke the stillness. Their tour guide approached a shell-shocked Dawes.

"Your car, yes?"

"Yes," she whispered raggedly.

"You must tell them, at the visitors' center."

Dawes couldn't tear her gaze from the gray-green water. She kept staring at the spot where the Peugeot had disappeared. One white-knuckled hand gripped the other, as if she were praying that the statue of Saint Michael perched on the steeple above her head would command the seas to part and the car to miraculously reappear.

"You must tell them," the tour guide insisted. "At the visitors' center."

Cutter's mind had been racing since he'd first spotted the bobbing vehicle. Whatever else Dawes might have intended to do with the data disk, his gut told him this little drama hadn't figured into her plan. It hadn't figured into his, either, but he sure as hell wasn't going to pass up the opportunity that had just been handed to him on a big, golden platter.

"This hasn't been your day, has it?"

The comment jerked Dawes's head around. She'd whipped off the sunglasses she'd used as a shield up to now, so this was Cutter's first glimpse of her eyes. Caramel-brown and flecked with gold, they were flooded with dismay…until they dropped to the puckered skin below his chin. Then the emotions Cutter had seen too many times to count clicked across her face. Curiosity came first, followed quickly by embarrassment at being caught staring.

Apparently Dawes was made of tougher stuff than most. Either that, or she understood how it felt to be gaped at. She didn't color up and quickly look away. Instead, her gaze lifted to his.

"No," she admitted, raising a hand to hold back her wind-whipped hair, "it hasn't."

Cutter had grimaced when Field Dress had saddled him with this bland businessman's cover but decided it would work like a charm in this situation.

"Maybe I can help. I have some contacts who know this area."

Like Nick Jensen, aka Lightning, who'd grown up in the back alleys of Cannes before being brought to the States and adopted by one of OMEGA's top agents. Any strings Mike Callahan couldn't pull through official channels, Nick could through his own.

Mallory struggled to hold back her hair and the hot tears stinging her eyes. Any other woman in her situation would have jumped at the offer. Any woman, that is, who hadn't been savaged by the media and made into a walking bull's-eye for predatory males.

Granted, this one had already come to her aid once. Yet those cool gray eyes and powerful shoulders didn't exactly put him in the tame category. Then there were those scars…

"Do you always go around rescuing women?"

The question came out sounding more suspicious and hostile than Mallory had intended. He answered with a raised brow and a shrug.

"Only those who seem to need it. Obviously, you don't. My mistake." With a nod, he turned away. "Good luck salvaging your car."

God! That mess with Congressman Kent had

turned her into a real bitch! Disgusted with herself, Mallory stopped him with a brusque apology.

"I'm sorry. It's just… Well…"

She decided he didn't need to know the sordid details behind her recent distrust of all things male.

"I'm sorry," she said again. "I, uh, appreciate the way you handled that jerk down in the village and I'd welcome any help retrieving my car. My suitcase is in the trunk. *And* my passport," she remembered on a new wave of dismay. "And all my traveler's checks!"

Stunned all over again, Mallory spun around to stare at the spot where her rental had disappeared. The sea now completely covered the mud flats. Except for the causeway, the island was cut off from the mainland.

As it had been for hundreds of years, when pilgrims had dared the treacherous sands to buy indulgence for their sins. Mallory was in no condition to appreciate the irony.

"Do you think…?"

Gulping, she tried to swallow her panic. All she had with her was a single credit card and the few francs tucked in the purse slung over her shoulder. Like a fool, she hadn't even carried her receipt for the traveler's checks on her person. The past weeks had shaken her to her core, it was true, but that was no excuse for sheer stupidity!

"Do you think they can get my car back? Or at least retrieve my passport and traveler's checks?"

"Maybe. Depends on how strong the riptide is and how far it carries the vehicle."

She whirled again, grabbing at the fragile hope he'd offered until he gently shattered that.

"I suspect you aren't the first tourist to lose a car to the tides, so I'm guessing there are probably a number of salvage companies in the area. It'll take time to mount that kind of an operation, though, and some big bucks. You'd better check with the rental company to see what their insurance covers."

Mallory's stomach took another dive. She'd barely glanced at the half dozen or so insurance clauses she'd initialed when she'd rented the Peugeot. Now phrases like *negligence, collateral damage,* and *criminal acts* popped into her head.

Surely the rental company couldn't hold her responsible for the loss! Okay, there were signs posted all over Mont St. Michel. And yes, she'd heard the muffled sounds of what might have been a warning announcement.

But... But...

Mallory forced her mind to stop spinning in empty circles. She wasn't completely irresponsible. Nor was she helpless. She'd worked for the Commerce Department for several years before accepting the offer from Congressman Kent to join his staff. She understood bureaucracy, knew she had to get the wheels turning. Buttoning down her panic, she constructed a mental list.

First, she'd verify with the authorities here on Mont St. Michael that she was the driver of the vehicle that had been swept out to sea. She'd need statements from them and other witnesses as to what happened to the car when she contacted the rental agency. Then she'd call the U.S. embassy and find out how to obtain a temporary passport. After that, she'd get American Express to replace her lost traveler's checks. She'd also check with them about travel insurance and coverage for her lost suitcase and clothing.

Relieved to have a plan, Mallory turned to the man beside her. "Would you be willing to provide a written statement detailing how I, uh, lost the car?"

"Sure."

She swept a hand toward the stairs leading down to the village. "I need to let whoever's in charge around here know that was my vehicle. Then I need to make some calls. You don't happen to have a cell phone with you, do you?"

Something flickered in his cool gray eyes. Mallory thought it might have been amusement, but it was gone before she could be sure.

"As a matter of fact, I do."

"Would you mind if I use it?"

"Not at all."

"Thanks. Again," she added, embarrassed now by the memory of her less-than-cordial response when he'd tossed the tipsy tourist into the horse trough.

If he remembered it, he gave no sign. Matching his stride to hers, he accompanied her to the stairs leading to the exit from the hilltop abbey.

"My name is Cutter Smith, by the way."

Mallory hesitated. She could hardly refuse to provide her name after all he'd done for her, but anticipation of his reaction when he connected her to the headlines made her cringe inside.

"I'm Mallory Dawes."

"Nice to meet you, Mallory. I'm sorry it had to be under these circumstances."

His grip on her elbow was warm and sure and strong. His expression didn't telegraph so much as a flicker of recognition. Relieved, Mallory flashed him a smile.

"You and me both."

Chapter 4

Cutter had suspected she'd be a looker when she jettisoned her sour expression, but he'd underestimated the result by exponential degrees.

When Mallory Dawes smiled, she was more than mere eye candy. She was all warm, seductive woman. The smile softened her mouth and gave her cinnamon eyes a sparkling glow. It also damned near made Cutter miss his footing on the steep stairs.

Feeling as though he'd taken a hard fist to his chest, he recovered enough to escort her down a million or so zigzagging stairs and through the village to the main entrance. Mallory halted just outside the massive barbican gate, surveying the scene.

"I can't believe this. It's so…so surreal."

Cutter had to agree with her. The tide had swept in with a vengeance. Beyond the gate, the causeway shot straight and narrow across a broad expanse of silver-gray water. Except for that man-made strip of concrete, Mont St. Michel was completely cut off from the rest of France.

A large crowd lined the western edge of the causeway. Most were tourists busy clicking away with their cameras. Others looked like locals. Gesturing extravagantly, they shouted encouragement as a wrecker battled valiantly to keep Tour Bus 57 from being swept out to sea. They'd managed to attach tow chains to the bus and had it strung like a giant whale while it slowly took on water.

As Cutter and Mallory watched, transfixed, the sea reached the level of its windows and poured in through several that had been left open. The bus sank right before their eyes and settled in eight or ten feet of water, with only its top showing.

The tourists continued to shoot photo after photo. A man whose white shirt and nametag suggested he was the tour bus driver paced back and forth. Flinging his hands in the air and gesticulating wildly, he poured out a stream of impassioned French to a uniformed gendarme.

The officer took notes in a black notebook, somehow managing to look sympathetic and supremely bored at the same time. Cutter guessed he probably dealt with drivers of sunk or missing vehicles several times a week and had little sympathy for idiots who ignored warning signs and loudspeaker announcements.

Mallory had obviously formed that same impression. Chewing on her lower lip, she turned to Cutter. "This could get dicey. How's your French?"

"I can order a beer and ask directions to the bathroom. How's yours?"

"Two years in college. I can find my way around, but I never learned the proper phrase for 'My car is now at the bottom of the ocean.'"

"I think he'll get the drift."

"Hope so."

Actually, Cutter could communicate fairly fluently with authorities on several different continents. He'd already decided how to capitalize on this situation, however, and his plan didn't include making things easy for Ms. Dawes. Accordingly, he stayed in the background when she approached the police officer.

"*Excusez-moi.*"

"*Oui,* mademoiselle?"

"*Ma voiture, uh, été perdue.*"

At his blank look, she fell back on English and the universal language of hand gestures.

"My car. It's gone. Out there."

"*Oui,* mademoiselle." Heaving a long-suffering sigh, the officer hefted his notebook and pen. "Tell me, please, the license number."

"I don't know the license number."

"The make and year?"

"It was a Peugeot. A little one. Blue."

The gendarme was too well trained to roll his eyes, but it was obvious to everyone present he wanted to.

"You have rented this car, yes?"

"Yes. From an agency at the Paris airport."

"We shall call the rental agency and get the information I must have for my report. This way, *s'il vous plaît.*"

The glance Dawes threw Cutter's way sent a spear of intense satisfaction through him. He was an ally now. No longer a stranger, not quite a friend, but a familiar face in a sea of trouble. Ms. Dawes didn't know it, but they were about to get a whole lot better acquainted.

He nodded encouragement as she accompanied the gendarme to the police van parked at midpoint on the causeway. While the officer got on his radio and requested a connection to an operator at the Paris airport, Cutter eased out of sight at the rear of the van and made a call of his own.

Mike Callahan took his succinct report of the

sinking of the Peugeot along with the request he draw on Lightning's particular expertise.

On the other side of the Atlantic, Mike whipped around to check the electronic status board on the wall behind him. The blue light beside the director's name indicated Nick was alone and at his desk downstairs.

"Lightning's on scene," Mike advised Cutter. "I'll get back to you in ten."

"Roger that."

Shoving back from the console containing an array of screens and phones that would have made his counterparts in the CIA and FBI turn green with envy, Mike strode toward the elevator. The titanium-shielded bullet zoomed him down three stories with stomach-bouncing efficiency.

Grimacing at his reflection in the highly reflective door, Mike scrubbed a hand over his cheeks and chin. He'd been at the control desk without break since the op had kicked off. No big deal compared to some of the stretches he'd pulled. Still, he could have scraped off his whiskers during the down hours between contacts with Slash. There was a reason OMEGA maintained sleeping quarters, shower facilities and a fully-equipped gym for controllers and their backups.

Mike's mouth twisted. Hell! Who was he kidding? He'd never given a thought to his whiskers before. Nor had any other male operative, until a certain blue-eyed babe with a killer smile and a body to match had volunteered to fill in for the recuperating Elizabeth Wells.

He could see Gillian now, courtesy of the hidden cameras that made regular sweeps of the elegant first-floor offices. Although they appeared empty of visitors, Mike pressed a button to signal he wanted entry and waited for Lightning's temporary assistant to give him access.

Okay, he lectured himself sternly as the elevator door whooshed open. *All right.* No need to get his shorts in a bunch. He was thirty-five years old, for God's sake. He'd spent the past seven years as an OMEGA operative. When not dodging bullets, he trained sharpshooters for a list of agencies that read like a governmental alphabet soup.

No damned reason his insides should turn to mush because Adam Ridgeway's daughter swiveled around in her chair to greet him.

"Hi, Mike."

"Hi, Gillian-with-a-*J*."

It was a stupid joke, one he'd pretty well worn out in the years since Adam had brought his coltish teenaged daughter to the shooting range and she'd solemnly introduced herself as Gillian, spelled-with-a-*G*-but-pronounced-with-a-*J*.

The teenager had gone on to graduate magna cum laude from Georgetown, had landed a job at the State

Department and snared a plum first assignment at the
American Embassy in Beijing. Daddy's connections
had no doubt had something to do with that. Mike
suspected her Uncle Nick had probably weighed in,
as well. Now Gillian was home between assignments, filling in for Elizabeth Wells for a few months
and making Mike's life a living hell.

He was too old for her, he reminded himself for
the hundredth time. Too damned rough around the
edges. She'd grown up in the country-club set. He
preferred not to think about the cesspool he'd sprung
from. Rumor had it that she was getting snuggly with
some buttoned-down Ivy League type, and that he
was the reason she'd decided to take this hiatus
before accepting another overseas assignment. That
alone should have prevented Mike from going hard
and tight when Gillian asked what she could do for
him.

Should have, but didn't.

Ruthlessly suppressing several inappropriate
thoughts of what he'd *like* her to do for him, he
growled out a terse reply.

"I need to see Nick."

"Sure." Crossing one knee over the other, she
reached for the intercom. "Hang on a sec."

Sweat popped out on Mike's palms. The girl—
woman!—was all leg. Damned if she wasn't well
aware of it, too.

Jilly hid a smile as she buzzed her godfather and honorary uncle. She knew she shouldn't tease Mike. Her father, mother *and* godfather would all lace into her if they had any idea she'd deliberately let her skirt slide up. Or that she was taunting an operative with Mike Callahan's reputation.

Problem was, she'd nursed a world-class crush on Callahan since he'd positioned her in front of him, wrapped his arms around her, and helped her line up a paper target in the sights of a Walther PPK. She just might have to take a refresher course, Jilly mused as Nick picked up.

"Hawkeye needs to see you," she advised.

"Send him in."

Exercising severe mental discipline, Mike put the long-legged temptress out of his head and gave his boss a quick update. Lightning's reaction was one of amusement.

"The car sank?"

"Like a rock. Slash says he saw it go under, taking Dawes's suitcase, passport and traveler's checks with it."

"I've been to Mont St. Michel a good number of times. Amazing what tourists leave in their cars while they trudge up to the abbey."

Every OMEGA agent knew the story. Nick Jensen, born Henri Nicolas Everaud, had once run numbers and picked pockets in his native France.

He'd also offered to pimp for Maggie Sinclair, Gillian's mother, during a long-ago op. Judging by the small smile that flitted across his face, he still had a hankering for the good ol' days.

"What about the disk?"

"It's still in the vehicle," Mike advised, "and sending signals."

"Does Slash think this business with the car was intentional? That the Russian will attempt an underwater retrieval?"

"If that's the plan, Slash doesn't believe Dawes was in on it. He says she's genuinely upset. Apparently," Mike added with a grin, "she's turned to him for help."

"I'm not going to ask how he managed that!"

"He wants to play the Good Samaritan and keep her on a string as long as possible. I've already made a call to State. Dawes won't get a replacement passport any time soon. I'll work American Express when I get back upstairs. What I need from you is a recommendation for a good spot for Slash to go to roost in the area."

"I know just the place."

His enigmatic smile returning, Nick lifted the phone.

"Jilly, please get me Madame Yvette d'Marchand."

"The shoe designer?"

"That's her." He checked his watch. "She's probably at her Paris office, on the Boulevard St.

Germain. If not, her secretary will know where she can be reached."

Mike walked out of Nick's office a few minutes later with directions to a seaside villa and assurances that its staff would be primed and ready to receive Monsieur Cutter Smith and companion.

Gillian-with-a-*J* gave him a wave and another glimpse of those mile-long legs. Mike's jaw had locked by the time the elevator door swished shut.

"A villa?"

Cutter threw a quick glance at the police van to make sure Mallory was still engaged with the gendarme.

"I was thinking more in terms of a hotel room where I could maintain close surveillance."

"So was I," Hawkeye relayed, "but Lightning says this place is airtight. The owner ran a string of high-class call girls until she married one of her clients and he set her up in another line of business. She's since made millions as a fashion designer. Lightning says she's an avid art collector, and has all of her homes equipped with start-of-the-art surveillance. You won't have to worry about security."

"What's my cover?"

"You're a wine broker, in France for the fall tastings and lot auctions. A friend of a friend knows the villa's owner. She offered to let you use it as a base while you search out select vintages in the

Calvados and Loire regions for your extremely dis-
criminating clients."

"Hell, I don't know Calvados from Calvin Klein.
You'd better zap me a short course in French wineries."

"It'll be waiting for you at the villa."

"Roger that. Gotta go. The target just parted
company with our local gendarme and looks ready
to bite nails."

Not just bite them, Cutter decided as he slipped
the phone into his pocket. Chew them into little
pieces.

"Problem?" he asked politely.

"Yes," she ground out. "The rental agency says
they have to check with their insurance company
before they can authorize another vehicle. They've
also put a hold on my credit card until full damages
and liability are assessed."

She raked back her hair, threading the silky
strands through her fingers.

"Looks like I'm stuck here until American
Express comes through. May I use your phone?"

Hawkeye had promised to take care of American
Express; Cutter needed to give him time to work it.

"Sure, but you'll need something to write with
once you get hold of the information. I've got a pen
in my car. It's right over there."

He lowered the windows to let the sea breeze in
while she struggled with the information operator.

She couldn't know every word was being recorded, or that Cutter derived a sardonic enjoyment from her mounting frustration.

"I know I should have made a record of the check numbers," she said after a short exchange with whomever she'd reached, "but I didn't. Can't you look me up in the computer?"

She waited, tapping her borrowed pen against the notepad Cutter had thoughtfully provided.

"You did! Thank God!"

The happy grin she zinged Cutter's way lit up her face. Seconds later, the grin collapsed.

"No, I can't come to the Paris office to present my passport as identification. I'm currently without cash and any means of transportation. I'm also without passport."

Another lengthy pause.

"Excuse me, but we're not communicating here. It doesn't matter where the closest American Express office is. I don't have the money to get to Paris *or* Nantes *or* Marseilles and I've lost my passport along with my traveler's checks."

Her expression grew more thunderous by the second.

"Yes, I understand you're not authorized to fork over the funds without proper identification. Can't I go to a bank or post office? Or a notary. You have notaries in France, don't you? He or she could verify my ID from my driver's license and fax you the verification. No. No, I don't. Oh, for heaven's sake! Hold on."

Her eyes stormy, she appealed to Cutter.

"He has to get authorization from his superiors to accept a notarized signature. It may take a little time. He needs a number where he can contact me."

"Give him mine."

Magnanimously, Cutter jotted it down for her. She relayed it to the clerk and snapped the cell phone shut. Her glance strayed to the island looming just yards away.

"Lord, I hope there's a notary somewhere on that pile of rock."

He let her down gently. "You might have to look farther afield. I read somewhere that Mont St. Michel has only about fifty or so permanent residents."

He made that up to twist the screws a little tighter. It worked. Dawes's muttered expletive would have done any of the OMEGA operatives proud. Glancing sideways, she caught Cutter's grin and colored.

"Sorry. I'm, uh, a little rattled by all this."

"Not to worry," he chuckled. "I've heard worse."

Mallory would bet he had. His expertly tailored sports coat and Italian loafers shouted money, but she'd seen the man in action. He'd handled the beefy tourist who'd accosted her with unruffled ease. She suspected he hadn't come by those powerful shoulders working out in a gym. Then there were those awful scars....

Wondering how he'd acquired them, she flipped up his cell phone again. The sun was a red ball slipping toward the sea. She'd better finish her calls and find some place to stay the night.

All too well aware that a hotel or inn would require a guest's passport, she wrestled the number for the American Embassy from the information operator. The embassy was closed, but a recording gave her a twenty-four-hour emergency number. Unfortunately, the duty officer who answered didn't classify a lost passport in the same emergency category as death, dismemberment or attack by suicide bombers.

Mallory argued the point for some minutes before gritting her teeth and informing him she would call back tomorrow. *During* duty hours.

"God! Bureaucrats! I can't believe I'm one of them. Or was," she amended darkly.

Snapping the phone shut, she handed it back to Cutter. What the heck was she going to do now?

Spend the night sitting at a table in one of the little bistros, she supposed, if she could find one that stayed open twenty-four hours. Judging by the departing tour buses and rapidly emptying causeway, Mont St. Michel was a day-tripper's town. Mallory had the sinking feeling it rolled up its streets at night.

Cutter's deep voice dragged her from the dismal prospect of roaming dark alleys and narrow lanes in search of a spot to rest her weary bones.

"I don't like leaving you stranded like this."

"I'll manage."

Somehow.

"How about we walk back into the town and get you a hotel room for the night?"

Mallory was too relieved to mouth even a polite refusal. "Would you? I'll reimburse you, I promise. Just give me your business card or mailing address."

"No problem. Or…"

When he hesitated, her heart sank. Visions of dark alleys once again filled her head.

"Look, you're going to need a base camp for a few days to get this mess straightened out. I've been invited to put up at a villa not far from here. You're welcome to stay there for as long as you like."

Wariness replaced weariness. Her face stiffening, Mallory retreated behind the defensive walls she'd erected in the past month. "Thanks, but I don't think so."

As if reading her mind, he gentled his voice.

"It's okay. I'm not like the jerk who harassed you this afternoon. I promise I won't hit on you."

A smile crinkled the skin at the corners of his eyes.

"Unless you want me to."

Chapter 5

Doubts pinged at Mallory during the thirty-minute drive to the villa.

Cutter's invitation had seemed genuine enough. So had his promise to keep his hands to himself. She wanted to believe him. She was too exhausted *not* to. Yet the ugliness of the past month kept coming back to haunt her.

What if he'd recognized her from the vicious stories in the newspapers and on TV? Or overheard the nasty remarks that creep had tossed out this afternoon? Mallory's ready capitulation and acceptance of his offer to share a villa would have reinforced the rumors of her alleged promiscuity.

On the other hand…

He'd come to her rescue twice now, each time with quiet and extremely effective competence. Despite her prickly doubts and still-raw wounds, she felt comfortable with him. And, as crazy as it sounded, safe.

Besides, she didn't have a basketful of options at this point. Every bone in her body ached with weariness. All she wanted was a bed. Any kind of a bed.

"You said you're a bureaucrat. Or were."

His voice came to her through the autumn dusk now filling the car's interior.

"What kind of work did you do?"

She dragged herself from her near-catatonic state and searched for an answer that wouldn't open Pandora's box.

"I worked at the U.S. Department of Commerce for five years."

And then she'd accepted the position on Congressman Kent's staff.

Lord, what a mistake that had been! But Dillon Porter, Kent's senior staffer, had lured her up to the Hill with tantalizing visions of helping shape laws and policies that would affect the nation's balance of trade for decades to come.

"Commerce, huh? What did you do there?"

"Nothing very glamorous. I was an analyst with the Market Access and Compliance Branch of the International Trade Administration. Basically, I crunched numbers to track U.S. exports to and imports from Canada."

"Sounds like a big job."

"It certainly kept me busy. More than half a trillion dollars in goods flow between the U.S. and Canada every year. Most of the trade is dispute-free, although things got dicey for a while over softwood lumber." A note of pride crept into her voice. "I helped draft the agreement that finally settled that decades-long dispute."

"I'm impressed."

Looking back, Mallory had to admit that was her finest hour. She'd played a minuscule role in the landmark agreement, mostly providing historical trending stats, but her input had been valuable enough to win her a spot at the signing ceremony. It had also brought her to the attention of the House Committee on Banking and Trade.

How swiftly the proud can fall. Swallowing a sigh, Mallory skirted that dangerous ground.

"You said you're a wine broker. How often do you log onto the International Trade Administration's database?"

"When I need to."

The vague reply aroused her professional pride.

"You should check the database regularly. ITA updates it daily with the latest data on markets and products. You can also use that system to report unfair competition and dumping by foreign competitors."

Cutter was on shaky ground here. What he knew about the Department of Commerce and the International Trade Administration would make for an extremely short conversation. If he didn't want to trip himself up, he'd better steer the conversation into different channels…like Ms. Dawes's most recent occupation.

"I'm surprised you stayed at Commerce for so long. From what I've seen as an outsider looking in, a good number of Washington's brightest bureaucrats get lured into the political arena and end up either as lobbyists or working on a Congressional staff."

Her glance was quick and suspicious. Cutter kept his eyes on the road ahead and let her mull over her answer. A signpost at the juncture of the road gave her an out.

"Look, there's the turnoff for St. Malo. Don't your directions say the villa is only two kilometers ahead, on the right?"

"On the left," he corrected.

He'd let her off the hook for now. With Hawk back at OMEGA control, inserting spikes into every wheel, she wasn't going anywhere soon. Cutter would have plenty of time to worm Ms. Dawes's secrets out of her.

"Looks like this may be the place," he announced after a few minutes.

Slowing his rental, he pulled up at a set of iron gates decorated with gilded scrollwork and mythological creatures. Cutter noted with approval the tamper-proof screens protecting the security cameras mounted above the gate. Pressing the call button, he identified himself to the disembodied voice that answered.

"*Bon soir,* Monsieur Smith. We have been expecting you."

The gates swung open to reveal a long drive that wound through acres of manicured lawn and led to a château perched on the rocky cliffs overlooking the sea. Complete with towers and turrets, the castle was right out of the fifteenth century.

Mallory's jaw dropped. Cutter caught his just in time.

"This is your seaside villa?" she asked incredulously.

"I, ah, heard about it through a friend of a friend. He didn't indicate it was this grandiose."

Crushed stone crunched under the tires. Cutter's trained eye detected more cameras mounted at strategic intervals and the glint of what he suspected were passive sensors laced throughout the grounds.

The drive ended at an arched passageway that once might have contained a portcullis. The passageway gave access to an inner courtyard. Two individuals waited inside the walled yard. The one on the right was tall and lean, with short-cropped salt-and-pepper hair, a neat mustache and a dignified air. Coming forward with a stately tread, he assisted Mallory from the car and introduced himself as Gilbért Picard, the majordomo and property overseer. With him was his wife, Madame Picard, a shy, rotund woman with rosy cheeks.

Gilbért was as smooth as butter and didn't so much as bat an eyelash when Cutter emerged from the vehicle. His wife's startled gaze went instantly to the scars, however. Just as quickly, she looked away.

Used to the reaction, Cutter introduced himself and Mallory. Gilbért apologized for paucity of staff here to greet them and retrieved Cutter's carryall from the trunk. If he wondered at Mallory's lack of baggage, he was too well trained to comment on it.

"Madame brings her maid and masseuse when she travels down from Paris," he explained, leading the way inside. "We have two girls from the village who come each day to clean. I will ask one to see to Mademoiselle Dawes's personal needs, *oui?*"

"I don't need a maid," Mallory protested. "Just a place to crash."

"Pardon?"

"All I want is a bed."

"But of course."

With a measured tread, he led them down a long

hall wainscoted in glowing golden oak. The alcoves lining the hall contained ultramodern sculptures with sharp angles and odd shapes. The pieces should have looked out of place in this ancient castle, but old and new somehow blended seamlessly.

Mallory peeked through open doors as they passed, stealing glimpses of salons and sitting rooms and a library stacked floor to ceiling with books bound in leather and etched with gold print on the spines. The grand ballroom and music room were on the second floor, the guest rooms and madame's private suite on the third.

On this floor, as on the others, both past and present came vividly alive. Baronial banners with richly embroidered coats of arms hung above suits of armor gilded with silver and gold. Yet the place of honor went to a Picasso spotlighted above a refectory table that might once have graced a twelfth-century cloister.

"We have put mademoiselle in the blue bedchamber," Picard announced as he opened an ornate set of double doors halfway down the corridor. "I hope it will be satisfactory."

Mallory stepped inside and felt as though she'd wandered into a Mediterranean grotto. *Blue* hardly described the shimmering azure of the drapes and upholstered chairs in the sitting room, or the richly embroidered coverlet on the four-poster bed. The bathroom beyond was accented with lapis lazuli trim, gold fixtures and sinks shaped like seashells. As in the rest of the château, modern sculpture and artwork coexisted beautifully with antique furniture.

"Monsieur is in the green chamber, next door."

Picard made no reference to the connecting doors between the two suites.

"Do you wish the dinner before you retire?" he asked politely. "Something light, perhaps? The omelette? Or the vol-au-vent, with fresh asparagus and our most delicious Normandy mussels?"

"Well…"

Hunger and exhaustion waged a fierce war using Mallory as the battleground. Her stomach beat the rest of her into submission. The lunch in Caen had been delicious, but hardly filling.

"The vol-au-vent sounds wonderful. If it's not too much trouble…"

"Not at all. Madame Picard baked the pastry shells only this afternoon. I shall tell her to set a table in the petite dining salon. In thirty minutes, *oui?*"

Mallory would have preferred a tray here in her room, but awareness of how much she owed Cutter made her reluctant to appear rude. Or too demanding of his time, she thought belatedly.

"Please don't let me alter any arrangements you've made for this evening," she said with a smile. "I'll be fine here. *More* than fine," she amended, making another sweep of the elegant bedchamber.

"All I had planned for this evening was to catch up on some paperwork. I'll see you downstairs in thirty minutes."

He disappeared with Gilbért, leaving Mallory to shrug out of her blazer and head for the bathroom. To her delight, an enameled casket offered a selection of shampoos, scented soaps, body lotions, bath gels and tooth powders. The thoughtful hostess had even provided her guests toothbrushes in hygienically sealed containers. A twenty-first-century hair dryer and lighted mirror shared space on the dressing table with a silver-backed brush, comb and hand mirror that might once have belonged to Marie Antoinette.

Mallory ached to sink into the tub but settled for a quick shower. Wrapping herself in one of the fluffy robes hanging in the closet, she slathered on lotion delicately scented with lilies of the valley. The creamy lotion moistened her skin and permeated the bath with flowery perfume.

Once back in the bedroom, she cringed at the prospect of pulling on the same clothes she'd worn for more than twenty hours. Madame Picard's arrival obviated that necessity.

"*Pardonnez-moi,* mademoiselle. Monsieur Smith says you have lost your suitcase to the tides at Mont St. Michel. They are so treacherous, these tides." Tsk-tsking, she shook her head and held out an arm draped with garments. "Madame keeps a spare wardrobe here at the château. These items, I think, will fit you."

"Oh, no! I couldn't."

"But you must. Madame d'Marchand would be most displeased if Gilbért and I did not see to the comfort of her guests."

Overcoming Mallory's protests, she laid the garments on the bed. The gown and matching negligee were lavender silk, lavishly trimmed with blond lace. The briefs and demi-bra were also silk.

For outerwear, Madame Picard provided a gorgeously patterned blouse by Hermès and nutmeg-colored slacks in fine Italian merino wool. She'd even thought to bring a pair of net anklets still in their plastic wrapper.

"Madame sells these in her boutiques," she advised Mallory. "You will wish to wear them with these, yes?"

From her pocket she produced a pair of slip-on mules in a leopard print splashed with bright red geraniums. The shiny metallic heels were the same eye-popping red and shaped like hourglasses. When Mallory glimpsed the label inside the mules, the light came on with blinding brilliance.

"Omigod! Is your Madame d'Marchand the shoe designer, Yvette d'Marchand?"

"Oui." Pride beamed across the housekeeper's face. "You have visited her boutique in Paris? Or in New York, on Fifth Avenue?"

"No, I haven't."

Like Mallory could afford a pair of shoes by Yvette d'Marchand! Movie stars and presidents' wives engaged in fierce bidding wars over her one-of-a-kind designs.

"Perhaps you can arrange a visit before you leave Paris," the housekeeper suggested, depositing the shoes beside the garments. "The petite dining salon is in the conservatory. Monsieur Smith awaits you there. It is just beyond the main dining salon."

"Thanks."

Mallory debated for all of thirty seconds before sloughing off the robe and sliding into the decadent briefs. The matching bra was too large, so she left it off and just went with a silky camisole. The shoes needed a little tissue at the toes, but otherwise fit beautifully.

Amazing how a shower and a pair of designer shoes could revive a girl!

Weary but rejuvenated, Mallory descended the stairs and followed Madame Picard's directions through the main dining salon. Four magnificent Limoges chandeliers graced the banquet-hall-sized room, which featured a still life that had to be the work of Paul Gauguin. French doors lined one side of the room and gave onto the glassed-in conservatory.

Mallory paused just inside the French doors, taking in the splendor of the setting. The conservatory's fanciful Victorian ironwork, profusion of potted plants and fan-backed wicker chairs produced a gloriously decadent belle epoque feel, while the glass walls provided an unobstructed view of the Normandy coast, now fading into the dusk.

A breathtakingly beautiful chess table set with ivory and ebony pieces occupied place of honor amid scattered lounge chairs at one end of the conservatory. The petite dining salon occupied the other. The round, glass-topped wicker table was set with linen and an array of covered dishes. Candles flickered in tall silver holders. Crystal water goblets sparkled in the candles' glow.

Cutter stood at the windows close to the table. A highball glass in hand, he appeared riveted by the spectacle of incandescent waves crashing against the rocky coast. He'd showered, too, Mallory saw. His short dark hair curled in still-damp waves and the bristles that had darkened his cheeks were gone. He'd traded his sport coat and shirt for a silky black turtleneck that molded his wide shoulders and, coincidentally or otherwise, hid most of his scars.

What in the world was she doing here? Mallory wondered, in this fairy-tale castle, about to have dinner with this stranger? The ordeal of the past weeks had made her gun-shy and wary around men. With good reason. She couldn't count the number of sly innuendos and outright insults she'd endured since becoming the butt of so many raunchy jokes tossed out by late-night talk-show hosts.

Even if the media hadn't made her a target, she would have had second thoughts if she'd encountered Cutter Smith on an empty street or in a deserted parking lot. Despite his expensive loafers and superbly cut sport coat, he carried himself with a tough, don't-mess-with-me air that would have made Mallory give him a wide berth.

Yet, after knowing the man for all of four or five hours, she'd driven off with him to this isolated château and was about to sit down to an intimate, candlelight dinner for two. Worse, she found herself wanting to trust him, wanting to believe he really was as kind and considerate as he seemed to be.

Not that it mattered. They'd go their separate ways tomorrow. For tonight, though, maybe she could let down her guard enough to simply enjoy his company.

The sound of her borrowed mules clicking against the tiles brought his head around. When he took in her altered appearance, a smile softened the harsh lines of his face.

"I see Madame Picard came through for you."

"Yes, she did. Thanks for mentioning my lost suitcase, although I have to confess I feel odd invading our hostess's home *and* wardrobe. Did your friend of a friend tell you what she does for a living?"

"He mentioned she designs clothing."

"Not clothing." Tugging up one leg of her borrowed Italian wool slacks, she waggled her foot. "Shoes. Hand-crafted, one-of-a-kind, thousand-dollars-a-pair shoes."

"Mmm," Cutter murmured, eyeing the slender ankle above the flashy leopard-and-red slipper. "Nice."

When she finished waggling and he'd finished admiring, he nodded toward the array of crystal decanters on a sideboard framed by feathery palms.

"Would you like a drink before dinner? Or wine? Gilbért brought a very nice Pouilly-Fuissé up from the cellars."

He had his spiel all prepared. As requested, Hawkeye had assembled and text-messaged several cheat sheets he'd labeled Wine for Dummies. If Mallory asked, Cutter was all set to expound on the dry, medium-bodied white wine from the Burgundy region of France. Made from the chardonnay grape, Pouilly-Fuissé was not to be confused with Pouilly-Fumé, made from the sauvignon blanc grape variety in the southeastern portion of the Loire Valley.

Thankfully, she didn't ask.

"I'd better pass on both. As tired as I am, alcohol might land me face down in the vol-au-vent. Which," she added, sniffing at the tantalizing aroma emanating from the covered dishes on the table, "smells incredible."

Cutter could take a hint when it whapped him in the face. Grinning, he set his drink aside. "Shall we eat, then? I told Gilbért we'd serve ourselves."

"Yes, please!"

When he went around to pull out her chair, he had to admit she smelled every bit as good as their dinner. Her skin carried a faint, flowery scent that reminded him of alpine meadows in spring.

"Want me to do the honors?" she asked when he'd taken the seat opposite.

"Be my guest."

While she wielded silver tongs and ladles, Cutter stretched his legs out under the table and revised his strategy. He'd planned to loosen her up with wine, charm her over a drawn-out dinner, and get her talking. The utter fatigue underlying her movements told him he'd better speed things up or she might fall asleep here at the table.

She helped by taking the lead. First she filled two plates with pastry shells topped by cream sauce swimming with chunks of mussels and fish, then added spears of tender white asparagus. Passing one plate to Cutter, she picked at the other.

"I'm curious," she commented. "How did you get into the wine business?"

"By accident."

That was true enough.

"I pulled a couple of hitches in the Army. During

one of them, I was stationed at a small site in Germany. I got to know the locals pretty well."

That was true, as well. His gut tightening at the thought of one particular local, Cutter ruthlessly slammed the door on the memory of the traitorous bitch who'd almost incinerated him before he'd taken her down.

Would this one try something equally desperate?

"One of the people I got to know was a wine wholesaler," he told Mallory, improvising from that point on. "We kept in touch after I left Germany. When I was looking for something to do after I left the Army, I contacted him and we went into partnership."

She speared a tender mussel with her fork but didn't bring it to her lips. "What did you do in the Army?"

He knew what she was edging around and decided to bring it out in the open.

"I trained as an explosive ordnance specialist before I transferred to the Rangers. Thought I knew all there was to know about cluster bombs, combined effects munitions and IEDs. Individual Explosive Devices," he translated at her blank look. "Turns out I didn't know as much as I thought. One of 'em blew away half my face."

He didn't add that the IED was part of a cache of stolen weapons he'd been tracking...or that his NATO partner on that op was a cool Scandinavian beauty who'd been playing a dangerous double game that had ended when their collaboration literally blew up in Cutter's face.

Months of reconstructive surgery and skin grafts had followed. The docs had wanted to do more, but Cutter had finally called a halt. He'd left the Army soon afterward, lured to OMEGA by Mike Callahan. His first mission had been to track down the woman who'd betrayed him and her country. Now, all these years later, he was working the same kind of op with another blonde.

Almost the same, he amended. His gut told him Mallory Dawes was at best an unwitting accomplice, at worst a mule transporting something she didn't know the value of. He'd watched her every move, listened to every nuance in her voice when her car sank. She'd panicked, sure, but the only real concern she'd expressed was for her passport and traveler's checks. There'd been none over her suitcase or what it contained.

Until Cutter knew how the disk had found its way into her suitcase, however, he wasn't ready to let her off the hook...or out of his sight. Smoothly, he redirected the thread of their conversation.

"I have to admit, I'm enjoying my new line of work more than the old. I've got an appointment with a local vintner tomorrow morning. Why don't you come with me?"

"I'd love to, but I can't. I need to find a notary and

fax my signature to the American Express office. And follow up with the embassy about my passport. And sort out this mess with the rental-car agency."

"I'm sure Gilbért knows the location of a notary. We'll stop by and obtain his or her chop on the way to the vintner. You can make any calls you need to on my cell phone."

"Thanks, but I've already imposed on you too much."

"Why don't you sleep on it? We'll talk again in the morning."

"Speaking of sleep…"

Her shoulders sagging, she laid down her fork. She'd taken only a few bites of her dinner. Cutter could see that was all she'd manage. The color had seeped from her cheeks and left them gray with fatigue.

"I'm afraid I'll have to poop out on you. Jet lag is catching up with a vengeance."

"No problem." He rose and came around to slide back her chair. "I'll see you tomorrow. Sleep well, Mallory."

"You, too."

As she turned to face him, her flowery scent teased his senses again. Cutter resisted the urge to brush a wayward strand of corn-silk hair off her cheek. If her allegations against Congressman Kent held even a grain of truth, Ms. Dawes didn't take kindly to being touched.

He wanted to, though, with a sudden, gut-twisting

urgency that surprised the hell out of him. Controlling the urge, he stepped away from her.

Cutter Smith wasn't like the others.

The thought teased at Mallory's tired mind as she dragged up the stairs.

She'd seen that spark of heat in his eyes a few moments ago. Felt the sudden, subtle tension sizzle through the air between them. But he'd promised she'd be safe with him.

He'd also promised he wouldn't hit on her unless she wanted him to. Now here she was, wishing she'd given him the green light.

Was she an idiot, or what?

Chapter 6

Still on Central American jungle time, Cutter's internal alarm failed to go off in time for his usual dawn run. He didn't jerk awake until his cell phone buzzed.

The ring tone sounded ordinary enough, but he was so attuned to the sequence of musical notes that he went from total unconsciousness to fully alert in two seconds flat.

"Yeah, I know," Mike Callahan said when his craggy face appeared on the screen. "It's early as hell."

"It is for me," Cutter agreed, scraping a hand over his chin. "Late as hell for you."

Callahan must have stayed at Control a second

night in a row. Wondering what had kept him there, Cutter threw off the duvet and swung upright. He'd left the windows open to the sea breeze last night. The air carried a damp bite this morning, but that wasn't what prickled the skin of his bare chest and arms. Callahan wouldn't have initiated contact without good reason.

"What's up, Hawk?"

"Thought you might want to know about your friend, Walters."

Cutter's mind clicked instantly to the heavyset tourist who'd accosted Mallory yesterday. Robert Walters. Age: fifty-three. Siding and storm doors. High roller.

"Did you pull his phone records?"

"I did," Mike confirmed. "Found some very interesting threads, but that's not why I contacted you. I intercepted State Department message traffic a few hours ago. The Bureau of Consular Affairs is trying to locate Walters's next-of-kin. Seems he met with an unfortunate accident yesterday, a few hours after your run-in with him."

"What kind of an accident?"

"He tumbled down some steps at Mont St. Michel and broke his neck."

An image of the steep, narrow passageways cut into solid rock flashed into Cutter's head. The steps were accidents waiting to happen, particularly to unwary tourists who'd imbibed one glass too many in a local bistro.

"What do the preliminary police reports say?"

"Although they're treating it as a 'suspicious' death and conducting a full investigation, they've found no witnesses or evidence to indicate the fall was anything but accidental. The inventory of the deceased's personal effects raised a red flag at *Direction Centrale,* however."

The hair on the back of Cutter's neck lifted. France's central director of police also served as head of their Interpol Bureau. As such, he played an integral role in combating international organized crime.

"Turns out our boy Walters had a soggy piece of paper in his wallet. The writing on it was blurred and almost obliterated…"

Surprise, surprise, Cutter thought wryly.

"…but they managed to lift an address. It checks to a small-time hood in Marseilles with suspected ties to the Russian."

"Well, hell!"

"I thought that might be your reaction," Mike drawled. "I checked the schedule of the tour Walters and his buddies were on. After visiting the Normandy beaches, they were scheduled to cut south to Bordeaux, then west to Marseilles before hitting the Riviera and the casino at Monaco."

Gripping the phone, Cutter paced to the windows.

The heavy drapes were open, the gauzy curtains fluttering in the damp breeze. He barely registered the chill blowing in as his mind ran with the possibilities.

Had Walters's horny tourist bit been an act? Was he the go-between designated to retrieve the disk from Mallory, either with or without her knowledge? Had he been instructed to deliver it to this thug in Marseilles?

If so, Cutter had interfered by busting up that little scene in the alley. After which, he'd spirited Mallory away and sequestered her here in this isolated château.

Then Walters had tumbled down a flight of steep steps. Was it an accident, or retribution for failing to retrieve the disk?

The last possibility presupposed the Russian had someone else shadowing Walters and/or Mallory. If so, had that someone witnessed her car floating out to sea? Did they know the disk was still in the trunk?

Dammit! It irritated the hell out of Cutter that he still had a *helluva* lot more questions than answers. Not the least of which was Mallory Dawes's role in all of this.

"You haven't had any movement on the disk, have you?" he asked Mike.

"Negative. It's still resting at the bottom of the sea. I've confirmed that the rental agency isn't going to attempt to raise the Peugeot, by the way. A salvage operation would cost more than the car is worth."

Frowning, Cutter turned away from the window and marshaled his thoughts.

"Okay, here's how I want to handle this. First, I'll work from the assumption that Walters was the designated go-between, sent to retrieve the disk from Dawes and deliver it to this thug in Marseilles. Second, I'm going to assume his death was no accident. That means there was someone else on scene, someone who engineered Walters's fall, either in retribution or anger over his bungled attempt. Third, unless and until a diver tries to retrieve the disk from the submerged vehicle, I'm assuming whoever wants the damned thing believes Dawes had it with her when she trudged up the ramp at Mont St. Michel to rendezvous with Walters."

"In which case, that someone has to believe she's still got it with her."

"Exactly."

"So you're going to use her as bait."

It wasn't a question, nor was there a hint of censure in Mike's voice. Cutter knew Hawk would do exactly the same given the circumstances. Staking out suspects like sacrificial goats was all part of the job. Cutter just wished this particular goat wasn't starting to get to him. He hadn't forgotten the fierce urge to touch her that had gripped him last night.

"Don't see that I have much choice," he bit out. "This place is a modern-day fortress. The Russian can't get to Mallory or the disk here. I'm taking her with me on my 'business' call to the local vintner you set me up with this morning."

"You got the cheat sheets I sent you, right?"

"Right. Good thing you warned me the Calvados region is more known for its brandy than its wine."

"That came from Lightning. Evidently this Monsieur Villieu provides private stock for Nick's restaurants. He said for you to confirm his order for the entire lot of 1989 Prestige blend, by the way."

Cutter was more of a beer-and-pretzels man than a brandy aficionado. If Nick Jensen wanted the entire stock of this stuff for his string of high-priced restaurants, though, it had to be something special.

When Cutter followed the aroma of fresh-brewed coffee to the petite dining salon some time later, he found Mallory ensconced in one of the fan-backed wicker chairs. The mist was fast burning off the cliffs outside but Cutter didn't spare the spectacular view a glance. His attention was centered on the woman slathering butter on a flaky croissant.

"Good morning."

When she looked up, her smile was warm and welcoming and plowed right into him. "Good morning."

"How do you feel?"

"Like a new woman."

He had to admit she looked like one, too. She

wore the same outfit she'd had on last night: jewel-toned blouse, slim brown slacks, frou-frouey shoes. But she'd swept her hair up into a twist that showed the smooth, clean line of her neck and jaw.

Her cheeks had regained their color, he noted. The gray tinge of exhaustion was gone. So was the wariness that had kept her voice cool and reserved. If she had lost sleep over a bungled exchange with Robert Walters, Cutter couldn't see any sign of it.

Filling a demitasse cup with coffee strong enough to substitute for roof tar, he carried the cup to the glass-topped wicker table. Mallory eyed the undiluted coffee with a raised brow.

"Don't you want some cream in that? It's high-octane."

"No, thanks."

Cutter welcomed the jolt to his central nervous system. After Mike's call, he needed it. While he ingested the caffeine, his breakfast companion nudged a basket of croissants and a small brown crock across the table.

"Well, you *have* to try this apple butter. Madame Picard says it's made from apples grown here in Normandy. After my first taste, I regretted every nasty word I muttered when I was stuck behind all those tractors hauling the fall harvest yesterday."

Cutter took advantage of the opening she'd just handed him to segue into his role. "That's not all they make from apples around here. The vintner I'm going to visit this morning produces some of the world's finest grape-based apple brandy."

"Grape-based apple brandy? Sounds almost like a contradiction in terms."

"It does, doesn't it?" Tearing apart a still-warm roll, he loaded it with creamy butter. "The appointment is for ten-thirty, but I can slip that if we need more time to locate a notary."

"Oh," she mumbled around a mouthful. "About that."

She flicked her tongue over her lower lip to capture a stray crumb. Cutter followed the movement with an intensity that annoyed the hell out of him.

"I really don't want to impose on you or your time. I'll get Gilbért to drive me to town."

Not hardly, he thought. He wasn't letting Ms. Dawes out of his sight.

"No sense both of us driving that way."

He took a bite and felt his taste buds leap for joy. Swallowing, he stared at the other half of his croissant.

"My God! This stuff is amazing."

Mallory had to grin at the expression on his face. He looked like a kid who'd just discovered a hidden stash of chocolate.

"Told you," she said smugly.

When he took another bite, the play of his throat muscles drew her gaze. He was wearing the silky black turtleneck again, paired with tan pleated slacks and a leather belt holding his clipped-on cell phone. The turtleneck covered most of the scars, but enough remained visible to tug at Mallory's heart.

She could only imagine the agony he must have suffered when the bomb he'd told her about last night exploded, taking part of his face with it. Thinking about his anguish, about how he must have had to fight for his life, made Mallory's own ordeal seem trivial by comparison. Slowly, inexorably, the tight knot of fury she'd carried around inside her for so many weeks loosened. As the knot unraveled, chagrin replaced the bitter, corrosive anger.

How stupid she'd been to lose all perspective the way she had! How egotistical to think her problems were so earth-shattering. People all over the world were battling cancer or dying of starvation or losing all they owned to war or the ravages of nature.

Yet here she sat, bathed in bright Norman sunlight, munching on warm croissants and apple butter, in the company of the most intriguing male she'd met in longer than she could remember. She'd be fifty times a fool not to savor every moment of this escape from harsh reality.

Those thoughts were still tumbling through her mind when Cutter downed the rest of his croissant and swiped his napkin across his mouth.

"That settles it. If the locals can work this kind of

magic with apples and butter, imagine what they can do with apples and brandy. You're going with me this morning."

Mallory capitulated with a rippling laugh. She'd tackle the American Embassy and the rental-car agency this afternoon. For now, she'd savor the bright sunshine and Cutter Smith's company.

"Okay, I'm going with you this morning. Let's get directions from Gilbért on how to find a notary."

Mallory hadn't counted on the French propensity for ignoring posted schedules.

Despite Gilbért's call to confirm the office hours of the town clerk, Mallory and Cutter sat on a bench and waited for more than twenty minutes for *le notaire* to pedal up. He offered a nonchalant apology, stuffed his beret into his jacket pocket, and led them to an office musty with the smell of old documents and wood imbued with damp from the salt-laden sea breeze.

To Mallory's relief, a computer and fax sat side-by-side with ranks of cloth-bound ledgers that looked as though they were left over from the 1800s. The clerk booted up and set out the tools of his trade.

"You wish me to witness your signature, yes?"

"Yes. Then I need to fax the authentication to the American Express office in Paris."

"Bien." He waved her to the chair beside his desk. "We begin."

While he and Mallory took care of business, Cutter wandered over to examine an array of yellowed photos displayed on one wall. Mallory joined him a few moments later. One glimpse at the photographs explained his grim absorption.

The stark, unretouched images portrayed the epic battles that had raged along the beaches to the north during the Second World War. Coils of wire gleamed in the gray light, encircling turrets. Anti-aircraft artillery peeked from cement blockhouses. Machine-gun emplacements sat perched high on rocky ledges. And far below, at the base of the cliffs, row after row of lethal steel spears protruded from the surf.

"My grandfather takes these photos," the clerk said, coming to stand beside them. "He was an old man, you understand, and crippled, but he bicycles north to Côte de Nacre—what you call Omaha Beach—to make photos of German defenses and provide them to *la résistance.*"

His chest puffing with pride, the clerk directed their attention to a framed document.

"General Eisenhower sends my grandfather a letter after the war and thanks him for his pictures. He says they helped to liberate our country. I have the copy here, but the original is in the museum at Arromanches."

Cutter dragged his gaze from the document and swept it over the photos again. As a former Ranger,

he knew the history. The initial wave of the First
Infantry Division, the Big Red One, had hit Omaha
Beach at 0630. The second wave came ashore at
0700. The Rangers and the 116th Infantry regiment
landed two hours later and were forced to wade
through the bodies of their comrades before they
finally cracked a breach in the German defenses.
Supported by tanks and two destroyers delivering
continuous bombardment, the Americans pushed
through the breach and liberated the surrounding
towns by the late afternoon.

"You will visit the museum?" the clerk asked.
"And the American Cemetery? It is not far, on the
road between St. Laurent and Colleville-sur-Mer."

With real regret, Cutter shook his head. "We'll
have to visit the museum another day. This morning
we go to Villieu Vintners."

"Ahhhh!" His face folding into paroxysms of
delight, the clerk kissed his fingers. "You will sample
the finest of Calvados brandies at Villieu. The best
in all of France."

Afterward, Mallory was never quite sure how the
day slipped away from her. She'd fully intended to
return to the château by noon, untangle her affairs,
and resume her interrupted vacation.

But after a short stop in the village so she could
purchase a few items of clothing and toiletries, they

drove northeast toward St. Lo. The dappled sunlight sifting through the trees wiped away much of Mallory's guilt that she wasn't back at the château, working the phones. Monsieur Villieu's ebullience and generous hospitality washed away the rest.

Or it could have been his brandy. The tingling scent of potent spirits surrounded her the moment she and Cutter arrived at the stone buildings housing Villieu et Fils Distillery.

Lean and spare, with cheeks chafed red by wind and sun, Villieu beamed as he walked his visitors through vineyards first planted by the Romans and orchards groaning with the weight of their fruit.

"The grapes, they do not grow as fat here as they do in Bordeaux and Cognac. The climate is too damp, the soil too flinty. Aaah, but when we blend our tough little grape with the apple and the pear…"

He kissed his fingers and opened the door to the fermenting sheds with a flourish. A sour-mash smell rose in waves from the huge vats and almost knocked Mallory back a step. Nose wrinkling, eyes watering, she breathed through her mouth until they exited the fermenting shed and entered a different world.

Here it was the heat that hit like a slap to the face. Sweat beading on her temples, Mallory followed Monsieur Villieu along rows of copper pots that looked like big, squat gourds with long necks.

"Here is where we boil the wine. It must heat to 212 degrees Fahrenheit for fourteen hours."

While Mallory discreetly dabbed at the sweat beading her upper lip, her host pointed to the tubes coiling from the necks of the copper pots.

"And there is where we capture the vapors that become Calvados. We boil seven hundred gallons of wine, yes? From that we get two hundred gallons of *eau de vie.*"

She understood the goal was to capture only the purest of the vapor, but she lost him when he tried to explain the difference between the heart, tailings and heads. The end product was a clear, amber liquid that was then stored for two to four years in Limousin oak casks inside caves cut into the hillside behind the distillery.

The potent fumes inside the caves were starting to get to Mallory by the time they emerged into the sunshine. The fresh air cleared her head enough to nod and smile when Monsieur Villieu insisted his visitors join him and his wife for lunch at a table set under an ancient oak tree.

As scarecrow-thin as her husband, Madame Villieu heaped bowls and plates for her guests before doing the same for herself and her husband. Her English was as spotty as Mallory's French, but the banquet she set out crossed all language barriers. A tureen of potato soup was followed by *salade Niçoise* and gargantuan platters of tomatoes, cheese, spicy sausage and sliced mutton. Following their host's lead, Mallory and Cutter slapped slab upon slab of meat, tomatoes and cheese onto fresh-baked baguettes.

In the midst of the feast, Monsieur Villieu poured stiff shots of his award-winning Calvados. "For *le trou Normand*, yes?"

"The Norman hole?" Mallory translated dubiously.

"Oui," he beamed. "We Normans have the long tradition. We drink Calvados in the middle of a meal such as this. It makes the hole, you understand, for more food to follow."

Tipping his head, he tossed back the brandy and thumped his glass on the table. His wife did the same.

"Now you," he urged.

Mallory glanced at Cutter, caught his grin, and raised her glass. *"Le trou Normand."*

"Le trou Normand," he echoed.

The Calvados slid down her throat like buttery apple cider. She tasted a hint of vanilla and rum raisin and started to smack her lips. Then the brandy hit her belly.

"Whoa!" Breathing fire, she fanned the air and regarded her empty shot glass with awe. "That is some potent stuff!"

Delighted by her pronouncement, Monsieur Villieu waved aside her protests and filled her glass again. She sipped cautiously this time and still had most of the brandy left when Cutter and his host excused themselves to talk business.

The women tried to converse during their absence. After a few moments of labored conversation, Madame Villieu got up to clear the table. Mallory helped by toting the tureen into the stone farmhouse that had probably stood on this site as long as the gnarled fruit trees and twisted vines.

They had the table cleared when the men returned. Their negotiations must have gone well, Mallory mused. Monsieur Villieu practically skipped across the lawn and Cutter wore a satisfied smile.

Feeling *extremely* mellow from the sunshine, good food and fine brandy, Mallory accepted the gift of a bottle of Monsieur Villieu's best before bidding her host and hostess goodbye and climbing into the car.

Cutter followed a different route back to the château, one that wound away from the coast. As she had the day before, Mallory found herself gazing across vast orchards. Now, however, she nursed a new appreciation for the apples of lower Normandy. Her head lolled against the seat. The breeze teased her hair.

Her mellow feeling dissipated somewhat when she noticed the time, but she couldn't bring herself to regret a whole day spent roaming the French countryside…especially with a companion as relaxed and easygoing as Cutter.

* * *

The château welcomed them home with windows gleaming gold in the afternoon sun and the roar of the sea loud against its cliffs. When Cutter pulled into the courtyard and came around to help her out, Mallory felt the sizzle again. It was there, arcing through the crisp fall air, tingling from the touch of his skin against hers.

Her breath snagged. Her eyes locked with his. She couldn't read the message in their cool gray depths, but she knew with everything female in her that Cutter had felt the heat, too.

Now, what the heck would they do about it?

The question was front and center in her mind as she returned Gilbért's greeting and followed him inside. Halfway down the long hall, she spotted a folded newspaper lying atop a stack of mail. The newspaper was French and local, but the black-and-white picture on the front page stopped her in her tracks.

Chapter 7

When Mallory came to an abrupt stop, Cutter was only a couple of paces behind her. He took a quick sidestep to avoid a collision while Gilbért turned in surprise at her involuntary groan.

"Oh, *nooo!*"

The fuzzy warmth engendered by her day in the sun and the hours spent with Cutter evaporated on the spot. Her insides twisting, Mallory pointed to the newspaper lying atop the hall table.

"It's him."

The newspaper showed only a partial head-and-shoulders shot, just enough for her to identify the man who'd accosted her yesterday at Mont St. Michel. That was enough. She knew with absolute certainty that when she unfolded the newspaper, her photo would appear beside his.

He must have seen her car float away and mouthed off to the people around him about the owner. Having such a notorious American lose her vehicle to the tides would make for a nice local news splash.

Gilbért glanced at the photo before politely handing her the paper. "You know this man, mademoiselle?"

"No, not really. I, uh, bumped into him yesterday at Mont St. Michel."

"It is *tragique,* how he dies."

"He's dead?"

"But yes. He falls down the stairs, there on the island."

Shocked, Mallory whipped open the folded paper. No mug shot of her, thank God, but the words *American* and *mort* leaped out from the caption below the photo.

The recently deceased had been loud and boorish and uncouth. Mallory felt no particular regret at his demise, only surprise and a guilty relief that her name hadn't been paired with his.

"I guess that's what happens when you combine steep steps and too much wine," she commented.

"Guess so," Cutter replied from just behind her.

His odd inflection brought Mallory's head around.

Disconcerted, she found his cool gray eyes narrowed on her instead of the photo.

"Hey, don't look at me. I didn't push him down any stairs, although I might have been tempted to if he'd pawed me one more time. In fact…"

Her joking tone faded. Brows drawing together, she glanced from Cutter to the photo and back again.

"In fact," she said slowly, "the last time I saw the man, you were holding his head under water."

Shrugging, Cutter disclaimed all responsibility. "He was still in the horse trough, swearing a blue streak when I left him. Too bad the dunking didn't sober him up."

Mallory's sudden and very uncomfortable pin-prick of doubt faded. She'd spent more than twenty-four hours in Cutter Smith's company now. She couldn't remember the last time she'd felt so relaxed around—or been so attracted to—a man with his charm and rugged masculinity.

It was the comfort level that made her dismiss her momentary doubt as ridiculous…and the attraction that kept her lingering in the hall after Gilbért had confirmed they'd dine in that evening and departed in his slow, stately tread.

"About yesterday, when this guy grabbed me…"

She saw the question in his eyes. He had to be wondering where she was going.

"Yes?"

"I, uh, could have been more grateful when you came to my rescue."

"I wasn't looking for gratitude."

"I know." Remembering how she'd had to force a single, grudging word of thanks, Mallory grimaced. "It's just that… Well… I've become a little gun-shy around men lately."

Not to mention curt, suspicious and distrustful. She could do better. And Cutter certainly deserved better. He didn't know it, but he'd given her an incredible gift today. The relaxing hours in his company, the lunch under the trees, the long drive in the sunlight, had loosened the anger that had tied her in such tight knots these past weeks.

"Does that include me?" Cutter asked, hooking a brow.

"Not any more." The smile in her eyes matched the one in her heart. "Thanks for today, Monsieur Smith. I had a wonderful time. Calvados will be my brandy of choice from now on."

Mallory lifted a hand, aching to curve it over his cheek, but the no-grope rule worked both ways. She'd filed sexual harassment charges against a powerful legislator for inappropriate touching. In the process, she'd destroyed both her career and the warm spontaneity that had once been an integral part of her. The old Mallory might have completed the contact. The new Mallory hesitated.

This time, though, the urge to touch was recipro-
cal. She could sense it with everything that was
female in her. Still, she hesitated, too scarred by the
ugliness of the past months to follow through. She'd
collected almost as many wounds as Cutter, she
realized with a catch in her throat, except hers were
on the inside.

Her hovering hand had started to drop when he
resolved the matter by simply leaning forward. The
warm skin of his cheek connected with her palm. His
breath mingled with hers. She lifted her gaze, felt her
pulse stutter.

Cutter's body reacted to the unspoken invitation
even as his mind shouted at him to break the contact
and back away.

Now!

She was his target, for God's sake! A possible
traitor, intending to sell data that could do irreparable
harm to her country. He'd played this game once, had
ignored his instincts and fallen for a woman who'd
damned near killed him—literally. It had taken long,
painful months to recover from that fiasco.

Problem was, his instincts worked against his in-
tellect this time. Common sense said to back off, but
his gut said Mallory Dawes had no knowledge of the
disk planted in her suitcase.

Cutter went with his gut.

Bending, he covered her mouth with his. He kept

the contact light, the kiss gentle. This was her show. He'd let her take it wherever she wanted it to go.

Okay, maybe a perverse corner of his mind was waiting to see if the stories about her were true, if she was as hot and hungry as her lovers had suggested.

If so, she had her hunger under control. His, on the other hand, bit into him with unexpected ferocity. His entire body protested when she broke the kiss and stepped back.

"I, ah, better go make some calls."

Cutter had to clench his fists to keep from reaching for her again. "I'll see you at dinner."

"Mmm. Hopefully, I'll have some good news about my various lost possessions by then and we can make it a farewell celebration."

"Hopefully," he agreed, still battling the ridiculous urge to drag her against him and take another taste of those soft, warm lips. He didn't breathe easy until she'd mounted the stairs and disappeared into her room.

Madame Picard had raided her employer's closet again. A long, multitiered skirt lay atop Mallory's bed, shimmering in a rainbow of rich jewel tones. Next to it was a short, boxy jean jacket trimmed with lace and sparkling crystals. The slip-on mules were also done in denim and lace and pouffy peacock feathers that ruffled in the sea breeze drifting through the windows.

Stroking the soft feathers, Mallory tried to picture Cutter's face when she glided into the petite dining salon decked out in Yvette's finery. Would she see the same hunger she'd glimpsed in his eyes a few moments ago? If she did, what would she do about it?

She knew darn well what she *wouldn't* do. She wouldn't back away after a mere brush of her mouth against his. Her pulse was still skittering from the kiss. She wanted more from Cutter Smith than one kiss, she acknowledged. Much more.

Her heart thumping at the thought, she blew softly on the peacock feathers. To heck with the legal bills still piled up at home. Before she left France, Mallory vowed, she'd treat herself to a pair of Yvette d'Marchand originals. She darn well deserved them. Assuming American Express came through for her, that is.

Setting aside the mules, she scrounged in her purse for her list of telephone numbers and seated herself at the desk in the sitting room. The first call had her tapping her foot. The second came close to shredding her temper. By the third, she was gritting her teeth.

"Excuse me, but I did exactly as you requested. I had a notary witness my signature and faxed you his stamped certification. What more do you need to reimburse me for the lost checks?"

She gripped the receiver, quietly seething. She knew it wouldn't do any good to lose her temper, but she could feel it oozing through her fingers like slimy dough. When the officious clerk at the other end of the line indicated that he needed yet another level of approval before reimbursing her, Mallory asked to speak to his supervisor. The woman who came on was calm and apologetic.

"I'm so sorry this is taking so long, Miss Dawes, but there's a flag on your account."

Mallory counted to ten. "I'm sure there is. I lost my traveler's checks."

"Yes, I know, but…"

"But what?"

She heard the sound of a keyboard clicking.

"I really don't understand the hold," the supervisor said after a moment. "I'll research it and get back to you. I'm sure we'll resolve the matter soon."

"How soon is soon?"

"By tomorrow, hopefully. We have the cell phone number you gave us, also the number where you're staying. We'll contact you as soon as we obtain approval to release the funds."

Mallory resisted slamming down the phone— barely!—but her jaw was locked as she dialed the American Consulate. It remained tight all through the runaround she got from the Foreign Service officer.

Disgusted, she thudded the phone into its cradle and started to push away from the desk. Desperation convinced her to make one last try. With a mental note to reimburse her hostess for all these calls, she dialed the country code for the United States followed by Dillon Porter's private number at the Rayburn House Office Building.

She wasn't surprised when she got a recording. It was midmorning back home, and Dillon attended as many meetings as Congressman Kent. Chewing on her lower lip, Mallory waited for her former coworker's voice mail to end in a loud beep.

"Dillon, it's Mallory. I'm in France. Wish I could say I'm having a great time. Unfortunately, I lost my passport and can't seem to get hold of the right person at the American Consulate in Paris to authorize a temporary replacement. I'm getting a first class runaround."

No need to go into detail about everything else she'd lost. The sorry tale of riptides and sunken Peugeots would only make her sound as stupid as she felt.

"I know it's a lot to ask, but would you pull a few strings at State for me? Please?"

She cringed inwardly at the irony of her request. She'd accused Kent of sexual impropriety and left his employment in a huff. Now here she was, asking his senior staffer to throw her former boss's name around on her behalf.

"I'd appreciate anything you can do. Here's the number where I'm staying until I get this mess sorted out."

She rattled off the number, repeated it more

slowly, and hung up. After that, there was nothing to do but fill the tub with perfumed bubbles and soak away the irritation generated by the calls.

The bubbles helped. So did the elegant skirt, lace-trimmed jacket and feathery mules. But it was the sight of her dinner companion in his tailored slacks, silky black turtleneck and a rust-colored suede sport coat that put the glow back in her day. He was waiting for her at the bottom of the stairs, an elbow resting on the carved newel post.

"Madame Picard insists her veal Normandie can only be properly appreciated if eaten in the right setting. I've been sent to escort you to the main dining salon."

He crooked an elbow, and Mallory slid her arm through his. The suede felt buttery soft under her fingertips. The flesh beneath it was hard and smooth. Heat transferred from the material to her palm as he led her into the dining room.

The two place settings should have looked lonely all by themselves at the far end of the long banquet table. But candles, sparkling crystal and a tall spray of blood-red gladioli in a porcelain vase created a small island of elegance.

"Are we celebrating?"

The question jerked Mallory from her contemplation of the play of sinuous, suede-covered muscle.

"Huh?"

"You said when you went upstairs that you were going to make some calls and, hopefully, be ready for a farewell celebration at dinner. Do we pop a cork?"

"No. Everything is still a tangled mess."

She had to work to keep her spirits from taking another dive as Gilbért came forward to seat her in one of the throne-like chairs. She was wearing Yvette d'Marchand, Mallory lectured herself sternly. Basking in the glow of Limoges chandeliers. About to chow down with a man whose kindness was steadily chipping away at her unflattering opinion of the male of the species.

She continued the self-lecture while Gilbért set out a tray of antipasto and prepared an aperitif tableside. The elaborate ritual involved drizzling water through a slotted spoon holding a sugar cube. The water infused an anise-flavored liqueur called pastis and slowly turned the cloudy yellow liquid an opaque white.

Pouring the drinks into tall glasses, Gilbért presented them with a flourish. *"Voila."*

"Merci."

Mallory had learned her lesson with the apple brandy. She took only a few cautious sips, savoring the licorice tang that enhanced the flavors of the olives and prosciutto-wrapped melon slices.

"Care to give me a status report?" Cutter asked

when Gilbért had left them to enjoy their aperitifs. "Maybe I can help with the untangling."

"The status quo hasn't changed. The rental-car agency is still dithering over liability, American Express says there's a flag on my account, and you wouldn't believe the runaround I got from the U.S. Consulate. I called a friend back home who has some pull with the State Department. He should be able to help."

She tried for a Gallic shrug and was pretty proud of its nonchalance until the import of what she'd just said pierced her breezy facade. Like a backhanded slap, it wiped the smile from her face and knocked the breath from her lungs. Her eyes huge, she stared at Cutter in mounting dismay.

"Mallory?" Frowning, he set aside his glass. "What is it? What's the matter?"

"I—I just realized… The bureaucratic run-around… All these delays…" She could barely breathe. Swiping her tongue over suddenly dry lips, she croaked out an anguished whisper. "They may be deliberate."

Cutter went still. She wasn't surprised at the wary look that leaped into his eyes. He had to be wondering just what the heck he'd gotten himself into.

"What makes you think they're deliberate?" he asked with a cool edge to his voice.

She had to tell him. Much as it killed her, she had to hang the dirty linen out for him to see.

"I caused a stink back in the States, one that involved a very influential man. I wouldn't put it past him to retaliate by having one of his pals at the State Department label me in the system as a troublemaker, or worse."

Mallory couldn't believe it hadn't occurred to her before this moment. Like an idiot, she'd asked Dillon to drop his boss's name and pull a few strings without once considering that Congressman Kent could pull a whole bunch more. He hadn't spent twenty-plus years in Congress without building a wide circle of cronies who owed him favors.

"That's how they play the game in Washington," she said, struggling to keep the bitterness out of her voice. "You scratch my back, I'll scratch whatever portion of your anatomy you point in my direction."

Cutter regarded her for several silent moments. She could only imagine what he was thinking.

"Why don't you tell me who you crossed and how?" he said slowly.

"My former boss, Congressman Ashton Kent."

His lips pursed in a soundless whistle. Hers twisted in a wry grimace.

"I know, I know. Nothing like pitting yourself against one of the most powerful men in the United States."

"What happened?"

"Kent grabbed my ass once too often, so I filed a sexual harassment complaint."

Blowing out a ragged breath, Mallory stripped weeks of torment down to the sordid basics.

"Kent claimed I dressed too provocatively. That I left the top buttons of my blouse undone to entice him. He even produced a picture of the two of us, taken shortly after I joined his staff. There I was, smiling up at him in what he asserted was an open invitation."

Try as she might, Mallory couldn't hold back the tortuous doubts. They swamped her now, as they had so many times in the past weeks.

"I admired the man, Cutter! At first, anyway. Ashton Kent is a living legend in American politics. I was pretty jazzed to be asked to join his staff and probably didn't hold back when I was with him those first few weeks."

She cringed now at the memory of her initial, awestruck admiration for the silver-maned legislator. Maybe she *had* flirted a little. Maybe her eagerness to be considered a team player *could* have been interpreted as a come-on.

Then there was that business with her blouse.

"We were working late on draft legislation," Mallory related. "I'd slipped off my suit jacket. I didn't notice the top button on my blouse had come undone until Congressman Kent leaned over my shoulder and got an eyeful. That was the first time he fondled me."

Cutter said nothing, for which Mallory was profoundly grateful. The telling was difficult enough without editorial commentary.

"I was as surprised as I was embarrassed, but made it clear I wasn't interested. That's when the congressman informed me that I hadn't been hired for my brains."

Her listener broke his silence then. The pithy, one-syllable oath eased the tight knot in Mallory's chest.

"That's pretty much what I thought, too. So the second time Kent grabbed me, I filed a complaint. What followed wasn't pretty."

"No," Cutter growled, "I would imagine it wasn't."

She slumped against her chair back, relieved she didn't have to hide her dirty little secret from him any longer. "I'm surprised you didn't recognize me. My face, my personal history and detailed accounts of my sexual proclivities made just about every paper in the country."

"I travel a lot." His glance softened as it swept over her. "I'm guessing the media were a lot harder on you than they were on the congressman."

"You got that right. He came out looking like the poster boy for Viagra. I was painted as the promiscuous slut who tempted the poor man to sin."

Her dinner companion snorted. "Who in their right mind would believe Kent was a helpless victim?"

"His wife, for one. The arbitrator, for another.

And a dozen or so jerks like the one who hit on me at Mont St. Michel, all convinced Mallory Dawes was good for some raunchy, no-holds-barred sex."

Cutter toyed with his aperitif glass. He had strong hands, she thought, big and blunt-fingered.

"You sure that's why that guy hit on you?"

"I'm sure."

"He didn't just spot a beautiful woman sitting by herself and forget his manners?"

"Thanks for the compliment. God knows, I wish that was all it was. He made it clear, though, that he recognized me from the news stories and fully expected me to live up—or down—to my reputation."

She shrugged, feeling fifty pounds lighter now that she'd unburdened herself. "Sorry, Cutter. I guess I should have warned you that you were hooking up with the next best thing to a porn star."

She didn't expect the laughter that rumbled around in his chest. His gray eyes invited her to share in the joke.

"I didn't know there was a next best thing," he commented, grinning.

An answering chuckle gurgled up, surprising Mallory. She couldn't believe she was actually trading jokes about the degrading incident that had left a permanent stain on her psyche.

Okay, maybe not so permanent. The blot seemed to lighten a little more with each hour spent in Cutter's company. She was searching for a way to express her gratitude when Gilbért returned and held the door open for his wife to roll in a heavily laden cart.

The antipasto tray was whisked away. Wine goblets replaced the pastis glasses. Domes came off an array of silver serving dishes. With a beaming smile for his wife, the majordomo presented a platter garnished with parsley and cleverly carved lemon swans.

"I give you *le veau de la Normandie.*"

Chapter 8

Mallory's account of her run-in with Congressman
Kent gave Cutter a good deal more to chew on than
Madame Picard's succulent veal.

Her account, brief as it was, tallied with the detailed summary in the background dossier OMEGA
had put together on the Kent incident. She hadn't
tried to gloss things over or minimize her part in the
mess. If anything, she seemed to take a dispropor-
tionate share of the blame, and that left Cutter quietly
seething.

He'd crossed paths with Ashton Kent. Twice.
Once while Cutter was still in uniform and Kent had

been part of a Congressional junket touring the Middle East. Again at Nick Jensen's high-priced D.C. restaurant, when Kent had disappeared into one of the private rooms with the well-endowed widow of a wealthy campaign contributor. Both times the old goat had struck Cutter as a walking, talking prick.

He didn't doubt for a minute Kent had felt up his bright-eyed new staffer. What really pissed Cutter off was that Mallory appeared to have taken most of the heat for it.

Had that made her bitter enough to walk away with a disk containing personal financial data belonging to millions of government workers, up to and including the President of the United States?

No way in hell!

His conviction grew firmer by the hour. Problem was, it was still based more on gut feeling than fact. He needed something definitive to eliminate her as anything more than a possible unwitting courier.

He waited until they'd finished dinner and agreed to Gilbért's suggestion they take coffee and dessert in the conservatory before steering the conversation back to the subject of retribution.

"So you think Kent may be retaliating against you by asking a pal to hold up your replacement passport?"

"I think it's a distinct possibility."

"How would he know you lost it in the first place?"

"Good question."

Mallory drifted to the tall windows, her gaze on the moonlit seascape outside. Cutter did his best to ignore the play of light and shadow on her profile as she scrunched her forehead and considered the possibilities.

"Maybe the State Department contacted my place of employment to verify my identity before issuing a temporary passport. Or maybe," she said slowly, "the contact came from American Express. They said there was a flag on my account. Congressman Kent chairs the House Committee on Banking and Trade. He exerts tremendous influence over the entire industry. He also works closely with NSA and Homeland Defense. I wouldn't put it past him to have flagged the financial records of everyone on his staff. Maybe everyone on the Hill. All in the name of national security."

"He wields that kind of power?" Cutter asked with a carefully manufactured blend of curiosity and outrage. "What happened to our right to privacy?"

The answer came swiftly and without the least hesitation.

"9/11."

Abandoning the moon-washed cliffs outside, Mallory turned and jammed her hands in the pockets of her lace-trimmed jacket.

"We're at war. An undeclared war, some argue, but everyone agrees that it threatens all Americans. Desperate times call for desperate measures. By following the money trail across international borders, we've located countless Al Qaeda cells and their financiers."

He didn't miss the collective *we*—or that Mallory Dawes identified with the good guys.

"I can't speak for anyone else," she continued, "but I'm more than willing to let Uncle Sam peek into my personal financial dealings if it will help take down bin Laden and his thugs."

Cutter and the rest of the OMEGA operatives served in the front lines in the war against terror. Personally, he didn't give a rat's ass about the rights of a suspected suicide bomber. Professionally, he'd respect those rights for the simple reason that violating them might screw the case against the suspect. He made no comment, however, until Mallory came off her soapbox with a look of embarrassed chagrin.

"I guess I'm just not real thrilled that Kent may be one of the ones doing the peeking."

"I can understand why."

As Cutter studied the moonlight dappling her upturned face, he had to admit there was something seriously wrong with this picture. Here they were, surrounded by the earthy perfume of the conservatory's potted palms, with stars studding the sky outside and the sea crashing against the cliffs below. His overwhelming urge was to take advantage of the exotic setting to kiss Ms. Dawes senseless. Instead, he was doing his damnedest to get her to incriminate herself. Grimly, he plowed ahead.

"Have you thought about getting back at Kent for all he's put you through? May still be putting you through?"

"God, yes!"

The vehemence sent a sudden chill through him, icing his veins. The rueful shrug that followed started a slow thaw.

"But I tried that once and failed dismally." She gave a small, self-deprecating laugh. "I can be pretty stubborn at times, but I'm not into self-flagellation or masochism. I decided before I left for France that I wasn't going to beat myself up over Congressman Ashton Kent any longer."

She slanted him a sideways glance and hesitated a moment before adding shyly, "You reinforced that decision, you know."

"Me? How?"

"By coming to my rescue the way you did. By giving me a glorious afternoon in the sun and two nights like this. But mostly, by reminding me not all men are like Kent."

Cutter's conscience started to squirm. He'd done exactly what he'd intended to do. Isolated the woman. Made her dependent on him. Gained her trust. So why the hell was he now feeling like a world-class heel?

"Don't pin a halo on me, Mallory. Kent and I have more in common than you think. You don't know how hard it was for me to keep my hands off you this afternoon."

"There's one significant difference," she said quietly. "I *want* your hands on me."

Sweating now, he was reminding himself of all the reasons why he shouldn't take her up on her starry-eyed invitation when she drifted closer.

"I liked touching you, Cutter."

He managed to resist until she dropped her gaze to his mouth.

"And I liked kissing you."

Well, hell! He'd never made any claims to being a saint. What's more, he'd given her fair warning.

Slamming the door on his conscience, he did what he'd ached to do earlier that afternoon. His arm snaked around her waist. His stance widened. Cradling her hips against his, he tunneled his free hand into her hair to hold her head steady and took what she offered.

The desire that had bitten into him earlier didn't compare to the hunger her eager mouth and hands now roused. Tightening his arm, he crushed her lips under his, as if daring her to unleash the beast.

Mallory slid her palms up the lapels of his jacket, felt his muscles straining under the suede, and surrendered to a rush of mindless pleasure.

This was the way it should happen. *This* was the way it was supposed to be. Desire feeding desire. Heat stroking heat. No politics. No sexual power plays. Only his mouth greedy on hers and her hands frantic to burrow through layers of fabric to get at the hard contours beneath.

She had to smother a curse when the rattle of wheels announced the arrival of Madame Picard and her serving cart. Cutter wasn't as restrained. With a muttered expletive, he released her and rolled his shoulders to settle his sport coat while Mallory tugged down the jacket that had ridden up over her hips.

They weren't quite quick enough. Madame Picard's glance went from one to the other as she rolled her cart across the tiles.

"You wish me to serve dessert?"

"That's okay," Cutter said, taking charge. "We'll serve ourselves."

With a smile and a small bow, madame departed. The interruption hadn't lasted more than a few seconds. Just long enough for reason to prevail...if either of them was inclined toward reason.

Mallory certainly wasn't. After so many weeks of doubting herself, of hiding behind sunglasses and avoiding men's glances, she reveled in the heat in Cutter's eyes when they whipped back to her. Her pulse skipping, she scooped a two-tiered plate from the cart.

"I've got the chocolate truffles and strawberries. You bring the whipped cream."

Dessert was the last thing on Cutter's mind as he snatched up the silver pot containing fresh, frothy cream. Visions of where and how he would spread the stuff damned near had him tripping over his own feet.

He maintained his balance and enough presence of mind to snag their unfinished bottle of wine from the cooler as he followed Mallory through the grand dining salon. Once they'd mounted the stairs and closed the door to her sitting room behind them, however, the bottle, silver pot and two-tiered plate were set aside and forgotten.

Mallory came into his arms with unrestrained eagerness. The ugly insinuations and allegations of promiscuity flashed through Cutter's mind, only to die an instant death the moment she went up on tiptoe and locked her arms around his neck. She gave as much as she took, but the giving was warm and generous, the taking anything but rapacious.

He was the one who yanked open the buttons of her jacket. *He* almost choked when he peeled down the denim and saw the lacy camisole beneath. *His* heart jackhammered against his chest when she angled her head and nibbled her way from his lower lip to his chin to his throat.

Cutter had to fight to keep from tossing her over his

shoulder and hauling her to the bed in the next room. The instincts she stirred in him were primitive, almost primeval. He couldn't remember the last time he'd wanted a woman as much as he wanted this one. Hell, he'd *never* wanted one as much as he did Mallory.

Not even the Danish beauty who'd arched and panted and hooked her legs around his waist only hours before she triggered the device that created such carnage and devastation.

The realization locked Cutter's jaw. He stepped back, fists balled, every muscle and tendon in his body raw with the memory.

"I'm so sorry." Stricken, Mallory touched a feather-light finger to the scars she'd just kissed. "I didn't think… I didn't realize… Do they still hurt you?"

They did, but not in the way she thought.

Cutter almost ended things then. He was pretty sure he would have, too, if she hadn't proceeded to yank the rug out from under his feet.

"I'm sorry," she whispered again, leaning forward to drop a tender kiss on the underside of his chin. "I'll be more gentle. I promise."

The irony of it hit before the absurdity. In her own words, she'd been publicly branded as the next thing to a whore. Yet she stood there with sympathy swimming in her big brown eyes, reining in her natural urges, promising to go easy on him.

On *him!*

His doubts sank out of sight. Insides turning to mush, he chuckled and tugged her against him.

"You just let rip, sweetheart. I'll do my best to grin and bear it."

All inclination toward laughter had disappeared by the time he scooped her up and carried her into the bedroom. So had any pretense that he was a passive player in the game. He was rock-hard and hurting when he dragged down the silken coverlet.

Stretching her out on the pale-blue sheets, he stripped off her lacy camisole and briefs. The need to possess her made his hands unsteady as he shed his own clothes, but he managed to fish a condom from his wallet.

A strangled sound came from the bed. Throwing a quick glance over his shoulder, he saw Mallory propped up on one elbow.

"What's that slogan?" she choked out as he joined her on sheets as soft as snow. "'Never leave home without them?' Reminds me of a certain financial institution that shall remain nameless at this… Oh!"

Cutter smiled at her breathless gasp and shifted his weight. They fitted together perfectly, her mouth within easy reach of his, her breasts flattened against his chest. He shifted a little more to the side and stroked his hand from her breasts to her belly and back again.

She was incredible, he thought while he could

still think at all. Her skin was smooth and creamy and flushed with heat. Her belly hollowed under his palm. The pale hair of her mound was soft and silky to his touch.

Cutter fully intended to draw out the foreplay as long as possible, priming her, testing his own limits. But when he found the slick flesh between her thighs, his mind shut down and his body took over. Fitting himself against her, he locked his mouth on hers and sank into her wet, welcoming heat.

They found a rhythm as old as time. Mallory's skin grew damp with sweat. Her nipples ached from Cutter's nipping, sucking kisses. She rolled atop him to return the favor and had contorted to work her way down to his chest when her entire body went taut.

She jerked upright. Hands, teeth and thighs clenched as her climax slammed into her. Wave after wave of pleasure ricocheted through her belly. She thought she heard Cutter groan. She knew his muscles bunched under her bottom just before he thrust upward.

She collapsed onto his chest seconds later. Or maybe it was hours. She didn't have a clue. The only reality that penetrated her sensual haze was the hammer of his heart under her ear.

Mallory floated slowly back to earth, vaguely aware of the cold air prickling her backside.

Flopping onto the mattress, she dragged up the tangled sheet and nuzzled into Cutter's side. She must have dozed a little before she came awake with the scent of their lovemaking teasing her nostrils. Burying her face in the angle between his neck and shoulder, she touched her lips to the warm skin.

"Mmm. You taste salty."

"I am salty. And thirsty." Easing his arm free, he leaned over her and dropped a kiss on her still-tender lips. "How about I retrieve the wine?"

"Great idea. Bring the other goodies, too." She scrambled upright and hooked the sheet under her arms. "We'll have our own private picnic."

Cutter did as asked. He brought the dessert tray and pot of still-frothy whipped cream first, then went back for the wine. Mallory had bitten into her second truffle when he returned.

"You are *not* going to believe how wonderful these are," she gushed. "The first one was mocha, flavored with Cointreau. This one is chocolate, hazelnut and rum. Here, take a bite."

Smacking her lips in exaggerated ecstasy, she offered him the remaining morsel. He bent to take it, but she didn't see her playful mood reflected in his expression. He'd turned thoughtful during his two trips into the sitting room.

Okay. All right. So he wasn't into postcoital picnics. No big deal.

She reached deep inside for something blasé to cover the awkward moment and came up empty. When he stood beside the bed and looked down at her, though, she knew the moment had stretched too thin to simply ignore.

"Is something wrong?"

He hesitated a few seconds too long.

"Wait," Mallory said, her heart sinking. "Don't tell me. I can guess. You're having a sudden attack of conscience."

She'd hit the mark. She could see it in his face. Dismayed, she shook her head.

"I should have known this little romantic interlude was too good to be true. That *you* were too good to be true."

"Mallory…"

"You're married, aren't you?"

"No."

"Engaged."

"No."

"In love with a twenty-two-year-old cowboy from Montana."

"What?"

If she hadn't been so mortified by his withdrawal, she might have derived immense satisfaction from his stunned expression.

"Hey, I saw *Brokeback Mountain*. I pretty much fell in love with Heath Ledger myself."

His mouth opened. Snapped shut. In a tone that sounded like glass grinding, he refuted her allegations.

"Did it feel like you were in bed with someone nursing a taste for twenty-something cowboys?"

"I don't know. Let me think about it for a minute."

"Oh, for…!"

Tangling a hand in her hair, he tugged her head back. His eyes weren't cool any longer, she noted.

"In case you haven't noticed, my taste runs to twenty-nine-year-old blondes who run around losing passports, sinking rental cars and smearing chocolate all over their lips."

When he proceeded to kiss away the aforementioned chocolate, Mallory's doubts subsided. Temporarily. Only after he broke the kiss to lick at the corner of her mouth did her thoughts reengage. Curious, she cocked her head.

"How did you know?"

"Know what?"

"How old I am. Was that just a lucky guess?"

"I must have overheard you give the information to the gendarme at Mont St. Michel."

"I don't remember giving my age," she said, a frown gathering. "My name, yes. And your cell phone number. Not my age."

Impatience flickered across his face as a sick feeling churned in the pit of Mallory's stomach.

"Oh, God! You knew."

Dragging the sheet with her, she scrambled to her feet. Strawberries and truffles spilled everywhere.

"You knew all about me, didn't you? You *did* read the papers, or saw the reports on TV. You knew about me, yet you sat there at the table and listened while I spilled my sad little tale."

He didn't try to deny it. He couldn't. The truth was stamped all over his face.

"Yes, I knew who you were."

Her chin lifted. She'd indulge in some serious self-flagellation and name-calling later. Right now she just wanted him gone before she burst into tears.

"Glad I gave you some fun, Mr. Smith. Now get out of my room."

"Listen, Mallory, I did know who you were, but…"

"But what?" she jeered. "You lied about not reading the news stories because you wanted to see if they were true? If I was hot as they said? Well, now you know. They're true. Every one of them."

"To hell they are."

"You can go home, sell the latest chapter in this squalid serial to the tabloids, make millions."

"Dammit, just listen a moment! I didn't see any TV specials or pore through the tabloids. I studied the dossier put together by the outfit I work for."

"You got a dossier?" Her face went slack with surprise before morphing into a full-fledged scowl. "On me?"

"Yes."

"Why? You're a wine broker, for pity's sake. Why would you…? Oh!"

Swirls of conversation came back to her. Reeling, she recalled how Cutter had cleverly pumped her for information about her job at the Department of Commerce.

"Oh, Lord! How much of an idiot can one person be? This has to do with my job at the International Trade Administration, doesn't it? What did you think you could get from me, Smith? Preferential status on ITA's market listing? Inside information on your foreign competition?"

Cutter came within a breath of telling her the truth then. *Not* because of his mounting guilt for taking advantage of her vulnerability. Or the odd, indefinable emotion that had jolted through him when she'd pressed her lips against his puckered flesh.

It wasn't love. He'd only known the woman for all of two days. People didn't fall in love that quickly, except maybe in movies. Like *Brokeback Mountain.*

Christ!

No, he wanted to level with her for purely professional reasons. Mallory Dawes didn't have any knowledge of the disk tucked in a pocket of her suitcase. Cutter would stake his reputation on that. Correction, he'd stake what was left of his reputation after pulling an 007 and hopping into bed with his target.

She might, however, be able to help him determine *how* the disk got into her suitcase. For that, he needed her full cooperation.

Before he could read her in on the situation, though, he had to clear it with OMEGA's director. Lightning trusted his agents' instincts, gave them complete authority in the field, but this particular op involved the President of the United States.

"Mallory, listen to me. Please."

He figured he had all of thirty seconds to convince her he didn't rank right up there with Congressman Kent as a total sleaze.

"I did receive a dossier on you, but it had nothing to do with the wine business or your job at the International Trade Administration. I can't explain what it *did* concern. Not yet. You'll have to trust me a little longer."

Her chin jutted. Fury put bright spots of red in her cheeks. "Give me one good reason why I should."

She had him there. Cutter didn't think she was in any mood to appreciate a reference to the hours they'd spent together. Or to the fact that they both still wore each other's scent on their skin. All he could do was curl a knuckle under her chin and tip her face to his.

"I can't give you one, sweetheart. But I will. As soon as I make some calls, I promise. Just trust me a little longer, okay?"

"I'll think about it." Her eyes stormy, she jerked away from his touch. "Now get out of my room."

Chapter 9

The coded signal came in just as Mike Callahan was about to turn the control desk over to his relief.

It was only a little past four in the afternoon, D.C. time, but it was late evening on the coast of Normandy. Mike had taken Slash's report several hours ago. He'd figured on grabbing a few hours sleep while his field operative did the same.

His pulse kicking up a notch at the unscheduled contact, Mike nudged his relief aside and brought Slash's digitized image up on the screen.

"Thought you were locked down for the night, buddy."

"I was. I am."

Sliding into his seat at the console, Mike noted the rigid set to Cutter's jaw. Someone or something had gotten to him.

"What's up?"

"I want to read Dawes in on the op."

"Roger that."

Callahan didn't question the abrupt change in plans. He trusted Cutter Smith's instincts implicitly. He should. The two of them went back a long way. Over the years they'd shared ops, beers and the occasional night out with whatever females they happened to be involved with at the time.

Those years had forged bonds that went beyond friendship. Danger had further hardened the bonds to tempered steel. On one memorable occasion, Slash had manned a Black Hawk helicopter's 20mm cannon to hold off more than fifty enraged rebels while Mike scrambled for the hoist cable that would extract him from the sweltering jungle. On another, Mike had jumped in a Navy jet and flown halfway across the world to accompany Slash on the agonizing medevac flight home after a certain traitorous bitch had left him bleeding, burned and unconscious.

Neither of them talked about that long, horrific flight. Or about the woman Cutter had later tracked down. Some things didn't need discussing. Reading a target into an operational mission with such top-level interest, however, did.

"I'll have to run this by Lightning."

"I know."

"He's going to want to know the rationale."

"Tell him…"

Slash's hesitation was as uncharacteristic as his scowl. Mike waited a beat, wondering what the hell had happened in the scant hours since his last report.

"Tell him I'm convinced Dawes didn't know the disk was in her suitcase. I want to work with her, see if she can shed some light on how it got there."

"You sure she'll cooperate? She might not take kindly to learning that you've had her in your sights all this time."

"She's already tipped to the fact that I have more than a friendly interest in her." He paused again, then added a gruff postscript. "Considerably more, as it happens. Things, uh, got personal tonight."

Mike had spent too many years undercover to react to that bit of news, but he had to work to hold back a low whistle. The only other time Cutter had led with his dick instead of his head, he'd wound up in a burn ward.

"You sure you know what you're doing, buddy?"

"Yeah, I'm sure." Cutter stared straight into the camera. "Get back with me as soon you talk to Lightning."

"Will do."

Mike didn't need to check the electronic status board to know Lightning wasn't on site. He'd departed some hours ago to participate in a charity sports event at the Army-Navy Country Club. Wearing his Presidential Envoy/millionaire restaurateur persona, Nick Jensen and his wife, OMEGA's chief of communications, were knocking tennis balls around the court at something like a thousand dollars a whack.

So was Nick's executive assistant, Mike remembered with a sudden kink in his gut. Gillian had called up to advise Control she'd be at the country club with Nick and Mackenzie.

"You've got the stick," Mike instructed his relief. "I don't want to catch Lightning in midswing and throw him off his game. I'll deliver Slash's request in person."

Shrugging into his red windbreaker with its Military Marksmanship Association patch on the breast pocket, he dug his car keys out of the pocket of his jeans and descended to the tunnel that led to OMEGA's specially shielded underground parking facility.

His tan Blazer sat in its usual spot. The vehicle was only two years old but had already logged over a hundred thousand miles. Mike knew it was good for another hundred-plus. Drew McDowell, code name Riever, owned and operated a chain of classic car restoration shops in his civilian life. Drew had personally replaced the rods and adjusted the timing. The Blazer could go from zero to sixty in three-point-six seconds.

The acceleration came in handy when Mike wasn't in the field, working an op for OMEGA, and had to eat up road between his Alexandria condo and the Firearms Training Unit at Quantico, where he taught agents from a half dozen federal agencies the fine art of blowing away bad guys.

The familiar stink of the solvent he used to clean his weapons after a shoot permeated the Blazer. Mike kept a complete kit in the rear well—bores, brushes, rods, gun vise, wood and metal polish—all the tools of his trade. He carried his Mauser 86sr in a concealed compartment, as well. NATO snipers trained with a military version of Mauser, which featured a ventilated stock to dissipate heat and a detachable box for quick switching from high- to low-penetration rounds. Mike's had been custom built to his specifications.

Exiting the garage, he opened the car windows and let the brisk September air blow away the stink. Fall was in full swing, he noted absently as he negotiated the pre-rush hour rush. The oak and chestnut trees had already begun to turn. Fat yellow mums nodded from pots and planters along Massachusetts Avenue. His eyes shielded from the bright sun by mirrored sunglasses, Mike cut over to the Theodore

Roosevelt Bridge to avoid the usual logjam on 395 and cruised along Memorial Parkway. As always, the solid bulk of the Pentagon stirred memories of his years in uniform.

His first months had been rough. He'd arrived at boot camp with a chip the size of Rhode Island on his shoulder and a mouth to match. It hadn't taken long for a lean, wiry DI to cut the new recruit down to size. By the time Mike graduated from boot camp, he'd found a home and the family he'd never had.

He'd started in law enforcement, a rookie cop with few skills except the ability to put every round dead center at the practice range. That skill had served him well after transferring to an ultra-secret, highly mobile Special Ops forward insertion unit.

Mike would still be in uniform if Nick Jensen hadn't convinced him he could serve his country just as effectively in a different capacity. The transition was a wrench, but Mike had never looked back. OMEGA was every bit as tight as his Special Ops unit.

And Nick Jensen made one helluva boss, he thought as he pulled up at the gatehouse of the hallowed Army-Navy Country Club, a scant mile south of the Pentagon. Two guards manned the gate, along with a civilian-type Mike immediately identified as Secret Service. Wondering which of the President's numerous progeny were participating in the tennis tournament, he flipped open the ID case that cleared him for access to any government installation.

With a respectful nod, the guard activated the wrought-iron gates. "Welcome to Army-Navy, sir."

"Thanks."

Tucking away his ID, Mike navigated the winding road that cut through the superbly manicured grounds. Founded in the early 1920s to provide recreational facilities for military and civilians assigned to the nation's capital, the sprawling complex covered more than five hundred acres of wooded Virginia countryside. Mike played an occasional round of golf at the club, but didn't go out of his way to rub elbows with the generals, admirals, senators and foreign ambassadors who made up the bulk of the membership.

The indoor/outdoor tennis courts were some way past the redbrick, white-pillared clubhouse. A festive crowd had gathered to watch the matches underway on all four outdoor courts. Cheers rose with every returned volley, while groans abounded after each missed shot.

Nick and Mackenzie were hard at it on court number three. Mike could see the sweat streaking his boss's dark-gold hair. Mac had drawn her mink-brown mane back in a ponytail that whipped from side to side with every strong-armed swing. They were matched with a hook-nosed reporter from the

Washington Post and his partner, an angular, gray-haired woman Mike recognized as an undersecretary of defense.

But it was the couple on court two that riveted Mike's attention. Gillian's blouse and thigh-skimming pleated skirt were both pristine white, but she'd topped them with a hot pink sleeveless V-neck sweater. Her sun visor was the same neon pink, trimmed with sparkling crystals. And when she stretched to return a killer serve, she flashed a glimpse of matching briefs.

Mike's throat went dry. He knew damned well tennis stars like Venus and Serena Williams were glamming up the courts with colorful outfits and sequined shoes. He just wasn't prepared for the sight of Gillian Ridgeway in pink panties with a crystal heart etched on the right butt cheek.

Or for her partner's reaction when she scored the winning point. Whooping with delight, the jerk caught her up and whirled in a full circle before planting a kiss on her laughing lips.

"Game, set and match to Ridgeway and Olmstead," the announcer intoned while Mike's eyes narrowed to slits behind his sunglasses.

The urge to smash his fist in this guy Olmstead's face was completely irrational. That didn't make it any less atavistic. Jaw tight, he jammed his hands in his pockets.

They were still there, bunched into tight fists, when Gillian gathered her gear and came off the court. She accepted the congratulations of several spectators before she spotted him off to the side of the crowd.

"Mike!"

A smile sparkled in her vivid blue eyes. A *friendly* smile, he lectured himself sternly, the kind she'd drop on any casual acquaintance.

"Did you see the match?"

"Only the last few minutes." Which would, he knew, replay repeatedly in his head for nights to come. "You're good."

"I'm okay. My golf game is better, though."

Dragging up one end of the towel draped around her neck, she daubed at the sweat plastering tendrils of her jet-black hair to her temples.

"I understand you've been known to hit the fairways," she commented. "Maybe we should get up a foursome some weekend. You and I could take on Uncle Nick and my father. Dad is always looking for fresh blood."

Mike couldn't think of anything that would throw off his concentration more completely than sharing a golf cart with Gillian Ridgeway while two of OMEGA's most lethal operatives watched their every move.

"Or I could pair up with Dayna," she suggested with a grin, referring to an OMEGA operative who just happened to be an Olympic gold medalist. "We girls could take on you boys."

He was still trying to adjust to being classified as a "boy" when Gillian's partner strolled up and draped an arm across her shoulders.

"Hey, Jilly. We need to sign the score sheet."

Mike had made a career in the profession of arms. He could bring up his weapon, fix a target in his crosshairs and squeeze off a shot in less time than it took other men to chamber a round. With the same split-second precision, he sized up Jilly's partner as arrogant, over-confident and possessive.

"In a minute." Looking too damned comfortable in the circle of the man's arm, Gillian made the introductions. "Wayland, this is Mike Callahan. Mike, Wayland Olmstead."

Mike knew the name and the rep, if not the face. Yale undergrad. Harvard law. Hotshot young attorney carving a niche for himself at the National Security Agency.

"Good to meet you, Callahan."

The grip went with the man. Too strong and too long, as if signaling his power. Mike resisted the impulse to crunch the jerk's knuckles.

"I see you're a shooter," Olmstead commented, eyeing the Military Marksmanship Association patch.

"Not *just* a shooter," Gillian corrected. "A world champion. Mike instructs at the Federal Law Enforcement Academy at Quantico," she added, supply-ing his civilian cover. "He's the man my father strong-armed into teaching me to shoot."

Adam Ridgeway was more than capable of teach-ing his daughter how to handle weapons. So was her mom, for that matter. Maggie Sinclair's exploits were still the stuff of legend at OMEGA. But both parents had preferred a professional instructor, insist-ing that Mike could be more objective in assessing Gillian's strengths and weaknesses. Shows what they knew.

"You did a heck of a job," Olmstead said, squeezing her shoulders. "Jilly knocks down more sporting clays than I do every time we take out the Blassingames."

The message was about as subtle as a rifle butt to the bridge of the nose. A used Blassingame, if you could find one, went for a cool fifty thousand.

Idiot.

"I think you should know," Gillian warned, her eyes twinkling. "Samantha and Tank have been pes-tering Dad for lessons, too."

Mike had no problem with teaching Jilly's col-lege-aged sister to shoot, but the prospect of putting a gun into the hands of her teenaged brother drained every ounce of blood from his face.

Gillian had to laugh at his expression. He couldn't have looked more horrified if she'd shrugged off

Wayland's arm, gone up on tiptoe and given him a class-A liplock.

Something she'd thought about doing more and more frequently, she mused as a roar rose from the bleachers surrounding court three.

"Game, set and match to Jensen and Jensen."

"Good for Nick and Mackenzie!" With another squeeze, Wayland steered Gillian back toward the courts. "Let's go congratulate each other."

"Coming, Mike?"

"I'll wait here." He adjusted his sunglasses and gave her one of his Uncle-Mike-to-little-Jilly smiles. "Tell Nick I need to talk to him when he gets a minute."

One of these days, she vowed as she accompanied Wayland through the milling crowd, she'd have to convince him she was all grown up.

After consulting with Lightning, Mike waited until he was back in the Blazer to contact Cutter. Traffic was a bitch, crawling along like a snail on tranquilizers, belching diesel fumes into the slowly gathering dusk.

The traffic snarl matched Mike's mood. He could have gone all month without that glimpse of Olmstead tipping a champagne glass to Gillian's lips.

Hell, all year.

With a surly sneer for the unbroken stream of red taillights ahead, he punched a two-digit code into his phone.

"Lightning gave the green light," he relayed when Cutter's image appeared on the screen. "You can read Dawes into the op."

"Roger that."

The leap of satisfaction in Cutter's face had Mike biting back a warning. Slash knew what he was doing. He wouldn't fall for another female with a soul as flawed as the one who'd damned near killed him.

"When do you plan to tell her?"

"First thing in the morning."

"Good luck."

"Thanks, Hawk."

Cutter woke early the next morning.

A cold wind rattled the windows, causing the château to creak and groan with the prerogative of age, but he didn't hear a sound from the suite next door.

That was fine with him. He needed a good run to clear his head. He'd lost several hours of sleep to the image of Mallory's angry face and stormy eyes when she jerked away from his touch. Even more to the vivid memory of her slick flesh and low, throaty moan when she'd climaxed in his arms. He'd have to talk hard and fast to recover the ground he'd lost last night. Faster still to get her into bed again.

With various strategies for how he'd break the

news that she was the primary suspect in an identity theft of massive proportions kicking around in his head, Cutter pulled on the jogging suit OMEGA's Field Dress Unit had included in his hastily assembled kit. He would have preferred his usual Nikes and well-worn gray sweats but had to admit the chocolate-brown velour designer job felt as soft as a fuzzy kitten against his skin.

He followed the scent of fresh-brewed coffee and rising yeast to a kitchen aglow with copper pots. Gilbért was seated at a peg-and-board oak table with his jacket hooked on the back of his chair and the remains of his breakfast in front of him. Madame Picard stood at a granite slab of a counter and rolled pastry dough with floured arms.

"'Morning."

Abashed to be caught in his shirtsleeves, Gilbért scrambled for his jacket. "*Excusez-moi,* monsieur. I did not hear the bell."

"I didn't ring. Please, sit down. I just want some coffee before I head out for a run. May I join you?"

"But of course."

The coffee was thick and tarry black, the cream light and frothy. One cup led to another, then to a brioche fresh from the oven. Regretfully, Cutter passed on a second until after his run.

The morning mist swirled gray and thick when Gilbért disarmed the security system and Cutter exited into the cobbled courtyard. Discreetly placed cameras tracked his progress through the gate and onto the long, sweeping drive.

Instead of following the drive to the main road, he opted for a path that led along the cliffs. A mile at a slow trot loosened muscles that hadn't been exercised in several days. With the ocean hidden by the fog but roaring loudly in his ears, Cutter gradually lengthened his stride. Salty mist dewed on his face. Damp air filled his lungs. Thoughts of Mallory Dawes looped through his head.

Six miles later, the velour was drenched with sweat and Cutter had decided on a direct approach. He wouldn't gain anything by pussyfooting around the issue. First he'd shower and shave. Then he'd tell Mallory about the disk, inform her that he'd had her under close surveillance since Paris, and brace himself for the firestorm that would follow.

He accomplished the first two items on his agenda with minimum fuss and maximum speed.

His cheeks tingling from the rapid scrape of his razor, he tugged on slacks and a lightweight knit sweater in a peacocky blue, compliments of Field Dress, and rapped on the door to Mallory's suite. When she didn't answer, he tried the small dining salon, the oak-paneled library and the music room before once again making his way to the kitchen.

Madame Picard was still at the counter, peeling apples for the pie shell she'd baked while he was running.

"The run?" she inquired politely. "It is good?"

"Very good. Has Mademoiselle Dawes come down?"

"*Oui.*" The paring knife made a small circle in the air. "She comes, she goes."

"Goes?"

"*Oui.* The telephone rings, and mademoiselle, she asks Gilbért to drive her."

"Drive her where?"

"Into town, to the train station."

Cutter smothered a vicious oath. "How long?"

"*Pardon?*"

"How long have they been gone?"

Her shoulders lifted in that quintessential Gallic shrug. "Five minutes, perhaps ten."

Cutter spun on his heel and sprinted for the stairs to retrieve his car keys, cursing all the way.

Chapter 10

Mallory stared unseeing at the mist-shrouded pines drifting past the windows of Madame d'Marchand's Rolls Royce Silver Cloud. Beside her, Gilbért hummed to himself as he steered through the forest that edged right down to the cliffs on this stretch of coast.

She should have been feeling like a princess. After all, she'd spent the past two nights in a castle and was now being conveyed to town in a chrome-laden behemoth that glided along with slow, ponderous grace. Instead, she wanted to bite something. Or someone.

She supposed she should thank Cutter for waiting until last night to bring the walls of her fairy-tale castle tumbling down around her. At least she'd got to spend a whole day roaming the French country-side, lazing in the sun, sipping apple brandy. An evening filled with sparkling crystal and *le veau de la Normandie*. And let's not forget that hot, sweaty session between the sheets.

She ground her teeth, and Gilbért raised an in-quiring brow.

"Yes, mademoiselle?"

Shifting in her seat, Mallory glanced at the stately majordomo. He appeared so calm, so dignified, with his salt-and-pepper hair, neatly trimmed mustache and spiffy tweed driving cap.

"Mademoiselle is disturbed?" he asked, unbend-ing enough to tip her a look of friendly concern.

She started to deny it. Shielding her thoughts and emotions had become a necessary survival mechan-ism over the past months. She was feeling just raw enough, though, to blow a long huff of self-disgust.

"Did you ever make a fool of yourself over someone? A total, twenty-four-carat fool?"

"But of course. I am French. It is required."

"Wish I could use nationality as my excuse," Mallory said glumly. "With me, it's just plain stupidity."

"What is life without such folly, eh?" His lips curving, Gilbért relaxed his gloved hands on the steering wheel. "Madame Picard was the belle of our village. All the men puff their chests and strut like the peacock when she strolls by. She tortures me, *ma petite Jeanette,* until I go mad with despair and decide to drown myself in the village well. It is a gesture, you understand, a foolish gesture. I have gone down the well many times as a boy, but now I am too big and become stuck. It takes a team of horses to pull me out, while the whole village watches. We laugh about it still, Madame Picard and I."

Gilbért's rich chuckle invited Mallory to share in the absurdity of life in general and love in particular.

Okay, she thought, smiling at his tale, so maybe she wasn't the only woman in history to fall for a sexy smile and a body to match. Throw in a propensity to appear just when a girl needed him most and a seemingly sympathetic ear, and it was no wonder she'd let desire cloud her judgment where Cutter Smith was concerned.

The stupid thing was, deep down inside she still wanted to trust him. Against all reason, despite every bitter lesson she'd learned in recent months, she wanted to give him the time he'd asked for. How stupid was that?

She was squirming inwardly at the answer when a figure darted out of the forest. Planting himself in the middle of the road, he waved his hands above his head and signaled for them to stop.

With a low grunt, Gilbért stomped on the brakes. His eyes narrowed under the brim of his tweed cap.

"I know this one. He is the son of the baker in town."

Judging by the curl to Gilbért's lip, he didn't hold the baker's son in particularly high esteem. Mallory's glance cut back to the man on the road.

Skinny and spike-haired, he looked to be in his early twenties. His jeans were fashionably ragged, showing large patches of bare skin. His jacket was also denim. The black T-shirt he wore underneath sported a heart skewered by a stiletto dripping blood.

"Wait in the car, mademoiselle." Gilbért put his shoulder to the Rolls' heavy door. "I will see what he wants."

Whatever it was led to an escalating exchange of words and gestures. Mouths twisted into sneers. Arms were flung. Chins were flipped. When the kid dragged an arm across his nose to wipe it, an obviously disgusted Gilbért turned and stalked toward the car.

Before he'd taken more than a few steps, the baker's son whipped something out from under his jacket. Mallory caught only a glint of metal before he raised his arm and brought it down on Gilbért's skull. The older man crumpled like an old suit of clothes.

"Hey!"

Mallory was out of the car before Gilbért hit the ground. The kid spun toward her, clutching what she now saw was a small but lethal-looking revolver.

She froze, her breath thick in her throat, as he let loose with a torrent of French. The volume rose with each agitated phrase, until he was almost shouting at her.

"I don't understand." Her voice cracked. Her mind fought to find the right translation. *Je, uh, ne comprend...*"

"I will have it!"

"Have what?"

"Everything. The purse. The wallet. What you carry in the car."

Drugs, she thought when her brain unfroze enough to register anything except the gun barrel aimed at her midsection. The wild eyes. The runny nose. He had to be on drugs. Only someone really messed up in the head would risk a robbery in broad daylight with a man who could easily identify him lying in the dirt at his feet.

The realization she was facing an armed junkie would have scared the crap out of her if a second realization hadn't hit right on top of that one. *Because* the man lying in the dirt at this guy's feet could identify him, he might not be inclined to leave either Gilbért or Mallory behind as witnesses.

"The purse," the kid shouted, his gun shaking with the effort. "Throw it down, in the road. Then move away from the car."

Struggling desperately to recall the tips imparted in her self-defense course, Mallory tugged at the strap of the purse draped across her chest and one shoulder. Most of the advice had to do with avoiding dangerous situations. Never pick up hitchhikers. Stick to well-lighted areas. Travel in pairs.

The options narrowed down considerably when confronted by an armed robber. Don't resist. That was rule one. Her life was more valuable than her possessions. Except in this case, she didn't have many possessions and she couldn't shake the sick certainty that her life hung by a very thin thread with this guy.

Rule two, don't make any sudden moves that might make the attacker think she was reaching for a concealed weapon. Dear God, what she wouldn't give for a concealed weapon!

Rule three… Do whatever you could to get away if he tried to force you into the car and run like hell in a zigzagging pattern.

Her hand shaking, Mallory dragged her purse over her head. She could zigzag it into the trees lining the road. Maybe. If she ran, though, she'd leave Gilbért at the mercy of this crackhead.

"Here." Her mind racing in frantic circles, she dangled the purse. "This is all I have. Just take it, okay?"

"Throw it down onto the road and move away from the car."

She tossed the purse, but not onto the pavement. With a twitchy jerk that was ninety-nine percent nerves and one percent desperation, she managed to land it in the weedy grass beside the road.

Okay. All right. Mallory's breath came fast and shallow as the kid stalked towards her to snatch up the purse. He was closer now. Almost within reach.

She sucked in her gut, trying to work up the courage to propel her body through the air while he tore open the purse and viewed its meager contents.

She waited a fraction too long.

"Pah!" Pocketing her one credit card, he threw the purse into the weeds again. "There is more, yes?"

"No! Nothing! I swear."

"You come from the château. You are the guest of Madame d'Marchand. You have the suitcase. The furs. The jewels."

"I'm staying at the château, but I don't have any jewels or furs. You've got the wrong girl."

"I think not. Move away."

She took one step to the side. One slightly forward. Another…

Gilbért's groan was hardly more than a whimper, but the small animal sound provided the only distraction Mallory knew she would get. When the kid threw a swift glance over his shoulder, she sprang.

She knocked into his shoulder, threw him off balance, lunged again. This time she hit him from behind.

Locking one arm around his neck, she clung to his back like a monkey and made a desperate grab with her free hand. She caught only a corner of his jacket sleeve, but it was enough to keep him from angling his gun in her direction.

Cursing, he bucked and humped like an enraged bull. Mallory bounced on his back like a rag doll, but wouldn't loosen her stranglehold or release his sleeve. Knowing she had to bring him to his knees before he shook her off, she tightened her arm around his throat and squeezed for all she was worth.

"Mademoiselle!"

From the corner of one eye, she saw Gilbért stagger to his feet.

"He's got a gun!" she shouted.

The possibility Gilbért might join the fray spurred the kid to renewed fury. Choking, he spun in a circle and pumped off wild shots.

The first went into the air. The second plowed into the Rolls' shiny chrome grill. Cordite stung Mallory's eyes. Percussive shock waves hammered at her eardrums, so loud and painful she almost missed the roar of a car tearing down the road at top speed.

The kid picked up on it the same moment she did. Every bit as desperate as Mallory now, he staggered toward the Rolls and spun her into its side. Her hip slammed into the tank-like fender. Pain screamed up her spine.

Still she hung on. Or tried to. A second ramming jarred every bone in her body. Her chokehold loosened. His sleeve tore free of her grasp, but it took a vicious elbow to her ribs to knock her off the bastard's back.

She fell to the pavement. Heard Gilbért shout something in French. Then another shot cracked through the air.

"No!"

Mallory rolled onto all fours, prepared to see the butler stretched out on the pavement, fully expecting she would be next. Instead she heard an unbroken stream of curses from Gilbért, punctuated by the thud of running feet. Her head whipped toward the sound.

Cutter raced toward her from the car skidded sideways across the road some yards back. Mallory's dazed mind registered the pistol gripped in his hand. Gulping, she cranked her head around and spotted the baker's son sprawled face-down in a slowly spreading pool of blood. Her joints turning to jelly, she plopped down.

"Are you hurt?" Cutter crouched beside her, his grim glance raking her from head to toe. "Mallory! Sweetheart! Were you hit?"

"No." She raised a shaking hand to shove back her tangled hair and winced. "Not by a bullet, anyway. Bastard got me with an elbow."

"An elbow?"

"Right in the ribs."

Cutter sat back on his heels. His blood still thundered in his ears. His lungs hadn't pulled in a breath since he'd spotted the humpback figure gyrating wildly beside the Rolls. He'd aged a good ten years when he'd identified Mallory as the hump. Another ten in the two or three seconds it had taken him to jam on the brakes, leap out of the car and yank his Glock from its ankle holster.

"Stay here," he bit out.

Glock in hand, he joined Gilbért. The majordomo was on one knee beside the shooter, feeling for a pulse. Cutter didn't expect him to find one. He hadn't had time for a precision take-down.

"He's dead," Gilbért confirmed.

With a grunt of pain, the older man pushed to his feet. Cutter hooked his arm to help him up.

"You okay?"

"Yes." Disgust riddled his voice. "Like the fool, I turn my back and he hits me from behind."

Cutter kept a steadying hand on Gilbért's arm. His face was ashen and his cap had slipped down over one ear, but otherwise he appeared whole.

"Madame Picard and I feared it would come, sooner or late, with that one."

"You know him?"

"He is Remy Duchette, the son of the baker in town. He's had trouble with the police, you understand, but nothing that makes me think he carries a gun. I would not have stopped if I thought him dangerous."

"Why *did* you stop?"

"Remy comes out of the woods just there and waves to us. I think he wants a ride. Too late it becomes clear he waits for us."

Cutter slewed toward the treeline. The kid had picked a good spot for an ambush. A bend in the road, where the Rolls had to slow to make the turn. Plenty of cover to hide behind until his prey appeared.

"Remy knows this car," Gilbért continued, his disgust mounting with every word. "He knows madame entertains guests of great wealth. He has probably heard in the village that you and mademoiselle stay at the château and decides to wait in hope of robbing you."

"So that's what you think this was? An attempted robbery?"

"*Oui.* I hear him tell mademoiselle he wants her purse and the furs and jewels from her suitcase."

Cutter said nothing, but the warning lights already blipping inside his head flashed a sharper red.

"He said he wanted her suitcase?"

"He wants what is in it. Mademoiselle tells him she has only her purse with her, but he does not believe her and orders her to move away from the car."

"He acted all jumpy and twitchy," Mallory chimed in as she joined them. She gave the sprawled body a quick glance and looked away. "I think he was on drugs. My guess is he needed money for a hit."

"We must call the gendarmes." His face grim,

Gilbért extracted a cell phone from his pocket. "Then I must go into town to explain to my friend the baker how his son dies."

Cutter nodded. The sooner they got the police on the scene, the sooner he could get Mallory back within the walls of the château.

"I'll cover the body. Is there a blanket or a tarp in the car?"

"A tarp, in the trunk."

With the ease of long practice, Cutter reached down, hiked his pants' leg, and slid the Glock into its ankle holster. Mallory followed the movement with a crease between her brows.

Cutter knew he'd blown what little remained of his cover. Before he explained the Glock, though, Ms. Dawes needed to do a little explaining of her own.

"You're still green around the gills." With a firm hand on her elbow, he steered her back to the Rolls. "You'd better sit. It'll take a while for the police to get here."

She eased onto the seat with an awkward movement that told him her ribs were still hurting and sat sideways, shoulders hunched, while he searched the Rolls' cavernous trunk. It yielded both a neatly folded tarp and a supply of emergency road beacons. Cutter set several as a warning to any approaching vehicles to slow down.

He itched to search the woods for evidence that

would either support or disprove Mallory's theory that this was a drug heist gone bad, but he could wait for the police on that. Right now he was more interested in her reasons for departing the château so abruptly.

Hooking an elbow on the open back door, he conducted a swift assessment. Her face had lost its pasty hue, but the crease was still there, pulling at her brows. Cutter knew the questions were piling up behind her frown and decided to slip his in first.

"Madame Picard said you got a phone call and asked Gilbért to take you to the train station. Why didn't you wait for me, tell me where you were going?"

"You were out jogging. I was in a hurry." Her glance dropped to his ankle. "Do you always carry a gun?"

"Most of the time."

"You weren't wearing it last night."

"It wasn't necessary inside the château." Doggedly, he steered the conversation back to her abrupt departure. "Why did you just up and leave this morning, Mallory? Where were you going?"

"I told you. Into town."

"Why?"

"The stationmaster called. He said a package had come for me on the overnight express train from Paris, and that I had to sign for it personally. I thought it had to be either my passport or replacement traveler's checks, so I asked Gilbért to drive me to town."

If Cutter had any doubts about this roadside attack, she'd just resolved them.

Neat, he thought grimly. Very neat. Dangle the bait. Lure the prey out of her protected lair. Arrange an ambush on a deserted stretch of road. The only question in his mind was how the hell the hunter could be sure she would bring her suitcase with her.

"Your turn," Mallory snapped, breaking into his thoughts. "Why do you have a gun strapped to your ankle? Is the wine business so dangerous and cut-throat? Or was that all a lie, too?"

"Pretty much."

Her breath left on a long, slow hiss. "You're starting to really torque me off, Smith."

"Brace yourself, Dawes. It gets worse. I work for the U.S. government. An obscure agency you've never heard of. We've had you under close surveillance since Dulles."

Chapter 11

Mallory sat in the passenger seat of the Rolls. Stunned by Cutter's revelations, she nursed her aching ribs with slow, dazed strokes while he and Gilbért briefed the officer who'd arrived on the scene.

He'd followed her from the Paris airport.

He'd orchestrated every move, from their initial meeting to the passport delays to this romantic getaway at a French château.

He and this shadowy agency he worked for suspected her of stealing personal data on millions of government employees!

Every word, every touch had been a lie.

Last night he'd asked her to trust him, to give him time to make some calls before he filled in the blanks. Fool that she was, she'd tried to talk herself into doing just that.

"Mademoiselle Dawes?"

The police officer's sympathetic face loomed in the window of the Rolls. She and the French gendarmerie were becoming well acquainted, Mallory thought on a bubble of quickly suppressed hysteria.

"I understand this has been a shock, but I must ask you some questions."

The police officer seemed to ascribe her disjointed answers to nerves and the language barrier. Using great patience, he took her statement before speaking once again with Gilbért and Cutter.

Their colloquy resulted in more phone calls and a search of the woods. In the ensuing wait, Mallory's shock gave way to a slow burn as more and more personnel arrived on the scene. The local mortician, who evidently doubled as coroner's assistant, drove up in his hearse. A Crime Scene Unit appeared shortly after that, followed some time later by two men in civilian clothes.

They conducted a lengthy dialogue with Cutter and cast several pointed looks in Mallory's direction but didn't speak to her directly. Accepting the business cards they gave him, Cutter passed them one of his own before striding back to the Rolls.

"Let's go. We'll take my car."

When he reached down to help her, Mallory sent him a look that froze his hand in midair. The message was lethally clear. Touch her and he died.

Ice on the outside, smoldering at her core, she didn't say a word during the short drive. Neither did Cutter. They both knew the thin veneer of silence would shatter once they reached the château. Too many furious questions, too many outraged emotions roiled around inside the confines of the car to keep them bottled up for long.

First, however, they had to get through Madame Picard's barrage of shocked exclamations. Her husband had called and related the gist of the attack, but she needed the assurances of both Mallory and Cutter that Gilbért had sustained no injuries other than a slight dent to his head. After much hand-wringing and head-shaking, the apple-cheeked cook retreated to her domain with promises to deliver a pot of coffee and fresh pastries to the library.

Her footsteps were still ringing on the parquet floor when Cutter braced his hips against the gilt-trimmed desk that dominated the library and eyed Mallory's angry expression.

"You've had time to digest what I told you. I can see it didn't go down well."

"How very astute of you, Mr. Smith. If that's your real name," she added on a scathing note.

"It is. Where do you want to start?"

Arms folded, she faced him across the width of the oriental carpet. "How about this disk you say was in my suitcase."

He nodded, his stance as relaxed as hers was rigid. A framed portrait by an artist Mallory didn't recognize hung in a lighted alcove behind him. All sharp angles and glaring colors, the painting was probably a masterpiece, but she was in no mood to appreciate art right now.

"The disk is a standard, seventy-megabyte CD," Cutter said crisply, "the kind available to every government employee. A baggage inspector at Dulles found it in a side pocket of your suitcase, tucked inside a case for a CD by blues singer Corinne Bailey Rae."

His steady gaze never left her face. Hers lanced into him like a pointed stake aimed at his heart.

"Go on."

"The baggage inspector recognized the General Services Administration logo on the disk and showed it to his supervisor, who popped it into a computer. It contained only one file. I told you what was in it."

"Yes," she ground out, "you did."

She was still struggling with that. After a VA employee admitted he'd loaded millions of personnel files onto a home computer that was stolen in a burglary a few years back, every federal agency had tightened controls over personnel data. Yet someone had used *her* pass code to access *her* computer and collect the names, social security numbers, and financial information on twenty million of her fellow government employees.

"What I didn't tell you," Cutter continued evenly, "was that our lab techs found only your prints on the disk."

If she'd opened a new box of CDs and handled the contents before walking out of Congressman Kent's offices for the last time, Mallory didn't remember it.

"All that proves," she countered, "is the person who put it in my suitcase was very careful."

"Agreed. What we need to do now is determine who that person was."

She supposed she should be grateful for the *we* and for his calm deliberation. Then again, why the hell shouldn't he be calm? She was the one tagged with identity theft on a massive scale.

The possibility she might land in the middle of another media blitz, this time as a suspected traitor, was so demoralizing Mallory had to bite down on the soft inner tissue of her lip to hold back an anguished groan.

The pain helped, but her voice still came out thick and heavy. "I'm not sure I should talk to you about any of this until I consult with a lawyer."

"That's your call, Mallory. We'll work it any way you want."

There it was again, that seductive, sympathetic *we*. As if they were on the same team. Partners. Friends. Lovers.

"But we *have* to work it," he insisted with maddening deliberation. "I don't have any proof at this point, but I suspect this morning's attempted robbery was an attempt to retrieve the disk."

Mallory had pretty much come to the same conclusion. Nothing else made sense, as Cutter proceeded to point out.

"Duchette wasn't there by chance. Someone alerted him to the possibility that you would drive into town this morning to pick up the package waiting for you at the station and, presumably, resume your interrupted vacation. Someone who doesn't know your suitcase floated away with your rental car and is currently resting at the bottom of the Bay of St. Malo."

"The same someone you hoped I would lead you to."

"That's right."

The blunt, unapologetic response ripped a hole in Mallory's heart. She'd convinced herself Cutter was different. Worse, she'd fallen a little bit in love with him. Maybe more than a little.

Even after last night, after he'd dropped that bomb about the dossier, she'd granted him the grace period he'd asked for. Still hoping, still clinging to the ridiculous notion that he hadn't played her for a complete fool, she'd decided to hang around for the explanation he'd promised.

Well, now she had it. She was the bait he wanted to dangle in front of a shadowy, international thug. Hugging her arms to hold in the hurt, Mallory lifted her chin and waited for him to continue.

"We know him only as the Russian. We believe he's responsible for previous coordinated identity thefts, but nothing on quite this scale."

Cutter watched her face and knew he slashed into her with every word. Shoving his hands in his pants' pockets, he balled his fists and carved the next slice.

"We want him, Mallory. *I* want him. He and his kind have caused untold misery to hundreds of thousands of people. This gig would have been bigger, caused even more damage. If he'd gotten his hands on that data, the bastard could have brought our government to a temporary standstill."

"This is all so unreal. And so ironic. Congressman Kent took the floor of the House just a few months ago and gave a speech stressing the urgent need for additional safeguards on personal financial data." Her lips twisted in a mocking smile. "I wrote most of it."

"Which makes you the perfect sacrificial goat if anything went wrong. You possessed an insider's knowledge of the weak links in data protection. You could access restricted systems in your official capacity. You had damned good reason to want to get even with Kent."

"And if I got caught," she said bitterly, "I proved Kent's point. Our information systems are so vulnerable that any disgruntled employee can walk away from the job with a disk full of unauthorized data."

Cutter stiffened. "What did you just say?"

"You heard me. Our systems are so vulner…"

"No! Before that."

"Do you mean the bit about proving the pompous ass's point? Trust me, Kent could turn even a theft by one of his own employees into a political advantage. Not only do I show myself for the predatory female that he painted me, I help get him reelected by making more headlines for him."

"Kent's up for reelection this year?"

"Don't you read the papers?"

"I told you, I've been out of the country." Dismissing her sarcasm with an impatient shake of his head, he strode across the room. "What's the story with Kent? Does he have locks on his seat?"

Startled by his bulldog, in-her-face aggressiveness, Mallory shed some of her own prickly attitude.

"Not this time. He's facing a tough challenge from his state's former lieutenant governor. Or was," she amended, "until the sexual harassment charges I filed edged his competitor out of the headlines and into obscurity. You wouldn't believe how many points Kent gained in the polls after the charges were dismissed. My boss played the noble legislator, wrongly accused, to the hilt."

"Jesus!"

Cutter paced the length of the library and back again, his mind churning with new and intensely disturbing possibilities.

What if they'd followed the wrong scent? What if the Russian wasn't involved? Or involved only on the periphery? What if this was all an elaborate setup, with Mallory fingered to take the fall while racking up more points in the polls for her former boss?

Whirling, he strode back to the woman watching him with wary distrust.

"Sit down," he snapped. "We're going to take this from the top. I want to know who knew you were leaving for France, who had access to your computer, and everyone who stands to gain if and when Congressman Ashton Kent is reelected."

Not until hours later, after they'd expanded the list to include everyone who stood to *lose* if Kent *failed* to win reelection, did they begin to zero in on a name.

By then Gilbért had returned from town and Madame Picard had substituted the tray of untouched pastries with a heaping platter of ham-and-goat-cheese sandwiches. Cutter downed two, but Mallory only picked at the accompanying salad garnished with walnuts and crisp apple slices. She wasn't quite sure what to make of the intense grilling. Was she still a suspect or what?

"This guy, Dillon Porter," Cutter fired at her between man-sized bites. "You say he tried to talk you out of bringing charges against Kent?"

"Dillon is Kent's senior staffer. He's been around the Hill a long time. He knew how tough it would be for me to make the charges stick. He also warned me to expect a vicious media backlash. He hit the bull's-eye on both."

"Is he on Kent's payroll, or a permanent employee of the House Banking and Trade Committee?"

"He works directly for Kent, but…"

"And he's the person you called yesterday to help expedite your passport?"

"Yes, but…"

"What did you tell him? Exactly."

"I didn't speak with him personally, just left a message on his voice mail. I told him I'd lost my passport and had run into a bureaucratic wall trying to get a replacement. I asked him if he could look into it from his end and pull some strings."

"You didn't mention losing anything else?"

"No."

"Nothing about the traveler's checks or rental car or suitcase?"

"No. But I did give him the number here, so he could contact me if necessary."

"Someone with Porter's connections wouldn't have any trouble tracing the number to Madame d'Marchand's country estate."

Cutter downed the last of his sandwich, his jaw working on the crusty bread while afternoon sun poured in through the library windows. Light sparkled on the old, uneven glass and picked out reddish highlights in his dark hair that Mallory had never noticed before.

She wouldn't have noticed them *now* if not for the fact that he'd planted himself in the upholstered armchair set at right angles to hers, with only a round, leather-topped drum table between them. Dusting his hands on a napkin embroidered with the château's crest, he leaned forward and pinned her with a hard look.

"Did this Porter character know you were leaving for France?"

"*Everyone* at the office knew. I'd been saving and planning for it for ages. I—I almost cancelled. The arbitrator took so long to make his determination. But after the decision, I had to get away."

"Did you take your suitcase to the office at any time before you left for Dulles Airport?"

She shook her head.

"You didn't use it when you cleaned out your

desk? Or swing by to say goodbye to friends on your way to the airport?"

"I didn't have many friends left after the hearing." She covered the still-sharp sting of abandonment with a shrug. "Most of the other staffers didn't want their names associated with mine."

In fact, they'd bailed like rats fleeing a burning tenement building. All except Dillon. He'd never once compromised his loyalty to Congressman Kent, yet had offered Mallory brutally honest advice when asked and a shoulder to cry on when she'd chosen not to follow it.

He'd also, she recalled with a sudden catch to her breath, delivered the written copy of the arbitrator's decision.

"What?" Cutter asked, his gaze sharp on her face.

"I just remembered. Dillon stopped by my apartment the day before I left. Just for a few moments, to drop off some paperwork."

"Where was your suitcase?"

"I don't know." She scrubbed the heel of her hand across her forehead, struggling to recall those last, chaotic hours before she'd made her escape. "In the hall closet, I think. Or I may have carried it to the bedroom to start packing."

Cutter didn't need to hear more. Shoving out of his chair, he unclipped his cell phone and stalked to the window. Feet braced, eyes narrowed on the topiaries trimmed into fanciful shapes in the formal garden outside, he waited for Mike Callahan to acknowledge his signal.

He'd already apprised Hawkeye of the incident in the woods. His controller was working the Remy Duchette connection hard, searching for ties to the Russian. Cutter's terse call propelled him in a new and potentially explosive direction.

"Congressman Kent's senior aide?"

Looking as happy as a lion with a thorn embedded in its paw, Lightning shoved a hand through his sun-streaked mane and paced the length of his office.

"Is Slash sure about this?"

"He sounded sure to me," Mike confirmed grimly.

He'd spent most of the afternoon digging into Dillon Porter's past, present and anticipated future. In a town where who you knew carried considerably more weight than what you knew, Porter had racked up an impressive set of credentials. Seventeen years on Capitol Hill, first as a page, then an intern, then a professional staffer, had solidified his power base and made him indispensable to Congressman Kent. The fact that he'd stuck with Kent despite the legislator's rumored extracurricular activities suggested Porter was every bit as ambitious as his boss. Longevity carried its own cachet on the Hill.

"As far as I can tell," Mike informed his boss,

"Porter's clean. I've screened his financials, his contacts with registered lobbyists, every overseas junket he took with his boss. I couldn't find anything that even suggested a link to the Russian."

"So Slash thinks the data theft may be a setup, with the ultimate goal of making Kent look good for pushing for tighter controls over personal financial data?"

"He thinks it's a possibility. Kent was facing a tough challenge for reelection until the publicity resulting from the Dawes allegations painted him as a combination of unjustly accused and sly old dog."

"Knowing Kent, he parlayed both roles into a solid block of votes."

"Yeah, he did. The latest polls indicate the good ol' boys back home are solidly in his camp, but some women voters are still on the fence."

"They'd topple off quick enough if Mallory Dawes was branded a thief as well as an oversexed temptress."

"That's the working hypothesis."

Lightning shoved back his suit coat and splayed his hands on his hips. He knew as well as Mike they were walking a political minefield here. The President himself had stumped for his good pal and longtime political crony. Kent's reelection was essential to the party's midterm legislative agenda.

"What's your game plan, Hawk?"

"I'm going to get up close and personal with Porter. He doesn't know me from squat but, seasoned staffer that he is, he'll certainly know that the Military Marksmanship Association has more than ten thousand members."

Not to mention strong ties to the NRA. Mike had his opinions about gun control, which didn't necessarily coincide with those held by many of his fellow sharpshooters. He suspected Dillon Porter would see only dollar signs, however, when he linked Mike with the powerful lobbying organization.

"When are you going to establish contact?"

"Tonight. I obtained a copy of Porter's schedule. He's on the Hill until six, then he and his boss head over to a reception in honor of the new Secretary General of the World Bank."

"The World Bank?" A smile spread across Lightning's tanned face. "Well, well."

Mike matched Nick's grin. They couldn't have orchestrated the initial contact any better if they'd planned it. Adam Ridgeway, OMEGA's former director, now headed the International Monetary Fund, the operating arm of the World Bank.

Keying his intercom, Lightning summoned his executive assistant into the office.

"Do you know what your folks have on the agenda tonight, Jilly?"

"They're attending a function for the IMF. Wayland and I were supposed to go with them but he had to fly up to New York on a case. Why? What's the deal?"

"Hawk wants to connect with someone attending the soiree."

Her glance slid to Mike. He'd steeled himself for the impact of those sapphire eyes…or thought he had. Damned if it didn't hit him with the force of a 40mm rubber-tipped, riot-control bullet.

"That works out perfectly. You can be my escort."

The protest came fast and straight from his gut. "That's not a good idea."

"Sure it is. I'll be your cover, Hawk. Pick me up at seven."

Chapter 12

Mike had landed in a number of desperate situations since joining OMEGA. He couldn't ever remember feeling as hinky as he did when he pulled into the circular drive leading to the home of Gillian Ridgeway's parents, however.

Set on a wooded lot in McLean's priciest neighborhood, the two-story brick residence wore a graceful patina of age. Ivy climbed up the mellow brick. Boxwoods framed the walk to the door. Leafy maples and oaks shaded the house, molting bright layers of orange and red onto the carpet of lawn.

Mike drove up the circular drive and parked his

newly washed Blazer under the pillared portico. The scent of wood smoke filled his lungs as he mounted the front steps. One thought filled his head.

This was an assignment. Just an assignment. Gillian Ridgeway's sole purpose was to provide an entrée into her father's set. With that admonition firmly in mind, Mike rolled his shoulders to settle his tux and leaned on the doorbell.

Instant chaos erupted inside. When the door jerked open a moment later, the noise shot up another ten or twenty decibels. Maggie and Adam's teenaged son added to it by bellowing at the top of his lungs.

"Would you please *shut up!*"

The sheepdog lunging frantically in the kid's hold ignored the booming command. Tongue lolling, jowls flapping, it howled an ecstatic welcome and went up on its back legs to paw the air. Mike was treated to a hairy chest, a freckled pink belly, and a sack of balls that would have made a stallion strut. The dog was hung like a Clydesdale.

"Shut up, I said!"

Grunting with the effort, Adam Ridgeway II— Tank to everyone who knew him—hauled on the hound's collar to drag him away from the door. Dark-haired and brown-eyed like his mother, the kid gave every indication he'd soon match or exceed his father's height. Both parents lived in mortal fear of the not-very-distant day Tank would qualify for his learner's permit and hit the streets.

"Sorry 'bout that," he shouted over the still-ecstatic barking. "He's just a pup. Hasn't learned to mind real well yet."

No kidding.

"C'mon in." Planting his sneakered feet, Tank struggled to control the leaping, cavorting animal. "Been meaning to ask you. When are we going to the range?"

Thankfully, Maggie's intervention saved Mike from having to answer. Grimacing at the unceasing din, she shouted over the rail of the circular stairs.

"Tank, please! Take him outside."

Muscles straining under his maroon-and-gold Washington Redskins sweatshirt, the teen hauled the hound down the hall.

The sheepdog thought the rough handling was great fun. His claws scrabbled on the marble tiles. His tail scissored back and forth. He made repeated lunges, woofing joyously and almost knocking Tank on his butt several times before both disappeared through a side door.

"Sorry, Mike." Smiling ruefully, Maggie Sinclair, code name Chameleon, descended the rest of the stairs. "Radizwell Senior passed all of his energy and none of his manners to his numerous offspring."

The original Radizwell had exhibited even less re-

straint than his progeny, but Mike knew better than
to badmouth Maggie's beloved pet. The Hungarian
sheepdog, along with a completely obnoxious lizard
she'd picked up during a mission to Central America,
had ruled the Ridgeway household for as long as
anyone could remember.

Radizwell I had succumbed to old age after
spawning several successive generations. Terence
the Lizard was still around. Somewhere. Mike snuck
a quick look at the chandelier gracing the entryway
to make sure the evil-tempered creature wouldn't
drop down on his head before taking the hands
Maggie held out to him.

"I believe this is the first time I've seen you in a
tux, Hawkeye. You look very distinguished."

"You look pretty darn good yourself, Chameleon."

She looked better than good. Her slinky black
cocktail dress hugged a figure that could still turn
heads on any street in any city. Laugh lines fanned
the skin at the corners of her sparkling brown eyes,
but those tiny wrinkles were the only indication she
could have a daughter Gillian's age, another in
college, and a son as tall and skinny as a scarecrow.

"Jilly's almost ready. While we wait, you can brief
Adam and me on what's going down."

Tucking her arm in his, she steered Mike into the
den. Her husband was already there. As cool and
contained as Maggie was warm and spontaneous,

Adam Ridgeway looked up from the pitcher of martinis he was stirring. The gleam that lit his eyes when they skimmed over his wife was nine parts admiration, one part smug male possession.

"New dress?"

"Yes, it is. Do you like it?"

"Very much. Hello, Hawk. Martini?"

"I'll pass, thanks."

Nodding, Ridgeway passed his wife a long-stemmed glass. His gaze turned several degrees cooler when he took his own glass in hand.

"Have a seat," he invited in a tone that had Mike unconsciously squaring his shoulders, "and tell me just what kind of op you've involved my daughter in."

Mike thought the grilling by the father was bad. Making the rounds at the crowded reception with the daughter's body tucked against him was worse.

Much worse.

Gillian had dressed for the occasion in a strapless, flame silk sheath that revealed more than it concealed. Decorated with tiny beads that sparkled when they caught the light, the dress and its wearer drew every eye in the place, including Mike's.

She'd added killer three-inch stilettos in the same heart-stopping red that brought her shoulder almost level with his. She'd also swept her thick black hair up in a cluster of curls that left her neck bare except for the tiny baby hairs on her nape. Those soft, feathery curls snagged his eye every time she turned to greet another friend or acquaintance. Since she seemed to know everyone in the place, every curl had burned into Mike's brain by the time he spotted Congressman Kent.

His face animated beneath his carefully styled silver mane, the legislator was evidently relating some inside joke to a circle of cronies. When he finished, the men around him burst into raucous laughter. The lone woman in the group rolled her eyes.

Mike's nerves began to hum with something other than acute awareness of the woman on his arm. Wherever Kent was, his aide wouldn't be far away.

A moment later, Gillian leaned closer. "There's Porter," she murmured. "Second in line at the bar. Gray suit, yellow striped tie, rimless glasses."

The staffer looked a good five years older than the photo in the file Mike had pulled up. Then again, bag-carrying someone like Kent would probably add years to anyone. He was still on the job, Mike saw, working the line at the bar, engaging both the man ahead and the one behind with the skill essential to a politician's aide.

Mike bided his time until Porter had procured two drinks and delivered one to his boss. Kent took it with a careless nod and turned back to his cronies. His aide lingered at the edge of the group for a few moments before drifting toward a newscaster for one of the local affiliates.

"Okay, Jilly. Let's move in."

Cutter received Mike's update early the next morning, European time.

He was just out of the shower after a grueling dawn run. He'd needed the run to clear the cobwebs from his head. If he'd slept more than a few hours last night, he'd be surprised. His mind had gnawed restlessly at the problem of the stolen data. The rest of him had remained tense and edgy, all too aware of the fact that Mallory slept just on the other side of the connecting door.

Only two nights ago she'd flamed in his arms. He could still feel her body taut and straining under his, still hear her hoarse groan when she'd climaxed. He'd come within an ace of knocking on that door a half dozen times and trying his damndest to recover the ground he'd lost with her.

He might have done it if she hadn't been wrung dry by the incident in the woods yesterday morning, not to mention the grilling he'd put her through for most of the afternoon. After that exhausting session, she'd opted for a tray in her room and an evening on her own to try and sort through everything he'd dumped on her.

The report Cutter had just received from Mike

wasn't going to help with the sorting. Slicking back hair still damp from his shower, he rapped on the connecting door.

Mallory took her time answering. The dark smudges under her eyes suggested she hadn't slept any better than he had. Bundled from neck to ankle in a plush terrycloth robe, she read the news on his face.

"Your friends didn't find anything on Dillon, did they?"

"Not yet. They're still digging, but at this point he looks squeaky clean."

Too clean, in Mike and Cutter's collective judgment. Everyone had skeletons in their closet. Porter couldn't have spent all those years at the center of power without acquiring one or two himself.

"So we're back to square one," Mallory muttered wearily. "With me dangling at the end of your hook, bait for this Russian character."

"Let's talk about that."

When she sank onto the edge of the rumpled bed, her robe parted at the knee. Not much. Only enough to give Cutter a glimpse of smooth, bare calf. Ruthlessly, he slammed the lid on the insidious thought that Ms. Dawes was halfway to naked. He'd done some hard thinking in the dark hours before dawn.

"I think it's time to switch gears. That incident yesterday morning scared the crap out of me." Cutter wasn't going to forget seeing her go down any time soon. "I don't want you hurt, Mallory."

The admission elicited a small huff. "I'm not real thrilled at the prospect, either."

"If Remy Duchette's attack *was* linked to an attempt to retrieve the disk, whoever wants the data is getting both frustrated and desperate. That makes him dangerous. We need to send him a signal, make it clear you don't have the CD."

"How do you plan to accomplish that?"

"We'll use the media."

"Please tell me you're kidding!"

"I know, I know. They ate you alive at home. With a few words dropped in the right ears, they'll do the same here."

Cutter hated the idea of feeding her to the sharks again but didn't see any other option at this point.

"We'll put you in front of the cameras. Have you relate your sad tale of the riptide carrying off your rental. You'll stress that you lost everything, including your suitcase and all its contents. Then I put you on a plane back to the States and hang around Mont St. Michel to see if someone tries to recover the disk."

Manfully, he kept his gaze on her face while she fiddled with the flap of her robe and mulled over his plan. He could see it didn't thrill her.

"I know you came to France to escape the media, Mallory. I don't like asking you to put yourself out there again, but it's the only way I could think of to throw any would-be predators off your scent."

"I can handle the media."

"What the problem, then?"

Dammit, he wished she'd stop playing with the flap of her robe. The thick fabric bunched, was smoothed flat, bunched again. Cutter was starting to sweat when she finally voiced her objections to his plan.

"I skipped lunch for almost a year to save for this trip. It started as a vacation, but morphed into my escape from the ugliness at home. I'm not ready to wade back into the mess yet."

"I understand. I do."

He'd watched her unfold during those hours in the sun, when they'd sipped Calvados and picnicked with Monsieur Villieu and his wife under the apple trees. Warm color had dusted her cheeks. Laughter had sparkled in her eyes. Now the shadows were back, and it ate at Cutter's insides that he'd been the one to put them there.

"You can't just pick up your vacation where you left off," he said quietly. "Not while whoever put that disk in your suitcase thinks you might still have it."

Chewing on her lower lip, she smoothed the terrycloth several more times.

"Okay," she said after a moment, "here's *my* plan. We orchestrate the media blitz as you suggest. I admit

I lost everything. Let the world know my suitcase went to sea with my rental car. Then, after we've thrown whoever wants the disk off my scent, as you so delicately put it, I go my way and you go yours."

"No good."

The swift, uncompromising negative took her aback. "Why not?"

"I can't let you wander around the countryside on your own."

"Let?" she echoed, stiffening.

"I'll rephrase that. I don't want you wandering around France on your own. There's no guarantee this media ploy will work. Word that you don't have the disk in your possession might not reach the right people. Or they may not believe it. You could still be a target, Mallory. I can't… I don't want to take that risk."

"If they think I still have the data, I wouldn't be any safer at home than I am here."

Yes, she would. Cutter had requested 24/7 surveillance for Mallory and her apartment. She wouldn't take a step without someone right there, behind or beside her.

He couldn't tell her about the tag, however. Not yet. *He* was convinced she hadn't stolen the data but until he proved it, she'd remain under watchful eyes.

"We don't have to decide this right now," he said with a shrug that suggested her imminent return to the States wasn't a done deal. "Let me dangle the bait, see if we can gin up some media interest. You may be ready to go home after dealing with them."

"After they start feasting on my flesh again, you mean. You're probably right."

Her shoulders slumped under the robe. He could almost hear her desperate hopes for obscurity crash down around her.

"Okay," she conceded after a long silence, "we'll play it your way."

Knowing that his mission took precedence over her vacation plans didn't stop Cutter from feeling like a total heel.

"You'll have other opportunities to wander through the countryside, Mallory. I promise."

Her chin lifted. A healthy anger leapt back into her eyes. "I don't want your sympathy, Smith, and I sure as hell don't trust your promises."

She pushed off the bed, dismissing him with an imperious, impatient flap of her hand.

"Go do whatever you need to do. I'll start pulling on my body armor. Again."

Cutter's strategy worked exactly as planned.

Ordinarily, a botched robbery and the death of a small-time local hood like Remy Duchette wouldn't stir much interest outside the immediate vicinity. The fact that Duchette had attempted to rob a guest of a famous Paris designer upped the interest considerably. All it took was one call from Hawk to make sure the word leaked to the right ears.

The local stations began calling the château soon after lunch. Following the agreed-on game plan, Mallory refused to grant any interviews. She knew all too well there was nothing like a reluctant subject to rouse the media's hunting instincts.

Sure enough, by the time the early-evening news hit the airwaves, reporters had linked Mallory to the woman who'd made so many headlines back in the States. A stringer for Reuters had also connected her to the police report filed by the gendarme at Mont St. Michel. The phone rang incessantly from then on.

Every major network carried the story on the late-night news. Writhing inside, Mallory huddled in a corner of the sofa in the downstairs sitting room and watched replays of her exit from the Rayburn Congressional Office Building after the arbitrator's ruling that there was insufficient evidence to support her allegation of sexual harassment. Sunglasses shielded her eyes, but her rigid shoulders and tight jaw telegraphed her disgust at the decision. The networks followed her terse replies of "No comment" with excerpts of a news conference held by a smug, vindicated Ashton Kent.

"Bastard," Cutter muttered as the phone shrilled yet again.

As instructed, Gilbért took names and numbers and advised that Mademoiselle Dawes would return the call should she decide to speak about her recent unfortunate experiences. When he delivered the message to the sitting room, Cutter hit the remote to mute the TV.

"We've stirred the pot enough. Please call them back and tell them Ms. Dawes will speak to the press tomorrow at eleven."

"Yes, of course."

"We'll leave for Paris shortly after that. Ms. Dawes wishes to return to the States. I'm putting her on a plane tomorrow afternoon."

"Most understandable." The butler's glance shifted to Mallory. "I am so sorry, mademoiselle, that you will take home such unpleasant memories of your visit to Normandy."

"They're not all unpleasant." She dredged up a smile. "I stayed in this beautiful château, had my first taste of Calvados and sampled Madame Picard's *veau de la Normandie*. Those memories I'll cherish."

There were others, ones she wasn't so sure about. Like the memory of Gilbért crumpling to the ground and skinny, spike-haired Remy Duchette pointing his pistol at her middle. And Cutter…

She didn't look at him. She couldn't. She knew darn well her memories of him would remain as confused as the emotions he roused in her. Worse, she suspected the remembered feel of his mouth and hands and sleek, powerful body surging into hers would blot out her anger at his lies and deception. Eventually.

But she wasn't there yet. She wasn't anywhere near there.

"You must come again," Gilbért pleaded. "Perhaps in the spring, when the apple and pear trees bloom. They shed their petals and cover the earth like snow."

"Perhaps I will."

When he departed the sitting room, Mallory decided to do the same.

"I'm going upstairs. It's been a long day."

Long and draining and filled with mounting dread over the ordeal she'd face tomorrow. She refused to link that hollow feeling in the pit of her stomach to the fact that she'd say goodbye to Cutter shortly after the news conference.

He'd lied to her since day one, for pity's sake! She should be overjoyed to put an ocean between them.

"I'll see you in the morning."

Cutter nodded. Much as he ached to take her in his arms and kiss away her weariness, it was better this way. She'd be on her way home tomorrow, out of his reach until he wrapped up this op.

Now if only he could get her out of his head.

He stayed downstairs until well past midnight. No light showed under the connecting door when he let himself into his suite. Wavering between relief and regret, Cutter stripped down to his shorts, slid between the sheets, and locked his hands under his head.

The sea murmured restlessly outside. Inside, the castle settled into sleepy semisilence. The wind whistled down stone chimneys. An occasional water pipe pinged. The clock on the mantel bonged the quarter hour, then the half.

Cutter had resigned himself to another long night when one sound separated itself from the rest. His glance zinged to the connecting door. Not so much as a sliver of light showed under the sill.

He picked up another soft creak. Two seconds later he was out of bed and dragging on his slacks. His head told him that it was probably Gilbért or his wife coming up the stairs with such a stealthy tread, trying not to disturb the guests. His gut said different. Sliding his Glock from its holder, he put his back to the wall and cracked the bedroom door.

A shadow slid over the top step. Elongated. Danced along the darkened hallway.

The shape was stretched and distorted. Cutter could see it belonged to neither Picard. Eyes narrowed, blood pumping, he thumbed the Glock's safety but didn't shove through the door until a loud clatter shattered the silence.

Chapter 13

"Dammit!"

As if tripping over a creaking stair wasn't bad enough, Mallory hit the oak railing on her way down and landed on her butt with a jarring thud.

Her late-night snack flew off the plate she'd carried up with her. The cheese slices she'd cut from the towel-wrapped wheel Madame Picard had left out landed in her lap. The round-bladed knife she'd brought to spread it with scattered with a half dozen or so crackers. A ripe, juicy apple bounced down the stair, ponging noisily on each tread.

Mallory managed to catch the pear before it

suffered a similar fate, then lost her grip on it when a nasty snarl came out of the darkness behind her.

"What the hell are you doing, creeping around at this time of night?"

"Me!" Her heart pinging, she threw an indignant glance over her shoulder at the half-naked male who materialized out of the shadows. "You just took five years off my life…and no doubt bruised my pear!"

"Was that what went airborne?" The taut set to his shoulders relaxed. "Hang loose, I'll retrieve it for you."

First he detoured to the lacquered chest at the top of the stairs and deposited an object that gleamed dully in the faint light. Mallory's pulse bumped when she realized he'd come into the hall armed.

"There's an apple down there somewhere, too."

He descended the stairs like a sleek jungle cat. His bare feet didn't raise so much as a creak on the stairs that had protested *her* weight. The dim light made a moonscape of his back and shoulders and deepened the gap that appeared between his low-riding slacks and the small of his back when he stooped to retrieve the runaway fruit.

"What did you do?" he asked, dropping down to sit knee-to-knee with her on the step. "Raid the fridge?"

"The kitchen table. Madame Picard left a platter of goodies out."

"I'm going to miss that woman." Cutter eyed the recovered stash hopefully. "Got enough for two?"

"If you don't mind broken crackers and slightly dented fruit."

"Feed me, woman."

So much had happened since Mallory boarded the plane to Paris that she would have sworn she was beyond being surprised by anything. Yet here she was, huddled on the stairs of a centuries-old château in a borrowed bathrobe with a man who'd lied to her from their first meeting. What surprised her even more was that she was in no hurry to end their late night tête-à-tête.

Frowning, she tried to rekindle her earlier anger. She was still seriously ticked at Cutter. Not to mention hurt that he'd used her as a pawn in his dangerous game. So why was she spreading cheese flavored with crunchy hickory nuts for him?

Because she was leaving tomorrow, the nasty voice of reality mocked. Leaving France. Leaving Yvette d'Marchand's château. Leaving him. Her dream-vacation-that-never-quite-was would be over. All she had left of it was a few more hours and this temporary, fragile truce with Cutter.

Refusing to dwell on the grim reality of going home to hunt for a job and an employer who'd hire someone who'd made allegations against her previous boss, she spread a cracker with the soft, creamy cheese.

"Here."

Cutter popped the cracker into his mouth. While he crunched down, Mallory cut and peeled a slice of pear with the blunt-tipped knife. The fruit was firm and succulent. Juice dribbled onto her palm with each cut.

She gave Cutter the first bite and nibbled on the second. He munched contentedly, his elbows resting on the stair behind him. Mallory licked the juice from her fingers and let her glance slide along his outstretched length.

Shadows played across his flat belly and sculpted the planes of his chest. The air in the drafty hall was cool enough to make her grateful for the fluffy robe, but Cutter seemed impervious to the chill.

"I've arranged to have someone meet you at the airport in D.C.," he told her, breaking the stillness.

"Why?"

"I thought you might need a friend."

"A friend? Or a watchdog?"

"Both," he admitted without a trace of apology. "His name is Mike Callahan. He'll keep you safe until I wrap things up over here."

She didn't particularly care for the idea that she had to be "kept" by anyone, but the incident in the woods had shaken her more than she was ready to admit.

"What happens when you wrap things up?" she asked. "You resume watchdog duties yourself?"

"If we haven't nailed whoever slipped that disk into your suitcase."

"And if you have?"

"Then I'm hoping you might still want a friend."

She didn't have many of those left, Mallory acknowledged silently. Yet the idea of being Cutter's pal turned the sweet taste of pear sour and left an empty feeling in the pit of her stomach.

She was still trying to deal with the hollow sensation when he levered upright. His shoulder nudging hers, he angled around and removed the knife from her sticky hands.

"Just a precaution," he said when she raised a brow. "The thing is, I'd like to be more than friends. And I really want to kiss you right now."

"We both know that's not a good idea."

"Granted. That doesn't make the want go away."

He cupped her cheek. His palm was warm against her skin, his breath a soft wash that mingled with hers. Mere inches separated them. Tomorrow, it would be an ocean. After that, who knew?

Maybe that was why Mallory didn't pull back when he leaned in, why her head tilted and her lids drifted down. Tomorrow, she decided as his lips brushed hers, would just have to take care of itself.

His mouth moved over hers, tasting, tempting. Heat stirred in her veins. The muscles low in her belly clenched. Then Cutter slid his palm from her cheek to her nape, anchoring her head, and molded his mouth to hers.

The half-eaten pear rolled off Mallory's lap and thumped down the stairs again. The broken crackers scattered. She had no idea where the cheese slices went and didn't care. Her body eager, her hands greedy, she matched him move for move.

Within moments she was semiprone on the wide wooden stairs. His free hand yanked at the tie to her robe. The lapels parted, exposing her to chill air and Cutter's smooth, hot flesh.

She could feel him hard and straining against her hip. Wiggling a little, she added to the pressure on his fly. The sensual friction soon had him grunting and dragging his mouth from hers.

"If we're going to stop," he rasped, "it had better be now."

Her blood pumped in heavy spurts. Desire raced like liquid fire through her veins. She wanted him naked and locked between her thighs.

"If we *don't* stop, we need to change positions. Or geography. This stair tread is putting a permanent dent in my spine."

"That, Ms. Dawes, is easily remedied."

He scooped her up and took the stairs two at a time, reminding Mallory of that powerful scene from *Gone with the Wind.* Except she wasn't Vivien Leigh, fighting him every step of the way and her Clark

Gable retained presence of mind enough to retrieve his gun before striding down the hall toward his half-open bedroom door.

The hard butt of the pistol handle against her hip sobered Mallory and reminded her again why Cutter was here...until he kicked the door shut and carried her to bed in the finest Rhett Butler style.

The scent of fresh-baked croissants pulled Mallory from total unconsciousness. Lifting her face from the satin-covered pillow, she blinked owlishly and followed the general direction of her nose until her sleepy gaze collided with Cutter's.

"'Bout time you woke up."

He, obviously, had been up for some time. His jogging suit lay over the arm of the chair. Muddy sneakers sat on the floor beside it. He must have gotten in an early run, showered and changed while she remained dead to the world.

As he deposited a tray on the bedside table, the tang of his aftershave teased Mallory's nostrils and vied for supremacy with the yeasty scent of the rolls. Wiggling upright, she shoved her hair out of her eyes and helped herself.

"What time is it?" she asked around a flaky mouthful.

"Almost ten."

"Ten!" The croissant lodged partway down her

throat. With a painful gulp, she swallowed the half-chewed bite. "I'm supposed to go in front of the cameras at eleven! Why did you let me sleep?"

"You told me to. Remember?"

Now she did. She'd mumbled the order sometime after her second out-of-body experience. Or was it her third? As best as Mallory could recall, every inch of her had shivered with delight and exhaustion.

Those emotions contrasted starkly with the ones that crept over her now. The prospect of facing a barrage of reporters stripped away all trace of morning-after joy. Her arms as heavy as lead, she dropped the roll back onto the tray.

"I'd better get dressed. Think I could fit into one of those suits of armor in the hall?"

Cutter was well aware of her reluctance to put herself out there again, but her attempt at levity brought home just how deeply she dreaded it. Nudging her aside, he sat on the edge of the mattress.

"I'll be right there with you."

"That's another thing. How do I explain you?" Frowning, she plucked at the bedcovers. "What's our story, Cutter? Do we have a history, or are you just one more notch on my bedpost?"

"If the subject comes up…"

"Trust me," she said bitterly, "it will."

"…we tell them we met in France, fell for each other and aren't worried about the past, only the future."

"They won't buy it." Dragging the covers with her, she slumped against the padded headboard. "We've known each other less than a week. Hardly long enough to fall in love."

For her, maybe. Cutter wasn't sure when he'd taken the plunge.

He suspected it was there in Monsieur Villieu's orchard, with the sunlight on her face and her laughter as potent as the apple brandy. Whenever it had happened, he knew he wanted her safe and this op over more than he'd ever wanted anything. Or anyone.

He'd loved only once before, or thought he had. Jogging along the mist-shrouded cliffs this morning he'd realized that whatever he'd felt for Eva Hendricks didn't come close to the protective and fiercely primitive instincts Mallory Dawes roused in him.

Which was only one of the reasons he'd made a quick trip into town after his run. The other was the horde that would descend on her in less than an hour.

"Maybe this will convince the reporters we're serious."

He positioned the jeweler's box on the tray beside the basket of croissants. Her brow snapping into a line, she stared at the blue velvet box suspiciously.

"What's that?"

"Your protective armor."

The ring was an antique, its square-cut diamond mounted on a wide, white-gold filigree band that looked like old Victorian lace. Smaller baguettes circled the central stone in a delicate swirl.

"There was only one jeweler in town, so I didn't have much of a selection to choose from."

With Mallory watching in slack-jawed surprise, Cutter slipped the ring out of the box and onto her finger. The band was a little loose. He'd had to guess at the size.

"You didn't have to do this," she said, still frowning.

"Yeah, I did."

Feeling as though the moment required a more extravagant gesture, Cutter raised her hand and dropped a kiss on her fingers.

"If you look at the filigree closely, you'll see it's carved in the shape of vines and fruit. Apropos, wouldn't you say?"

She studied it in silence for several moments before lifting her gaze to his. "It's beautiful, Cutter, and will certainly add credibility to our story. I'll give it back to you right after the press conference."

"The ring is yours, Mallory. A souvenir of your trip to France."

Ignoring her protests, he dropped another kiss on her hand and pushed off the bed.

"You'd better get dressed. A couple of TV crews have already arrived to set up their equipment."

* * *

For long moments after the door closed behind Cutter, Mallory simply sat amid the rumpled covers and stared at the white-gold band.

If she'd searched every store in Paris, she couldn't have found a ring that delighted her more. She loved the antique look to it, with the graceful swirl of baguettes anchoring the center stone. But it was the delicate filigree band that filled her heart with a bittersweet ache.

The intricate vines, the tiny leaves, the fruit—as Cutter said, so very apropos of Normandy and the short time they'd spent here. She couldn't believe he'd gone to so much trouble to erect the facade they'd present to the media, or that he'd found such a perfect vehicle to do it.

Then presented it to her here, she thought on a sigh. Amid the rumpled covers, with her hair a tangled mess and her eyes still gritty from sleep. The man needed to work on his timing, if not his technique. Even a fake engagement warranted brushed hair and teeth. With another sigh, she threw off the covers and padded to the bathroom.

She left the blue bedroom thirty minutes later. Rather than appear in borrowed feathers, she wore the jeans, white blouse, and navy blazer she'd had on when she arrived in France. Luckily, the ever efficient

Madame Picard had restored them to pristine neatness. The ring sparkling on her left hand demanded something better than rubber-soled mocs, however. Making her final appearance in a pair of Yvette d'Marchand's exclusive designs, Mallory descended the grand staircase.

A brief smile settled around her heart as she remembered going *up* the stairs the night before, but it died when she spotted the equipment cases scattered across the black-and-white tiles of the entry hall. A babble of voices rose from the library, punctuated by intermittent flashes as the camera crews tested their strobes.

Dread coiled and writhed like a living thing in Mallory's stomach. Dragging in quick, shallow breaths, she forced herself to continue down the stairs.

"Elle est là!"

She had no trouble translating the excited exclamation. Her throat closing, she heard the others pick up the cry.

"There she is!"

"It's her!

Like baying hounds on the trail of a fox, a dozen or so reporters spilled out of the library into the hall. Mallory froze as still cameras flashed, blinding her with a barrage of white light. The questions flew fast and furious until Cutter's deep voice sliced through the din.

"Ms. Dawes will be more than happy to answer your questions, but not here in the hall."

Tall and authoritative, his scars a deliberate and very visible warning that he wasn't a man to be taken lightly, he mounted the stairs and tucked Mallory's hand in his arm. She managed not to clutch at his sleeve like a frightened child, but her knees felt like the custard filling in one of Madame Picard's pastries as they waded into the fray.

"Ladies. Gentlemen," Cutter said calmly. "In the library, as agreed."

A battery of TV cameras, some mounted on tripods, some shoulder-held, captured their entrance. Cutter positioned Mallory in front of the gilt-trimmed desk and slipped a lover-like arm around her waist. The modernistic portrait in its lighted alcove formed a dramatic backdrop. The oriental carpet provided a tapestry of jeweled colors at their feet.

Mallory tried not to wince as the klieg lights came on, adding their glare to the flashes from the still cameras. Boom mikes poked over the heads of reporters who machine-gunned the questions at her.

"Mademoiselle Dawes, how do you come to be at Yvette d'Marchand's château?"

"Did you know Remy Duchette?"

"What happened at Mont St. Michel that caused you to miss the turn of the tide?"

"Have you been in contact with Congressman Kent during your time in France?"

"Is Monsieur Smith your latest lover?"

Mallory knifed the reporter who'd shouted the last question with an icy glare. Before she could respond, however, Cutter drew her closer within the circle of his arm.

"Not her latest," he corrected.

He smiled at her, playing to the audience yet somehow giving her the sense that his words were for her alone.

"Her last."

Okay, this was only pretend. A very skillful act for the cameras. Even if it hadn't been, Mallory knew better than to believe Cutter's smooth lies. That didn't prevent a raw, scratchy lump the size of the Eiffel Tower from clogging her throat.

Chapter 14

If Cutter hadn't already suspected he was in over his head where Mallory Dawes was concerned, watching her perform for the cameras would have done the trick.

He knew how much she'd dreaded the inquisition. Felt her flinch as the questions went from personal and prying to just plain vicious. Chin high, she responded to those questions she chose to while ignoring the rest.

Cutter deflected as many of the barbs as he could by referring all inquiries about Remy Duchette to the local police. He also played the new man in Mallory's life to the hilt, staking his claim with every possessive smile. Yet not even this very public branding could protect her from increasingly salacious questions about her alleged affair with Congressman Kent. Finally, he'd had enough.

"That's it," he said abruptly, fighting hard to keep his anger in check. "Ms. Dawes and I need to leave for the airport. Gilbért will show you out."

Leaving the gaggle to pack up their gear under the butler's watchful eye, Cutter steered Mallory into the hall. She kept her arm tucked in his and a smile pasted on her face as they mounted the stairs. Once out of camera reach, though, she wilted right before his eyes.

"You okay?"

"Yes." A shudder rippled through her slender frame. "I know they're only doing their job. They just…kind of get to me."

"You didn't let it show."

"You think?" She gave a small laugh. "I must be getting better at this. God knows I've had plenty of practice. When do you want to leave?"

"As soon as you get your things together."

This time the laugh was a little more genuine. "That won't take long."

"Knock on the connecting door when you're ready."

Mallory entered the room she'd come to think of as her own and rested her shoulder blades against the door. The circus downstairs had drained and humiliated her, but she regretted more the fact that her stay in this elegant suite with its shimmering azure drapes and four-poster bed was over. That, and the knowledge she would soon say goodbye to Cutter.

She wanted to believe his promise to follow her home as soon as he could. Ached to believe the hours they'd spent locked in each other's arms last night had seared him as much as they had her. Despite his lies and elaborate deceptions, everything inside her wanted to trust him.

Catching her lower lip between her teeth, she raised her left hand. Cutter had insisted she keep the ring. As a souvenir. Curling her hand into a fist, Mallory tilted it this way and that, setting off colorful sparks as the diamonds caught the light.

Her hand stilled. The rainbow of colors dimmed. Sighing, she went to gather her few things.

"You must come again," Gilbért pronounced on the steps leading to the cobbled courtyard. His wife endorsed that with a vigorous bob of her head.

"I cook for you," she promised. "Pears *en croute*, yes? With buttered brandy sauce."

That alone was enough to make Mallory wish she had more to give them as a parting gift than the bottle of Calvados from Monsieur Villieu's private stock.

They, in turn, presented a hibiscus-colored shopping bag with gold cord handles and an instantly recognizable logo. A shoebox sat inside the bag.

"These are from madame's spring collection," Gilbért said. "She hopes you will accept them with her apologies that you should come to harm while a guest in her home."

Lust and guilt battled for Mallory's soul. "I can't accept such an expensive gift."

"But you must," the butler insisted, pressing the bag into her hands. "Madame wishes you to have them."

She suspected it was Gilbért and his wife who wanted her to return home with something other than a mixed bag of memories and the bruises she'd collected from Remy.

"Thank you." Going up on tiptoe, she kissed his weathered cheeks. "And you, Madame Picard."

"*Au revoir,* mademoiselle, *et bonne chance.*"

Cutter stowed his carryall and the small tote holding the items Mallory had purchased in town in the backseat of his rental car. After shaking hands with Gilbért and dropping kisses on Madame Picard's apple-red cheeks, he settled Mallory in the passenger seat and slid behind the wheel. She twisted around to wave as the car rattled through the arched passageway. Once they were on the sweeping drive, the château dwindled to a fanciful, turreted image in the side mirror.

Mallory said little during the long drive to the airport on the outskirts of Paris. Cutter, by contrast, was a whirlwind of activity. Dividing his attention between the traffic ahead and the road behind, he eliminated every obstacle Mallory had been tripping over for the past week. By the time they nosed into the bumper-to-bumper traffic on the airport loop, he had everything arranged.

"Your temporary passport was delivered to the Delta Business Class reservations desk. It's waiting for you with your ticket."

"Okay."

"There's an American Express kiosk inside the terminal. They'll reissue your traveler's checks."

Horns blared as he cut the wheel and pulled onto the ramp for short-term parking.

"The rental-car company wants you to sign a release of liability, but you can take care of that when you get home. Mike Callahan will be at the gate when you deplane. Look for a big bear of a man, almost as ugly as I am."

She smiled dutifully at the sally. She could think of a whole slew of adjectives to describe Cutter Smith. *Ugly* wasn't one of them.

Scarred, yes. *Rough around the edges,* definitely. Yet capable of such incredible tenderness that Mallory's heart ached with the memory of it. Wrenching her gaze from his profile, she let it drop to the filigree band on her finger.

"Mike will be wearing a windbreaker with the

insignia of the Military Marksmanship Association
on the pocket. Rifles crossed over a bull's-eye." He
shot her a quick look. "Got that?"

"Rifles crossed over a bull's-eye. Got it."

The short-term parking garage was jammed, but
Cutter lucked out and found a slot only a few yards from
the second-story walkway to the departure terminal.

He carried the tote, Mallory the brightly colored
shopping bag. She couldn't believe she'd crossed
this same walkway less than a week ago, blithely
unaware she was being stalked by the man at her side.
Her little burst of resentment quickly fizzled. Too
much had happened, and her feelings for Cutter were
too confused, to work up much of a mad at this point.

The replacement passport was waiting at the Delta
Business Class desk, as promised, along with a
revised return ticket.

"We bumped you up to Business Class," the
helpful clerk advised after issuing a boarding pass.
"Do you have any luggage to check?"

With a strangled laugh, Mallory shook her head.
"Not this time."

"Very well. Your aircraft will begin boarding at
Gate 42B in approximately one hour. Have a good
flight home, Mademoiselle Dawes."

"Was Business Class your doing?" she asked as
Cutter took her arm to weave a path through the
throngs of travelers toward the shops at the end of the

concourse. The distinctive blue-and-white sign above the American Express kiosk stood out like a beacon.

"I figured you deserved at least that much of a break after…"

He broke off, his grip tightening. When his eyes narrowed on something beyond her, Mallory twisted around to see what had snared his attention. Shock rippled through her as she spotted her face staring back at her from the giant TV screen mounted above the heads of the travelers.

There she was, backdropped against the stark, modernistic portrait in Madame d'Marchand's library. Same shoulder-length blond bob. Same wary brown eyes. Same navy blazer. The commentary was in French and muffled by the noise in the terminal but Mallory got the gist of it when the screen split to display Congressman Kent's image alongside hers. A moment later, both were replaced by a mug shot of Remy Duchette.

"Didn't take long for them to get the footage on-air," she commented, her throat tight.

"That was the idea," Cutter reminded her. "The story's probably been running every half hour since the interview."

"Hold this a moment, would you?"

Passing him the shopping bag, she fumbled in her purse for her sunglasses. She hadn't hidden behind them in days. Something inside her died a little at having to resort to their shield again.

The clerk in the American Express kiosk responded with the same efficiency as the airline representative. It was obvious he'd seen the news flash. Curiosity prompted several sidelong glances, but he refrained from comment except to request Mallory's signature in several places. She walked out of the kiosk fifteen minutes later with money in her purse for the first time since the day she'd arrived.

"Wonder what happened to the flag on my accounts?" she drawled while she and Cutter once again threaded through the crowds.

"Beats me."

His totally fake innocence scored a huff from Mallory. A moment later, she bumped to a stop.

"Look."

Her pointing finger drew his attention to a display of plastic snow globes in the window of a souvenir shop. Amid the bubble-encased Eiffel Towers and Arc de Triomphes was the cathedral of Mont St. Michel, rising from a blue plastic sea.

"I *have* to get one of those."

She found a boxed globe easily enough, but the long line at the register moved at a snail's pace. The business with American Express had eaten a chunk out of her hour prior to boarding. The long lines at security would devour the rest. Disappointed, Mallory put the globe back on the shelf.

"I'll pick one up after I see you aboard the plane,"

Cutter promised. "Do you need to make a pit stop before we hit security?"

"I'm okay."

She assumed they'd say goodbye at the security checkpoint, since only ticketed passengers were allowed beyond. Cutter, evidently, had other plans.

When they approached the checkpoint, he produced an ID and an official-looking document and pulled one of the security inspectors aside. That worthy individual skimmed the paperwork, pursed his lips and gestured to a fellow officer. Mallory caught only snatches of the intense conversations that ensued, but picked up several references to Interpol. Cutter finally broke away and strode back to her.

"Seems to be a problem here with my permit to carry concealed," he said, his voice low and for her ears only.

"You're armed?"

His hooked brow made her realize how stupid that sounded. Of course, he had his gun strapped to his ankle. This was his job. *She* was his job.

"I need to talk to the director of security," Cutter told her. "Wait for me here. Right here."

"It's getting close to boarding time."

"I'll square this away as quickly as I can. If I'm not back in ten minutes, go on through. I'll meet you at the gate. If they call your flight, get on board. You know what to do when you deplane."

She covered her sudden, sinking sensation with a brisk nod. "Look for Mike Callahan. Big. Ugly. Crossed rifles. Bull's-eye."

"Be sure to tell him about the ugly part."

"I will."

"Just in case, you'd better take this with you."

She assumed he was referring to the tote he'd carried through the terminal with her. Before she could reach for it, however, he wrapped his hands around her upper arms and pulled her forward for a long, hard kiss.

"Wait here," he growled, when he released her. "Ten minutes."

Cutter stalked back to the two security officials, torn between the need to get Mallory on that plane and the equally fierce need to keep her in his sight until she was aboard.

It took one call to Interpol and another to OMEGA to untangle the confusion over the permit. By Cutter's watch, he was back at the security checkpoint in nine and a half minutes. His brows slashing together, he skimmed the entire vicinity. Mallory wasn't anywhere in sight.

Spotting the official who'd stopped him in languid conversation with another employee, he thrust through the crowd. "The woman I was with," he bit out. "The blonde. Did she pass through security?"

"No, monsieur. She waits for you, then goes back to the concourse."

"Dammit!"

If Mallory had decided to use the delay to buy that snow globe, Cutter would rip her a new one.

"She comes back soon," the inspector added helpfully. "I hear her tell her friend she has not much time."

"What friend?"

"The woman who greets her. She carries a shopping bag, too. The same as mademoiselle's."

Cutter whirled, his mind racing. Who the hell had Mallory hooked up with? A fellow shoe addict? A representative of Yvette d'Marchand, bearing more gifts? Yvette herself, driven by curiosity about the houseguest who'd generated such a spate of publicity?

Or someone else? Someone who'd tried to use Mallory's connection to d'Marchand once before to get to her?

His stomach clenching, Cutter barged around clumps of travelers and swept through the gift shop on the run. Customers scattered. The clerk at the register shouted a protest. A string of muttered curses followed him out again.

His heart jackhammered against his ribs when he burst onto the cavernous concourse and skidded to a stop. He spun left, searching the crowd, praying for a glimpse of Mallory's navy blazer or pale gold hair.

He swung to the right and had started for the Delta

reservation counter when he spotted her through the glass windows. She was on the walkway leading to the parking garage, arm-in-arm with a slender brunette in designer jeans and a mink vest. They moved at a good clip but both, he saw with a jolt of disbelief, were laughing.

Cutter's step slowed. Ice coated his veins. The noisy terminal faded, replaced in his frozen mind by a dark, silent munitions warehouse.

Eva had left an urgent message for Cutter to meet her there. Said she'd put the squeeze on one of her sources and learned that the stolen munitions they'd been tracking were in a crate hidden inside the warehouse. He'd slipped over the wall an hour early, intending to reconnoiter. A half dozen yards from the entrance to the warehouse he'd picked up the murmur of voices…accompanied by the unmistakable timbre of Eva's low, rippling laugh. Then a truck had rumbled up, the warehouse doors opened and she'd walked into the spear of headlights.

Cutter never knew which of them fired the shot that ignited the munitions stored inside the warehouse. He wasn't even sure she'd screamed his name before the explosion knocked him on his ass and the flames consumed him.

Now, with the echo of her laughter ringing in his ears, the agony of those months in the burn ward gripped Cutter like a vise. Needles of pain seemed to shoot through his jaw and neck. He couldn't breathe, couldn't move, couldn't force any thought through his frozen mind except one. Mallory was walking away from him. Arm in arm with a stranger. Laughing.

"Keep walking."

The woman in the mink vest reinforced the soft command by digging her gun in deeper.

"I'm telling you the truth," Mallory said desperately. "I don't have the damned disk."

"So you wish me to believe." The brunette's smile belied the menace in her eyes. "I saw your performance on TV. It was worthy of the Bolshoi. How fortunate that I was in Paris and could intercept you at the airport."

Her English was as flawless as her face, but the reference to the Bolshoi generated the sickening suspicion that she worked for the nameless, faceless Russian Cutter was after.

"I wasn't performing! I *did* lose my suitcase to the riptide at Mont St. Michel. I *am* going home."

"You've caused me considerable inconvenience, Ms. Dawes. Please don't try my patience further. Walk." The gun gouged into her ribs. "And smile for these nice people."

Mallory stretched her lips at the travelers hurrying in the opposite direction, but inside she screamed with frustration and fear and a fast-growing fury.

She'd been standing less than a half dozen yards from the security checkpoint when this svelte brunette had sauntered by. Catching sight of the gold-embossed shopping bag, the woman held up a similar one of her own and strolled over. To talk shoes, Mallory assumed. The next thing she knew, she had a gun sticking in her side and was being hustled toward the exit.

She could guess what Cutter would think when he discovered she'd skipped. He'd believe she knew about the disk all along, that she grabbed this opportunity to escape.

The brunette must have been reading her mind. "This man you were with. The one you kissed. Does he know about the disk?"

She was damned if she'd tell the woman anything. "No."

"So it is just you and your Congressman Kent who make this deal?"

"*Kent?*" Mallory stumbled, numb with shock. "Are you saying *Kent* burned that data to disk?"

"Do you think you're the only woman he pawed?" Amusement laced the reply. "He is a pig, that one, and easily led by his dick. And now he pays dearly for his pleasure." Satisfaction thrummed through her voice. "The data he pulled off your computer is worth millions. My best haul to date."

Reeling, Mallory realized she wasn't dealing

Chapter 15

Mike Callahan was waiting when Mallory and Cutter deplaned at Dulles an exhausting thirty-six hours later.

They'd spent most of those hours holed up at Interpol. While Mallory watched through a one-way mirror, Cutter and several very skilled interrogators grilled the woman they soon identified as Catherine Halston, aka Fatima Allende, aka Irina Petrov.

Cool and unruffled, Petrov had admitted to a half dozen other aliases. In exchange for the promise of a reduced sentence, she also offered to provide video of her afternoon trysts with Ashton Kent in a posh D.C. hotel—including segments detailing his reluctant agreement to provide identity data as the price for keeping silent about his illicit liaison.

After the session at Interpol, Mallory had contrived a quick visit to Yvette d'Marchand's Paris boutique to thank the designer in person for the shoes now adorning her feet. Brilliant aquamarine crystals studded the thick wedge soles and decorated the straps that crisscrossed over her feet, wrapped around her ankles, and tied midway up her calf.

The glittering three-inch platforms gave her the necessary boost to meet Mike Callahan eye to eye. Almost. He was as tall and tough-looking as Cutter had indicated, but nowhere near as ugly. When she told him so, he shot his fellow agent a dry look.

"Thanks, Slash."

"I calls 'em as I sees 'em, Hawk."

Cutter used the drive in from Dulles to provide an update on the results of the interrogation. Callahan, in turn, shared the dossier he'd compiled on each of the Russian's various aliases.

"The woman got around. Remember the op that came apart on us in Hong Kong?"

Cutter let out a low whistle. "That was her?"

"That was her."

The thick file Callahan passed over his shoulder prompted a question from Mallory.

"Do you have a copy of the dossier you compiled on me?"

"I don't know." He glanced in the rearview mirror. "Do I?"

"You might as well show her," Cutter said. "I've already taken a ration of grief over it."

Mallory had to admit this OMEGA gang was nothing if not thorough. The file she thumbed through contained everything from her taste in music to her preference for cookie dough and chocolate chip ice cream, as extracted from records of her credit card purchases. She was still poring through the file when they drove into an underground parking garage.

Fifteen minutes later, Cutter and his partner whisked her onto an elevator that appeared out of nowhere. After a short, swift ride, it opened in an elegant anteroom. The woman who rose and came around her desk to greet them had coal-black hair, blue eyes and a smile that lit up the room.

"It's a pleasure to meet you, Ms. Dawes. I'm Gillian Ridgeway, filling in as executive assistant to the Special Envoy. He's expecting you. Before I buzz you in, I have to know…"

Her eager gaze dropped to Mallory's feet.

"Are those the Yvette d'Marchand's? The ones you used to deck the Russian?"

"They are."

Hiking up her jeans, Mallory displayed the lethal weapons. The aquamarine crystals caught the slanting sunbeam and threw it back in a zillion points of light.

"Oooh! I want a pair of those."

"There was a catalog in the box. They come in every color. You should get sapphire, to match your eyes."

Mike Callahan made an inarticulate sound that could have been a grunt or a mere clearing of his throat. Whatever it was, the small noise recalled the woman to her duties.

"I'll tell Uncle Nick you're here. Mac is with him, by the way."

Escorted by Cutter and Mike, Mallory entered a sunlit office redolent with the scent of polished mahogany and well-soaped leather. When the President's Special Envoy came from behind his desk, she felt her brows soar. Cutter had warned her to expect smooth and sophisticated. He'd left out the drop-dead gorgeous part.

Nick Jensen was as tall as his two operatives, but the similarities stopped there. Cutter and Mike were both dark-haired and more rugged than handsome. With his tanned skin, blue eyes and tawny hair, Jensen looked like an older and more polished Brad Pitt.

"Sorry we put you through the wringer in Normandy," he said with a smile Mallory suspected had raised goose bumps on more females than he could count. "I hope you understand the necessity."

"I do now. If you'd asked me a few days ago, I might not be so ready to forgive or forget."

"The situation got a little rougher than expected."

"It always does."

That came from a long-legged brunette in a severely tailored gray pantsuit with a gigantic pink peony pinned to the lapel. Pushing off her perch on the conference table, she came forward. Lightning made the introductions.

"This is my wife, Mackenzie Blair-Jensen. She was working some communications issues upstairs when Hawk—Mike—called to say you were en route, and she decided to hang around."

The vivacious brunette took Mallory's hand in a firm, no-nonsense grip. "I *had* to meet the woman who took down an international thug with a thousand-dollar pair of shoes. Way to go, Ms. Dawes."

Her glance, too, zinged south.

"Is that them?"

"It is."

An obliging Mallory once again showed off her trophies. The sparkling platforms infected the other woman with instant greed.

"Guess what I want for Christmas, husband of mine."

"Duly noted. Now if you ladies don't mind, we should talk business instead of shoes."

The mood in the sunny office immediately sobered. Suggesting everyone take a seat at the mahogany conference table, Nick Jensen laid out his plan of attack.

"I've set up an appointment with Congressman Kent a little more than an hour from now. Cutter and Mike will accompany me. Kent thinks I want to discuss the President's new counter-terrorism initiative. He *isn't* expecting me to show up with you two. Or with the House of Representatives Master at Arms, two detectives and a U.S. district attorney."

That should get Kent's attention, Mallory thought with unrestrained glee.

"We'll show him the airport surveillance tapes," Jensen continued, "and ask if he recognizes the woman accompanying Ms. Dawes. Only then will we produce sworn statements by Irina Petrov."

Jensen's glance swept the table.

"That's when we ask him what he knows about the disk containing the stolen data pulled off a computer in his office."

Mallory saw only one problem with the proposed plan and voiced it in no uncertain terms. "I want to be present when you do."

"We've discussed that," Cutter said evenly.

They had, she acknowledged with a curt nod. In Paris and on the long flight home. His argument that Mallory's presence would alert the reporters who prowled the halls of Congress held weight. Just not enough to convince her to sit on her hands while they confronted the man who'd made her life a living hell.

"I'll wear a disguise if necessary, but I want to see Kent's face when you tell him about the video tapes."

"Mallory…"

"I'm with Ms. Dawes." The support came from Mackenzie Blair-Jensen. "She's earned the right to be in at the kill. Plus she'll add to the shock value when Kent sees her."

Lightning drummed his fingers on the conference table and deferred to his field agent. "It's your call, Slash."

"No," Mallory countered swiftly, "it isn't. I didn't ask to be part of this operation, but now that I am, I want to see it through to the end. Correction, I *intend* to see it through to the end."

The men exchanged glances. Even Mackenzie looked surprised. Mallory suspected few people stood up to Lightning, but she refused to cave. Jaw set, she folded her arms and matched Cutter glower for glower.

"Okay," he conceded. "You're in. On one condition. We still don't know how that disk got in your suitcase. We're guessing Kent used an agent. We're also guessing that was his chief of staff, Dillon Porter. We don't *think* either of them will try to resist or turn violent when confronted, but we can't rule out the possibility. You take your cues from me. If the situation looks like it might deteriorate, you do what I say, when I say. Understood?"

"Yes, *sir!*"

A look of amusement crept into Jensen's eyes as they shifted to his wife. "She sounds a lot like someone else I know."

"I can't imagine who." With a flip of her hair, Mackenzie shoved away from the table. "Come with me, Ms. Dawes. I'll take you upstairs while the boys work out the final details. Give our wizards in Field Dress fifteen minutes and your own mother won't recognize you."

The vivacious brunette whisked Mallory out of the office. The door had barely shut behind them, however, before she pounced.

"Okay, the shoes are fantastic, but I want the real story on that ring."

"So do I." Abandoning her desk, the dark-haired executive assistant joined Mackenzie to ogle the diamonds and white gold.

"We saw the news conference," she confided. "We couldn't wait to meet the woman who brought Slash to his knees."

"Cutter was just performing for the cameras."

Mackenzie gave a snort. Gillian sniggered.

"Do you know how Slash got those scars?" the older woman asked.

"He said it was an explosion."

"Did he say who ignited it?"

"No."

"Make him tell you sometime. Until then, take my word for it. Cutter Smith wouldn't put a ring on *any* woman's finger unless he meant for it to stay there."

After that startling disclosure, the confrontation in Ashton Kent's office proved something of an anticlimax.

Mallory's auburn wig and subtly altered features got her past the palace guard without so much as a flicker of recognition. Even Dillon Porter gaped when Nick Jensen identified her along with the two detectives and U.S. district attorney. Congressman Kent blustered, protesting her presence, until Jensen cut him off at the knees.

After that, matters moved at warp speed. Mike Callahan and one of the detectives led a protesting Porter into another room. The second detective advised Congressman Kent of his rights. Each thinking the other had ratted on him, Kent and Porter soon admitted to a conspiracy to cover up the congressman's illicit affairs and use Mallory as a mule to deliver the blackmail payoff. Less than an hour after entering her old office, Mallory watched as her former boss was handcuffed and led out.

Someone had alerted the media. They'd assembled in droves and forced Kent to run a brutal gauntlet. Still in disguise, Mallory stood off to the side. She experienced none of the euphoria she'd

expected at seeing the once-mighty legislator
brought low.

"You okay?"

Sighing, she turned to Cutter. "I thought this
would make up for some of the humiliation and hurt."

"Didn't it?"

"No. It just made me feel…sad."

They stood side by side until the circus trailed
down the steps of the Capitol.

"I was thinking…"

Cutter hesitated, sounding unsure of himself for
the first time that Mallory could remember.

"You were thinking…?" she prompted.

"I got back from Central America and hopped on
a plane right for France. Barely had time to shave
between flights."

He scraped a hand over his jaw, as if feeling for
the whiskers he'd grown in the jungle.

"The thing is, I've racked up more vacation time
than I know what to do with. I thought maybe you
might want to go back to France, finish that trip you
planned in such meticulous detail."

"When?" she asked, her heart starting to pound.

"I'm ready whenever you are."

They'd crawled off a plane less than four hours ago.
Mallory hadn't slept in longer than she could recall.
She knew darn well her skin sagged like an old sponge
under the makeup OMEGA's Field Dress Unit had so

skillfully applied. Yet joy sang through her as she framed Cutter's bristly cheeks between her palms.

"Let's go now. Right this minute."

Epilogue

Mallory stood at the window of the small pension. Moonlight washed over her. A cold, damp breeze blew in through the open panes. Hugging her arms for warmth, she filled her lungs with the sharp sea air.

Instead of following the itinerary Mallory had planned originally in such meticulous detail, she and Cutter had holed up in this tiny hotel carved out of the ancient walls. The pension wasn't as grand as Yvette d'Marchand's château or anywhere near as modern. Cutter had lugged their hastily packed bags up three flights of stairs, grumbling with every step over the lack of modern conveniences like elevators and man-sized showers. His good-natured complaints had died when he'd taken in the view from their balcony window, however.

Mallory drank it in now, her spirits soaring. Floodlights illuminated the tall spire topped by the gilded statue of St. Michael slaying his dragon. Below and beyond, the moon-washed waters of the Gulf of St. Malo stretched as far as she could see.

"The tide's in," Cutter commented.

"So it is."

Padding across the bedroom on bare feet, he slid his arms around her waist. Her head drifted back against his shoulder.

They and the other inhabitants of St. Michel were completely cut off from the rest of the world. Just the way they wanted it.

"Wonder if any cars or buses washed away?" she mused.

"Probably." A chuckle rumbled up from his chest. "With any luck, ours was one of them."

Then he bent to nuzzle her neck and Mallory forgot the tide, forgot the view, forgot everything but the sizzle he ignited just under her skin. Alternating kisses with stinging little nips, he fanned the sparks to a five-alarm blaze.

"Have I mentioned that I love you?" he muttered between bites.

"Not in the last hour or so."

"I do, you know."

"I know. Same goes." Twisting around in his arms, she kissed the underside of his chin. The tough, puckered skin tugged at her heart. "Mackenzie said I should ask you who ignited the explosion that caused these. I got the impression it was a woman."

"It was." His palms cupped her face. "She's history, sweetheart, and not worth wasting this moonlight on."

He was right. The present was too full, and the future held no room for shadows from the past. Taking his hand in hers, Mallory led him back to bed.

* * * * *

AWAKEN TO DANGER

BY
CATHERINE MANN

Catherine Mann writes contemporary military romances, a natural fit, since she's married her very own USAF research source. Prior to publication, Catherine graduated with a BA in fine arts: theatre from the College of Charleston, and received her master's degree in theatre from UNC Greensboro. Now a RITA® Award winner, Catherine finds following her aviator husband around the world with four children, a beagle and a tabby in tow offers her endless inspiration for new plots. Learn more about her work, as well as her adventures in military life, by visiting her website: catherinemann.com. Or contact her at PO Box 41433, Dayton, OH 45441, USA.

With deep admiration, I humbly dedicate this book to a real life "Scorch", who won his personal battle through an incredible strength of will and spirit. (You know who you are.) Many thanks for discussing your own recovery journey with me as I wrote this book.

"God grant me the serenity to accept the things I cannot change, courage to change the things I can and wisdom to know the difference."

(Serenity Prayer, made well-known through Alcoholics Anonymous by Reinhold Niebuhr who attributes the inspirational saying to Friedrich Oetinger.)

Chapter 1

Where was she, and where the hell were her clothes?

Flat on her back in a strange bed, Nikki Price stared up at the ceiling fan moving slower than the spinning ceiling. *Click, click, click.* Blades cycled overhead in the dim light, swaying the chain with a tiny wood pull dangling from the end.

"Ohmigod, ohmigod. *Oh. My. God.*" What had she done last night?

She tried to look around but her eyeballs seemed stuck, all swollen and gritty in their sockets, her head too heavy to lift off the fabric-softener-fresh pillow, sheets equally as soft against her bare skin. All over bare. Goose bumps prickled over her *completely* naked body.

"Not right," she whispered to herself, her quiet voice bouncing around the quieter room sporting a hotel-generic decor. "Not right, not right."

Her bedroom fan pull sported a miniature soccer ball with tiny flowers painted on the white patches, a gift from her brother last Christmas. "Okay, I'm not totally losing it if I'm noticing silly details like overhead fixtures, right?"

No one answered. Thank God.

Still, nothing was familiar in the dim bedroom, only a hint of early sunrise streaking through the blinds. Voices swelled outside the walls. Her stomach clenched.

Okay, almost definitely a hotel.

She inched her fingers under the covers across the mattress, farther, farther again. Empty. She searched her mind for clues before she would have to turn her head and confront whoever might be in the room with her.

Panic stilled her more than even the nauseating ache stabbing through her skull. She hadn't drunk much the night before. Had she? She scrolled through the evening, getting ready to go to Beachcombers Bar and Grill for the live music—and a neutral place to break things off with Gary. But she couldn't recall much of anything after asking for a second amaretto sour. She wasn't an angel, but she'd never expected to wake up in a strange bed.

Of course she hadn't expected to do a lot of the reckless things she'd done over the past seven months since Carson Hunt tromped her heart. Truly tromped. Not the sort of temporary hurt that came from having a crush go south or getting dumped by a guy she'd just met. No. He'd deep down damaged her soul so much that even thinking about him still made it difficult to breathe. The ache of betrayal by her first real love might never go away.

Although these days she was more mad than hurt.

Could she have been mad enough last night to do something beyond reckless? Something totally stupid. Apparently she had since here she was. She'd thought she was ready to break up with the latest loser she'd been dating in hopes of filling that empty spot left by Carson. Finally she would move on with her life.

Okay, so she dated Air Force pilots—like Carson. From the base where Carson was stationed. And most of them happened to be tall and blond like, well, *Carson*. It had only taken her seven months to make the connection—hello?—but once she had, she'd resolved to set her life right again and end things with her latest Carson substitute, Gary Owens.

No wonder she'd frozen up when any of those dates so much as kissed her. She wasn't interested in *them*. Which made her feel even worse. No guy—even a loser—deserved to be used as a replacement for another man.

Her stomach rebelled. So why was she naked in a hotel room? Apparently she'd gotten over her kissing aversion.

She swallowed down fear along with a prayer that whoever she'd been with had used a condom. From here on out, *she* would stop being such a loser. She risked a deeper breath, inhaling the scent of laundry detergent. Masculine cologne—ohmigod.

Breathe in.

Breathe out.

Breathe in...cologne and an air of something else, an unfamiliar smell she couldn't quite identify, but her body shivered in disgust all the same. Somebody was in the room with her. Still asleep? Or in the bathroom?

Please, please, please at least let it be Gary, even if they'd never slept together before. He hadn't been at the bar last night for those few minutes and couple of drinks she *could* remember, but he'd been the one to set up the meeting by sending her an e-mail asking her for a date.

Bracing herself for the worst anyway, she arched her aching body, her head pounding as she rolled onto her side under the cotton sheets. Fresh pain pounded as her cheek met the pillow, but she stifled the urge to moan. The room appeared as empty as the bed. She gulped in gasping breaths, her heart now hammering harder than her head, relief making her darn near dizzy. At least if he was in the bathroom, she would have a second to collect herself.

Palms flattened to the mattress, she angled up, cool morning air prickling along her skin. Winters in South Carolina were all the chillier for the humidity. Cold and damp, like the ancient tombs her junior high students were currently studying in honors history class—and ohmigod, she was going to be late for work.

"Hello?" Her voice crackled up her parched throat. "Uhm, I would really appreciate it if you wrapped a towel around yourself before coming out."

She didn't risk guessing a name.

Nikki waited, but still no sounds from the shower or anywhere else. She squinted to look through the dim morning light across the room. The tiny bathroom seemed abandoned. Relief rode a shuddering exhale racking through her.

She would worry later about the rest when she swiped the fog from her head. She wasn't off scot-free thanks to those unaccounted for hours, but she didn't have to confront the awful awkwardness—and horror—of facing some guy she couldn't even remember picking up.

New leaf turnover time.

Hell, she would turn over a whole flipping tree. She was done feeling sorry for herself just because Carson "Ultimate Loser" Hunt had drop-kicked her heart in one unforgettable night. She would take control of her life and her emotions.

Pressing the heel of her hand to her melon-heavy head, she swung her feet to the floor. *Thud.* Her toes struck something solid rather than carpet. She toppled forward, her heart double-timing to marathon pace.

Arms flailing she grabbed for the end table, slammed to her knees, her teeth jarring together. Pain sliced through her head. She squinted in the faint light….

And stared straight into the unblinking eyes of the dead man on the floor.

Major Carson "Scorch" Hunt was dead tired and he hadn't even eaten breakfast yet.

Of course he hadn't fallen into bed until two in the morning due to an emergency on the flight line and he was back at his desk by dawn, hoping for a more peaceful day. No such luck.

Now thanks to a phone call from the security police, peace was on hold for far longer than the sausage-and-egg croissant he'd picked up at a fast-food joint. On his way out the office door again, he jammed his arms back into his leather flight jacket that had never made it onto the brass anchor peg before his phone rang.

A lieutenant from his squadron was dead.

Damn it. His fisted hand snagged inside the sleeve. He punched it through.

He'd braced himself for the possibility of losing someone in battle, but not at home. Worse yet, the young pilot was Carson's responsibility as second in charge, since the commander was deployed to the Middle East with the other half of the squadron.

Shrugging the jacket over his shoulders, he bolted down the hall, through the glass door and out into the parking lot. Early-morning traffic clogged the base streets, adhering to the so-damn-slow speed limits. Screw it. The VOQ—visiting officer's quarters—was only about a mile away. On foot would be faster, taking him there in under five minutes. He sprinted through the web of parked cars, tucked through the creeping traffic, ignored the honks.

The phone call from base security police hadn't said more than Lieutenant Gary Owens was found dead in the VOQ with a woman.

Owens had an apartment downtown, but sometimes guys checked into one of the rooms for the night if they were partying nearby and too drunk to drive home—or if they lucked into unexpected plans for the night. *With a woman.*

Boots pounding pavement, Carson tried to block thoughts of exactly *which* woman Owens had been dating for the past month. Of course stemming thoughts of Nikki Price had been damn near impossible for a long time. For over two years, actually, since a pool party at a squadron member's apartment when he'd realized his crew member's daughter had grown up. Really grown up. Smart, sexy, twelve years his junior and the daughter of a man he respected and admired. Not to mention Carson wasn't in a place to offer any woman a secure, stable happily-ever-after.

Catherine Mann 13

And still he had weakened and betrayed his friend by sleeping with Nikki. Once. A mistake he couldn't repeat even though his pulse rate jackhammered through him at the mere possibility Nikki could be in trouble.

Carson left the road for a shortcut across the lawn, past pine trees and bare-limbed oaks. He had no claim to Nikki, and yet here he was, running like hell for her as much as the dead lieutenant. Her boyfriend.

He couldn't stomach thinking about her with Owens. But who else could be in that room? And if the guy had been cheating on Nikki with another woman then somebody deserved an ass kicking.

Except damn, damn, damn it all, Owens was already dead, a screwed-up kid who'd just gotten his life back on track. Carson had been so sure he'd helped the baby pilot, but had he intervened soon enough?

Think. Focus. If Nikki was inside that brick building, then she needed him, even if he was the last person she would want to see.

Each huffing bootstep drawing him closer, Carson trained his eyes on the security cop cars—at least a dozen—encircling the three-story building along with an ambulance. Looked like everyone who wasn't guarding the gates had been called. Police in camo and blue berets secured the scene. An SP—security police officer—guarding the front entry held up a hand.

Before the military cop could speak, Carson nodded. "I'm Lieutenant Owens's commander."

The SP nodded and saluted. "I'll radio ahead and let them know you're on your way, sir. Down that hall and around the corner."

"Thank you, Sergeant." Carson slowed his feet, if not his pulse that still slugged from dread more than the mile sprint.

He cleared the front desk and strode down the narrow carpeted hallway, taking the corner on a sharp pivot. The corridor hummed with organized pandemonium, more cops and base medical personnel, a couple of agents from the Air Force OSI—Office of Special Investigation.

His eyes scanned past to home in on one person.

A woman sat huddled in a chair outside a VOQ room, blanket wrapped around her while her teeth chattered, security cops on either side. He didn't need to see a face to recognize *her.* Nikki Price.

Hell.

She looked up, the motion jerky from shock most likely. Her eyes locked on his down the length of the passageway, dark circles underneath. Hair even darker tangled around her head in a silky mess that begged his fingers to comb through, to rest on her shoulders and pull her to his chest for the comfort she no doubt needed.

Her fingers went slack around the deep red blanket until the edge slid open to reveal her clothes. Jeans and a silky pink shirt, misbuttoned as if hastily snatched up and on—the same clothes she'd been wearing when he ran into her the night before. He stuffed back the kick of jealousy and moved closer. Still she didn't speak, a slight tightening of her full lips the only indication she registered his approach.

He wrestled with the detachment he would need to get through the next hour, a difficult battle. He looked past her into the room to the sheet over a body on the floor. Closing his eyes, he swallowed and winged a quick prayer for the dead man. There was nothing more he could do for Owens.

Nikki needed him.

Carson knelt beside her, too aware of the cops standing guard a few feet away. "Nikki?"

Finally, he let himself look at her face again even as he steeled himself for the unshakable draw combined with guilt that made it tough to think around her, much less speak. He worked to read her expression, but her face was blank. Still he couldn't miss the pale cast under her olive complexion.

She glanced up, frowning, confused. Or disoriented? Her shaky hand rose toward his face. "Your mustache. It's gone."

What an odd thing to notice, but then she had reason to be in shock. Her wounded eyes seemed so much older than her twenty-three years right now, a dangerous thought for him to have since their twelve-year age difference helped him keep his distance.

He stroked his freshly bare upper lip. "That's what I get for shaving on the fly when I was running late." Because his few hours at home during the night had been filled with thoughts of running into Nikki outside Beachcombers on her way in to meet up with another man. "What happened here?"

She shrugged, the blanket slipping farther. "Gary is dead." Her voice was low, overly calm but thready, a thin substitute for her normally husky and—God help him—sultry tones. "You probably already know that."

"How?"

"We're not sure. Sometime during the night he hit his head."

Hit his head? Drunk and stumbling around in the room? Possible. Yet something was still… off. "I'm sorry this had to happen to you. What can I do to help? Tell me and I'll do my damnedest to make it happen."

"Gary's the one we should be sorry for." Her fingers twisted in the burgundy blanket even as her face stayed composed. "Thank you for coming over, but the SPs have everything under control."

So why were they keeping her around?

God, he wished she were anywhere else right now. She should be on her way to work. She often went in early or on Saturdays to tutor at-risk students from other classes and schools. He shouldn't know so much about her, but his ears always tuned in when her father bragged about his daughter's graduation from college, her junior high teaching job, her latest marathon race.

Damn. He was a freaking sap when it came to this woman. Always had been.

Tearing his eyes away from her before he did something dumb like scoop her up and take her away, he stared at the shrouded body being hefted onto a gurney. "Owens was in my squadron. I have to be here for him, and your father would want me to look out for you."

Her father, a cargo plane loadmaster, was deployed to the Middle East. The last thing the Price family needed was more stress with J.T. in a war zone and his wife taking care of a toddler with another late-in-life baby on the way.

"I *am* okay." Nikki's teeth chattered faster in contradiction to her seeming composure.

"Right. And you're not in shock, either. Uh-huh." Carson shrugged off his jacket. No way did he want to think of her father right now or all that guilt would drive him to his knees.

He'd betrayed the man in the worst possible way, a man who was more than a friend, more than a comrade in arms. They'd been POWs together, the strongest of bonds.

He owed J. T. Price better than screwing the man's daughter. He couldn't make up for the past, but he could take care of the present by hauling Nikki out of whatever mess she'd landed her most excellent ass in.

Carson passed his jacket to her. She stared at the coat so long he wondered if she might simply ignore his offer. Finally, she took it from him carefully, without touching his hand.

The blanket slid around her waist as she shoved one arm then the other into his coat, a final shiver rattling her teeth. "I'm sure my dad will be grateful."

Not hardly.

He wanted to tell her he'd come for her, too, but that wouldn't be wise with a cop within earshot.

The gurney wheeled past with the sheet covering the outline of a body. She went even paler under her deep tan. She tanned easily thanks to her mother's Greek heritage—and what an inane thought in the middle of hell. "You still haven't told me what happened? How did he hit his head?"

Maybe he should pull the SP aside and speak with him instead, but he couldn't bring himself to leave her sitting alone.

"I don't know. I had a couple of drinks over at Beachcombers. I was nervous about—"

Please don't let her say she was nervous about sleeping with Owens.

"—about breaking up with him."

Thank God.

Or maybe not because that gave them all the more reason to have fought.

"I don't remember anything after the second drink. I can't even recall leaving Beachcombers, just waking up here."

Nikki didn't remember? Or was too embarrassed to say? Either way, he could tell now wasn't the time to push her.

He could see the fear in her wide eyes. Her foggy eyes? Something wasn't right. Her dilated pupils stared back at him in spite of the early-morning sun through the windows and overhead light flooding the hall. Nikki didn't use drugs. He would bet his life on that.

Except no one ever believed his wealthy uptight parents were users, much less addicts, until his tenth grade English teacher. She hadn't been able to get the administration to do crap for him since his parents were six-figure contributors to the private school, but she'd pointed him toward Alateen. His parents weren't alcoholics, but the counseling principles had still applied for the child of addicts.

His teacher had also steered his parents toward enrolling him in a military prep school for his junior and senior years. A school far-the-hell away from his neglectful, abusive home life.

If Nikki had a problem, she needed help from someone better than him with his own secrets and demons.

"Maybe I should call your mother." He reached inside his thigh pocket for his cell phone. Nikki's mother, Rena, was also a counselor, even if she was on maternity leave.

"No!" She gripped his wrist with quiet desperation. Her slender fingers seared through his uniform sleeve. "Please. Mom has enough on her plate right now with Dad deployed, not to mention being over forty and pregnant again. She hasn't wanted people to know, but she's having a tough time with nausea, even a false labor scare. Please, don't call her. Okay?"

"You shouldn't be alone. Is there a friend I could call for you?"

She shook her head, tangled hair brushing her shoulders. "I don't want *anyone* to know, not yet at least."

"All right, but that means you're stuck with me." He shoved to his feet by the SP. "Have you finished questioning her?"

"For now. The lead OSI agent said he has more questions for later."

Carson glanced back into the room where two men in suits were crawling around the floor looking under the bed. The OSI was made up of part civilian investigators, part active duty military. Since the incident had happened on base, involving a service member, civilian police wouldn't even be involved. Would that be better or worse for Nikki? Who the hell knew anything right now except he had to get her out of here. "Then I'll take her home."

The cop stepped closer to Nikki's chair. "I'm afraid we can't let you do that, sir. She has to be checked out by a doctor first."

Doctor? They'd said *Owens* was the one who hit his head. Had something happened to her, too? That would account for the pupils and the confusion over what happened. "A doctor?"

He reached to brush back her hair for a better look at her face. She jerked away, flinching. From him or pain? Either way her hair swished to reveal a bruise on her cheek. What the hell had Owens done to her?

Scenarios he hadn't wanted to consider blared through his

head. He'd assumed Owens died in a freak accident—slipped in the bathroom or tripped over his pants or rolled out of bed. Carson pinched between his eyebrows. He didn't want that image of Owens in bed with Nikki. But the image of Owens hurting Nikki…

Hell.

Rage threatened to blind him. He blinked the red haze clear enough to function.

He scoured her clothes as if somehow he could develop Superman X-ray vision and find marks on her skin. No such luck, a curse and a blessing. But he did find other details he'd overlooked earlier—missing buttons on her silky shirt tugged on over a tank top. One of the knees of her jeans seemed more threadbare than the other, as if she'd skidded recently. He would wager money he would find a bruise beneath the denim.

There'd been an attack. A struggle. And somehow Owens had died.

"Nikki, did he hurt you?" Or worse. He blinked back the red fog again.

"I told you, I don't remember." Pride and a paper-thin bravado braced her shoulders. "Even if I did, this isn't your business or problem."

"Are you sure you don't want me to call your mother? She's going to find out eventually."

"And maybe we'll have a few more answers by then. I would like to get through—" she sucked in two shaky breaths "—the doctor's exam first."

She might not want his help, but he wasn't leaving her alone. He would protect her until she could take care of herself again.

He turned back to the SP. "She needs to leave. Now. Can't you see she's about to pass out? Who the hell knows what happened here but it's clear she was assaulted and needs treatment."

"Major, we're just doing our job and the investigator still needs to question her."

"He can do that at the hospital." He let all his anger seep steel into his words. "If she's been abused in any way and you've kept a traumatized woman sitting here alone—"

"We're moving things along as quickly as we can, Major, without compromising the crime scene."

"Is she being detained?"

"No, sir."

"Then she's ready to leave for the E.R." He slid an arm around her shoulders and eased her to her feet trying not to remember the last time he'd touched her this way or how many times he'd been tempted to put his hands on her body again.

His only defense had been distance. And now it looked as if he wouldn't be leaving her side anytime soon.

Chapter 2

Nikki tugged a surgical scrub shirt over her head and stifled a wince at the lack of underwear since all her clothes had been bagged for evidence. As if she didn't already feel exposed enough today.

At least the E.R. held more answers for her than her still-foggy head. She'd pulled it together enough during the police escort over to call in sick at school. Truth be told, she did feel sick, heartsick and body sore.

Paper crackled under her as she gingerly slid off the gurney, her toes hitting cold tile. Not as much of a shock as it could have been since she already felt chilled to her soul.

Bracing a hand on the cabinet full of gauzes, tongue depressors and latex gloves, she tugged on the surgical pants and knotted the tie before sliding her feet into the flimsy hospital slippers the nurse had given her. For the first time in her life she was grateful she could go braless. She could have sent Carson to her place to pick something up, but he wouldn't leave the hospital and she really didn't want him rooting through her underwear drawer.

What a silly thought. Except her brain seemed to hitch on the oddest details as if to fill empty space left by missing memories. At least the doctor reassured her it didn't appear that she'd had sex or been raped. She shuddered.

Any bruising stayed confined to her arms and ribs and Gary had been wearing his pants—even if they'd been around his ankles. All signs indicated if she'd killed him, she'd done so before penetration.

Her stomach cramped at the thought she could have taken a life, even in self-defense. She couldn't live with having killed someone, anyone, and to have known that person... Would she spend the rest of her life wondering what she could have done differently?

Or worse yet, never know.

Had she struggled and thrown him off? Or hit him with something? She was strong enough to do it after years of training on her university soccer team. She squeezed her eyes shut tight against tears so close to the surface, as if maybe she could find the memories from the night before glistening behind her eyes.

But nothing.

The shrink the E.R. had sent down for a consultation couldn't offer definitive answers, but he did say the memories could trickle back once her mind had a chance to adjust to the trauma of what happened.

Distraction. She needed a distraction and normalcy. She

snagged her cell phone from the rolling tray and settled into a steel-back chair rather than the exam gurney that held too many invasive memories. The message symbol flashed on the LCD screen. No surprise. She clicked through the numbers. Two from friends and then her mother's number—four times. She wouldn't be able to hold her off much longer and she certainly didn't want her mom to panic.

She would never be able to forgive herself if her mother lost the baby because of stress Nikki rained on her family's already overloaded life. A call should buy her a little time at least. She retrieved the stored number and waited—for only a ring and a half.

"Mom, hi, it's me. What's up?"

"Nikki Janine Price, you were starting to worry me." Her mother's voice held more concern than rebuke. "Are you all right? Where are you?"

Uh-oh. She recognized that tone well. Mom already knew the answer, or at least part of it.

But she wasn't a sixteen-year-old trying to hide a C on her report card. "I'm obviously not at work."

A benign response until she figured out how much her mother already knew. She'd learned a lot about finagling words after listening to her young students try to play her.

"I know that much. I called the school to leave a message for you and they said you're home sick today. You sound stuffy."

Duh. Because she'd cried her eyes out all over a nurse about an hour ago. At least her mom didn't seem to know about Gary Owens's death yet. "I'm just a little congested, nothing a steamy shower and a nap won't fix."

Liar.

She'd held strong all morning only to lose it when the doc put her in the stirrups. God, she'd gritted her teeth through pap smears before—bleck, nobody liked those after all—but she'd already felt so exposed, violated and outright scared to death. Tears were so darn embarrassing, even though the doc had patted her knee and said to take her time while the nurse passed Kleenex and comfort. Their sensitivity only served to make extra tears well up even remembering it now.

Her emotions were so fuzzy and out of control—like standing in a batting cage with one of those baseball pitching machines, and her reflexes too muddled to keep up with everything pelting toward her. All the more reason to stay away from her mom for a couple more hours.

She would go to her mother's house this afternoon and tell her in person before the rumor mill kicked in around base. Although the fallout in the press could be limited because of the exclusively military investigation.

"You didn't pick up at home, either. Are you at the doctor's?"

Mom radar. Its accuracy was scary. "Yes, I've seen a doctor." True enough. "Why did you call in the first place?" A new fear slithered through her hazy brain. "Are *you* okay?"

"I'm fine. Everything's wonderful in fact." Her mother's happiness darn near vibrated through the phone lines. "I had an ultrasound this morning and, well…"

The reason for her mother's call. Of course. "You wanted to share the excitement of the moment with someone since Dad couldn't be there."

"Pretty much, and who better to share it with than my daughter?"

Nikki pulled her tattered nerves together enough to speak

a while longer, for her mom, for her dad, too. "Everything looks good?"

"Perfect so far for a forty-two-year-old mother-to-be. I just need to keep my feet up after the spotting and cramping scare." She laughed low. "Am I crazy to do this?"

"You and Dad are great parents." They'd just sucked at being married for the first twenty-two years. Now that they'd finally figured it out, they seemed determined to start over in every sense of the word, including with a new pair of kids since their first daughter and son were already grown.

She admired her mother's determination, even as she resolved not to put herself through the hell of waiting for years for a man to get his head out of his butt and commit emotionally. "Could the technician see if it's a boy or girl?"

"Yes," Rena paused, "but I want to tell your father first."

"You know how I hate secrets." Her parents had tiptoed around telling their kids the truth about their problems, as if she and her brother Chris couldn't hear the fights and feel the dark silences afterward. She and Chris had kept their schedules packed as teenagers trying to avoid the tension.

"You'll be the first to know after I get in touch with him."

Nikki scrubbed a hand over her eyes. The dizziness kicked into overdrive, exhaustion nailing her. "I'm glad everything's cool with Freckle. I'll be looking forward to seeing the pictures later today. Okay?"

"Are you sure you don't need—"

"I just want a nap, then I'll come by later this afternoon. I promise." She swallowed hard. "I love you, Mom."

She disconnected, already dreading the conversation to come and the burden she would place on her family because of whatever the hell she'd done last night, because of her poor judgment in choosing Gary Owens. Her father was flying in a hot zone and so didn't need the distraction of worrying about her. Although there was nothing she could do to stem the eventual tide of gossip that would flow through e-mail overseas.

Being an adult and independent meant accepting responsibility. What she did affected others—like her family.

Turning her back on her too-pale reflection in the medicine cabinet glass, Nikki scooped a rubber band from a rolling table and gathered her hair away from her face. She needed to get her life together and work on putting this behind her. No more nursing a ridiculous broken heart for a man who flat-out didn't care. She wouldn't be like her mother, losing years of her life waiting for a guy to realize what he was throwing away.

Besides, she had bigger concerns right now. Like getting through the interview with the OSI agent due to walk in the exam room.

Why wouldn't Nikki call a lawyer?

Thumbing the disconnect button on his cell phone call from work, Carson kept his eyes locked on the exam room door while he paced past the row of vinyl-covered chairs and sofas. If only he could infuse his will through the panel into the idealistic woman on the other side.

Growing up, he'd watched countless guilty-as-hell people get off with a slap on the wrist because of expensive counsel, greased palms and a few wealthy connections. How could she simply trust her entire future would be okay if she just told the truth? What little she could remember. He couldn't stomach even the possibility of Nikki losing her freedom when he knew without question that woman was *not* a murderer.

He'd spent the past couple of hours on the phone taking care of crises at the squadron, arranging for an officer, chaplain and doctor from a base near Owens's parents in Nebraska to make a notification visit. He wished the couple lived closer so he could have made the visit himself. But he would travel from Charleston to Omaha to attend the funeral, along with every squadron member available. Regardless of what Owens had done last night, he'd still been an officer under Carson's command.

The door swung open. The OSI agent ambled out, slow, but Carson wasn't fooled by the guy's sleepy-eyed act. Special Agent David Reis's cynical eyes were taking everything in, and Carson wasn't so sure cynicism would work in Nikki's favor.

Nikki stepped through a few paces behind the agent, speaking with the nurse at her elbow flipping pages on a metal clipboard, stray words drifting about lab results and release forms for her to sign. She seemed okay, steady on her feet and confident even in surgical scrubs that somehow managed to accentuate her mile-long legs and skim over gentle curves he had no business noticing, especially today.

Good God, regardless of how strong she looked, bruises still marked her arms and heaven only knew where else. He forced his hands not to clench. He kept tracking her moves, searching for answers—or at least clues—as to what happened when the uneasiness settled with the weight of a stare boring into him. Slowly, Carson turned.

Special Agent Reis stared back with those half-open assessing eyes.

Carson nodded toward Nikki. "She's free to go?"

"Yes, sir, as soon as she finishes signing her release papers. We've covered everything for now. She just needs to stay in town until we have a few more answers." Absently, Reis reached into his inside jacket pocket, frowned then brought his hand back empty. "You're going to take her home?"

"Yes."

"Good." He fished into his pants pocket and brought out gum this time. "No matter what shook down in that VOQ room, she's had a helluva shock."

Carson tugged his leather jacket off the back of a waiting room chair. "Guess you can't tell me what she said."

"You'd guess right." He folded a piece of gum into his mouth. "Sorry."

"You're only doing your job." He understood all about that. He wouldn't get anything more out of the detective, but it wouldn't hurt to be amiable and form a connection that might lead the guy to give him a heads-up about info in the future. Carson nodded to the empty gum wrapper in Reis's hand. "Just quit smoking?"

Reis grin-grimaced. "Yeah, I still reach for the cigarettes. Doublemint sticks aren't helping much."

"Try drinking everything with a straw for a while."

"Like a drag from a smoke." His working jaw slowed. "Good call. Addictions suck."

"That they do." And since the opening was there, he continued, "Speaking of addictions, you need to know that Owens had a gambling problem. He seemed to have it under control, but..."

"Sometimes old contacts can still be hard to shake."

Nodding, Carson reached to stroke his mustache—damn it—only to find it gone. "I just thought you should know."

More than that he couldn't say without betraying confidences, and he really didn't know more that would be helpful. Still, he'd stuck to the standard squadron knowledge. Reis would have found out eventually. Carson had only sped up the process for safety's sake.

Reis studied him through half-open eyes. "Not that you have any reason to send me in a direction other than Nikki Price."

"I just thought you should know," he repeated.

"Duly noted." Reis tucked his gum pack back in his pocket and pivoted away.

Carson chewed on a curse harder than the investigator chomped gum. So much for keeping his damned drooling over Nikki a secret.

He could deal with the rest of the world knowing. But it was far tougher—and more essential—to keep the rogue attraction hidden from Nikki.

Rohypnol, a date-rape drug, had somehow been slipped into her drink last night.

Nikki settled into the bucket seat of Carson's sparkling Ford F-250, still rocked to her toes by the lab results that had arrived while Special Agent Reis questioned her. She hadn't been able to determine from the detective's expression if the news worked in her favor or not. Worst of all, there was less chance of her remembering now since the memory loss wasn't simply a by-product of trauma-induced stress.

A long sigh swelled low in her chest, rolling up without any real release in the tension kinking her muscles. The drizzly day outside Carson's windshield and pattering on the cab roof mirrored her mood. Thank goodness she wouldn't have to hold it together much longer. Another twenty minutes and she would be in her apartment.

Riding home with Carson was preferable to her trip over in the ambulance with Special Agent Reis. Barely.

Except she owed Carson big for the hours he'd spent looking out for her today so she wouldn't have to upset her mother. Sure he'd done it for her father, but he had seemed concerned for her, too…

God, she was already weakening around him again, the warmth and scent of his leather jacket more enticing than it should be. And while she'd always found his mustache sexy, his fully-revealed sensual upper lip was all the more enticing.

A dangerous thought.

Still, she should answer the unspoken questions lurking in the clammy air between them. "The doctor said I wasn't raped."

His knuckles went white on the steering wheel, even as his face stayed blank, aviator sunglasses hooked on the collar of his flight suit. "You didn't have to tell me, but thank you."

"Of course I would tell you." She scavenged a smile. "And you would have found out all the details anyway since you're Gary's commander."

He kept his eyes forward on the traffic-packed road, watching the streetlight. "I would have found out because I'm worried about you."

She let herself soak in the concern in his voice until the light turned green.

"Thank you." She blinked against the glare streaking through the window as the sun peeked from behind the clouds.

Her head thunked back to rest and she watched the telephone poles whiz past as they drove toward the winding bridge. Everything blurred from exhaustion and more. Definitely more than she wanted to acknowledge because then she would have to admit that spending time with Carson was important. "The hospital put a rush on my lab work. Someone slipped Rohypnol in my drink last night."

His curse hissed long and low. "And somebody's going to pay for that, no damn question."

"At least I understand the memory loss." Although that piece of knowledge came with another sense of having been violated. Who'd done it? She'd finished one drink before Gary arrived, and been almost through the second when he slid up beside her, elbow on the bar smiling as if totally unaware that their relationship was going nowhere. How could he have not realized?

Or had he? "I should be relieved I'm not suffering some mental break from trauma, right? Instead I'm just…"

"Pissed off. Of course you are." He glanced over at her, gray eyes steely with a repressed anger glinting through. "You have every reason to be upset."

Damn it, he'd given up the right to be her friend a long time ago. "Please quit being so nice."

"You want me to be an ass?"

She cranked the heater higher even though she knew the chill went bone deep from things that had nothing to do with dreary January weather. "I'd like an excuse to holler."

"I could take you out on my boat to the middle of Charleston harbor and let you yell if you think it would help."

"It won't."

"Are you sure you don't want me to call your mother?"

"No. I'll tell her. Later though—" She stopped short as an awful possibility pushed through her muzzy mind. "Do you think what happened will hit the news soon?"

"The basics, but the names are being withheld until Owens's family is notified."

She squeezed her eyes shut, guilt pressing hard against her chest over the crushing pain Gary's parents would suffer. Because of her?

"The investigator is withholding your name for your own safety."

What? She shifted in her seat to face him. "I thought they believed I'm guilty."

"They saw the wisdom of at least considering other options."

"Thank you."

"I didn't do anything."

"Thank you anyway for staying with me today."

"Your father would have my ass if I didn't look out for you. Sharing an enemy prison cell forges a bond I can't explain."

Those days when her father's crew had been missing, then reported taken by enemy warlords, had been hellish. She'd feared for her father's safety as well as for the man she'd thought she loved—even if at that time Carson had not noticed her beyond a kid sister kind of way.

Until later.

She so didn't need to think of later right now with him sit-

ting so close and her in need of comfort in a big way. Who
wouldn't be rocked by what had happened? But she was
strong. She could hold on until she got in her apartment where
she would have a long soggy cry in her bathtub. A man was
dead, a man she'd cared about enough to date. A man she'd
kissed and apparently nothing more, thank heavens, but he deserved to be mourned. Even if he'd done something so horrible she'd struck out and killed him.

Bashed in his skull.

Bile burned high in her throat. "Pull over."

"What?"

"Pull over or you're gonna need your carpet cleaned."

He whipped the truck across two lanes and onto the shoulder. She jerked her seat belt free and lurched from the cab to
the swaying reeds and tall marsh grass.

Thank God he didn't join her while she heaved up her
empty guts. If only she could pitch the horror of the day into
the marsh grass, as well.

Finally, she straightened again, weaving as she sucked in
chilly winter air until the double vision of afternoon traffic
meshed into a single world again. Turning back, she found
Carson leaning against the passenger-side door, waiting in
case she needed him, but not intruding.

Emerging sunlight glinted off his blond hair and sunglasses
now shielding his eyes, his body every bit as tall and strong
and appealing as the first time she'd seen him strutting across
a tarmac when she'd been waiting to welcome her dad home
from an overseas tour. She was too tired and heartsore to feel
attraction, but God, how she yearned to rest her head on that
broad chest.

Instead, she planted her feet into the grassy incline and made her way back up slower than she'd descended.

She stopped beside him. Traffic whooshed past in blasts of wind.

Carson passed her a handkerchief without speaking. She took the small folded linen from his hand, three tiny initials embroidered in the upper corner. She studied the larger "H" with a "C" and "A" on either side. Who carried monogrammed handkerchiefs anymore? Apparently Carson. She'd thought he was a friend, had even shared a bed with him and didn't even know he carried a handkerchief, much less what the "A" stood for.

Nikki swiped the cloth across her mouth before clutching it in her fist. "Thanks."

"Are you all right now?"

"Who would be?"

"Right answer." His curt nod gave away less than his shielded eyes as he stood in the freezing mist without the least shiver. Maybe he seemed so perfect because he wasn't even human. "It'll take the drugs a while to wear off."

She sagged to rest beside him against the truck, drags of the prickly cold clearing her head. "So I didn't hurl because I'm an emotional wreck after all?"

"Over in Rubistan, after your dad and I were rescued, I barely made it to the barracks bathroom before I lost the MRE the soldiers gave me."

She pressed her fingers between her eyes against the ache his image brought. She'd hurt for him then and wasn't anywhere near as distant as she wanted to be now. "I appreciate your telling me that, especially since it must be difficult for you to talk about that time. My dad still doesn't discuss what happened over there very much."

Carson shrugged it off his broad shoulders as if it were no big deal when they both had to know otherwise. "We handle crap like that in different ways. The important thing is that you deal with it."

"Even if that means hurling in a ditch."

"Hey, join the trauma-hurling club." The strengthening sun glinted off his smile as brightly as it did his golden hair.

"And you're a badass." A badass who happened to look like an angel who could lead a saint to sin.

"So are you."

Ohmigod, everything had been easier when she could keep her distance from him. She could almost delude herself into thinking he wasn't as—charming?—no, that wasn't quite right. Carson had seemed nice, a flat-out nice guy she'd liked, admired, wanted so much she'd been a blind idiot.

She really needed to go home fast. "Thanks for the quick reflexes in pulling over. I'm ready to leave now."

"Are you sure you'll be okay alone?"

"You can't be offering to stay with me?" She knew full well he had to get back to the squadron. Already he would have to work late into the night to clear through all the work and crises that would have piled up while he was out of the office—

Whoa. Stop.

Why had she taken so much note of his work schedule when she'd been dating other guys? It had been bad enough before when she took note of everything about him, back when she'd thought he felt the same attraction.

Carson swiped his sunglasses off and dried them on the leg

of his flight suit. "I do have to get back to work, but I could pull together supper for you before I go. I haven't eaten today either, and I'm actually a competent cook."

"I know."

He stopped midswipe on a lens. "You do?"

Oops. Might as well fess up. He probably knew anyway and pretending she hadn't once followed him around like a silly puppy would only hint she still had feelings. While she might still have feelings, they sure weren't the tender kind anymore. "I used to pay all sorts of attention to what you did back during my 'crush' days."

His smile pulled tight. With guilt? He hooked his glasses on the neck of his uniform again. "So let me cook for you then."

Invite him into her apartment? Not a chance. "Thanks, but the drugs and the whole…everything…are still making me nauseous."

"Then I can sit and pass you crackers."

Definitely guilt.

She so didn't want him taking care of her out of obligation. "Thank you, but you have work. I have papers to grade and laundry to do. You've done enough already."

Understatement of the year.

She could see he wanted to argue…but his cell phone rang again. His forehead creased with frustration, his hand gravitating toward his phone even as he obviously battled the urge to ignore it.

"You know you can't ignore the call. Take it. I'll be fine."

And she would.

If only his intense blue eyes didn't shout that he wasn't done with her yet.

Chapter 3

He was done.

Carson leaned against the quarter panel of his truck and stared past the pool up at Nikki's apartment. She was safely inside, thank God. He'd walked her to the door. She hadn't invited him in—no surprise—but he'd waited until she assured him the place was safe and empty.

Now he could return to the pile of messages waiting for him at the squadron since he'd accomplished all he could from a cell phone for one day.

So why was he hanging out in a half-empty apartment parking lot, rain drizzling until it dripped from his hair onto his forehead? If he loitered around, staring up at Nikki's image moving around inside for much longer, somebody would call the cops on his ass. If he didn't freeze to death first even though he had his leather jacket back. Damned if the thing didn't smell like her now, a light flowery perfume and something unmistakably *her*. And double damn, but why could he still recognize her scent even after seven months?

He should just lose himself in work, order a deep-dish pizza and dig in for another 2:00 a.m. punch-out. Given the time change over in the Middle East, pulling a few extra hours at night worked well for speaking with the deployed squadron commander about routine business. Sure he could ask the new boss for advice on the whole mess, but the guy was swamped with duties overseas. Their old commander, Quade, had left two months ago and moved his family to the Pentagon for his next assignment, so he wasn't on hand to ask for advice, either.

Mentors were in short supply to help him out with this one. He was on his own in a job he hadn't asked for, wasn't even sure he was ready for yet. But the position had come to him anyway and he refused to screw it up.

The phone rang in his hand—again. He tucked the headset piece in his ear. "Major Hunt."

"Captain Lebowski from scheduling." The Chicago area accent cut through the earpiece. "We've got a problem I know you're going to find hard to believe, but when Reach 2-1-3-1 landed in Hawaii, the plane broke."

A broken plane and a crew in search of a tan. Great. Just what he needed today. "Yeah, amazing how that always happens on flights to Hawaii and never in Thule, Greenland. Let me guess on the ETTC—" estimated time to completion for a return home "—is a week right?"

"Of course it's a week. Who can get a decent tan in under a week?"

"All right, what's broken? Where's the part gotta come from? Do we need to ship maintenance guys out?"

Carson listened while continuing to scour the parking lot for—what? Something. Anything he could find that might be off and account for the mess of the past twelve hours. Because if he could find the cause, he could fix it like that broken plane.

He should drop his sorry butt into his truck and leave. He'd done more for her today than required, and the attention would not go unnoticed in his small community of aviators once word leaked of the incident.

So go.

And he would.

But he wouldn't stay gone, just checking from a distance. He owed Nikki for how he'd treated her. She'd been there for him at one of the lowest points of his life and he had taken without giving a thing back.

He understood all about the importance of making amends except when those amends might harm someone. He'd stayed away for seven months because being close to her again would only risk hurting her more.

Well, now staying away wasn't an option.

"And that's it, sir," Lebowski wrapped up his summary, "I'll give you a SITREP at the end of business."

A situation report to add to the list of work, but at least his people were on top of things.

"Roger and out."

He thumbed the off button, relieved it wasn't another major crisis. The ADO—assistant director of operations—directly below him in the chain of command could have handled this one, but the old commander Quade had been such a micromanager that the personnel around him hadn't broken the habit of calling about every nitnoid detail, which made the job more time-consuming than need be.

Quade was a helluva flyer, had been a dedicated commander, and no doubt cared about his people, even if his gruff demeanor implied otherwise on more than one occasion. But Carson had often wondered what would have happened to the squadron if Quade died while in charge.

Delegation was important. Sure there were times he could do the job better than someone less experienced, but if someone else could do the job well enough, that was okay, too. Otherwise how did anyone learn if they never had a chance to stretch their wings?

But what did he know? He was too damn young to be in this job anyway. Even with delegating, he was working his ass off so much he was lucky to get breakfast.

Or lunch.

He tucked the phone back in his thigh pocket and stared up at the balcony marking Nikki's place, her UNC alma mater flag waving beside her sliding doors. His chest went tight again as he thought about finding her this morning, her spine so straight while she sat wrapped in that blanket. He would do anything to wipe away this horror for her. Any-damn-thing. Nothing would slip his attention in this investigation. And hell, suddenly he understood Quade's position a little better.

Because Nikki's safety was one responsibility he couldn't bring himself to delegate.

Nikki brushed her hand over the stack of sixth grade reports on farming techniques of ancient Egypt calling to her

for grades, but she resisted. Her students deserved her complete attention and a fully functioning brain.

She needed air, space, sun, all in short supply on this rainy
day. But at least her balcony would be less claustrophobic
than the tiny apartment that had seemed so big when she first
moved in last fall.

Nikki snagged her cordless phone from the cradle and slid
open the balcony door. She really craved a long run on the
beach but her aching body probably wouldn't hold up for any
length of time. Too bad the pool was closed for the winter.
The water, chilly though it might be, invited from below.

Dropping into a lounger, she started to dial her mother's
number when the phone rang in her hand before she could
punch the first number.

She checked caller ID and found "Caller Unknown."

Her stomach clenched. Residual nerves, no doubt. She
tapped the On button. "Yes?"

Silence stretched for a second too long. Her nerves flamed.
She started to hang up and sprint back inside when a cleared
throat on the other end stopped her.

"Nikki?"

Carson.

But he'd only just left. Standing, she scanned outside,
past the swimming pool and found him three stories down
in the parking lot, against the closed tailgate on his truck.
She rested her elbows along the wooden rail, phone pressed
to her ear as firmly as her eyes stayed locked on his tall,
lean body.

"Did you forget something?" She'd returned his jacket, although she did still have his handkerchief.

"I seem to have overlooked doing one mighty damn important thing for too long."

The weight of his words seeped through the telephone. Did he intend for there to be a deeper meaning? Could he be referencing their night together after all these months? That evening she'd thought finally he'd noticed her only to have him leave the next morning and pretend the whole night never happened.

She wished she could erase that night from her memory as easily as she'd forgotten the one prior. "At least one of us has good recall today."

"I'm not talking about today."

"I know." How silly to speak on the phone while they looked at each other, but with a swimming pool between them and three stories of height, they were safe from touching.

Could he be as affected by her as she was by him? The disturbing and tempting thought spread soothing warmth through her on an oh-so-cold day. "Maybe we shouldn't talk right now with everything so jumbled—"

"I'm sorry for the way I behaved that night and the next morning."

An apology months too late.

She wouldn't be drawn in again. She couldn't bring herself to believe he was total scum, but something was messed up in that head of his and she didn't want any part of the fallout again.

Best to shoo him away fast before she did something reckless like ask him to come back up and inside. "You're forgiven."

"I don't deserve your forgiveness, but thank you."

She didn't want his gratitude. She wasn't sure what she

wanted—okay, she knew she'd always wanted Carson—but more than that she wanted to safeguard her heart so she wouldn't spend the next two decades mooning over a man as her mama had done.

"Thank you for your help today. I really need to go now. Goodbye."

She hung up fast, a clean break, as she should have done the first time Carson had smiled a hello at a squadron picnic years ago. Better yet, she turned away, back into her apartment. She wasn't a twenty-year-old hero worshipping the new guy on her father's crew anymore.

God, had she really had a thing for Carson for nearly three years?

Nikki angled through the half-open sliding door and dragged it closed, phone still clutched in her hand. Time to finally place that call to her mother. She punched in her parents' number and waited through *ring, ring, ring.*

"Hello?"

Chris. Her brother.

Her hands shook with adrenaline letdown along with the need to talk to somebody, and her brother was *so* the only person she could hang with right now. They'd forged a tight bond during all their family moves and their parents' marital troubles. She didn't care why Chris was back early from his New Year's road trip with college friends, but thank God he was.

She shouldn't drive anywhere because of the drug and nerves. Her brother could come over and pick her up. She couldn't stall telling her family any longer.

"Hey, runt. It's me. Could you come over? I've had a really crummy day."

* * *

His crappy day—hell, week—was finally about to end.

Carson gripped the stick on the C-17 and hurtled the craft through the sky closer to his home base. Only a couple more hours left until landing with the squadron representatives who'd flown out to Omaha for Owens's funeral.

He'd paid his respects to the family and worked like crazy not to think about the unanswered questions from the night the man had died. Still he couldn't help but wonder if Owens had been the one to drug Nikki's drink. And how had it happened at Beachcombers, the last place he would expect something like that to occur? Beachcombers wasn't some rave club, just a low-key seaside restaurant and bar where flyers hung out.

At least her brother was watching her and didn't seem to mind the occasional check-in call from Carson—under the guise of keeping tabs on J. T. Price's family while the man was deployed. He would continue checking in with Chris and with Special Agent Reis, while keeping his distance.

Game plan set, boots rocking the rudders, Carson lost himself in the sky as he soared the cargo plane through the clouds the way he escaped through hours spent skimming his thirty-one-foot Catalina sailboat over the waves.

Blue, blue and more blue...

He lived to fly, whether it was through the sky or along the ocean. That's all he'd ever wanted. He hadn't planned on a commander gig, but here he was, responsible for people like the crew around him.

Back in the cargo hold were loadmaster Picasso and in-flight mechanic Mako.

Up front in the cockpit, new baby copilot Kevin Avery sat in the right seat and instructor pilot Nola Seabrook was strapped in a jump seat behind them.

God, when had he gotten to be the old guy? Except he wasn't that much older than these aviators. Somehow he'd landed on the fast track—he hoped because of his ability. Although he often wondered if his prestige-hungry parents had played some of their behind-the-scenes games in their high-power circles with congressmen who happened to be close buddies with a general here or there.

The military wasn't supposed to operate that way, but the whole thing had spiraled beyond his control. So he worked his ass off to be the best damn pilot, officer, leader possible in order to be worthy of his commission and whatever responsibilities came his way. Including checking on Nikki.

And did everything have to cycle back around to Nikki Price?

Jesus, he needed to start seeing other women. Except he didn't have the time or interest in anyone else. Work overload and stress maxed him out. He knew his limits and he recognized the danger signs if he pushed himself to the wall. He was trying to lose himself in the sky, and would have to find time to sail soon. All to fight the urge to take what he really wanted and could never have again.

A drink.

Too many people counted on him. He couldn't risk screwing up. Stats read that every alcoholic's drinking affected at least four other lives. Any mistake he made would ripple through the whole squadron.

In spite of Nikki accepting his apology, what he'd done was unforgivable. He'd been so damn arrogant that night, thinking he was holding it together. That he was somehow stronger than his parents because he'd battled and won against *his* addiction.

His fall had been swift.

Attending his friend's wedding should have been low stress. Sure, drinks would flow, but he resisted that temptation every time he partied with his crewdog pals. He'd even hung out with his wartime crew before Spike's wedding. Life had finally been good again, the hell of their shoot down and capture in the Middle East past. He'd been cleared in the initial mandatory pysch eval. He knew with his family history he needed to be careful.

Then when he'd least expected it, everything flew apart. Why had seeing Spike that happy left him so damn shaken, enough to weaken and do something he'd been fighting for over a year not to do—hit on Nikki?

Next thing he'd known, he was looking at the bottom of an empty shot glass, then another, more following until…he couldn't remember more than spotty flashes of tangling naked with her in the sheets. Amazing flashes.

Flashes he also feared may have been brief and not nearly as good for her. Wasn't that a kick in the ego? And also a well-deserved punch to his good sense.

His fist clenched around the throttle. He fought the destructive urge to be with her every day. He couldn't offer her a damn thing, had tried to settle for friendship but knew now he couldn't go for half measures in any part of his life. He wasn't as strong at resisting temptation as he'd thought.

He had enough on his plate staying sober and doing his job. Speaking of which, he had a young pilot here in need of leading right now. Being an Air Force officer was about more than flying. He had a duty to train, mentor, motivate future leaders.

The failure with Owens weighed heavily on his shoulders today. He'd been certain the man was shaking his gambling problem. He'd even begun attending support meetings with other addicts.

Carson thumbed the interphone button. "Lieutenant Avery, let's talk. Career planning can never start too early. What's your goal?"

The wiry young pilot who probably weighed all of a hundred and thirty pounds soaking wet answered, "To be the Chief of Staff, sir."

Seabrook snorted into the headset from the jump seat. "Lieutenant, it may have escaped your notice, but since Curtis LeMay died, all the Chiefs of Staff have been fighter pilots."

"Oh." The scrawny kid deflated in his leather seat.

Damn. You'd think she stole the kid's ice-cream cone. "She has a point, but things change. Military transport is the fastest growing airframe, and we're raking in those medals. So you never know. What's your plan for making Chief of Staff?"

"I plan to be the best aviator I can be, sir."

Ambitions were all well and good, but he definitely needed to have a sit-down with this kid later about specific choices for different career paths, or before he knew it, he would be in a job he hadn't foreseen, either. "How about we settle on a more immediate goal today, with tangible early results."

"And what would that be, sir?"

"You tell me?" Take some initiative, kid. Having a goal

was great, but setting attainable immediate goals to get there was even more important. In the last three months, Carson had tried to be the mentor to Owens he hadn't found around himself near enough. A.A. meetings had taught him well the necessity of guidance and support, one-day-at-a-time steps.

"I'd like to earn a call sign, a cool one like yours, sir."

Avery thought the call sign "Scorch" was cool? Jesus, it came from the mortifying moment of setting his own mustache on fire with the flaming Dr Pepper drink in a bar.

Seabrook laughed, husky and slightly wicked. "So you're not enjoying the call sign always reserved for the newest aviator."

Avery winced. "No, ma'am."

"Then get to work earning a new name, Bambi."

Carson smothered a laugh at the lieutenant's shudder of disgust over the undignified moniker. "I'll keep my eye on you and see what new handle I can come up with."

"Thank you, sir. If it's okay, I'd like to step in back for a walk-around before landing."

"Roger, cleared to unstrap."

Bambi unbuckled the harness holding him in the copilot's seat and ducked out of the cockpit for the stairwell leading to the cargo hold. Captain Seabrook slid into the empty copilot's seat on the right and settled behind the stick, scanning the control panel. "Tough to believe we were once that idealistic."

"Maybe because we weren't." In those days his only plans centered around escaping his family legacy. The rigid structure of the military provided a blessed relief to a childhood spent not knowing what to expect from minute to minute with coke addict parents.

Lately he worried about the stress load sending him over the edge, something he was always on guard against and a part of why he kept his personal life as uncomplicated as possible. He dated, but low-key. He'd even dated Nola Seabrook three years ago, back when they were both Captains, when he was senior only in years and not her supervisor in any way. She was far more suited for him than Nikki, closer in age, they both understood the pressures of military life, combat, even captivity since Nola had been snatched during a mission in South America.

Jesus.

Surely the crappy-luck odds were about played out for them?

Of course now with his new promotion in the squadron, a relationship was out of the question even if he was interested. Which he wasn't, because the chemistry wasn't there in spite of her bombshell-blonde looks…and he couldn't shake a certain leggy brunette from his brain.

He definitely needed to keep his personal life simple for at least as long as the squadron stayed under his command. Lives depended on it.

Thank God the runway neared. Time to pull his attention back on landing this lumbering beast of a plane. An instant before he could thumb the radio button to contact the control tower, the headset squawked in his ears.

"Major Hunt, there's a message for you at the command post from Special Agent Reis. Something about an accident over at Nikki Price's place, a loose balcony railing."

His muscles clenched as tight as the knot of dread in his

gut. Screw having someone else check on her and keeping his distance. The second this plane touched down, he'd be out the hatch and on his way to Nikki's side. Where he intended to stay.

Chapter 4

Enough already.

Nikki considered herself a tough person overall, but had somebody painted a bull's-eye on her back while she wasn't looking?

She toed off the water faucet in her steaming bathtub that hadn't come close to easing the kinks and cold from her tumble off her balcony into the pool. At least she'd been able to control her fall enough to land in the water when the wooden railing gave way. Thank God for all those gymnastics classes her parents had paid for when she was a kid.

Her stomach still lurched just thinking about those horrifying seconds in midair. She rested her head back and wished she'd thought to turn on her stereo before she sank into the bubble bath. She could use all the help relaxing that she could scavenge.

Three stories was a helluva long way to fall and hope that the dive angle you'd taken would land you in the pool rather than smack you onto the cement instead. She'd no doubt made a record breaking cannonball splash. EMS techs called by her neighbor declared her unharmed, although she would be black-and-blue by morning.

What happened to her nice boring life? She was a junior high teacher whose biggest concern should have been whether or not her students made it to regionals for the history fair.

Her doorbell echoed.

Peace over.

She hauled herself out of the water and grabbed for her jogging shorts and T-shirt resting on the edge of the vanity.

The doorbell pealed again. Her mother, no doubt, since the gossipy little old man next door had called her family's house two seconds after phoning EMS. She really could have used a beach towel from him instead. It was darn cold in that pool in January, even in South Carolina.

When she'd told her mother about Gary's death, her mom had—no surprise—freaked. Nikki had calmed her down by tapping into her mother's training for suggestions on regaining her memory. Keeping a dream journal and making an appointment with a hypnotherapist didn't feel like much, but at least she was taking action, already unearthing snippets of memories.

When she wasn't busy diving off a third-floor balcony.

The doorbell stuttered while she tugged her clothes onto her damp body. "Hold on, hold on, Mom." She hopped, one leg at a time into shorts. "I'm coming and I'm gonna chew you out for not putting up your feet like the doctor—"

a building sneeze tingled through her sinuses, down her nose "—aaaachoo!"

She snitched Carson's freshly washed and folded handkerchief from the stack of laundry on her sofa and tried to ignore the teacher voice inside of her that insisted tissues were more sanitary than a cloth holding germs. And was this stuffy nose cosmic justice for lying to her mom about having a cold last week?

She tugged the door open. Rather than "concerned Mama," she found "pissed-off hunky flyboy." Her fingers fisted around the handkerchief, tucking her thumb to hide the telltale corner peeking out.

Carson gripped the door frame, his sensuous lower lip pulling tight. "You're okay."

"You don't have to sound so mad about it."

His hand slid from the frame and before she could blink— or head back into her apartment away from temptation—he hauled her to his chest. "Jesus, Nikki, you could have died. I damn near had a heart attack when command post patched through an in-flight call about this."

Hunky, awesome-smelling flyboy, who'd raced straight over after a flight just for her. Muscle, leather and all that concern made for a heady sensory combination, especially when she was already susceptible to this man. Her body obviously wasn't near as smart as her mind.

But her will was stronger. She edged her shoulders free, stepping back without meeting his eyes. "I landed in the pool." What was she doing staring at her bare feet beside his boots? She forced her gaze up to meet his full on, no flinching.

His hand gravitated to her damp hair. "How long ago did it happen if your hair's wet?"

She held still under his touch, the heat of his fingers steaming her skin from a simple brush of his knuckles across her cheek. Better to let him think the water was from her impromptu swim than mention she was naked in the tub sixty seconds ago. "Why did they call you?"

His hand fell away. "Your mother phoned my secretary at the squadron to track me down. She wanted me to check on you since her doctor has her on bed rest."

"Figures." Where was Chris when she needed him? "You'd think I was still in college."

"I think you're lucky to have a family who cares. Was she a little intrusive? Maybe. But I don't see her here hovering."

"You're right. I am lucky, and I don't mean to sound like a brat."

She might not want a relationship with him anymore, but her ego still nudged her to be careful. They were inching toward dangerous—tempting—territory every time they spoke.

He strode past. She grabbed the door frame to support her suddenly shaky knees.

She watched him saunter into her apartment, a place he'd never stepped inside before. Seven months ago she'd been finishing up at UNC. Their one night together had been at his place, a beach community bungalow he'd bought from another military family when they'd moved.

She wondered what he thought of her bargain-basement Pier 1 knockoffs and the scattered plants she'd grafted from her mother's garden in an attempt to fill corners she couldn't afford to decorate.

Why was she thinking about appearances now when she'd never cared about material things before? If Carson Hunt—obviously from wealth—was only impressed by a price tag, then she was well rid of him.

He stopped short in front of her class's latest history project. "What the hell is this?"

She laughed and damn it felt good, almost as good as the rush because he'd noticed her most prized possession in the whole place. Her students had crafted the towering project which made it worth gold to her. Nikki walked deeper into the apartment, surreptitiously hiding the used handkerchief under a throw pillow until she could wash it.

Nikki tugged a tissue from the end table on her way to the six-foot-high papier-mâché creation she'd brought home from school strapped into the back of her Ford Ranger. "It's a sarcophagus."

"Ohhh-kay." Hands hooked in the pockets of his leather flight jacket, he studied the psychedelic coffin propped against the island counter separating the small kitchen from the rest of the dining area. "While I don't claim to be an interior design expert, why do you have one in your dining room?"

She ambled closer, determined not to bemoan the fact she was wearing nothing but ratty gym shorts and a threadbare T-shirt over her damp body. "My students are studying Egyptian history. The kids have been crafting papier-mâché items to go in the tomb, and we tried to build this in class, too, but Trey Baker spilled his lunch inside the sarcophagus and tapioca pudding totally stinks when it rots, so I had to cut that part out. Although what kid actually eats tapioca? Most children I know like chocolate pudding with candy sprinkles or gummies, or maybe a cookie crumbled on top."

"I liked tapioca when I was a kid."

"Geez, were your parents health food nuts or what?"

"Or what."

Welcoming the chuckle, she leaned an elbow against the counter bar and smoothed down a straggly corner of newspaper sticking from the still-damp section. "Anyhow, I'm patching over where I cut out the damaged part."

She'd taken a break from repairing the project to eat supper out on her balcony. Memories of Carson's apology had drawn her to the railing and before she'd known it, she was tumbling heart over butt toward the pool. "It should be dry enough to paint by tomorrow."

"Shouldn't you be resting?"

Reasonable notion except every time she closed her eyes she saw Gary Owens's vacant dead stare. "If I rest, I'll think. I'd rather work. Although building a coffin really isn't helping take my mind off this whole mess."

"Rather macabre."

"Macabre." She snatched up a piece of paper from under the phone.

"What are you doing?"

"Writing down the word." And trying to think about anything but the dead man and unanswered questions. She finished scrawling on the notepaper and tore the top sheet off from the soccer-patterned pad—a Christmas gift from one of her pupils. "I've got this student who's a word wizard. Feeding his brain is a full-time job. You use these words that are not the kind guys would usually choose."

"I can't decide if you're insulting or complimenting me."

"Neither. You just don't speak as informally as most guys I know."

"I'm older than most guys you know. Hell, I even eat tapioca, remember? If I said dude a couple of times, you wouldn't notice the other words."

"Still hung up on being a cradle robber, are you?"

His eyebrows shot up at her open acknowledgement of their past relationship. Relationship? One-night stand.

Ouch.

He thumbed the pad of paper, fanning through sheets until one piece peeled loose. "Shouldn't you be resting?"

"You already said that."

"Must be early onset Alzheimer's at thirty-five." Absently he picked up the stray piece of paper, leaned back against the bar and started folding. "I understand you need to keep your mind off things, but how about reading a book? Your body has been through hell the past few days. You should take care of yourself."

"I'm a young, resilient twenty-three, not an *old* thirty-five like you."

He stopped midfold on the soccer paper. "I'm guessing your mother and father encouraged you to speak your mind when you were a kid."

"What clued you in?" She smirked for a full five-second gloat before the fun faded with reality. "And how surprising that you always manage to bring up my dad anytime we speak."

"People have parents."

"You don't."

"Sure I do." His fingers started tucking and folding the paper again, drawing her eyes to his talented nimble hands.

Hands she remembered feeling over her skin too well right now. "Other than our tapioca conversation, you've never mentioned your parents once in all the time I've known you."

"I didn't crawl from under a rock."

She smiled slow and just a little bit impishly vindictive. "That's open for debate."

His laugh rumbled low and long, wrapping around her with far more languorous warmth than the ineffective bubble bath she'd stepped out of ten short minutes ago. Her body tingled with awareness, her breasts suddenly oversensitive to the brush of cotton against her bare skin.

"Damn, Nikki, you never did cut me any slack." Shaking his head with a final self-derisive laugh, he bent a last tuck on the paper and extended his hand to her with the finished product cradled in his palm—an origami bird.

She inched backward, then caught herself. This was her home, her life. She stood taller and stood him down. "Stop trying to be charming."

His beautiful smile and laugh faded to a mere echo. "I thought you accepted my apology."

"I did." She wadded the tissue in her hand, tossing it aside with a final sniffle. Cold. Not tears. No more tears over this man. "But you can drop the charming friend act. There's no going back to how things were. You had your chance, and you blew it, dude."

His mouth went tight, his eyes dropping away from hers. Pausing. Holding. Right at her shirt level.

A damp T-shirt she now realized clung to her breasts that happened to be hyperaware of the sexy blond hunk standing a reach away.

Carson's hands shook from resisting the urge to reach for Nikki and cup her breasts that he happened to know fit perfectly in his palms.

And damn it all, why did he have to remember the feel and taste and texture of her in his mouth right now? Washed-thin cotton clung to her skin and subtle curves, begging to be peeled up and off so he could dip his head and lick away whatever water remained on her skin.

Water.

He needed to remember what had happened tonight, how she'd almost plunged to her death, would have if not for the pool below. The thought alone served as an effective cold splash on his heated body. That railing shouldn't have given way. This was a new complex with pristine upkeep. He couldn't ignore the possibility that someone could have tampered with the balcony rail, someone who didn't want her to remember what happened that night in Owens's VOQ room.

He could be wrong, but it was a helluva lot safer to err on the side of caution. "You shouldn't stay here by yourself."

Her spine went straighter, which just so happened to press her peaked breasts tighter against the T-shirt. Counting to ten—twenty—he set the origami bird on the counter.

She folded her arms across her chest. "If you're offering to hang out with me, I'll have to decline."

"I never thought you would agree to that anyway. And quite frankly, I don't think it would be wise."

She bristled to her full five feet ten inches tall. "Because you're afraid I'll jump your bones? Well, you can be sure that even if I'd been the least bit tempted before, you've killed that spark."

Heard. Understood. And regretted.

"I'm more concerned with my own self-control." The words tumbled out ahead of his better sense. Not really a surprise considering how he always seemed to lose his head around this leggy dynamo who could outrace most men and kept a sarcophagus in her living room.

Her jaw dropped wide, started to close then went slack again. A bracing sigh later, she answered, "I don't know what you're expecting to accomplish with a comment like that, but you made it clear the morning after Spike's wedding that you don't want me in your life, and you didn't do it in a particularly nice way. If you had a sister—"

"I do."

"You do?"

Her jaw went slack again, tempting him to kiss the surprise right off her face. Coming here had really been a mammothly stupid idea.

But before he could drag his sorry, horny butt out the door she continued, "Quit distracting me. My point is, if someone treated your sister the way you treated me, you would kick his ass."

"You're right." More than she could even know. He shoved away from the counter and her too-cute sarcophagus and idealistic too-young heart. "And since I don't want *my* ass kicked by your brother or father, it's best I don't stay here. I just had to see for myself that you're okay and make sure you're safe."

Did she have to look so damn conflicted? He was having a tough enough time resisting her when she told him to shut up with all that fire and spunk he knew she brought to bed with her.

She skirted around the sofa full of inviting green pillows that would spread perfectly along the carpet to make a downy lawn for all-night sex. "Good night then. Have a nice drive home."

"Fine, but you're not staying here, either."

Nikki stopped short. "Why do I feel the irrepressible urge to put my hands over my ears and shout, 'You're not the boss of me'? Of course that would fit right in with your whole too-young-for-you mantra."

God, he liked her sense of humor. "You're good."

She snorted. "That compliment came about seven months too late."

"I meant at distracting *me*."

"Apparently not nearly good enough." She sagged to sit on the arm of the sofa. "Why are you so gung-ho on my not being alone?"

"With everything that happened with Owens, I'm concerned your balcony railing giving way might not have been an accident." He planted his boots deep in the plush carpet, the need to see her safe burning even stronger than the need to see her naked.

God, she hated being afraid of her own shadow.

But Carson's words kept rolling around in her head the next day as she parked her small truck in her parents' driveway. Late-afternoon sun dappled through the evergreens packing the yard surrounding the two-story white wood home.

She'd brushed aside Carson's concerns the night before, told him she would double bolt her door and think about what he'd said. She'd bristled out of pride and a need for independence.

Stupid. Stupid. Stupid.

About halfway through her PowerBar at lunch, she'd come to the conclusion that safety was too important. She wouldn't be one of those airheads in a horror movie who went walking in the dark woods at night even when half her friends had already been whacked by some psycho with a gas-powered garden tool.

So here she was with her truck and a suitcase full of clothes. She didn't need a reality check. She already knew. Bad crap was happening. Gary was very dead and she'd darn near died falling off her balcony. Even if it was an accident, she would have been more alert to her surroundings before this mess. Until she could get her life settled again, she needed to be extra careful.

Her mother was worried anyway and in need of extra help with her difficult pregnancy. Why not take her up on the standing offer to stay in the garage apartment?

She could still come and go as she pleased, but would have her brother nearby. Sure sometimes he'd been a wormy little pest who once dumped all her makeup into the sewer. But now that he'd shot up to six foot four inches, he made a fairly decent crime deterrent.

And she sure had plenty of time on her hands to help her mom repaint the new nursery.

Her principal had suggested she take a weeklong vacation. *Suggested* being a loose way of putting it. She suspected a parent or two had complained after getting wind of what happened the night Gary died. Whatever *had* happened.

Gossip could be hell. As much as she wanted to dig her heels in, she could see the principal's resolve. Pissing off her boss now wouldn't be wise.

Her whole life was crashing down around her. She needed control over something. At least she could still tutor her at-risk high schoolers or she would go nuts.

She threw open her truck door, stepped out and reached into the back to heft up her suitcase. Carson was right. She was lucky to have a family support system. Her parents had worked hard to build this for their kids and finally for themselves, too. She wouldn't settle for anything less when it came to building her own life.

And suddenly she couldn't help but wonder what sort of childhood had Carson had. He'd mentioned a sister and a love of tapioca, but nothing else.

Before she could tap on the screen, the front door swung open. Her tiny mother stepped into view with an unmistakable belly and a headful of dark curls lightly streaked with silver. "Nikki!" She swung the door wider, her gaze skating to the suitcase on the plank porch. "I'm so glad you decided to take me up on the offer of some pampering."

"The garage apartment—no pampering, though, please. I was hoping I could help paint the nursery." She reached to pat her mother's stomach and stifled thoughts of having kids of her own. Now definitely wasn't the time. "How's my little sister?"

"She's doing—" Her mother paused, eyes narrowing. "Wait. How did you know it's a girl? Did your father spill the beans in spite of our decision to wait to tell everyone when he gets home?"

Nikki pulled her hand back and hefted her suitcase. "Lucky guess. I figured I had a fifty-fifty shot of getting it right and tripping you up."

"Brat." She swatted her arm with her gardening magazine. "Your father always did spoil you."

"And you need some spoiling today, too. Now how about put your feet up and I'll come down to check on you once I stow my gear over the garage?"

Nikki backed down the steps and over to the outside stairs leading to the garage apartment her father had modified. If her dad was here now, no doubt J. T. Price would worry about everything with Owens. He was concerned enough with what few details he'd been told.

Her father was overprotective, always had been. She'd actually felt sorry for the poor skinny high school boys who made it to her front porch only to be confronted by her six-foot-four-inch weight lifter father. He didn't scowl. But he didn't smile at those fellas, either.

What a sucky welcome home he would have if she didn't get this mess straightened out. While she wasn't some woman in desperate need of daddy's approval, she also wasn't overly thrilled at the prospect of worrying or disappointing him, either.

One day at a time. She would have to trust the OSI and Special Agent Reis to do their job.

Meanwhile, the best thing she could do for her parents—and for herself—was keep life level, help her mother out with some yard work. Not stress about what she couldn't control.

Her cell phone buzzed in her black backpack purse slung over her shoulder, and with an instinctive awareness she didn't want and couldn't escape, she knew it was Carson checking up on her again.

Chapter 5

"Hello, Major, what can I help you with?"

Carson stepped deeper into the OSI agent's office, hoping for a few answers from Reis, who was currently slipping a tie over his head and tightening it to start his day. The guy stored ties in his office? A kindred workaholic, which boded well for solving this case faster.

And please God, clearing Nikki.

She hadn't answered his phone calls in two days, but he couldn't blame her. She'd left a message for him with his secretary, insisting she didn't need to speak to him directly, but that she was fine and staying at her mom's.

At least she was camping out where her college-aged brother could keep his eyes open. Carson refused to feel guilty for checking in with Chris, any more than he would feel guilty about stopping in to fact-check with Reis. "I'm here for an update on the Owens case and anything you may have uncovered about Nikki Price's accident."

His gut still burned from even thinking about Nikki plummeting from that balcony.

Distraction. He needed it. Pronto. So he studied the room for hints about this man who held Nikki's life in his investigative hands.

Framed soccer field posters from around the world splashed the walls with color—one even including a photo of Reis with a soccer trophy and bottle of champagne. He didn't need to avert his eyes from the liquor as he had in the early days on the wagon.

He could even remember now how Cabernet had been his vino of choice with steaks and Pinot Noir had accompanied him on more than a few sailing trips. He didn't crave as he used to, but the thoughts still crowded his mind.

Reis shoved aside an old carryout box marked from a gourmet deli. "How's Ms. Price doing after her tumble from the balcony?"

"Fine, barely rattled other than a cold from the freezing water."

"So you've spoken to her?"

Why was he asking? Reis probably already knew anyway. Carson avoided the question and simply stated, "Seems mighty coincidental to me, her railing giving way."

"Could be an accident."

"Or it could be someone trying to kill her before she remembers what happened."

"Do ya' think?" Reis quirked an eyebrow.

What an ass. But being openly antagonistic in return

wouldn't get the answers he needed. "Excuse me for being slow on the uptake, but I fail to see what's so damn funny."

Reis rocked back in his chair underneath an autographed photo of Pelé. "What's so damn funny? Watching you, Major. I've seen you work a crisis without flinching, with a calm I'd expect from someone more seasoned. But when it comes to a woman, you're just as human as the rest of us."

Well hell. While it might be true—all right, *was* true—what did this have to do with anything? He'd be irritated if he didn't admire the guy's no-bull attitude and sharp eye. "Call me Cro-Magnon, but it pisses me off when a woman—any woman—is in danger. It's my job to protect. I can't turn that off just because I'm not in combat."

"That's the only reason I'm not chewing your ass for thinking I'm idiot enough not to have considered the possibility someone may have tampered with her balcony. There're plenty of reasons somebody may have been angry enough to whack Owens over the head. His gambling habit. Or maybe Nikki Price had a jealous ex-boyfriend who didn't much like her getting busy with another guy."

An understandable possibility since thinking about Nikki dating other guys tossed acid onto his already burning raw gut even though he had no claim to her. He kept his hands loose, his face impassive. He'd mastered the blasé look with his new command duties.

Funny thing, though, Reis was giving him exactly the same blank expression. The investigator's words about ex-boyfriends being to blame shifted in Carson's head, settling into place a second before Reis leaned forward, elbows on his desk.

"So I guess you won't be surprised to hear you're on my suspect list, as well, Major."

How damned ironic that in spite of years of working to hide his attraction to Nikki, the agent had pegged it so fast.

If he was doing such a piss-poor job of keeping his emotions under wraps, then maybe it was time to confront this dogged attraction head-on with Nikki after all.

Nikki jogged alongside her brother, her running shoes pounding pavement with dogged determination. She shot puffy clouds of air ahead then plowed through the vapor. Too bad her cloudy memories weren't as easily dispersed.

Thank goodness Chris didn't want to talk because she had too much energy to work out. Instead, she kept her Walkman headset in place, hoping exhaustion and WWII era tunes— The Andrews sisters at present—would soothe her frustration over having her life hijacked.

She missed her apartment and independence. However as much as she wanted to return to her place and simply invest in a kick-ass security system, she couldn't forget her mother's strained face and difficult pregnancy. Her father was due home in another week. She could put her own needs on hold for a few more days.

Cars chugged past in the sleepy neighborhood, some turning around and taking detours for ongoing road construction, but she felt safe enough in the late afternoon with her brother alongside. Even Carson couldn't expect her to hole up inside indefinitely.

One foot in front of the other, she willed the runner's high to overtake her so she could block out the resurrected yearning to be with Carson, a light harmonic melody pulsing through her ears and thrumming in her veins. A swelling, sentimental ache she'd finally acknowledged the night she decided to break things off with Gary…

Nikki thudded along the planked boardwalk stretching toward Beachcombers Bar and Grill. Flight-jacket-clad bodies with dates packed the back porch, twice as many undoubtedly inside if the dull roar was anything to gauge by. Finding Gary could take hours in this wash of brown leather and jeans. Better to park her butt at the bar and wait for him to find her.

A marshy breeze blew in off the beach, cold, but not enough to drive the congregated smokers back inside. She charged closer while sailboats bobbed along the nearby marina, lines snapping and pinging against masts in a mariner's tune.

But she wouldn't be lured by that song of Carson anymore. Tonight would be her fresh start. No more self-destructive dating losers who happened to resemble Carson.

One of the first things on her agenda, stop coming to a watering hole populated with flyboys from nearby Charleston Air Force Base. Climbing the steps up to the hangout housed in a historic clapboard two story, she pushed the rest of the way through, smiling and nodding at familiar faces she barely registered. Same old crowd, even on a Sunday evening.

The bass from the band pulsed through the ground, beach music blending with old rock tunes from her parents' day that had round-robined back into modern remakes. She sucked in a bracing breath, prepping herself for the upcoming confrontation. Gary had been a little possessive in the past when guys hit on her, but not violent. Still just in case, she'd chosen a public meeting place.

She parted a circle playing quarters. "Pardon me. 'Scuse me." She ducked around an overendowed regular wearing Lycra and no coat in January. "Excuse me, Hannah."

Finally. The door.

Nikki dodged another couple between her and her destination—and slammed into a solid body. Her senses announced his identity before she even looked up.

Carson, full of musky scent mixed with a fresh ocean air, unmistakably him. She forced her gaze upward and her feet to stomp backward when she wanted to stay smack-dab where she was and just breathe for a few minutes—or days.

"Hi, Scorch."

She refused to duck and run. She had nothing to be ashamed of. He was the one who'd been a total jerk and if speaking with her made him a smidge uncomfortable, then too damn bad.

He hitched a foot on the step back into the main bar, shoulder on the door frame, a white paper sack clutched in his hand. "Hey, have you spoken with your father recently?"

And wasn't that just like him to bring up her dad every time they spoke? Thinking Carson stayed away because of her father stung a little less, since at least he had a reason—albeit a really stupid one. However if he'd simply been a user-jerk, then getting over him would be easier.

A lose-lose situation for her.

"Phone calls have been scarce, but the Internet has been awesome. He talks more through e-mail than he would over the phone anyhow."

"That's your dad."

"Are you meeting someone here?" Ah hell.

"No, just grabbing carryout on my way to a meeting." He lifted his hand gripping the paper sack. "Nothing like Claire's Southern barbecue wings after a day of sailing."

Claire McDermott was joint owner of Beachcombers with her sisters. Claire was a single attractive woman who happened to cook Carson's favorite food—and didn't jealousy suck? The guy was heading to a late meeting at work on a Sunday night, for goodness' sake. "So you're still sailing."

"I finally bit the bullet and replaced my old sixteen-footer with a used thirty-one-foot Catalina a couple of months ago."

She could so see him out on the water, sun bleaching his golden hair white, bronzing his chest while they both savored the waves and the day. She'd always admired his way of enjoying silence as much as a conversation. "Good for you. Life should be lived."

He stared back at her with eyes so blue she saw the ocean and really wanted to jump in, headfirst, no safety preserver.

He blinked first—thank God—and looked over her shoulder. "Are you meeting someone?"

She wanted to say no and see if he asked her to join him for supper, but she was smart enough not to act on that "want" with this man ever again. "Yeah, he should be here any minute."

His sky-blue eyes blanked. "I won't keep you then."

"Enjoy your wings and your meeting."

Nodding, he brushed past and heaven help her she watched his confident long strides since he couldn't see her unrestrained attention as he melded into the crowd. And how weird was it that suddenly she could see through that crowd just fine when it came to watching him?

Pain—and yes, anger—whispered through her veins. All of which strengthened her resolve to break things off with Gary. How unfair to date him when she still had this mess of feelings for Carson tangled tighter than those sailboat lines twisting in the wind.

He cleared the walkway and stopped. Waving?

She should look away. Leave. Quit staring after him like a lovesick dork. And she would in just a second.

Carson called to someone behind a beat-up truck but his words drifted away on the wind and out to sea. He waited to be joined by two men—an older, shorter man in a backward ball cap and another guy about Carson's age, taller in a plaid shirt. She couldn't make them out well from a distance and didn't study them overlong since she was too busy being more relieved than she should that Carson wasn't with a woman.

He walked with the two men toward his extended-cab truck where they all three climbed in. All? Apparently there wasn't a work meeting after all. It stung more than a little that he'd felt the need to make excuses.

Definitely time to leave and move forward...

Panting from her run, Nikki slowed on the sidewalk in front of her parents' next-door neighbor's, sifting through the mishmash of emotions from that night to simply analyze the event.

She'd already remembered that time prior to stepping inside, but relaxing did offer her a few more details—like the two men Carson met up with. Problem was that seemed so insignificant. She could only hope the relaxation techniques suggested by the hypnotist would help her recall more.

As if she'd conjured Carson from her thoughts, there he was, in the driveway with her mother, little Jamie barreling by the trailer hitch on his toddler scooter.

Her mom sagged back against the fender of Carson's truck, her hand pressed to her forehead. Nikki's stomach lurched up to her throat. Had something happened to her father? God, she'd been so selfishly focused on her own mess she'd all but forgotten that her dad was in the Middle East, not a safe place for military members on the ground or in the air.

Nikki ripped the headset from her ears and sprinted across the dormant lawn, over a low hedge toward her mother. "Mom?" She took her mother's elbow, determined to keep it together, be supportive. "I'm here. Breathe—"

"It's all right," Rena interrupted, straightening with a shaky smile. "Everything's fine. I only got a smidge spooked when Scorch drove up. I had a little flashback to the other time my husband's commander showed up on my doorstep. Of course I know you wouldn't come alone for a bad call. You would bring along a doctor and chaplain," she rambled, gasping. "But still…"

Carson jammed his fists into his leather coat pockets. "I'm sorry. I didn't mean to scare you. I just came to check on everyone. And you're right. I wouldn't be here alone and I wouldn't be wearing a flight suit."

He would wear his dress blues, all those ribbons across his chest. He could be a poster model for a recruiting office he filled out any uniform so well. What a silly superficial thought that made her wonder if her feelings were still the result of physical attraction and the old crush.

She didn't much like what that said about her.

He'd apologized, hadn't made excuses and seemed to be working on amends. Just because she didn't totally trust him, she didn't have to be rude. And the excitement circling laps around inside her stomach was simply nerves because of their history. Maybe she'd gotten it wrong over the past seven months by staying away from him. Perhaps spending more time with him would help her get over that.

Get over *him*.

He had to stop looking at *her* before her family noticed.

But Carson couldn't seem to reel in his attention from Nikki, her face glistening with sweat, her hair mussed, much like he imagined she would look during marathon sex. Which he would give his left nut to remember having had with her seven months ago.

The next morning, they'd been naked in bed together and he couldn't even recall shedding more than their shirts. He remembered well that incredible moment she'd unfastened the front clasp of her bra, freeing perfect pert breasts. He'd reached for her with both hands, could feel the shape and pebbling peaks of her against his palms even now.

His breathing hitched right along with a skipped heartbeat. How idiotic to think about sleeping with Nikki when standing in the driveway with her exhausted mother, worried brother and wild man baby brother currently trying to run over Carson's boots with his scooter.

Actually, it wasn't wise to think about getting naked with her at any time, because his self control was dwindling fast the longer he spent with her. But he'd figured out quickly in Reis's office that he wasn't fooling anyone, especially himself, by staying away. Best to convince her they could resurrect the light friendship they'd once had.

While keeping his flight suit zipped this time.

Nikki's brother Chris shuffled up beside them, his eyes locked on his mother's weary face, concern stamping a maturity beyond his years on his college-aged features. The kid had been bending over backward to help out around the house since his own brush with the law his junior year in high school. His part-time job at a restaurant then had almost turned deadly when the boy's boss had tried to use Chris as cash mule for drug money.

Damn, hadn't the Price family been through enough?

"Hey, Mom?" Chris cupped her elbow. "How about we go inside and I'll dig up some of that chocolate peanut butter and marshmallow ice cream you've been craving?"

Rena straightened from the car, her gaze shifting from Carson to her daughter and back again with too much perception for his comfort level. Rena tucked her hand in the crook of her lanky son's elbow. "That sounds wonderful, Chris. Then Scorch can finish, uh, *checking* on Nikki."

Nikki shifted from foot to foot, fidgeting in a way he recognized as her need to run. He completely sympathized, which steeled his resolve to make this right between them.

Carson tapped the earphones dangling around her neck, soft strains of something filtering through but unidentifiable. "What's playing?"

A smile teased at her full lips, no gloss needed. She had a shine all her own. "Want to guess?"

"Lady, I couldn't figure you out if I had a million guesses."

"Thanks, I think." She reached down to the CD player

clipped to her Lycra running pants and turned off the music. "My secret shame—I'm a big band, WWII music addict. Ragtime, too. Anything over sixty years old, and I'm there."

"God, you're full of surprises." How odd to realize he didn't know her any better than she knew him. He thought he'd been the one with all the secrets.

"That's me, unpredictable as ever, although I have to confess that these days I'm in the mood for a boring life."

The past few days had to have been scary as hell for her. Carson cupped her elbow, which seemed surprisingly frail even through the thick cotton of her pullover and a body he knew to be toned from running, workouts and even her membership on a local rec league soccer team. Thank heaven for those honed quick reflexes. Still, she had to be sore, bruised maybe.

He searched for signs of scrapes but found nothing visible. "Are you okay? You look tired."

She scrunched her elegant nose. "Thanks."

"Are you feeling any aftereffects from the fall? You didn't actually go into work today, did you?"

"I wish. But no work for me today. The principal thinks it's best I take a couple of weeks off."

"What the f—" He stopped short, biting back the word along with his anger at the injustice before shoving it all aside to focus on her. "I'm so damn sorry."

"Me, too. The principal was hanging tough until word leaked that DNA tests of the skin under Gary's fingernails matched mine, which of course still doesn't mean a thing since I was obviously there with him."

His jaw flexed with tension or—more unsettling—jealousy? "Having your life on hold must be hell."

"They're paying me, so I shouldn't complain, but my students…" She shook her head, ponytail swishing from the back of her Atlanta Braves ball cap. "I wanted to be there with them when they present at the regional history fair."

"The sarcophagus."

"At least we got to finish the display and the reports before my surprise vacation." She nodded toward the open garage door full of gardening supplies. "I'm keeping busy around here in the meantime. I figure I can sabotage most of Mom's gorgeous landscaping by the end of the week."

The perfect excuse to hang around here longer and launch his plan to resurrect their unlikely friendship.

"Want some help? For your dad, of course." He winked.

Snorting, she rolled her eyes. "You're picking on me, aren't you?"

"More than a little."

"I think I lost my sense of humor along with a few hours of my life." She scooped a second sweatshirt off the hood of her truck and tugged it over her head on her way to the garage. She could pull on five layers and his mind's eye would see the beauty underneath, his hands itching to tunnel inside for a second sampling.

"About my dad—" she sidestepped a table saw on her way to the wheelbarrow "—I had to tell him what's going on before the news filtered over there."

He walked up alongside her in the garage, the scent of motor oil arousing as hell when mixed with a hint of Nikki's soap. "That must have been tough."

"Totally sucked." She passed him a rake. "I was so proud of myself for being independent, and yet, here I am."

She emptied the wheelbarrow, tossing two bags of mulch on the cement floor and grabbing the handles to roll it outside. Empty oak branches swayed overhead along with evergreens. She'd run a couple of miles and now planned to cool down with yard work? This woman really did need a friend's support more than maybe even she knew.

"Independence doesn't mean stupidity." He scraped the rake over the yard, gathering a growing tidal wave of dead pine needles. "It's good, normal and damned lucky to have family you can count on who know they can count on you."

"What about your family?" She knelt to scoop up the growing pile of pine straw with her hands. "You mentioned a sister."

"My sister's married, lives with her husband in Ireland."

"Ireland? Wow, you don't hear that one all that often."

He rubbed his thumb against two fingers in the universal "money" symbol.

"Ah, lucky for them."

He shrugged, raking faster. The Prices seemed a helluva lot richer to him with their overflowing home and working class values.

She stared up as she rose to take the handles again. "The whole 'money doesn't buy happiness' notion? Hmmm… maybe not, but it sure pays the bills." She dumped the full wheelbarrow by the curb and rolled back to his next pile of straw. "What about the rest of your family?"

"Well, they don't have any problems meeting their bills."

"You have that look to you."

"That look?" He peered over his aviator glasses, liking the *look* of her so much it was tough to process her words.

"Prep school education. A far cry from my parents' garage jam-packed full of yard gear, greasy tools and workout weights."

Her implied censure gave him pause. He'd always known she had a crush on him. He knew he had his faults—big ass faults—but since she didn't know about his alcoholism, he'd never stopped to consider there might be other things she disapproved of about his way of life. That tweaked more than it should have. "I think you're insulting me."

"No. Only commenting on our obvious differences. Just because I feel you did a really scumbag thing a few months ago doesn't mean I believe you're an actual scumbag."

"Thanks." Sort of.

"But while we're on the subject of that really scumbag thing you did for which you have finally apologized but never explained…" She dumped another load of pine straw, her face averted a little too conveniently to be coincidence.

"Noticed that, did you?" He leaned on the rake, taking in the overstiff brace of her shoulders and wanting to kick his own ass.

"Tough not to notice." She slumped back against the tree, hands behind her. "So why did you walk out the door and never bother to call? Or better yet, why did you invite me through your door in the first place?"

And into his bed. That much, at least, he remembered along with the feel of her bare chest against his as they'd tumbled onto the mattress. He'd just lost most of the parts between bed and waking up. The good parts, stolen by a drunken blackout. Finding Nikki naked next to him in the morning and knowing he'd broken her trust, her father's trust and his own code of honor made him realize he'd bottomed out.

He'd rolled his sorry, hungover butt off the mattress and found an Alcoholics Anonymous chapter. A.A. meetings had saved his life. Slowly, he was regaining his self-respect.

One day at a time. Never take it for granted.

"Why did I go to bed with you?" The truth wouldn't hurt any worse. He flattened a hand to the tree beside her head and let what he was thinking and feeling show for the first time in…he couldn't remember when. "Because I really wanted to be there, for a long time, almost from the first time I saw you. You were legal, but damn, you were young. And on that day, I was truly too much of a scumbag to stay away—"

"Stop." She clapped a hand to his mouth.

"Stop?" Speaking felt too much like kissing her hand, which messed with his head more than any drink.

"I've changed my mind." Her hand trembled. "I don't want to hear this tonight. I want to rake leaves and talk like we used to." Her hand fell away.

Her soft touch lingered, a simple caress when they'd shared far more overtly sexual touches and still he went stone hard, wanting her so much his teeth hurt. "Before you realized I'm a scumbag?"

"Yeah."

Wasn't that what he'd wanted as well in coming here to-night? So go. Leave. "Do you think you can really forget what I did that night?"

"I can forget for an evening."

Less than he'd hoped for but more than he deserved. "Fair enough."

Since she didn't move away he let himself keep staring into her eyes. What could happen outside in her parents' front yard while traffic inched past? Branches rustled overhead raining more pine straw around them, some catching in her hair. He lifted his hand and still she didn't move away, apparently as caught in this insanity as he was. He swept his fingers over her head. Silky strands. So damn soft that before he knew it he'd cupped the base of her skull.

Her pupils went wide, her gray eyes stormier still until he could have sworn the sun was sinking faster. So easily he could urge her closer. Or step forward. Or hell, just lean and taste her because it killed him, absolutely freaking killed him, that he only had spotty recollections of what happened between them that night.

He would give anything to have at least the memory of those lost hours. Although he suspected remembering would torment him even more.

The front door blasted open a second ahead of her brother Chris loping through onto the porch. "Mom sent me out to ask if Carson would like to stay for supper?"

A mom probably smart enough to realize things needed breaking up out front before he snapped the thin thread of Nikki's returning trust.

Carson backed away, shoving his hands in his pockets. He didn't deserve that trust, but he would be damned if he would abuse it again. As much as he wanted to climb those steps and hang out with this awesomely normal family and listen to Nikki's even more amazing laugh, he knew better now. He'd made a step in reclaiming their friendship, but would need to tread warily to resist stealing more.

"Thanks, but I need to get back to the squadron."

Chapter 6

She really needed to get back to work, but there were no new breaks in the investigation.

Nostalgia and longing mellowing her, Nikki stared down the empty corridor at the high school, only the rumblings of Saturday in-school suspension swelling from the lunchroom. At least she still had her tutoring stints here with older students until she resumed her junior high position. She glanced at her Minnie Mouse wristwatch she'd bought on a lark because she thought it would charm her cranky fourth period class.

Ten minutes early. Good. That would give her time to set up in the library.

Her footsteps echoed down the hall as she passed a poster announcing an FCA meeting. Good luck banners stretched for the basketball team along with a sign for the drama department's upcoming production of *The Lion, the Witch and the Wardrobe.*

She ached to teach her students, to recapture the rush of that moment when youthful eyes lit with enthusiasm over learning something new. She even loved the challenge of breaking through with the surly ones. Junior high was such a pivotal time, building foundations and confidence to carry into this high school world with temptations and dangers beyond any she'd seen just a few short years ago when she'd graduated.

And the world beyond was definitely scarier than she'd ever imagined.

Who'd have thought she would yearn for lesson plans? Or even a tour of bus duty? She would sacrifice almost anything for a stack of ungraded papers to take her mind off what happened in the yard with Carson. Had she really almost kissed him again? And why was he working so hard for her forgiveness now?

Nikki rounded the corner into the library where she would meet up with Billy Wade Watkins. The kid didn't seem particularly interested in learning, but he preferred school to home. A start. Hopefully he would realize that education was a means to a better life. Not that social services had been able to prove squat. He'd been removed and returned to his alcoholic parents twice over the years. She'd even tried to work some magic for the kid through the base since his father was retired military, but no luck.

She scanned rows of books lining the walls, more partitioning aisles and study stations until she spied the top of a masculine head in a computer booth, a dark-haired male like

Billy Wade, apparently making use of the free Internet time. She rounded a large circular table on her way to the cubicle. Feet came into view—no ratty Nike runners, but rather *leather loafers?*

Not the standard student gear around this school. So where was Billy Wade?

The male stood, Special Agent David Reis emerging from behind the cubicle wall. The last person she expected to see here, and one guaranteed to scare the bejesus out of her.

Her stomach bolted up to her throat. What was he doing *here?* And on a Saturday?

Willing her nerves to settle, she dropped her grade book, papers and text on the table to give herself an extra second to regain her composure around the investigator. Thank God he didn't have handcuffs in sight.

"Is there something I can help you with, Agent Reis? Did you receive the e-mail I sent to your office with a list of all Gary's friends?" Babbling. Not good, but she couldn't stop the tumble of words from her mouth. "I also forwarded a copy of the post Gary sent me that night, inviting me to join him at Beachcombers."

"I got it, but that's not what I'm here for." Reaching back behind the cube wall, he lifted a paper bag. "Here is your purse back. I'm sorry to say we have to keep your clothes for evidence."

And why bring it here? Unease tickled up her spine in spite of the lack of handcuffs. She took the sack grateful they'd let her have her credit cards and license that first day. Her clothes, however, they could keep forever. "I could have come to the base to pick it up."

"Thought I would save you the trip since I already had business out this way." He shoved his hands in his pockets, fished out a pack of gum, offering her a piece—she shook her head—before folding a stick in his mouth. All the while, he never took his eyes off her.

She resisted the urge to fidget like a bug under a science lab microscope. But wait? He already had business out here? "You've been questioning people I work with?"

"That bothers you?"

"Of course it does." She tossed the sack onto the round table with such force it slid to a stop against her grade book. "I've already been put on a leave of absence at the junior high because of this mess. I need my work back—"

"I'm sorry for any financial inconvenience."

His expressionless stare reminded her of a circling shark peering through that microscope, and sheesh what a mixed-up image that was. She really needed to air out her brain before she returned to work full-time.

And to do that, she needed to help Agent Reis however she could. "It's not about the money. It's about my students who need consistency. It's about how much I love my job."

"It's also about a man who lost his life."

"I understand that better than most, wouldn't you think?"

"Then you'll appreciate why I'm here." His shark stare warmed with a hint of human compassion. "Actually, coming here could well clear you."

"Clear me? Gary never came here."

"As I told your major friend when he came to my office, I have to consider that someone may have gone after Owens because of you."

As much as she wanted to rejoice over any option that cleared her, she cringed to think that she could have caused Gary's death, even inadvertently. "Who? I can hardly wrap my head around this."

"I can't discuss details of an ongoing investigation."

Even being a suspect brought such a total lack of privacy she felt exposed. Her hands twitched to check her sapphire button-down shirt with her black slacks. She hated the vulnerable gesture, the near irrepressible need to be sure she was totally covered.

She forced her hands back to her sides and hoped Reis hadn't noticed—only to realize the shark-eyed investigator hadn't missed a thing. In fact his gaze was still locked on her clothes.

On her body?

Okay, now she was totally feeling exposed and completely freaked out. He couldn't be interested in her. Could he?

He was an intriguing man, no doubt, handsome in a dark and serious kind of way. Which made him completely not her type since apparently she had a real weak spot for fair-headed charmers. But how did she discourage this guy without embarrassing both of them? Provided she was even reading him right.

Thank God Billy Wade Watkins chose that moment to amble through the library entrance, silver chains on his baggy clothes jangling. "Ms. Price? Sorry I'm late. I had to drop off my dad at some church meeting thing so I could use the truck."

"Over here, Billy Wade." She backed away from the investigator. "Agent Reis, thank you for bringing my things, but I have to get to work."

"Of course. Let me know if you remember anything more." He leaned closer, his eyes over her shoulder. "Be careful. Schools aren't the safest places to hang out these days."

He brushed around and past, leaving behind his Doublemint gum scent and unwelcome doubts about her students, as well as questions about that whole strange once-over moment from Reis that still totally creeped her out. She'd been so looking forward to this tutoring session, yet suddenly she wanted nothing more than to rake pine straw with Carson.

And that unsettled her as much as the prospect of Reis prying in her personal life.

Prying the dog tag on his flight boot out of Jamie Price's mouth, Carson passed the toddler a graham cracker in exchange. If only adults were as easy to figure out as the pint-size versions. "There ya' go, kiddo."

The chubby-cheeked child snatched the treat and shoved it into his mouth in a shower of crumbs and cuteness. Carson ruffled the fella's dark curls, wiped the drool off the dog tag and climbed back up the ladder in the Price kitchen to replace the battery on the smoke detector.

He'd already checked every battery, furnace filter, window and door lock, and still it wasn't enough. Nothing would be enough until Nikki was in the clear and he knew exactly what happened the night Gary Owens died.

So he worked to fix what he could.

After leaving Nikki and her too-tempting rake, he'd run himself into a stupor until three in the morning. Not that sleep came easy with her eyes haunting the back of his eyelids. By sunrise, he'd decided his idea to spend more time with her may have been ill-advised. He would return to his original plan to check in with her family and Reis.

Except halfway to the marina for a day of sailing, he'd turned toward her parents' place to ask her to join him—just to keep her occupied and cheer her up after her forced sabbatical. Right.

Wrong.

Jesus. He hadn't been led around by his libido like this since high school. Still he waited for Nikki rather than simply leaving. And actually, hanging out with her mama and short stuff wasn't a great hardship. He suspected there were a lot of clues to what made Nikki tick to be found in this ivy-stenciled kitchen.

Rena reached into the cabinet and pulled down two Mason jars like the others perched on her windowsill. Water and plant clippings filled each glass container, some stems sprouting new root webs. "You're really going above and beyond in your acting commander duties."

He folded the ladder and propped it beside the fridge.

"The squadron's only at half power with the rest deployed overseas." This house brimmed with so much life—plants, kid, pregnancy, even rising bread—he could hardly take it all in. *Take.* He hated that word and was trying his damnedest not to be a *taker* like his parents.

She twisted on the faucet and slid a jar underneath the gushing flow. "Even at half power, you're still dealing with quite a load if you're giving everyone this much individual attention."

Of course she would know better. He was doing his job and pulling overtime, but even that didn't involve multiple home visits in a week. "These are extraordinary circumstances. Besides, J.T. and I have history from crewing together. He would look out for my family in the same way—if I had one."

Out of smoke detectors and furnace filters to fix, he dropped his restless butt at the table. For years he'd never questioned his decision to stay single, but parked in this kitchen, he couldn't ignore the regret tugging at him as strongly as the toddler yanking on the dog tag on his boot again.

The water overflowed. "Do we have reason to worry about Nikki?"

He held out his hands to the little guy on the floor to buy himself time to think. Plunking the kid on his knee, Carson tugged the dog tags from around his neck and passed them over. "I wish I had the answer to that one, Rena, but I honestly don't know."

She shuffled the jar to the counter and filled the other, then tossed two fern clippings inside before placing them on the sill. "She only tells me the basics about what happened with Gary Owens, so I worry all the more."

"The OSI agent leading the investigation seems sharp."

Rena sank into a chair across from him, nudging a line of tiny Tonka trucks across the table toward her son who ignored them in favor of his new favorite teething toy—dog tags. "So the worst that could happen is that Nikki—" she paused, swallowed, then continued "—killed him in self-defense as opposed to an accidental death."

The worst? Someone could be gunning for her, far worse. And there were two women and a child here with just a college kid for protection. He didn't like this at all. To hell with

worrying about treading warily while rebuilding a friendship. Damn straight he was concerned and he intended to talk
to Reis about protection options. This would be easier if Rena
and J. T. Price lived on base, except this whole mess had
started on base. So if someone else had killed Owens, that
someone had access to military installations.

All serious concerns, ones a pregnant woman didn't need.
He studied her face as she rubbed her swelling belly.

"How are you feeling?"

She swung her feet up onto a spare chair. "Like I'll go stir-
crazy sitting still for four more months."

"Seems to me there's plenty going on around here." He slid
a discarded piece of junk mail across the table and started
folding. "Don'tcha think, little guy?"

Jamie flashed him a gummy grin broken only by a few
baby teeth and the remnants of graham cracker. Damn he
was cute with all that dark hair and those saucer-wide dark
eyes, in fact resembled the baby pictures of Nikki packing the
house.

"You're good with children." Rena interrupted his
thoughts.

Uh-oh. He knew that matchmaking tone well. He folded
faster. "Uncle on-the-job training."

"You'll be a good father someday once you find that right
woman."

He needed to put a stop to this line of conversation as
quickly and politely as possible. He cranked a smile. "Why
do all women assume a man's only single because he hasn't
met the right woman?"

Her face pinked in sync with her embarrassed grimace.

"I'm sorry. That was presumptuous of me. Blame it on the inquisitive counselor not getting to log in those hours at work—" The phone chirped from the wall, interrupting whatever else she'd been planning to say.

Passing the kid the folded paper airplane to keep him quiet while Rena talked, Carson used the moment to gather his thoughts before the woman managed to wrench God-only-knew what else out of him. He definitely had too many secrets to let down his guard around her. He'd all but forgotten she was a shrink, she'd put him so at ease. Probably why she was reputed to be such a good one.

After the shoot-down and rescue in the Middle East, he'd been evaluated at a base in Germany. He'd managed to side-step the head examiners over there, a skill honed in his childhood.

Hindsight showed him his mistake. His alcoholism had flared after his return until he'd hooked up with A.A.

However sharing details in a therapeutic setting was totally different than spilling his guts to Rena Price. He was coming to terms with his childhood, but that didn't mean he wanted to take out a billboard about all his neglectful parents had forgotten to do for him and all the things their coked-up friends had tried to do *to* him. He couldn't understand how his sister managed to trust her genes enough to marry, much less procreate.

Procreate?

He could almost hear Nikki teasing him for his stuffy word choice. She was every bit as full of humor and life as this house.

Rena tucked the cordless phone under her chin and reached

for Jamie, clutching him close with an urgency that spoke of maternal fear. "I'll track down your brother to pick you up, sweetie."

Pick Nikki up? "What's wrong?"

She fished the paper airplane out of Jamie's mouth, hugging him tight again. "Nikki's stranded at the high school, car trouble."

Relief slammed through him. A simple spark plug or flooded car. Except wait. J. T. Price, a proficient mechanic, had taught his kids well. Premonition pricked a second before Rena continued.

"Someone slashed Nikki's tires."

Nikki kept her eyes on the access road leading into the high school parking lot, a preferable sight to her pitiful little truck with its deflated tires, currently being loaded on a flatbed tow truck.

Billy Wade shuffled from foot to foot, his baggy clothes defying gravity by staying on his body in spite of the weight of the mint of silver chains hanging off them. "Too bad we don't have four cans of that flat-fix-it stuff."

"It's okay, really. My ride's on the way. And honestly, I think my tires are beyond any can of foam repair."

"This really blows." Dyed black hair, long on one side, hung over his face in a greasy curtain. "When I find out who did this to you, he won't be bothering you no more."

"*Any*more. And thank you. That's sweet of you to worry, but once the school checks surveillance video footage, they'll probably be able to nail the person responsible."

He went stock-still. Too still. "They have cameras out here?"

"Yes, Billy Wade, they do." God, she hated suspecting him of doing anything illegal, but Reis's suspicions still rolled through her mind.

"I could, uh, just give you a ride, you know. My dad's truck might not look like much, but it runs real good and has four full tires."

"Your dad's truck looks a lot like my father's Ford."

"Really?" The teen's mask of bored insolence slid away for a rare second. "Your old man drives a beater, too? I wouldn'ta guessed we had anything in common."

He stepped closer. Too close. Into her personal space.

Okay, uncomfortable moment. Step back, keep her composure and take heart in knowing those surveillance cameras would show she hadn't made a single improper move with this kid. Although it saddened her heart that the days had long passed when a teacher could even pat a student on the back. A few pervs had ruined it for everyone else.

She crossed her arms over her chest. "Thank you for the offer, but I have a ride on the way."

"That him?" Billy Wade pointed to the turn lane.

And Carson's sparkling truck. That sure wasn't her brother behind the wheel.

Oh boy. Her mama was gonna have some explaining to do. Except that would necessitate showing how much it bothered her that Carson was the one picking her up instead of Chris, and in the middle of all those muddled emotions she was so darn relieved to see Carson driving their way. Four slashed tires, close on the heels of Agent Reis's warning really gave her the creeps.

"I can see why you'd rather go with him." Billy Wade's face returned to surly, a cover for insecurity—she was pretty sure.

The impulse to assert she and Carson were just friends bubbled up, then fizzed in light of better sense. Letting Billy Wade and any other boys around here think she and Carson were dating would work to her advantage. She wasn't much older than these students, so erecting boundaries was all the more important. "Thanks for hanging out to help."

"Sure. Whatever. Nothing else to do."

Billy Wade ambled over toward his father's rusted-out truck, chains on his saggy black pants jangling with each heavy step. He really was a sharp kid with a good heart, and a very real chance of landing in jail someday like his brothers.

Carson's truck shooshed to a stop beside her, hunky flyboy behind the wheel in a navy-blue windbreaker for sailing and a smile that turned her heart over faster than that big cylinder engine of his.

"I hear you need a lift."

She turned her back on Billy Wade and the new host of worries she couldn't do anything about today.

Her eyes slid from Carson's chest to his scowl—directed right at Billy Wade as the teen continued his badass strut right past his truck and melded into the smoking cluster of other in-school-suspension students.

Nikki circled around to the passenger side and stepped up inside, supple leather warming her. Heated seats? An awesome feature she hadn't been able to afford in her little econo-truck currently on its way to a garage for a set of tires she was hard-pressed to finance. "You can wipe that disapproving look off your face."

Scowl showing no signs of fading, Carson eased his foot off the brake. "He's twice your size and a thug. This so-called 'look on my face' is totally justified."

"Appearances are deceiving." She instinctively defended her student as Carson drove from the lot. "He's a kid who's had a tough start and doesn't stand a chance at making anything of his life if he doesn't get extra help. It's frighteningly easy for a child with problems or special needs to go unnoticed."

He went silent at that for two traffic lights, stopped at the next before turning to her. "What happened to make him fall behind?"

"Dyslexia, which is especially tough to diagnose in a kid with a gifted IQ. He's smart, really smart, which helped him skate by for years with average grades. Add frequent military moves into the mix and it was easy for him to fall through the cracks."

"He's a genius with some kind of disability?"

"It's not as unlikely as you would think. One in three mentally gifted children has some kind of learning disability. The numbers could actually be higher since it's easy for schools to miss out on diagnosing the gifted dyslexic, especially when they're surprised a kid from his background is even passing at all."

"I wouldn't have thought about it that way. It sucks to think how many students could get lost in the system based on misconceptions."

He was being more insightful on the subject than she'd expected. Perhaps she'd been a little quick to judge him based on his silver-spoon background. "There are complexities to the levels and every dyslexic student is different. Basically, we figure out ways to send the information through another channel of the brain, usually a multisensory approach."

"For example?" he asked, seeming genuinely interested rather than merely making polite conversation.

That was more enticing than a surprise peek at his pecs. Well, almost.

"I have younger students trace spelling words in corn meal with a finger."

"Why not have all students do it that way? Sounds a hel-luva lot more fun than gripping a pencil until your fingers go numb."

"I agree."

He flashed a killer smile her way, sun reflecting off his avi-ator shades, darn near blinding her with the vibrancy. "Where were you when I was drilling spelling words? Wait." He thumped his head. "You weren't born yet."

"Are we beating that dead horse today?"

"With your vintage music fixation and my tapioca pud-ding, maybe we're not so far apart in age after all.

Something dangerous fluttered to life in her empty stom-ach. "Took you long enough to figure that one out."

"Too late, I'm guessing."

Was he regretting that? Hinting for something now? And sheesh, but she hated how even thinking it flipped her hun-gry stomach around. Not gonna go that route again. "Seems so."

"At least I can take comfort in knowing I'm not a COG."

"COG?"

"Creepy Old Guy."

Not by a long shot. She chewed the lip gloss off her suddenly aching lips. "Thanks for the ride and for showing up so soon, but where's Chris?"

"I was at your mother's when you called so I offered to come instead rather than waste time trying to track down your brother."

"Oh." That threw her for a second. Her stomach was in serious peril. "Uh, why? Anything wrong?"

"Nothing's wrong."

So why had he been there? She waited. And waited. "Thanks for coming out."

"Good thing, too. Probably didn't hurt for those students to see a man in your life."

"This is not your problem."

"I'm a male. I can't ignore it."

"I'm careful. I'm never alone with a student. Teachers are given training on just this subject for our protection and the students'. That's a part of why I always tutor on school property."

"All right. But I'm still picking you up until we find out what went on with Owens."

How silly to argue. She'd had the same concerns today. Her mother was confined to the house. Her brother was in and out of town visiting his girlfriend during college winter break.

And she couldn't hide from the truth. She wanted to be around Carson if for no other reason than to figure out a way to forget him as completely as she'd forgotten that night last week. "Since I don't have tires, I gratefully accept. For now."

"Thank you. And you'll be careful around that kid you're tutoring?"

Of course she would, but wondered at Carson's continued insistence. "You don't trust anyone, do you?"

"This isn't about me."

"I think it just became about you." She hitched a knee up to turn and face him even as he kept his eyes forward on the road. "You say you want to apologize, and sure you're helping. But I'm still confused. Can we only relate if things are about me? When does it become about you, too? Otherwise this is a one-sided, um, friendship—" yeah, friendship was a good word "—that's not fair to either of us."

His hands tightened around the wheel and she thought for a while he would simply keep driving until he whipped into the next turn. At a fast-food parking lot?

He threw the truck in park and turned to face her. "My parents were drug addicts."

Huh? That was a little more than she'd expected. She was thinking more along the lines of… What? She didn't know much of anything about him, and she wouldn't know more if she didn't unglue her tongue from the roof of her mouth and participate in this conversation. "I thought you said you had a privileged upbringing."

"I said my family has money."

"Guess I'm just as guilty of making character assumptions as you were with 'Thug.'" She couldn't stop herself from placing a sympathetic hand on his forearm. "I'm sorry—for the assumption and for how difficult your childhood must have been."

His quick nod offered his only acknowledgment of her empathy. With a brief squeeze of comfort she took her hand back, the heat of him tingling through her veins until she clenched her fist to hold on to the sensation. Already she could piece together parts he'd left unsaid, how no one thought to suspect anything, which left Carson and his sister unprotected.

Carson cut a quick glance over. "You can ease up a little on the sympathy. My sister and I went to great schools, and thank God for the nannies or things would have been a helluva lot worse."

"Somehow I think it was plenty bad enough." She shuffled this new image of Carson around in her mind and couldn't help but soften. "Where are your parents now?"

"Dad almost died of an overdose about two years ago." He recited the information in emotionless monotones. "Some thought that would scare him clean, he even tried. They've both been in and out of rehab clinics a dozen times and it never seemed to stick. Bottom line, I don't think either of them wants to change."

The resigned acceptance in his voice stabbed through her.

He kept his face forward even though their parking spot under the golden arches enabled him to look wherever he wished. "So, no. I don't trust easily."

Yet she couldn't miss how he'd trusted her today with a piece of himself and his past she suspected very few—if any—knew about.

"Enough heavy crap for one day." He reached for the door. "I hope burgers are okay."

"What?"

"Burgers. As in lunch, with some salty fries and a couple of apple pies. I assume you haven't eaten yet."

"No. But—"

"We'll get them to go."

"And where are we going with these burgers?"

He smiled. "Trust me."

God help her, she did.

Chapter 7

Trust was a tricky thing. Much easier to live up to than to give.

Carson parked his truck in the marina lot, more than a little humbled by how easily Nikki had gone along with his mystery plan. Although given the wariness creeping into her clear gray eyes as she looked across the line of bobbing boats down to Beachcombers Bar and Grill, she seemed ready to revoke her easy compliance.

"My sailboat's docked here now that I invested in something larger," he explained.

"Oh. Right. I thought for a minute you planned to wrangle some memories out of me and honestly, I've found that forcing it doesn't work." She sagged against the seat, staring out toward the bar with a melancholy weariness staining her eyes. "They always sneak up on me best when I'm not expecting anything."

"You're starting to remember what happened with Owens?"

She turned her head on the seat toward him. "Almost right away actually, I've gotten these smattering bits and pieces that may or may not be helpful. I shared everything with Agent Reis, for what it's worth. I even let Mom contact a hypnotist colleague from work, but I never could get past thinking what an ugly watch he was using for a focus point."

"Resistant?"

"Scared to death."

"Thank you for trusting me today." He wanted to say more, but knew better than to let things get any deeper and thereby ruin the afternoon. "Come on. I don't have lazy days much anymore and I intend to enjoy the hell out of this one."

Reaching into the back, he grabbed an extra windbreaker and tossed it to Nikki before snatching up their fast-food bags. Seemed she needed this day out on the water even more than he did. He couldn't help but think how in the past he would have offered a woman a more romantic meal such as croissants, fruit—mimosas.

Except he'd left behind his days of setting his mustache on fire with a flaming bar drink. His call sign Scorch may have stuck, but his party ways were long gone. He just hoped the burgers and sodas he had to offer now would be enough.

Even on the chilly winter day, the marina hummed with activity. No one swam in the frigid waters, but plenty perched on boat decks and along the docks wearing downy wind-breakers and cinched hoods, fishing off the pier or lounging on a bow. Carson searched the faces, wondering how many of them may have been at Beachcombers that night. Damn it, why couldn't he remember who he'd seen on his way to pick up his barbecue wings?

He'd been so hell-bent on getting out of there, the scent of whiskey and rum taking him to dangerous mental places. Then once he'd seen Nikki, he hadn't been looking at anyone else. He'd been tempted to hang out and talk to her as he'd done too often in the past. Since he'd been so tempted, he'd hauled ass away as fast as possible.

Guilt hammered him like the rogue swing of a boat boom. If he'd stayed around, maybe he could have prevented what happened. Owens would be alive. Nikki's life would be normal—and he would still be dodging her.

Wouldn't he? His fist tightened around the sack of burgers, which made him think of those brown-sugar-rich wings and that night all over again, not to mention another time he'd tasted hints of the sugary sauce while kissing Nikki after their friends' wedding.

Jesus, he really was in a crapload of trouble if he could remember who catered a wedding seven months ago. His feet thudded down the planked dock, past everything from a tiny Hobie catamaran manned by two teens in wet suits to a Beneteau yacht with jeweled partiers, toward his thirty-one-foot Catalina, a bargain bought used. Good thing boats didn't age like cars.

Without stopping, which would invite conversation and gossip, he waved at the crowded deck on the Dakota-Rat, a sailboat owned by Vic Jansen, the brother-in-law of fellow crew member Bo Rokowsky. The Rokowsky family outing resembled nothing from Carson's past but exactly the sort he'd wanted right down to the little blond kid with pigtails and a wife.

Except there was an empty space in the family since Bo was deployed.

Nikki shouted a greeting out over the water which would no doubt start the rumor mill churning at the squadron. He should have thought about that.

Maybe other people would have stepped in to help her if he hadn't preempted everyone else. Was he keeping her from something better on a personal level, too? She should have a houseful of children. She was a helluva teacher. He'd bet she would be an amazing mother, much like her own.

And she would. With some lucky bastard he didn't want to think about. Someday. Later. After he got her through this nightmarish time in her life safely.

"I brought you here to relax, but I didn't think about Beachcombers being so close. If it's a problem we can leave."

He stopped beside his boat slip, considering something else he could do to fill the day, kicking himself for assuming she would enjoy sailing as much as he did.

"No, really. It's all right. If I hid from every reminder of this whole mess, I would never go anywhere." She extended her hand. "Help me aboard?"

There she went again, being so trusting when he deserved to crawl for what he'd done. He certainly deserved more wariness. All he'd offered her were a couple of unsavory facts from his childhood.

He took her hand, a strong hand with short nails and impossibly soft skin he remembered, too. His memory flamed with their out-of-control kiss at his door, her hands tunneling up under his shirt, gliding her softness over him at a time when raw pain heated him from the inside out. He owed her so damn much.

Carson held her hand tighter as she stepped on the rocking hull, palmed her waist for the final boost. She looked so right there he wondered why he'd never thought to bring her before.

"Catch." He pitched the rope to her, leaped aboard and finished launching from the dock.

Already the familiar roll of the waves rocking beneath soothed his soul like a cradle in motion shooshes a baby. He took his place behind the wheel, firing the small motor to power them out of the narrow channel, Nikki an arm's reach away, trailing her fingers in the light spray.

She pulled her hand out. "Are you doing this today for my dad, too?"

"What part of trust me did you not understand?"

She flicked her damp fingers, showering an icy spray on his face. "Just joking."

Laughing, he leaned low and popped in the CD he'd bought this morning once he'd realized he would be detouring to her parents' house. He cranked the volume as the best of the 1940's spun up some "Bing" along with the percussion of the waves against the hull.

"Oh, you're playing dirty today."

"Gotta work with what you've got." He revved the motor to clear the channel without creating too large a wake to damage the shore.

The croon of the engine and slosh of waves mixed with Nikki's off-key croonings that somehow took on a musicality all their own.

After they finished the final bite of apple pie, she glanced over at him. "Thank you. This is really nice."

"I've missed running into you."

"Missed me showing up all the time, you mean?" She tipped her face into the sun. "God, I can hardly believe now how obvious I must have been with that mega embarrassing crush I had on you."

Had. Past tense.

Of course he'd known, and done his best to treat her like a little sister—except for one major lapse. He should have kept well away all the time, but God, she was charming.

He cut the motor, ready to switch to sail power. In a minute. After he had the answer to one more question he had to know now. "What do you think we would have done today if I hadn't screwed everything up then?"

"Hmm. You would have asked me to come along and I would have pretended it was no big deal. So we would have been doing the same thing, except now we're both coming into this with no expectations and being totally true to who we are. And speaking of being totally me, do you mind waiting a few more minutes to set sail?"

"Whatever works for you. This day is about you relaxing."

"Sometimes there's nothing more relaxing than getting your heart racing."

Heart racing? She couldn't actually mean what his body hoped she meant even if his mind knew better. She'd just said she was over her crush on him.

Before he could reason through the maze of her words, she'd jumped from her seat and clambered over to the main mast.

And up.

Holy crap.

Those long legs of hers in jeans and strong arms in his windbreaker shimmied her higher, her ponytail swaying from the back of her ball cap. He'd done the same countless times, but this was different. Enticingly different. He held the wheel and watched her stare out over the scenery, gasp in air, totally in the moment.

Sunlight streamed down over her. No makeup. No jewelry. But plenty of bling just from…her.

Bling and Bing. Modern but timeless, with a breezy sophistication in her old-soul self. He was toast.

So for the moment he surrendered and simply enjoyed the view of her slim body, the sweet curve of her bottom so perfectly on display. Sensory memory returned of gripping her taut roundness as he rolled her beneath him…

Who knew how much time he spent staring at her before she inched her way back down again and settled in a seat beside him. "Wow, the view from there is amazing."

Amazing. Yeah. That summed her up. "You scared the crap out of me, but that's one helluva pole dance, lady."

She threw her head back in her full-out laugh, so much more "real" than anything he could ever remember hearing or seeing in the affected world of his parents' social whirl. He raised the nylon sails, easing out the line bit by bit, savoring the increasing pull on his muscles.

Nikki shaded her eyes with her hand. "Do you need help?"

"I'll let you know. For now, just enjoy the ride."

Too bad he couldn't seem to take his own advice around this woman.

* * *

Her eyes full of sun, sail and sky, Nikki lounged along the cushioned seat while Carson manned the wheel like a Viking captain of old, making minor adjustments while the star-burst-patterned nylon billowed. Why hadn't he named his boat? He obviously loved this vessel, and she could understand why.

Sailing offered a secluded slice of heaven.

He'd been right to bring her here. Tension from the investigation eased, even while another tension altogether kinked as she felt herself drawn in again by this man.

Except before, she never would have done something as impulsive and undignified as climb a mast while he could see her. How strange to realize that in those days she hadn't been true to herself. She hadn't shown him the total picture of Nikki Price. Or had she tried to morph herself into what she thought he wanted?

The craft picked up speed along the waves, biting through the wind like a plane cutting through the clouds. She imagined he looked much the same at the helm of his C-17. "If you love the water so much, why didn't you join the Navy?"

Feet planted and braced, his thigh muscles bulged against worn denim. "I didn't much like the idea of six months out on ship duty every year. Besides, the water's my hobby, my way of relaxing. If I turn it into work, I might lose that."

"Such as how I enjoy sports and running, but didn't want to be a gym teacher."

"Exactly." A gull winged low, dipping for supper in the

comfortable silence before he picked up the conversational thread again. "Have you sailed much?"

"Nope. This is my first time."

The wheel slithered through his shocked-slack fingers before he secured his grip again and redirected the bow. "You crawled up there blind? What if it hadn't been safe? Good God, haven't you pitched off enough high places into water for one month?"

His concern was more than a little touching. She brushed a reassuring hand over his thigh—whoa baby. She pulled her arm back. "You would have told me to stop."

"You're trusting me too easily."

"That's just my body, not my heart, pal. Two very different matters."

At least he had the grace to look away. "So this is your first boating trip."

"It's my first *sailing* outing, but I've been boating. My family camped a lot growing up. Dad had a little John boat." She'd forgotten about those outings until now, and took comfort from knowing her childhood hadn't been all about her parents' arguments. "He pulled it behind that old truck he still drives. I swear he'll be driving that same truck when he takes Jamie and the new baby off to college."

"Are you okay with these new additions to your family?" Alongside, a fish jumped and plopped.

"I'm a little old for sibling rivalry, don't you think?"

"Feelings aren't always reasonable."

She'd never even considered it, but searched her heart and came up with… "I feel more like their aunt than a sister, which makes me a little sad. But Mom and Dad are a lot

stronger as a couple this go-round. The kids will have everything they need and more. Actually, since Dad's coming up
on retirement in less than five years, he'll be pulling cupcake
duty for elementary birthday parties while Mom works."

"Now that's an image guaranteed to spread grins around
the squadron, a crusty old loadmaster stirring up a batch of
frosting with sprinkles."

"I'll try to slip you some pictures."

His laugh rolled out over the cresting waves rippling toward one of the ka-jillion small historic battlefield parks
throughout the Charleston area. "So you really are okay with
the new rug rat siblings."

"Totally. They're gonna have a great life. Don't get me
wrong, Chris and I had a good childhood in so many ways,
but for these children, things will be more stable."

He set the autopilot and shifted to stand beside her, leaning back against the side. "So when your dad says no flyboys
for his little girl, it's a sentiment you echo."

"That would be strange since I've spent so much time dating flyers." Was he only making idle conversation? Tough to
think and decide with his body heat blasting.

"I figured it was a rebellion thing against your father."

No way was she confessing to her real reason for her recent run of flyboy dates who happened to have preppy blond
good looks.

She shifted her attention to the boats in the distance and
the ones remaining in the faraway dock by Beachcombers.
More familiar memories of the place flooded her brain,
stuffed fish peering down from over windows with glass eyeballs and slack jaws. Netting full of shells, sand dollars and

coral stretched across the wall. Small lanterns rested on each wooden picnic table, the smoky blue glass letting little light flicker through, more mood setting than illuminating.

Nothing new, yet she still clung to every detail, searching for a hidden clue in the place where she'd run into Carson last week while waiting for Gary…

"Hey, babe," *Gary's greeting jolted through Nikki a second before he leaned an elbow on the bar and kissed her neck.*

She ducked to the side with the help of the spinning bar stool. "I was starting to wonder if you'd stood me up."

"Never." *He tapped her nearly empty amaretto sour.* "Could I get you another drink?"

The press of bodies stifled her. She wanted space. She wanted to go home.

But first she had to tell him what little relationship they'd had was over. "Two's my limit since I'm driving. I'll take some plain orange juice."

"You've got it." *He angled over her shoulder to place the order, his chest sealing against her back until she could feel the imprint of his favorite belt buckle against her spine—a cold metal buckle shaped like an overlarge casino coin.*

And the imprint of more steel, lower down.

Nikki hopped off the bar stool. "Let's find somewhere quiet to talk."

In public, but not right beside a table full of her father's fly buddies—Picasso, Mako and the new guy in the squadron, Avery, who she'd also dated a couple of times.

"Sure, just what I was thinking." *Gary fell in step alongside her, then stopped, skimming a touch along her arm.*

"Wait. You almost forgot your orange juice. Hold on and I'll go back and get your drink for you…"

"Nikki?" Carson's voice sliced through her memories like the hull slicing the waves.

"Yeah, uh right. Just daydreaming." Nikki clutched the side of the sailboat as if she could hold on to the memories already slipping away faster than the dispersing wake.

"Go right ahead." He shoved away from the side with muscle-rippling ease and a smile, closer. "This day's all about relaxing."

Even with the warmth of the sun on her face and her thick windbreaker protecting her from the misty spray, she rubbed her hands along her chilled arms, a deeper cold settling inside her at even the whisper of memory that helped her with nothing, except to hint further that Gary may have drugged her. He'd certainly had the opportunity. But hadn't she forgotten things from before he brought her drink? The effects of Rohypnol varied from person to person, with so many other variables factored in.

She searched her mind to recapture the faces that had been in the bar around her, all people she knew and simply accepted as part of her world. Why hadn't she paid more attention to details?

Okay, think. In addition to the crew sitting down for an after-flight meal, she'd seen Claire McDermott subbing for the bartender with her co-owner two sisters on hand waitressing. Hadn't one of them even dated Gary briefly? Which one?

She would call David Reis the minute she got home and tell him what little she could recall. Although he'd most certainly already interviewed everyone there that night, which made her feel exposed all over again, thinking of so many of her military friends knowing the details.

Damn it, she hadn't done anything wrong—that she knew of. She gave up recapturing the moment in the churning water and shifted her focus back to Carson, his face tipped upward to… Gauge the sail? The sun? Simply feel the wind?

She couldn't ignore the appeal of his strong features, the way his broad shoulders and lean hips turned her on and inside out all at once. What was it about him that called to her at a time when she shouldn't have been able to think about anything but the blind panic of clearing her name? He was good-looking, sure, in a preppy privileged kind of way that had never snagged her interest before she'd seen him for the first time and suddenly that had become her type for forever after, even if everyone else fell short.

As if sensing her stare, Carson looked down and over at her. His eyes narrowed. "What's with the frown, lady? Quit thinking so hard. Get back to your daydreaming."

She pulled a breezy salute. "Aye-aye, Major. Or would that be Captain since we're on your ship?"

"Either's fine as long as you smile."

Good advice, she knew. And wouldn't it be nice to settle into the circle of his arms, her back against his chest as they sailed the day away? Just the wind and sun and feel of his muscled chest.

Unbidden and unwelcome, a snippet from the memory flashed, of Gary's chest, that favored belt buckle of his biting into her spine….

Her mind hitched on the notion of Gary's belt, the one he'd been wearing the night he'd died. Or had he? She could swear there hadn't been a belt in his pants down around his ankles and she couldn't recall the security police having found one when they looked around the room while questioning her.

Blinking out of the fractured memory and into the streaming sunlight, she couldn't remember any more from that night. But she had one important question to answer.

Where was Gary's belt?

Chapter 8

Where was his head?

Sure as hell not in the job.

After a boring commander's lunch, Carson tossed his leather jacket over the brass anchor peg in his office on his last Monday as commander. The rest of the squadron was due back Friday and he could resume his regular job as the number two dude. He would be flying more again, but Nikki would have her dad back in town to check on her until Reis got his head out of his butt and figured out what happened to Owens.

And what would J.T. have to say about the time Carson had been spending with Nikki?

Their day sailing together had been good. Damn good, but he wanted to make sure he was a better man now so he didn't screw up his life again, or more importantly, didn't do anything to harm hers.

Tucking around his desk, he hooked a boot in the chair to roll it back while snagging a stack of performance reports off the top of his file cabinet. At least her memory was starting to trickle back. A missing belt wasn't much, yet remembering anything was a hopeful sign she might recall more. But if those memories revealed she'd killed Owens? Carson was certain she would have only done so in self-defense, which would put her in the clear legally.

All of which still didn't help him decide how to handle the next five days with Nikki.

He reached for the phone to check in with Reis about the security camera footage of the high school parking lot, only to be stopped short by a tap on the open office door. He glanced over to find Captain Nola Seabrook standing in the entryway. "What can I do for you?"

"Sir, I need to schedule a tactics class." The crisp blond officer stood at attention, even though Carson ran a more relaxed squadron than other commanders. "Is Wednesday at fourteen-hundred okay?"

"Wednesday?" He flipped though his day planner. "Uh… no. I've already scheduled confession for that time."

"Confession?"

"Flight safety meeting." He lapsed into his best Irish accent. "It's always better for the flyers to confess than have their sins pointed out by the bishop."

Laughing, she lost the starch in her spine. "Fair enough. How about we schedule the tactics meeting to follow when they're all softened up?"

"Roger." He nodded. "Spread the word."

Pivoting away, she ran smack into another person already

waiting. Seabrook laughed. "Guess we need to take a number to talk with the major today."

"Apparently so," answered his surprise visitor—Vic Jansen.

What was he doing here? Was it family business since his sister was married to one of the deployed flyers? Or personal, since Vic belonged to A.A., too.

Carson nodded to Seabrook. "That'll be all, Captain. And could you let my secretary know to hold calls for the next twenty minutes? Thanks."

Vic ducked into the room, a blond lumberjack-looking fella in flannel. The somber guy had lost his daughter in a drowning accident years ago, but recently started with the program because he feared he was reaching for a bottle too often.

"What brings you here?"

"Just dropping my sister off at the commissary. Since I had time to kill while she shops, I thought I would stop by, shoot the breeze if you have a free minute."

Carson rolled his office chair back an inch from the desk. "Sure," he said, even though he really didn't have twenty seconds to spare, much less twenty minutes. But something was obviously on Vic's mind and part of the program involved helping each other out. "What can I do for you?"

"Actually, I was wondering if everything's okay with you?" Jansen dropped into a seat across from the desk, blue eyes piercing.

The guy had seen him with Nikki yesterday, but that wouldn't be cause to ask if he was all right. Although pursuing this friendship with Nikki could well be termed insanity. "Why do you ask?"

"It's been a rough couple of months around the squadron with the extra duties overseas and now Owens's death," Jansen answered, his Dakota roots filling his rolling accent. "It's a tough time to be the king."

Ah, now the visit made sense. And damn, but the guy had a point. There weren't many people around this place Carson could talk to—none for that matter. But the A.A. bond of trust and confidentiality was a cornerstone. Solid.

"I could use some advice." The words fell out of his mouth.

"Hell, Carson, are you sure you want *my* advice? My track record sucks, don'tcha know." It was no secret that Jansen's wife had divorced him after the death of their daughter. But from what Carson could gather it sounded as if the woman's defection had been heartless, occurring before Jansen started drinking.

"I'll take any help I can get."

"Ah, so you want to romance Nikki Price."

"Who said we're talking about Nikki?"

"Last time I checked, they don't let morons graduate from veterinary school." The rugged large animal vet smirked.

Searching for the right words for thoughts he didn't even understand, he scooped up a miniature porthole clock from his desk and checked the battery, which of course was working just fine.

"Nikki and I have this—" tenacious attraction? "—bizarre friendship that seems to defy the whole twelve year age difference. I want to understand her."

"Good-freaking luck." Snorting, Vic hooked an ankle over his knee, work boot twitching. "If you figure women out, make sure you copyright the knowledge so you can retire a millionaire."

"I'm serious here." He thunked the tiny clock back on top of the stack of performance reports. "God, how do I explain this?"

"You like a woman as more than a friend, and she likes you back."

Might as well quit lying to everyone including himself. "So it seems."

"But the problem is…?"

"Problems. Plural. We tried things once before and I screwed it up." He ticked reasons off a finger at a time. "Her family would disapprove. I'm not sure I'm husband material and she definitely deserves it all."

"Whoa." Vic held up his work-scarred hands. "You're already using the M word. I thought you were talking about liking a woman and asking her out on a date. Don't you think you're jumping ahead of yourself?"

Didn't people date to see if something more would develop? And when a woman was obviously the happily-ever-after sort, wasn't it leading her on to date when he knew full well it wouldn't lead anywhere beyond a bed? Okay, so he was old-fashioned. He couldn't help it, probably went along with his tapioca pudding mentality.

"Did you apologize for what you did before, the time you screwed it up?"

He nodded.

"Have you done something to make up for it?"

Amends. A critical part of the twelve-step program, but also keeping in mind not to press for forgiveness if the action hurt that person worse. "I'm not sure I could make this one right."

"Did you try? Even if something can't be fixed, there's comfort in knowing the other person tried."

"I've been looking out for her, checking her security. Nikki's in a helluva vulnerable state."

"It must be tough for her to be so helpless."

"Nikki's a tough lady," Carson answered without even thinking—then stopped, the words and their truth kicking around in his head for a second before settling.

Why hadn't he realized it before? Sure Nikki had been dealt a raw deal right now, but he needed to stop viewing her as a victim. Had he done so as a convenient excuse to keep his distance?

He needed to quit thinking he was protecting her by ignoring the attraction, the connection. Not that he'd been all that successful. Relationships were a lot tougher to achieve than any Ivy League diploma on his wall.

Was he really considering asking her out on dates? Forget the age difference? Her father's objections. His own concerns about his ability to be an equal partner. A hefty dose of cons.

And only one reason in the pro column, a reason he couldn't even quite define. Something as nebulous as the way the wind in sails and the clouds against a windscreen soothed his soul. "You're right."

"Of course. No morons around here, remember?"

"We can only hope." He rocked back in his office chair. "Any suggestions for how I should make things right so I have a chance at moving forward?"

Jansen leaned forward, elbows on his knees. "There's no secret answer other than every woman is different. Quit trying to charge ahead with what you think she needs and just listen."

Another A.A. technique he should have figured out for himself.

Flipping his wrist to check his watch, Jansen winced. "I gotta make tracks." He shoved to his feet. "Give me a call anytime. Okay?"

"Will do."

Jansen paused by the door. "Hey, Carson?"

"What?"

"Good luck." The lumbering vet smirked.

"I'm going to need it figuring this lady out."

"That isn't what I meant." Jansen shook his head slowly. "I meant good luck, because Nikki Price's father is totally going to kick your officer ass."

Great. Just what every guy wanted to hear as he reached for the phone to call a woman.

Nikki strode along the wooden walkway toward Beachcombers chanting, "Idiot, idiot, idiot…" But a curiously excited idiot.

She'd looked forward to this outing since Carson called her yesterday and asked her to lunch. His invitation had quickly distracted her from the disappointment of learning the surveillance cameras at the school had been angled wrong to catch any helpful information about the vandalism to her little truck.

The planked path forked, one way snaking to the back bar and marina, the other route leading to the front entrance of the restaurant where she was *not* going on a date. Just meeting Carson at Beachcombers for a meal to help joggle more memories free. Regardless, thanks to a new set of tires on her Ranger providing transportation, she now stood outside Beachcombers.

She tromped up the steps to the sprawling wraparound porch that usually buzzed with conversation from the diners, but sported only sparse smokers in the cooler climate. Her stomach cramped with nerves, even more from the prospect of seeing Carson.

Pushing through the heavy door, she searched the crush of people in the wide hallway, a waiting area complete with gift shop stalls and cubbies. She weaved through the melee, the lunch crowd mirroring the weekend gang, but with a subdued workday air.

For the first time, she noticed the wide age range. She'd always been so focused on her friends—and yeah, the fly-boys—she hadn't noticed how many retirees frequented the place, as well. Were they around on the weekends, too? She would have to pay closer attention.

Flipping her wrist, she glanced at her Minnie Mouse watch. The second hand clicked past Minnie's glove.

Fifteen minutes early.

So much for appearing blasé. But she wasn't into game playing this go-round. She would be herself, totally—mast climbing, sarcophagus building, notoriously early Nikki Price.

Still no sign of Carson, but any number of crises at the squadron could have delayed him. She refused to turn into a quivering mass. He wouldn't be that important to her ever again.

Still, nerves whipped around in her stomach faster than

Minnie's second hand. Nikki fidgeted with the new gift shop items filling shelves along the waiting area walls—hand-painted T-shirts, seashell ornaments with Charleston's historic Rainbow Row inked in miniature. She mentally filed away craft ideas for her classroom during local history week. Her gaze settled on glazed sand dollars sporting a sticker of a C-17—the cargo plane flown by Carson.

Sheesh. Everything didn't have to be about Carson. Her dad and countless friends flew that same craft.

"May I help you with something?"

Nikki jolted and looked over her shoulder to find Beach-combers' proprietor, Claire McDermott. "Did you design these?"

Claire neatened the hanging racks of stenciled canvas bags in perfect descending order of largest to smallest. "My sister Starr did. I do most of the cooking, but we're short staffed out front today, so here I am. Our other sister handles the book-keeping." She straightened her apron on curvy hips Nikki had finally given up on ever developing by the end of high school. "It's a family effort we hope will pay off."

"From the crush today, it sure seems so."

No wonder Carson with his lack of family connection ate here so often, even moored his boat in the area. She wondered if that might be why he'd spent time with her before, because she came with a family. And man that sucked, wondering if you were liked because of your parents and brother. Or if he preferred curvy types like Claire.

Nikki stomped down feelings and thoughts that too closely resembled the insecure idiot she'd been over Carson months before. The present carried enough problems.

She could see the questions in Claire's eyes that she was too polite to ask about what happened a week ago. The woman had to be frustrated at even the least association with the scandal…yet the place was buzzing with activity. Sometimes bad press could be better for business than no press at all.

Claire's attention shifted beyond her. Bustling around the counter with brisk efficiency, she passed Nikki a pamphlet. "Here's a list of our upcoming performers in the bar, and don't miss the discount coupons on the bottom."

The woman disappeared into the milling customers, emerging on the other side near two men who seemed familiar…

Nikki shook her hands loose trying to relax for a memory to shimmer free. The shorter man wore a backward baseball cap and sports jersey. The other man loomed taller and burly in a plaid shirt.

The image gelled in her brain. Both men had met up with Carson that night out in the parking lot. Ball-cap dude, she didn't know. But the man in the plaid shirt was Bo Rokowsky's brother-in-law. What was the guy's name? Vic something-or-another.

A tingling started up her spine, a shift in the air, an awareness that Carson had arrived even though she hadn't seen him yet and no, no, no she didn't want that kind of surreal connection.

Maybe the feeling was—

There he was. Carson. Tall, slim and golden blond, his tan deep from a lifetime outside. She wished she could remember his tan line, but there had been covers by that point.

Whoops. Dangerous territory for her thoughts, especially in public. She glanced back up to his lean face, features angular and tense, phone pressed to his ear while he searched the crowd for...

Her.

Dimples creased—because of her. He nodded his hello from across the room as he continued to speak into his phone and make his way toward her. The tingle increased to an all-over body flush. Just a casual get-together?

She wasn't fooling anybody, most especially herself.

Only a fool would risk going out with this woman, but Carson had learned long ago, the word fit for him every time he came near Nikki.

Except he wouldn't sacrifice common sense and safety even though the whole meal had tempted him to toss both out the back hatch. At least they'd accomplished something at lunch, compiling a joint list of people they remembered Owens hanging out with, hoping they would recall something overlooked initially.

He'd insisted on following her home even though, yeah, she'd driven over on her own. Maybe he simply wanted their time together to last longer and it really wasn't that far out of his way. Lunch with her had been so natural and easy, too natural. In the past there had been the boundary of her crush, something that most definitely put him in an older man role. Now they met on more equal footing, even though she wore a Minnie Mouse watch that for some reason he found endearing as hell.

Slowing outside the Price home, he pulled up on the curb

behind her car, a perfect reminder of those slashed tires. No matter how tough and toned she appeared, she was still vulnerable to creeps who drugged drinks and tore her clothes.

The urge to protect pumped through his veins, thrummed in his ears, damn near blinding him. He could tell himself all day long to ease off the protector role because Nikki was strong, but in practice, she meant too much to him for him to be anywhere but by her side.

He blinked his vision clear and stepped from his truck just as she slid from hers, one slim leg at a time. Jeans never looked so good slung low on her slim hips, her jacket open to reveal a fuzzy sweater, bottom button undone to reveal a hint of skin.

Carson met her at her open truck door. "I'm sorry I was late for our lunch."

"You weren't late." She gripped the open door, Minnie Mouse waving from her wrist. "I was early, and I know things are insane at the squadron right now."

"Well, I wish I could have picked you up. Next time…"

Wind rustled pine needles from the trees overhead and lifted her hair while she chewed her lip and finally released the kissable fullness, slowly. "Next time."

There would be a next time.

Yes.

He covered her hand with his on the open door. "No new memories today?"

"Spotty stuff, mostly of when you and I talked." She scuffed her shoe through the dead grass, drawing his attention to her jean-clad legs—as if he needed an excuse. "I, uh, watched you walk away and meet up with two other guys."

Vic Jansen and Gary Owens's sponsor, on their way to a support meeting for families of addicts, not just alcoholics, but a catchall group. He couldn't tell her that, though, without breaking confidence. "Do you remember anything else?"

"Not really. It never works when I want it too much." Her gray eyes clouded, seeming wider when she didn't blink, just studied him until he wondered if they were still discussing lost hours a week ago.

"Then let's stop forcing the issue." He circled a finger along Minnie, then around to Nikki's wrist. "You said relaxing helps, so just let things happen."

Although a relaxed Nikki might be more temptation than he could handle.

"Okay, I have a question that's really been plaguing me." Her eyebrows pinched together with serious intensity that set him on edge.

"Sure, go ahead."

She tipped her head to the side, her hair teasing along his wrist. "Why haven't you named your boat yet?"

Tension rode out along his laugh. Relax. Right. Linking his fingers with hers, he slid their hands off the door into a true clasp rather than the sort-of-resting-here deal.

Tugging her forward, he reached past to close her door. "Naming a boat is like naming a new aviator."

"What do you mean?" She kept her hand in his.

Encouraging.

Arousing.

And so damn right he didn't let go.

"Well, for example, Lieutenant Avery is bucking for a call

sign to replace Bambi, but we've got to wait for the watershed event."

"Like your flaming Dr Pepper moment when you scorched your mustache in a bar."

Now there was a splash of reality. "Exactly. A watershed event that sums up a person."

As if sensing his darkening mood, she stepped away even if she didn't release his hand. "I imagine you need to get back to the squadron."

"I've got another minute." He should have returned a half hour ago to tackle rewrites on performance reports and promotion recommendations, review and sign check-ride forms, all before the Wing Staff meeting at fifteen hundred.

He wasn't sure what he was doing standing here with Nikki. Even if he could see his way clear to risking a more serious relationship, he was scared spitless of marriage, and he couldn't even wrap his head around the whole father-kid deal. He could almost hear Vic Jansen laughing at him again since he kept gravitating right back to commitment thoughts.

One day at a time.

"Would you like to go boating again this weekend? Your dad will be home to look after your mom." And holy hell, he would somehow have to explain to J. T. Price why he was seeing the man's daughter when the guy expressly didn't want flyboys for his baby girl. No doubt, Ivy League, officer flyboys would fall even lower down the list for the practical values of the crusty chief master sergeant.

Carson stroked his missing mustache. He would just have to get the guy alone and ease the news into the conversation.

They had a mutual respect for each other from shared crew experiences and POW hell.

"Boating?" Nikki asked, bringing him back to the moment.

Before he worried about talking to J.T., Nikki needed to agree.

"My plate will be clearer. We could moor up in a cove for lunch, maybe go ashore and backpack around for the day."

Her hand stilled, frozen like her blanked face. "Go boating to relax and take my mind off of Owens and my pathetic employment situation?"

"To spend time together. If that's okay."

Slack jawed for a painfully long second, she blinked fast. "Yeah, I think it is. As a matter of fact I'm sure it is." Her grin widened. "Although this time it's my turn to bring the food."

He liked the idea of her feeding him, him feeding her back, on the bow of his boat in the middle of the summer in a secluded bay where they could soak up the sun and each other….

Time to pull his mind off that fantasy, awesome though it was. And what was he doing having summer thoughts, months away? What had happened to taking things with Nikki one day at a time?

The rumble of an engine drew closer. Hair rose on the back of his neck. The neighborhood seemed sleepy and safe, but less than two years ago, Nikki's brother had a run-in with the law that brought threats from drug runners…a drive-by wreck and later a brick through the window.

He gripped Nikki's elbow. "I'll walk you to your door."

And check the security system for the umpteenth time.

The approaching vehicle slowed, a nondescript sedan. Carson hustled her faster up the walk. Once he got her inside, then he would deal with any problem, if there was one. The car stopped.

Agent Reis was behind the wheel.

What was he doing here? He couldn't be about to arrest her. No, no, and *hell no.*

The primal drive to protect—already on high alert—seared his nerves. He suppressed the urge to do more than tuck her away in the house. He burned to toss her in his truck and take her as far away as possible from any and every threat. God knew he had the money.

Nikki stepped around him and started down the walkway, toward Reis, so strong and resolute it damn near tore him up inside. She had a calm bravery under stress that would serve her well in combat.

He just prayed she wasn't about to enter the zone.

Reis tightened his tie, his coat flapping behind him as he charged up the curb. Sunglasses masked his expression, not that the man gave much away with full face showing. He extended a hand. "Major. Ms. Price. Glad I caught up with you so I can deliver some good news in person."

"Good news?" Carson pulled up behind Nikki, a palm to her back to brace her.

"Autopsy report finally came in, and Owens was definitely struck, and by a right-handed person. Since you're a lefty, that's good news for you. Even as fit as you are, it's unlikely you could have exerted such force with your right. While we haven't completely ruled anyone out, it's safe to say we're shifting our focus elsewhere for now. Although why that someone would want his belt…" He shrugged.

Nikki reached out to Carson, trembling a hint, her eyes still glued to Reis as he detailed more intricacies about the autopsy and height angles at the site of impact. Carson clasped her hand, a similar relief rocking him slam down to his feet. No one should have to carry the burden of having taken another life, even in self-defense.

Although since a large percentage of the world was right-handed, they hadn't narrowed the search much.

"I've already placed a call to your principal that you've been crossed off our suspect list. Given his sigh of relief, I imagine there's already a message waiting for you on your voice mail."

"Reis, I have to confess I'm not overly impressed with the protective drive-bys around here. A broken balcony, slashed tires, and all while she's being watched. Once word leaks that the investigation's no longer focused on Nikki, this person's going to get deadly serious in eliminating her before she remembers."

"I understand your concern, but we can't put someone in protective custody indefinitely." He chomped harder, faster on his gum. "But I've got connections downtown. I'll put some pressure on local police."

A fair offer, even if nothing short of a closed case seemed like enough now. "Thank you. And thanks for making the personal trip out."

"No problem. I need to ask her brother and mother some questions anyway, but I see now that their cars are gone. I should have called first."

Nikki's hand twitched clasped in his, but she stayed silent. "Have a nice afternoon, Major." Reis nodded. "Ms. Price."

Agent Reis slid into his nondescript blue sedan and pulled away from the curb. Once Reis's license plate disappeared around the corner, Carson hauled Nikki into his arms. "About time he figured out you couldn't have done something like that."

She trembled in his arms. "How could you be so sure?"

"I just knew, damn it." His arms convulsed tighter around her. "Although now there's not a chance you're going anywhere alone."

Nikki eased her head back to look up at him, not too far since she was tall, a perfect fit. "I'll worry about right-handed threats later. Right now, I'm so relieved at this sliver of hope."

"Fair enough. But I'm going to come back after work so we can all discuss more serious security."

Carson palmed the small of her back on the way up the side steps leading to the garage apartment. He scanned the single room efficiency, an open space with a futon, kitchenette and cubicle bathroom. Only one entrance in and out, with an alarm on the door as safe as she could be without him parking his butt with her 24/7, something she wouldn't allow anyway.

Although damn, what he wouldn't give for the pleasure of simply watching her sleep.

She slumped against the door frame. "Ohmigod, I knew I was stressed, but didn't even begin to know how much until now."

"You have reason to celebrate."

"Are you offering to celebrate with me?" Her loaded question broadsided him.

They were standing on the threshold of more than her apartment.

He cupped her face, fingers threading back into her loose hair. "What do you think?"

And somehow he was kissing her. He should pull away and make sure she wanted— Her lips parted under his and yeah. Just yeah. He tasted her and a hint of the barbecue they'd had for lunch.

Her hands skimmed along his back and up to loop around his neck. "No mustache," she murmured against his mouth. "Feels different."

"It's going to *be* different this time, too." His hands slid lower to cup her amazing bottom he'd admired as she climbed the mast. Hell, to be honest, he'd been checking her out since she'd strutted past him in shorts while subbing for a sick member of the squadron volleyball team.

All the reasons he should stay away faded under the onslaught of driving need to claim her as his, finally, totally, and damn it, memorize every second of the feel of her toned body under his hands because he wouldn't be idiot enough to treat her so recklessly again.

"Carson," Nikki whispered against his mouth, tugging him back to the present. "Either that's a phone ringing in your pocket or you're really happy to see me."

"Both." He dropped another quick kiss before pulling back. He fished out his cell phone, looked at the LCD panel and winced. "The squadron. I've got to take it." He flipped open his phone. "Hunt."

"Captain Seabrook. All hell's breaking loose here, sir. We need you back ASAP. There's been a bombing in the barracks overseas, the barracks housing our guys."

His gut burned raw with each forced even breath. He needed a status report. "SITREP?"

"One confirmed dead, more expected, but it's chaos there and here."

His gaze snapped straight to Nikki and her furrowing brow as she somehow picked up on his tension even though he'd kept his face neutral. Her father was over there along with so many of their friends, and there wasn't a thing he could do except be the bearer of the horrific details. With the taste of Nikki still on his lips, he was torn with the need to keep her close in case the news involved her.

But duty didn't give him that option.

"Hold down the fort. I'm on my way."

And he prayed when he came back to the Price home that it wouldn't be for an official notification visit.

Chapter 9

Six hours later, the phone rang on her mom's kitchen wall.

Slamming her memory journal shut, Nikki launched from her chair at the table to snatch up the cordless receiver and kicked herself for not placing it beside her, but she wasn't thinking clearly right now. Carson had told her there was a bombing overseas and to keep her pregnant mother away from the television until he could get details.

Please, God, let her father be all right.

And if her father wasn't okay, let her be strong enough when the time came to tell her mom. At least her mother was upstairs resting after supper, so Nikki would have time to pull herself together if the worst…

"Carson?" she gasped into the mouthpiece, her fingers numbing from her death grip. Death? Awful word choice. The smell of leftover spaghetti hanging in the air made her nauseous. "Is everything okay?"

Silence answered. A delay for a telemarketer recording? She glanced at the caller ID, which read "unknown" as she'd seen before when Carson used his cell.

She put the receiver to her ear again. "Carson? Is that you?"

Was the news so bad he was searching for the right words? But no. He was never that shaken. If anything, he became more focused in a crisis. She admired that about him, along with so many other traits she'd never noticed before, too caught up in her hormonal crush and a thousand other things that seemed frivolous now in light of how transient life could be.

Huffing breaths increased on the airwaves, sending a creepy chill down her spine. An obscene phone call? Or something far more sinister and dangerous?

Footsteps sounded from the living room, coming closer, loping—her brother.

"Hang up," Chris hissed, the television echoing Jamie's Disney flick from the other room.

"What?"

He yanked the phone from her and barked into the receiver, "The line's tapped, you bastard, so quit calling."

Chris nailed the off button and tossed the phone onto Jamie's empty high chair.

What was going on and why hadn't anyone bothered to tell her? "The phone's tapped?"

"We've been getting calls like that for two days, so Mom phoned that Agent Reis guy. Mom didn't want to scare you and since you stayed up in the garage apartment most of the time, you were never here when one came in."

Could that have been why Reis wanted to speak to her family?

And ohmigod, none of this even mattered if something had happened to her father.

Call, call, call. She touched the phone, willing it to ring with Carson on the other end. Her hand slid back to her side as she turned to her brother. "Were you going to tell me about the breather and speaking with Agent Reis?"

"Haven't had the chance since you've been so busy with your major squeeze." Her brother slouched against the counter with a leftover slice of garlic bread. "Major squeeze. Get it? He's a major?" When she didn't laugh, he frowned. "Is something wrong?"

No need for Chris to worry, too. Pulling a weak attempt at a smile, she pitched a pot holder at his head. "Major squeeze? That was pretty lame."

"So insult me or something. This is no fun if you won't fight back."

She dropped into a chair at the kitchen table, snitching up the cordless phone. "I'm just on edge." She nudged her memory journal aside, not that she'd been able to add anything to the blank page with worries for her father filling her head. "Now what about this mystery caller? What did Agent Reis have to say?"

The phone rang under her hand. She snatched it up, thumbing the on button, but wary of another call from "the breather." "Hello?"

"It's me." Carson.

She sighed her relief, only to have tension ratchet up all over again as she waited to hear what happened overseas.

"Your father's okay."

Thank God, Carson cut right to the chase. She grabbed the edge of the table to keep from falling off her seat, her whole body suddenly limp. Her silent, lumbering father would be coming home. She blinked back tears.

Chris frowned, starting toward her and reaching for the phone.

Nikki palmed the mouthpiece. "The call's for me."

"Sure, I can tell when I'm not wanted." He ambled back to the Disney flick, whispering "major squeeze" repeatedly. God, she loved her dorky brother who'd been so sweet helping out at home even after his classes resumed.

She slid her hand from the receiver. "I'm back. Sorry, but I wanted to send Chris out. Details? Please."

"Your dad wasn't even injured. I spoke with him a half hour ago." Carson rushed to reassure her. "I'm heading toward your house and I don't want your mother to freak out when I pull into the driveway."

"She's upstairs resting."

"Good," he answered, his voice so…dead? "Are you free?"

What did he need to say that couldn't be relayed over the phone? "Just hanging out with Chris and Jamie, watching *Jungle Book*."

"Could you explain to Chris what's going on so he can tell your mom if she wakes up and there's something on the news?"

"Sure, but do you really think there will be anything on TV?"

"It was bad over there, Nikki." Cell phone static echoed along with the silence and what sounded like a heavy swallow. "I'm pulling into the driveway now. Could you meet me outside?"

He was upset. Of course he was. And oh God, he'd come to her.

"Give me thirty seconds to update Chris, and then I'm out the door."

"Thank you."

His bass rumbled even deeper, hoarse with emotion. If the accident didn't involve her father, there could only be one reason Carson had driven over.

He needed her. A couple of weeks ago she would have expected to take satisfaction from that. Now, she could only think of racing out the door, her heart as heavy as his voice over the phone at just the thought of him being in pain.

Studying the tops of his flight boots, Carson slumped against his truck tailgate, not sure why he'd driven here, but knowing if he didn't he might land in the bottom of a bottle before morning.

Even though he'd wanted to run to Nikki from the start, he'd tried to find his sponsor. Nikki shouldn't have to deal with his crap. But his sponsor hadn't been at home or at work or even picking up his cell phone.

Streetlights flickered on, doing little to brighten his mood. He needed to stop thinking about the past hours spent informing a woman her husband wasn't coming home. Of more hours telling two other women their husbands were being flown to Germany for surgery and God only knew if they would survive.

Still checking out his boots and that lone dog tag attached to ID a dead aviator when his body was blown to bits, Carson heard the front door creak open and bang closed. Nikki's footsteps—he was too tired to question how he knew it was her without even looking—thudded down the porch stairs. Closer, until her gym shoes and the hem of her jeans appeared in view.

He looked up and let himself soak in the sight of her makeup-free face, hair straggling from her haphazard ponytail. He'd been right to come here.

Carson fished out his keys and passed them to her. "Feel like driving? I even brought along your CD."

"Sure. Who would turn down the chance to drive a great new machine like this?" She took the keys from his hand, lingering for a quick comforting second before pulling away as if sensing he couldn't take too much emotion.

Without another word—and God bless her, no questions, yet—she slid behind the wheel, cranked the engine and rolled down the windows.

She handled the vehicle with her typical confidence, so he relaxed, only as his eyes slid closed realizing he never sat in the passenger seat. Even in the plane, he was the aircraft commander. His copilot days were long past.

Having an equal partner was rare.

He homed in on sounds to blot out thoughts—cars roaring past, the road reverberation shifting in tune as they ascended a bridge. A barge chugged in the distance, a long mournful horn echoing.

Inhale. Exhale. Forget. Inhale beach air. Salt water. Marsh. The scent of Nikki's soap. He was being selfish making her wait.

He turned his head along the seat. "I guess you want to know what happened."

"You'll tell me when you're ready." She kept her eyes forward, hands at ten and two, a rock when he needed one so damned much.

"I'm ready to talk whenever you want to pull over."

"Okay then. I know a quiet place not too far from here." A few miles later, she took the next exit off the highway, down a two-lane road along the shore, finally turning onto a dirt road leading to a tiny deserted historical landmark. The small battlefield boasted little more than a couple of minicannons, a broken cement bench and a sign explaining what happened here over two hundred and twenty-five years ago.

Shutting off the engine, Nikki shifted in the seat, leather creaking. "How about we sit in the back of the truck and look at the stars?"

She understood him so well it shook him sometimes since he didn't much like people rooting around in the cobweb-filled darkness of his head.

Well damn. Could that have been a part of why he'd run so hard and fast in the other direction after waking up in her bed? Not a reassuring thought in the least since he'd always told himself he stayed away for her, rather than risk hurting her again.

He leaned over to the backseat and pulled a bedroll of blankets forward. "I sleep outside sometimes."

In the back of his truck or the deck of his boat, the solitude and stars called to him. Except tonight he needed Nikki beside him.

Carson turned the key to keep the CD playing, windows

down before he stepped outside and dropped the back hatch. He unrolled the bedding, tossing the sleeping bag for cushion and shaking out the extra blanket to wrap around them, trying like crazy to ignore the intimacy of the whole action.

The night wasn't that cold, high forties maybe, with a bit of a bite in the crisp air. He followed her into the truck bed, sitting beside her, draping the blanket over their shoulders, their legs stretched out side by side with a tree bower overhead. A few stars twinkled through, but the overall haven effect blocked out the world.

By instinct, he slid his arm around her waist and she didn't object, simply tucked her head on his shoulder while they both leaned against the cab and stared up at the sky. The time had come to talk. As much as he hated pouring out the horror of the day at her feet, here they were, and he was learning Nikki was a lot stronger than he'd known.

"There was a bombing at the barracks housing our crews. Two injured." His head thunked back against the glass. "One dead."

Her hand fell to his thigh in a steady weight of comfort. "Who died?"

"The young loadmaster, Gabby." So named "Gabby" because the kid talked all the time and now would never speak again. "I had to tell his wife. She's only twenty years old, Nikki. Twenty damn years old and already a widow."

Her fingers squeezed tight on his thigh. She stayed silent. What could she say anyway? There weren't words for this. God knew he'd looked for them when speaking to Gabby's wife, and he'd said *something,* undoubtedly inadequate. He'd taken flight surgeon Monica Korba and Chaplain Murdoch with him, but ultimately telling her was his responsibility, his squadron, his lost wingman.

Big band tunes from WWII teased from the truck cab, the pair of chipped cannons leaning. Symbols of so much loss.

"I don't know how the commanders during World War II handled all the deaths." His chin fell to rest on top of her head, the scent of her mingling with the ocean air to fill the hollowness inside him.

"You said two were injured?"

This had to be traumatic for her, too. These people were her friends. He cupped her shoulder and hugged her closer. "Bronco and Joker."

She gasped, just a slight hitch she swallowed back without looking up at him.

He rubbed her arm until her breathing settled again. "Bronco was pinned by a beam when the barracks collapsed. He's got a few crushed ribs and a punctured lung. Joker caught flying glass in the chest and face. I spoke to Joker's fiancée right before she was supposed to leave for work. She kept trying to find her shoes as if that would make everything all right."

Her arms slipped around his waist and she held tight, offering a comfort he wouldn't ask for but was grateful she thought to give.

He forced down the acrid taste in his mouth insidiously whispering for a shot of something smooth to wash it away. "We finally caught up with Bronco's wife. Since she's a military doc she kept trying to discuss everything in medical terms with Doc Korba, but her hands and voice were shaking so bad while she talked… Bronco's little girl was running around the living room like everything was fine and she didn't have a clue her daddy's on an operating table in another country."

His voice cracked. Damn it. He scrubbed his hand under his nose and started to stand. "We should go back now."

She reached up, clasped his hand and stopped him. "Do you have to return to the squadron?"

"No. There's nothing more I can do tonight." He looked down at her, her old-time music riding the breeze, moonlight streaming silver glints in her hair with a timeless hint of what she might look like in thirty years.

Nikki tugged. "Then let's stay here."

"I'm pretty messed up in the head and we both know what happens when I can't think straight around you."

"Have you been drinking?"

"No." He wanted to, but was hanging on now, thanks to her.

"Neither have I." She tugged again. "Stay. Let's look at the stars and talk if we need to or just be quiet. But I don't think either of us is ready to go back yet."

He knelt beside her. "How did you get so smart so young?"

"It's in the music."

He knew better.

The age difference excuses weren't going to work for him anymore. While there were certainly a legion of other problems they would have to deal with later, for tonight at least they were both on even footing and in need of something they could only find together.

Cradling her face in his hands, Carson gave up the fight and kissed her.

* * *

Nikki didn't even think of pulling away from Carson and the warm pressure of his mouth against hers. In fact, she didn't expect to pull away from him at all for a long time tonight.

Halfway through his outpouring about speaking with the families, her heart had softened the rest of the way toward forgiving him for what happened before. Any man who noticed the vulnerability in a woman spinning circles to find her shoes in a crisis…well, that man had a deep and tender heart.

She wasn't sure what she intended to do with him after tonight, but she would never be able to move forward if she didn't finish what they'd started months ago. What better place to be together than out in the open? Away from the world that seemed to intrude too often and insist they were wrong for each other, for a litany of reasons she couldn't remember because the bold sweep of his tongue stole every thought right out of her head.

What was it about him? Could it simply be his experience that made men her age seem like boys? He certainly did know his way around a nerve-humming kiss that made her forget the nip in the air. In fact she could swear her skin was steaming as hotly as the blood coursing through her veins. His palm sketched along her stomach, bared as her sweater hitched, the bottom button already open in a V.

Arching—was that a purr coming from her?—she savored his calluses gained from years sailing, the gentle rasp a tantalizing abrasion against her oversensitive skin. She wanted more, more kisses, touch, sensation.

Everything, here under the bower of trees and light of a harvest moon glinting on the water.

He leaned forward, or she angled down, or they both simply followed gravity to the sleeping bag. She wasn't sure and didn't care as long as they both were flat. Soon. Yes. She sank into the giving softness, his body blanketing hers while he braced on his elbows to keep his weight off her.

Her legs locked around his at the knees, her hands urging against his rippling shoulders. "I want it all tonight."

No half measures like their other time together.

Still he kept the full press of himself off her, the sleeping bag only offering so much protection from the steel truck bed. He peered down at her, blue eyes deepening to a midnight hue almost as dark as the sky. "Things are moving fast here tonight. Are you sure this is what you want?"

"Do you plan to walk out on me afterward?"

"I tried to stay away and we saw how well that worked for me. I've thought about you every damn second for seven months."

"Good." Nice to know she hadn't suffered this alone.

"So there's a vindictive streak in you after all." His mouth creased up in a smile she burned to explore with the tip of her tongue. "I was wondering how you could forgive me so easily when you're well within your right to be kicking my ass into eternity for what I did."

"Actually, I think I owe you an apology, as well, for what happened then. I knew you weren't in any shape to make an important decision like going to bed together."

It felt good to finally voice the guilt she'd been hiding for months. As much as his walking away had hurt her, it was about time she accepted her own role.

He flipped to his side, palming the bared patch of skin

above her low-riding jeans. "While I still think any culpability rests squarely on my shoulders, we can start clean tonight."

She liked the sound of that. "Does that mean we're back to a first date? Because I won't go to bed with a guy on a first date."

His hand tunneled a hint higher up her sweater. "How about a clean slate with a history of friendship and dates."

"Sounds good to me." Especially if he would keep stroking her rib cage.

He thumbed the underside of her breast, teasing the swell through satin. "Right now I wouldn't mind hearing exactly what you want."

"I want to be with you." She slid the top button free from her lemon-yellow sweater, cool breeze drifting along passion-heated flesh.

His blue eyes lit with shock—and desire. "Uh, I meant back at my place, or yours."

"What's wrong with here?"

A growl rumbled low in his chest, vibrating against hers. "Not a damn thing."

He tracked her hands, freeing button after button until her sweater parted. She wondered at her own boldness for an instant, then gloried in it as his gaze hooked on her breasts. The chill in the air puckered her nipples tight against the scant satin and lace.

His pupils widened with increasing passion. As if she couldn't already feel the evidence of his growing arousal throbbing against her.

She reached for the front clasp of her bra, and thank goodness she'd put on the good stuff this morning, pale yellow Victoria's Secret. On sale. And holy cow she was rambling in her brain to ward off embarrassment.

The cold kissed her skin a second before his mouth. Moist heat flowed from him through her veins until she longed to shrug away the heavy blanket, but her languid body wouldn't obey commands from her brain. Only instinct. Her frantic hands grappled over Carson, hungry to touch as much of him as possible after yearning for so damn long. Much more and she would combust.

His hands slid lower to her bottom, drawing her nearer. They rolled along the truck bed in a tangle of arms and legs that should have hurt but sensation suffused her to the exclusion of anything else.

Cocooned in the blanket, she kicked free of her jeans, needing to be rid of the confining clothes. Her sweater hung from her shoulders as her bare breasts brushed along the rough fabric of his flight suit as they lay side by side.

The flight suit unzipped from the bottom for easy access during flight, and she definitely intended for them both to fly now, with the sky and stars, sound of the waves in her ears, the best of both worlds.

"Birth control?" she mumbled against his mouth.

"In my wallet." He combed his hands deeper through her hair, holding her with an intensity that rocked her. "Nikki, I swear I'm going to be around after."

"Can we talk about that later?" She only wanted to focus on finally feeling all of him all over her.

"I'm just doing my damnedest to be honorable here."

One of the things she admired about him, but right now

he'd turned her inside out until she couldn't have run enough miles to burn off the frenetic energy zinging through her.

"It would be very dishonorable to leave me unsatisfied." Stretched beside him, she wrapped her fingers around the thick length of him, learning the silken steel texture of him. His groan thrilled her as much as his touch, knowing *she* brought him pleasure. She suspected the timeless tunes from the stereo would arouse her mercilessly from now on.

He tugged out his wallet, pulled free a tiny packet and sheathed himself with a speed that spoke of an urgency echoed inside her.

Hooking his hand behind her knee, he hitched her leg higher, over his hip until she realized what he intended. No missionary position tonight. Fair enough. She liked the idea of taking this journey side by side.

Then the thick blunt prodding stopped her thoughts altogether as she focused on this moment she knew would change things between them forever. Deeper, deeper still, she took him inside her body and more, slowly, carefully, staring into his eyes and soul in a way she never had months ago when she'd been too wrapped up in her hero worship to see the man.

She winced at the uncomfortable pinch and stretch, settled, waited for her body to adjust around him.

"Okay?" he asked, his jaw flexing from a restraint he couldn't hide.

"Totally." She rocked against him once, twice, again, his grip on her hips helping her find a matching rhythm of their bodies together. Moving. Rocking to increase the pleasure of his slick thrusts.

He shifted onto his back, holding her in place during the

shuffle, the blanket slithering down around her waist, her sweater flapping open while he laved attention over her breasts.

His hand slid between them, touching where their bodies met, circling in time with her writhing hips against him. Her womb clenched tight, tighter, as tight as her legs clamping him to her as she chased the release so close... closer...

Waves of pleasure sluiced over her, pulsing like the breakers gushing against the shore, then receding slowly and stealing her muscles from her body until she slumped on top of him. Two deep thrusts later, his arms convulsed around her in time with his hoarse growl of completion.

Slowly, her senses tuned back in on things other than the residual pleasure pulsing through her.

Waves surged and crashed while the stereo piped one of her favorite songs, "Don't Sit Under the Apple Tree." Now she knew why.

Nikki grinned against his neck, tasting the sweat on his skin. "After all our talk about being old and mature, here we are in the back of a truck."

His hands roved up and down her spine. "I've never made love in the back of a truck."

"Me, either." Nor had she made love anywhere else for that matter.

A fact she now knew for certain.

She'd been almost sure nothing happened with Gary. The doctor in the emergency room had reassured her there were no signs of penetration, and she'd believed intellectually, but her mind had felt so violated it had been difficult to look beyond that. Now at least she had physical reassurance that she had not slept with Gary Owens—or any man for that matter.

Because making love in the back of a truck had been a first for her in more ways than one.

Chapter 10

Nikki was a virgin.

Past tense now.

Carson still couldn't wrap his brain around the fact, even as they sprawled in bed—at her apartment, not the garage place at her parents. After they'd untangled themselves from the sleeping bag in the back of his truck, he'd hesitated to take her to his house because of the bad memories it might hold for her, so he'd suggested her empty apartment. Since it was now common knowledge she'd moved out, there was no reason to fear hanging out in the place for a few hours.

An arm tucked under his head, the other curved around Nikki while she slept curled against his side, he stared up at her ceiling fan clicking overhead, circulating the heat. A tiny soccer ball dangled from the chain, spinning lazy rings in the air. Her room surprised him. She was such a no frills and leanly honed person he hadn't expected something so…frou-frou. From her ruffly curtains to the poufy spread, patterned with tiny pink flowers and little green leaves.

Then there was that soccer ball chain pull overhead.

The dichotomy was somehow so totally Nikki the image settled in his brain as he grew even closer to this woman he'd fought hard to resist. How many other facets to her personality had he missed because of preconceived notions?

And the biggest mistaken notion of all… Damn it, he should have figured out she'd never made love *before* he came up against the hint of a barrier. Which shocked the hell out of him.

Although she was a quick study.

Still, if he'd known he would have…what? Turned away? Probably not, but at least he could have offered her a gentler, more romantic first time. Being with her blew his mind beyond anything he'd ever experienced. He knew now there wasn't a chance he could have been with her seven months ago and forgotten.

However now he wondered what *had* happened between them. When he reexamined their conversations about that night, never once did she say they had sex, only that they'd gone to his place. Not that they'd discussed it much—his own damn fault.

He remembered waking up naked together, so they must have gotten mighty damn close before he passed out. God. He owed her an even bigger apology than he'd thought.

Nikki stirred against his side and sighed over his chest before pressing a kiss to his shoulder, stirring a *good morning* down south even in the middle of the night. He willed away the erection—okay, it wasn't going down any time soon, but at least he reined himself in and simply rolled toward her for a simple kiss.

Simple? Not for long.

Carson sailed his hand along her naked spine. "You're awake."

Her fingers skipped down his chest. Lower. Gliding one finger from tip to base. "So are you."

He clamped a hand around her wrist. "As much as I would really enjoy an encore, again, you need more time to recover."

"Women don't have a recovery time like guys."

"That's not what I meant." He pressed a kiss to the palm of her hand and resisted the urge to taste more instead of talking about what promised to be a sticky subject. "You were still a virgin."

She stilled for six clicks of the ceiling fan overhead before flipping to her back, sheet clutched to her creamy chest. "I was wondering if you noticed that little fact."

Tough to miss. Just the memory of her tight heat had him throbbing all over again.

While he couldn't have all of her just yet, he allowed himself the pleasure of teasing her tangled hair along the pillow and rubbing a dark lock between two fingers. "Twice tonight was probably already one more time than was wise for your body. Tomorrow, though, I'll be more than happy to take you up on that offer."

"So we're done for tonight?"

Her obvious disappointment stirred him as much as any touch. If she was game, he had a few ideas of how they could spend the remaining hours before sunrise and a return to the real world. "Unless I can interest you in a bath?"

"A bath?" She sat up, flowered sheet slithering down to pool around her waist while she studied him with unabashed enthusiasm.

Forget oysters, this woman was a walking, talking, living, breathing aphrodisiac.

"A steaming bath would be good for all those new muscles you used tonight." He swung his feet from the bed and held out a hand for her.

Linking their fingers, she followed him into the bathroom, leaning to twist on the water—and whoa what a view. Passion fogged his vision.

Steady.

Stepping over her seashell-shaped bath mat, he lowered himself into the tub, then settled her in front of him while the faucet sluiced steaming water over their feet, her sweet bottom pressing a soft torment against him. Way to go, genius.

His skull was going to explode before he could get around to discussing the pink elephant looming in the middle of her ocean-themed bathroom. "I thought we had sex seven months ago."

Arms draped along the sides of the tub, she tipped her head on his shoulder to look at him, surprise sparkling in her crystal-gray eyes. "You don't remember what happened that night? I think you owe me a new apology."

Ah hell. Not a pink elephant at all for her, since she didn't have a clue what he'd thought.

This really was screwed up and now he'd made it worse. He needed to unscramble his brain to get through this, tough to do when his eyes were full of Nikki's legs...and more. "What did you think I was apologizing for last week?"

"For passing out on top of me seconds before the act." Pink tinged her cheeks, but he suspected it had nothing to do with the steam rising from the water around them. "And I figured you were apologizing most of all for walking out the next morning and never calling."

"That last part, absolutely. The first part, God yes, I'm apologizing for that now, as well. I'm sorry for being in no shape to ask you to stay the night with me and for being self-ish enough to do it anyway."

"I can't believe that for all these months you thought we slept together." Confusion smoked through her eyes. "At least you're off the hook for that."

"Not even close. Doesn't matter that my body shut down, the intent to make love to you remained even though I knew I should stay away." He rested his chin on her head, remem-bering enough of that night to know that nothing, nothing was more important to him then than being with Nikki. And that unsettled the hell out of him because he still felt the same.

"Maybe you would have had second thoughts if you hadn't passed out."

"I doubt it. I'd wanted to be with you for so damn long." Which brought them back to the present. "And here we are again."

"Except things went better this time." Her smile granted forgiveness he still wasn't sure he deserved.

"I want afterward to be better, too." He clasped her hands in his, linking them over her stomach.

"Although I can't image how the 'during' part could be any better."

His thumbs brushed along the soft undersides of her breasts, perspiration from the heated water dotting her chest and begging him to taste her. "I would take that as a compliment, but you had twenty-three years of buildup going."

"Who says I went totally without for twenty-three years?" Pure sensuality emanated from her smile. "I'm a woman who can take care of herself."

He choked on a cough. *Take care of herself?* She couldn't mean… He searched deeper into her narrowed eyes and holy crap, she most definitely meant exactly what he thought.

Carson linked their fingers tighter, holding hands as much touching as he could risk with his body on fire from just her words. "Now there's an image I could enjoy for a damn long time."

Nikki's smile widened and she guided one of his hands down her belly, dipping deeper into the water. "Or you could enjoy it along with me now for real."

His brain went on stun, then revved to life because no way was he missing out on a second of this fantasy come to life.

Nikki reclined back against his chest, her knees parting in the move of an awesomely bold innocent. She guided his hand lower, her hand over his cupping the core of her.

She brought their other fisted hands up over her breast, unfurling her fingers until she flatted his palm to her pebbled peak. Slowly she guided his hand along her skin, her impossibly tight nipple tightening further. He swallowed hard.

Her mouth tipped in a slight smile. She couldn't miss the sway she held over him and damned if he cared about his surrender so long as she continued to lead his touch, growing bolder as her pupils widened with unmistakable pleasure.

He throbbed harder against the sweet press of her bottom.

Her other hand, underwater over his, twitched, tangling his fingers in short dark curls, dipping into moist heat and rubbing slow circles with his fingers against the hidden bud beading as tight and hard as her nipple minutes before.

Much more of this and he would explode. He started to pull his hand away and she held him firm, her breathing faster, her heart hammering so hard he could feel it through her back against his chest…until her spine bowed forward in time with her gasp, another, then a low moaning exhale as she sagged against him again, a limp, soft weight.

He soothed her through the aftershocks with steady pressure, whispering in her ear, "Definitely an image to carry with me. You're one helluva woman, Nikki Price."

Her head lolling, she nuzzled his shoulder. "While I can take care of myself, I've found it's all the better with you along."

Tomorrow, he would take her up on that. For now, he held her while the water chilled around them, reminding him of the cold reality.

He was fast losing control of his feelings for this complicated woman.

So much for believing she could keep things uncomplicated with Carson.

Stretching her leg to toe on the faucet to reheat the bath, she couldn't decide whether to be totally mortified by what they'd just done or simply languish in the afterglow and warming water. Sheesh, when she decided to let down her boundaries, she really went all the way. "You were totally right about a bath relaxing me."

His light laugh ruffled her hair, uneasiness seeping from her toes.

Carson's arms tightened, their hands linked over her stomach. "Thank you for trusting me to be your first."

"You're welcome." Definitely not simple anymore. From the minute she'd met him, she'd wanted him to be her first.

Her last?

"Do you mind if I ask why you waited so long?" He stretched his foot to turn off the water.

He'd shared so much about himself and his growing-up years, it seemed selfish to hold back, especially when her past was so much less traumatic than his. "My parents had to get married when my mom was only eighteen. Mom was already pregnant with me. It's not something we discussed, but I always wondered if they fought because of me."

"You know better now, right?"

Sort of. "Chris told me he brought up my 'premature' birth once and Dad almost decked him."

"Since your father's one of the least violent men I've ever met, that says a lot for how much he must love your mom."

"Yeah." The silent tension had grown so thick over the years, she couldn't wait to leave for college. "Still, Chris and I weren't surprised when they drew up divorce papers. They had a tough start, followed by a rocky couple of decades before everything came together for them."

Saying it out loud resurrected memories of childhood nights crying in her bed while her parents fought downstairs. Crying harder when they stopped talking altogether. "So why did I wait? I just wanted to be really, really sure before I committed even a part of myself to a guy."

Would he freak out now? Or would she beat him to the punch?

Nerves pattered in her stomach as she realized how close she was to giving more than a part of herself to Carson, a man who didn't cry for himself, but teared up over Bronco's little girl possibly losing her daddy.

Jeez, how selfish of her to have forgotten what brought him to her in the first place tonight. "Are you okay after everything that happened this afternoon?"

"I'm leveled out now. Thank you for letting me spill my guts like that back in the truck." Before she could answer, he flicked the drain on the tub, water sucking out. "We should dry off before we turn into a couple of prunes."

Vulnerability might be long suppressed, but she'd seen his sensitive side now and couldn't forget. She hauled herself from the tub and grabbed a coral towel, reaching for another for Carson from the wicker basket, wishing they could simply dry each other off and go to sleep. Instead, she kept thinking about what demons must be rumbling around inside of him after a day like today. Leveled out wasn't the same as okay. She knew that well from watching her parents interact after her father's capture in the Middle East.

Carson's capture, as well.

Nikki tugged the towel into a knot between her breasts. "What happened today must have brought back some awful memories of your own time overseas."

He grunted, toweling his legs dry.

Carson never just grunted. He might dodge direct answers

but he was always, always polite. She thought about backing off and letting him have his space…but then she remembered how that tactic had nearly destroyed her parents.

Holy cow, was she thinking about being a couple? Well, she wasn't *not* thinking about it. She couldn't lie to herself. She had feelings for this man that deserved exploring, which meant no half-measure crushes where they never looked below the surface.

Towel drying her hair, she stared at his steamy reflection as he stood behind her tying his towel around his lean hips. "I heard my dad's version of what happened to your crew overseas." The towel slid from her shaking hands. Kneeling, she scooped it into the hamper. "It took him a while to talk about it, but after he and Mom started marriage counseling, they decided Chris and I should know what happened when he was shot down and captured by those warlords. We're adults after all. They both decided they'd sheltered us too much from things growing up."

"Do you agree?" He draped his dog tags around his neck.

Tugging the comb through her gnarled hair, Nikki wished her life could be as easily untangled. "Certainly Chris and I knew something was going on between Mom and Dad. It was tough growing up with him gone so much, and Mom pretending everything was fine."

She turned to lean against the vanity, taking in his golden gorgeous face marred only by a tiny scar along his jaw. A scar that somehow made him all the more handsome for the human imperfection.

A scar he'd gotten during his time in the Middle East.

She traced the faded white line cutting through his five o'clock shadow and wondered about the scars he carried inside from his childhood, as well. "Hearing the truth might have reassured us since sometimes reality isn't as bad as what you're fearing."

He enfolded her hand and pressed a kiss to her wrist, right on her racing pulse. "You're talking about something else now."

"And you're a perceptive man."

Carson dropped her hand and strode from the bathroom. "If you're thinking about my parents, the reality is at least as harsh as whatever you would imagine."

The tile chilled under her feet as she stood in the doorway. "They hurt you?"

His back to her, he snagged his flight suit off the rocking chair in the corner. "Coked-up people don't know their own strength and lose a lot of inhibitions."

She wanted to wrap her arms around his waist, press her cheek to his shoulder, but she also didn't want to risk stopping his flow of words. She sank to rest at the foot of her bed in the middle of tangled sheets and the scent of them together. His handkerchief rested folded on top of her laundry and she still didn't know what that middle initial stood for.

Had anyone ever cared enough for this man to know everything—even the darker things—about him? "I'm so sorry."

"Don't get me wrong. I could handle getting slapped around, and I could defend myself when one of Mom's stoned friends came barging through my bedroom door."

A gasp slipped free. Her fears hadn't even come close to the reality.

He glanced over his shoulder, face harder than she could ever remember seeing it. "I was fine, Nikki, but when I caught some high bastard on top of my sister…" Turning away again, he yanked the uniform zipper up his body. "I went to one of my teachers for help. Other teachers and even the cops had blown us off in the past—or my folks bought them off. Who knows? But this teacher, Mrs. Godeck, she was different. Stronger. She told my parents she was going to make their lives hell if they didn't send us both to boarding school. Somehow, she stood them down."

Thank God for Mrs. Godeck.

He dropped into the rocker and laced his black combat boots, left, right, done. "Are you ready to go back to your folks' place? I need to report in early today and take care of all the fallout from the barracks bombing."

She was sitting in her towel, for heaven's sake, and it was—she glanced at the clock—four in the morning. Unease prickled. He couldn't be walking on her again because she'd gotten too close….

"I'm not walking out," he echoed her thoughts so perfectly it spooked her. "I truly do head into work at five or six on a normal day."

"And this isn't a normal day."

Taking her hands, he knelt in front of her. "Not by a long shot."

His explanation made sense, but still, something wasn't right. "I understand about commitment to your job."

He squeezed her hands. "I want you to be careful when you go back to work."

"Of course I will."

He could take his distance and shove it. She kissed the faded scar. "I'm also checking in this week with Reis about some thoughts I've had."

And to find out more about those creepy calls to her parents' house. She wanted more facts before she told Carson so he wouldn't freak needlessly and lock her whole family in some hotel until her father returned.

Carson tapped her forehead. "Memories?"

"Ideas."

"Good ones?"

"Crummy ones, actually, but I hate feeling helpless."

His throat moved with a long swallow. "Helpless sucks."

For a second the connection between them shimmered to life again, a thin, fragile thread she needed to handle with a feather-light touch.

From his thigh pocket, his cell phone chimed—at four in the morning? The thread snapped.

He growled. "I'm starting to hate that damn thing." Rising, he dropped a quick kiss on her lips as he whipped his cell phone from his pocket. He glanced at the LCD, his face blanking. "Sorry. I have to take this."

Carson stepped out onto the balcony to talk in private, his voice low. Even with his reassuring kiss and words, she couldn't shake the feeling there was something more he was keeping from her. She thought about those two men she'd seen him with the night of Gary's death, and how Carson had neatly avoided saying anything about them when she shared the memory.

Staring at the broad plank of his shoulders as he stood outside taking his mystery call, she told herself they were still early in this relationship thing. Be patient. Build trust.

Except she couldn't help but think of how long her mother had told herself the very same thing.

Chapter 11

Sliding the balcony door closed behind him as he stood outside in the chilly night, Carson tucked the phone to his ear, his head still pounding from the discussion with Nikki. He was trying, but he couldn't miss the searching in her eyes, the need for something more he wasn't sure he had in him to give after his screwed-up childhood.

However at the moment, the person on the other end of the phone needed him. That loyalty had to be a top priority. Without the support system, none of them would be worth a damn to anyone. "Hello?"

"Carson? Will, here. Sorry to call so late." They used first names in the program, even when they knew the surname.

"How's everything going?" All right, he hoped, because as much as he tried to channel his thoughts into being supportive, he couldn't stop thinking about Nikki, being with her—and the mind-blowing discovery that they hadn't been together months ago before he'd passed out.

He'd always been a heavy social drinker. That sense of family in a gathering had sucked him right in and he would stay until the bell rang for last round. He'd tried a few times to cut back, but with no lasting luck—until he'd bottomed out that night with Nikki and realized he needed to join A.A. He still had a long road ahead, but his sea legs were back under him and he owed a debt for that.

Free time was in short supply, but he volunteered every spare second to a local support group that served as a catch-all for relatives of people with a variety of addictions. "Hey, Will? You still there?"

"Yeah," the older man cleared his throat, voice raspy from years of smoking to fill the empty hours without a beer at the racetrack, "Vic called."

Not Will's problem tonight, but rather the guy Will was sponsoring. Will had been sponsoring Owens, as well, since Will belonged to both AA and Gambler's Anonymous. "At four in the morning? Must be bad, but at least he called."

Vic Jansen had caught the potential drinking problem early, recognizing he was having a rough time since he'd lost his daughter, using alcohol to numb the pain. Carson had a feeling Vic would make it through, and once he had his life back, the guy had the makings of being a rock-solid support. But first, they had to get Vic to tomorrow.

"He needs someone to come over and talk. My boy wrecked the truck and I don't get it back until the morning…"

"I can cover it." Easy enough to drop in since Vic lived on

his forty-two-foot sailboat docked near Carson's smaller one. Hell, he understood well how tough the nights could be. At least Vic was making the call rather than landing on the wrong woman's doorstep. "Thanks for the heads-up."

"No problem. Let me know how it goes."

"Roger." Carson disconnected and stuffed the cell phone back into his flight suit pocket.

Now he needed to figure out how to leave without seeming to bolt through the door. He wasn't sure where he and Nikki were headed, but again she'd held him through a hellish night. As much as he didn't want to lean on anyone, he couldn't ignore the fact that he kept ending up on her doorstep when *he* needed someone.

Which cycled him back around to being a taker, the thing he hated most. So what the hell to do? Deal with it one day at a time until he got his head out of his butt.

He rolled the glass door open to find Nikki dressed again. God, she looked great in those short fuzzy sweaters, softness and bright colors calling to his hands, *touch me*. He cricked his neck through the temptation to explore tangerine angora. "I'm sorry. I have to go."

"Work." Kneeling, she nodded, fishing a canvas bag from her closet, the hem of her sweater inching up to reveal a strip of her creamy back. "I understand."

Work? Carson hesitated a second too long and she glanced over her shoulder. He wasn't fooling her for a second, but couldn't say more. "I would stay if I could."

He hated lying to her. For the first time he considered telling her about his alcoholism. Why had he held off so long? Had he been enough of an ass back then to keep the secret so as not to taint her hero worship? A distinct possibility he needed to make right, and soon.

At least then she would understand moments he had to leave at the drop of a hat for a non-work-related call when he couldn't give her the specifics. That confidentiality was crucial in A.A., something he couldn't break even for Nikki. It sucked bad enough that Reis had investigated Owens's sponsor. How he'd found out the confidential relationship, Carson didn't know.

Okay, so he would tell Nikki about his drinking problem, but it wasn't something he could drop on her then sprint out the door. And he *did* have to sprint. "We're still on for sailing this weekend?"

"Sure." Canvas bag at her feet, she tugged open a drawer and shuffled clothes into the sack.

Thank goodness she was packing. While he was okay with them hanging out here together for a few hours, having her move back in—alone—was another matter altogether. Hopefully this hell would be over before she needed to use all those socks.

And satin underwear. Mint-green. Grape-purple. Lemon-yellow and funny how the mind focused on food adjectives for tasting. Tasting her. Was she wearing tangerine-orange to match that sweater?

Think of something else, pal. Pronto.

His fingers grazed a notepad by her phone, tore off a piece of paper and started folding. He'd picked up origami on his own one dark night, desperate to keep his hands busy with anything other than a bottle.

"I'll call." And he would. She was just within her rights to doubt him. *Fold. Tuck. Don't touch Nikki.* "Come on and I'll drive you back to your parents' place—and don't even suggest staying here."

"I'm not reckless. I know that I'm not some supercop or investigator. I'm a teacher, something I hope I'll be allowed to do now that I'm off the official suspect list."

She slid a neatly pressed pair of khaki pants from the drawer and he realized she was packing work clothes. Of course she would return to her job now that her name was cleared. Back to students who slashed tires and schools with metal detectors.

He forced himself to breathe evenly and crease the edge of the tiny form taking shape. "Do you have a gun?"

"No." She dropped another sweater, purple to match that grape lingerie no doubt. "And I'm not going to keep one with Jamie around."

"Fair enough."

He knelt beside her, his hand falling on top of hers to stop her speedy stowing because too easily he could envision her someday packing up to walk out of his life for good. "I really am going to call."

"Of course you are." Her hair swished forward to hide her face. "Carson? What's your middle name?"

Huh? God, he would never understand women.

He cupped her head, silken strands sliding over his skin until finally she looked up at him. "Alexander. My full name is Carson Alexander Hunt the fourth."

Searching her translucent gray eyes, he found wary consent a second before her hand glided up to his shoulders. Her mouth met his, no doubt about the mutual move. Here at least there were no misunderstandings or hesitations, just a driving need.

And if he didn't stop soon they would be doing a lot more than kissing.

He eased back. "I don't want to rush all the things I have to say, but come this weekend, we need to talk."

Her fingers toyed with the nape of his neck, her lips teasing over his. "I'd rather do more of this."

He pressed the one-inch paper tulip in her palm. "Certainly possible."

If she didn't run screaming and packing for good after their conversation.

Her every nerve screamed with tension.

After a jam-packed week of waiting to be alone with Carson, Nikki batted three helium balloons down and out from the passenger seat of her Ranger, clamping a folded Welcome Home, Dad banner under her arm. The three Mylar balloons would be a flyaway mess on the flight line, but Jamie loved them so she'd decided they could just tie the red, white and blue trio to her little brother's wrist.

Patriotic balloons trailing after her, she made tracks toward the big blue Air Force bus that would transport the families out to the tarmac to greet the returning aircrews.

True to his word, Carson had called her, every day this week for that matter, always checking in with her brother, as well, for a security update. Carson had even sent her flowers the morning after they'd made love. Not generic red roses, but a dozen, each one a different color. The note read how they reminded him of her sweaters and the brightness she brought to his life.

She'd cried—who wouldn't?—and slipped the card into the plastic picture holder in her wallet along with the origami tulip so she could look at both again and again in hopes of overriding the impending sense of doom. Their quick conversations had done little to diffuse the anxiety. His workweek was insane with the bombing and returning flyers. And since her return to the classroom, she'd been playing catch-up.

They were talking, some of the conversation sexy and longing. He wanted her. No question. It wasn't like before. But still… She'd been hurt, then angry for so long, this shift left her a bit off balance.

Panting puffs in the cold, she made it to the bus and climbed up the steps with seconds to spare. She waved to her mom and brothers in back and plopped in the lone remaining seat up front. Surely she would feel better once her father was safely home, then she and Carson could have their sailing date.

Date.

For real this time. Her hands clenched around her purse with that silly-sweet note from Carson inside.

Brown and brick buildings sprawled on the other side of the windows, reminding her when somehow she'd ended up here in a VOQ room with Gary Owens. God, she'd done a one-eighty from before, being certain the time had come to leave Carson Hunt behind forever. Now that she wasn't so focused on jabbing pins in a Carson voodoo doll, she was reminded of all the things she'd liked about him the first go-round.

He had a way of finding a good quality in each person and relating to them on that level, rather than seeing the negative and judging. He excelled as a leader by giving everyone else a chance to succeed based on that strength, something she would do well to cultivate in her teaching.

The lumbering bus jerked to a halt on the tarmac, restless families standing, pouring down the steps. Rows of parked cargo planes loomed, waiting for their missing friends. Airmen lined up outside to escort the families and greet their returning squadron mates. Where was Carson? Somewhere in that crowd most certainly, since already in the distance, she could see the specks of approaching C-17s on the horizon.

Coming home.

Hugging her coat around her, she waited alongside the idling bus while people streamed out, her mom and brothers at the back of the line.

Kevin Avery peeled away from the other flyers in leather jackets and joined her. "Hey, Nikki. How's it going?"

She felt bad about the way she'd treated him back in "Anybody-But-Carson" dating days. He seemed like a nice guy, dedicated to his Air Force career. Thank goodness he was okay with being friends, and had even set her up with his buddy Gary.

Great. They all knew how that one had ended. "Everything's better. My dad's coming home and he's in one piece."

"Yeah, and I hear the investigators cleared you." He nodded, clean-cut hair, boots perfectly polished until they glinted in the afternoon sun. "That's good. I always knew it couldn't be you and I told Agent Reis the same."

Nikki scratched the back of her neck, but the itchy sensation persisted that she was being stared at. She turned, scanned the cement expanse. Carson was watching.

Watching her with Avery.

Darn it. Was Carson going to get all weird again and insist he was too old for her? She winced to think of herself two years ago *hoping* he would be jealous and notice her. How juvenile it sounded now. She truly had been too young for him then—what a surprise notion.

She wanted to reassure Carson that her eyes were so full of him that even when he wasn't around, no other guy existed. But he was working and she knew from years listening to her parents that PDAs—public displays of affection—while in uniform were frowned upon.

But a smile would be cool. Right? Just as she started to grin at him—

Carson winked. Quick. Then done. But the tingle lingered long after he turned away to speak with the aviators lining up in front of him.

And my goodness, she could sure keep staring at the tempting view of his oh-so-perfect tush in a flight suit, but someone might notice and she wasn't ready to go public with their relationship. Not yet.

If nothing else, she should let her parents know, although her mother had probably already guessed.

Her gaze skipped down and away, back to the present where… Oops. Kevin Avery had picked up on every bit of the exchange. She saw things through his eyes and her quick shuffle from Gary to Carson didn't look good. As Gary's friend, Kevin had reason to be confused, even pissed on his buddy's behalf. He had no way of knowing that she and Gary had already been finished. Even if she explained it, who's to say he would believe her?

She simply stared at him silently, fairly certain he wouldn't confront her if she didn't broach the subject.

He tipped his head toward the cluster of flight suit-clad aviators. "Guess I should line up with the rest of the welcoming committee. Glad you're doing okay."

As Kevin melded in with his friends, her mother sagged to sit on the bottom bleacher, the middle trimester of pregnancy already slowing her down while Chris followed with toddler Jamie.

Nikki extended a hand. "Hey Chris, let me see the little guy."

Rena grinned, taking the banner. "So Chris can catch me if I topple over the side."

"You said it, Mom, not me."

Squatting in front of Jamie, Nikki tied the ribbons around his chubby wrist, her heart squeezing as tight as the knot over how darn cute her youngest brother was. She hitched him up onto her hip and snuggled him close while pointing out airplanes.

Which took her eyes right back to the flyboys. Carson's eyes held hers across the tarmac. No wink needed this time. She saw it in his eyes, a warming. He definitely wanted her. She shivered.

"Are you cold, sweetie?" her mother asked.

Totally scorching inside. And oooh, wasn't that a tingly thought? Scorch inside her. "I'm fine, Mom, thanks. Just remembering how many times we've done this welcome-home gig."

And wasn't that a nontingly thought?

Then Carson's gaze slid to Jamie and her heart squeezed tighter, more so when something bleak sent clouds chasing through Carson's beautiful blue eyes. What could he want to talk about when they went sailing? They couldn't be jumping to a superserious level this quickly, and frankly, she wasn't sure she trusted him that much yet.

Shoot, she wasn't sure she trusted *herself* that much. None of which she needed to think about now anyway.

The cargo planes slowed to a stop, side stairs and back hatches lowering until each clanked on the ground. The high noon sun reflected off the lumbering beasts. People packed the bleachers and milled around at the side, excited chatter the common denominator.

How many of these had she waited through, waiting for her dad, holding her mom's hand tight like now? How many more might she wait through for Carson? He stood to the side with the rest of the squadron at attention as the cargo hold full of green-suited bodies came into view.

First down the ramp, a stretcher carrying Bronco. He'd made it through surgery, surprising everyone with his sturdy constitution by being cleared for transport to come home with his squadron. Never leave your wingman.

He would spend a couple more weeks in the hospital here, but with his doctor wife to keep him on his toes, he would be fine. Joker strode beside him with his arm in a sling, his free arm extended for his fiancée.

Yet even with the smiles there remained an underlying solemnity for the missing man. Gabby's body had already been flown to the small Maine town where he and his wife had been

high school sweethearts. The base had held a memorial ceremony that left her hands trembling, even now just remembering.

And then from the middle of the mayhem emerged her
burly father, big and alive, someone she'd alternately adored
and resented all her life, depending on which country he
parked himself in at the end of the day.

She liked to think she was past those childhood hang-ups,
but couldn't ignore how messed up her life had become lately.
She hated to think that her crush on Carson had been some
sad father-figure deal. Ugh. Regardless, she knew her feelings for Carson were anything but familial.

Her father pulled back from Rena and turned to his two
adult children, little Jamie scooped up in one arm.

"Hey, Daddy." Nikki stepped into his open arm. "Welcome
home."

"Thanks, baby girl." He dropped a kiss on top of her head,
a quiet stalwart man who somehow still left such a void of silence when he was away.

She blinked back tears she refused to let mar this homecoming and stepped aside. Rena returned to J.T.'s side, so
much love humming between them, Nikki inched farther
away to give them more space even in public.

Her mind winged back to her father's return nearly two
years ago after being shot down and captured, how her heart
had been in her throat waiting for Carson, too. By letting Carson into her bed, yes, she was entertaining ideas of forever.
She couldn't ignore it. Some folks had a more casual approach to sex, and that was fine by her, but for her life, she
simply wasn't wired that way.

She was well-equipped for military life, she understood it, she'd lived it. She knew all the jargon, headaches, *heart-aches*—the joys, as well. Yes, she could handle this with her hands tied behind her back.

But did she *want* to spend the rest of her life waiting on a tarmac with tears in her eyes?

Carson hated waiting. And waiting to get Nikki alone this week had been hell.

Only a couple more hours until duty could be placed on the back burner for the night. First, he had to finish in-processing the returning squadron members—paperwork, customs, turn in medical records and equipment while the families passed time at an informal gathering inside the squadron briefing room.

Not much longer and things would wind down. He strode through the corridor from his office back toward the buzz of voices. A door swung wide from the public bathroom. He dodged, just as Nikki stepped out.

Thank you. A reward at the end of a killer week.

He stepped closer without touching. "Hey you."

She smiled back. "Hey *you.*"

"I've been going crazy this week wanting to see you." He advanced again.

Nikki stayed put, her smile full but her eyes…sad? "I understand you're busy."

Did she want space? Jesus, he was thirty-five years old, way past college-type dating scenes. Honesty. If they didn't go with that, then they were screwed.

He cupped her elbow and ducked into his office, door still

open but out of the mainstream of nosy folks. Clear for the moment, he allowed himself to move closer, near enough to exchange body heat as he flattened his hand on the wall behind her. "Just because I'm busy doesn't mean I'm not thinking about you."

Her smile filled her eyes now, too, breezily confident Nikki meeting him one for one. On a sexual level they were able to communicate openly. "And what did you think about when I crossed your mind?"

While they were being honest… "You usually crossed my mind naked."

"Totally?"

"Would it be piggish of me if you were only wearing heels?"

"Do-me pumps? Hmm… I may own a pair."

"Really?" He couldn't disguise his surprise. She'd never been much for heels, but then her barefoot appeal turned him inside out more than any other woman in stilettos ever could.

"No, I don't." Her grin went downright wicked. "But I will by this weekend."

He let his growl of appreciation rumble up and out as finally he got to be near her again. "How much longer until we can be alone?"

"What color?"

"Color?"

"Heels." Just below his neck, she toyed with the tab on his uniform zipper. "Since I'm shopping you can put in your order. Red or black? What's your pleasure?"

"You." He canted closer, a whisper away from her lips glistening with a gloss he would have to kiss off soon. He ducked his head close to her ear to whisper, "And I very much want to be your pleasure once we're out on the ocean, away from the rest of the world, no heels, no clothes, no outside worries. I wish it was summer so I could love you on the deck, out in the open, kissing every inch of your body while the sun does the same."

Her hot, panting breaths puffed over him. "Close the door. Now. Five minutes. Nobody'll miss us."

His brain fogged with possibilities of what they could accomplish in five minutes.

"Scorch?" a bass voice echoed down the hall.

He hadn't even heard anyone approaching. Jesus, he was far gone. Carson jerked, kicking himself for being reckless with Nikki's reputation and glancing back over his shoulder to look at…

The father of the woman he was just propositioning.

Gulp. Carson braced. "Yes, sir?"

J.T. frowned, stayed silent.

Sir. Crap. Carson's hand fisted on the door. He, a major, had just called a chief master sergeant *sir.* Officers did not call enlisted troops *sir.*

But a man sure as hell said *sir* to the father of his girlfriend. So much for waiting for the perfect time to logically explain about his relationship with Nikki.

They were so…

So…

Busted.

Chapter 12

She was so busted.

Three hours later tucking her little brother into bed, Nikki knew the confrontation was coming, even if her father had pretended nothing was wrong at the time. A quick unspoken agreement had zipped between the two men as readable as any newspaper.

No scenes at the squadron. Not a surprise since she'd lived her life being told to wear her best face on base. Be a good reflection of her father. She knew the drill.

Carson had backed away, his sexy proposition still echoing in her mind and pulsing heat through her veins. They'd returned to the gathering as if nothing happened—except that her dad had stuck to her side like glue until they drove home.

She tucked the Bob the Builder sheets around her little brother in his new race car toddler bed. He already snoozed away on his stomach, diapered butt up in the air under the quilted spread.

She glanced over her shoulder at her mom in a rocker with her swollen feet propped on the edge of the mattress. Nikki settled on the remaining patch of bed, next to her mother's puffy toes. "Are you sure you don't want me to keep him up at the apartment so you and Dad can have the run of the house?"

Rena patted her rounded stomach. "I'm not so sure we'll be doing any running, but we may take you up on the baby-sitting service for an afternoon sometime soon. For tonight, I think Jamie needs routine and to be near his daddy."

She totally understood and agreed. "People say kids are flexible, but I see in the classroom all the time how they thrive on structure."

"There's so much about the military way of life that's not normal for kids, I've always tried to keep what I could constant."

"I turned out okay for the most part." Other than a dead ex-boyfriend.

"I hope so." Rena nudged Nikki's hip with her crossed feet. "We're certainly proud of you."

"Thanks. I'm trying my best, even if I screw up."

All that water retention in her mother's toes tugged at Nikki's heart as she thought of the grief she'd brought during an already stressful time. She may not have actually wielded whatever bashed in Gary's skull, but she'd been on a self-destructive path for months.

Could she trust her judgment to have magically improved now? "I'm sorry I've caused you and Dad so much heartache the past few months."

Her mother studied her through perceptive eyes, taking a slow swallow from her glass of ice water while a couple of trucks growled along the deserted night road outside. "Do you want to tell me what happened to send you into such a tail-spin last spring?"

"Not really. Sorry." Telling would only make her mother upset with Carson when their relationship was about to become public. Really public, if the frozen tension on her father's face was anything to go by.

She should say something to her father before bed, even though she and Carson had discussed speaking with her father in the morning. Her mother wouldn't be surprised. She must suspect from how much time Carson had been spending around the house.

Had she known before? That "Mom Radar" was a spooky, perceptive thing.

Nikki refused to fidget like a kid. She was an adult. She didn't need her parents' permission, but she didn't want to make things tough at work for Carson or her dad. "I should let you go so you and Dad can enjoy your reunion."

Rena showed no signs of budging from her comfy spot. "I can talk a little while longer. Your father's busy for the moment anyway."

"Busy?" Uh-oh. Premonition trickled down her spine like the beads of condensation on her mother's glass.

"He's out on the porch waiting to talk to Scorch."

"*Sir,* huh."

The sardonic words from an obviously pissed off papa echoed across the lawn as Carson opened his truck door in the Price driveway. Looming on the porch, J.T. pinned him with a shotgun-father look as piercing as any bullet, illuminated all too clearly by the lamppost.

Carson finished stepping from his truck, not at all surprised to find J.T. waiting for him. They'd both known he would come by, an unspoken agreement.

At least the irate father hadn't made a scene at the squadron in front of everyone, because Carson damn well wouldn't have stood for Nikki's name being tossed around. As if she hadn't already been through enough gossip lately.

Thank God, her father apparently felt the same.

But now, after all the welcome-home partying was done, there was no more evading the question that had dogged the man's eyes throughout the evening.

"About that 'sir' thing…" Carson climbed the front steps, meeting J.T. face-to-face. "You caught me unaware. My nanny ingrained in me young to respect my elders."

"Elders?" Biceps flexed inside his flight suit. "You're really not getting on my good side today…*sir.* And I'm thinking it's important to you to be on my good side."

No-damn-kidding. Nikki was tight with her family, one of the many things he respected about her, and he refused to cause friction in the Price household. "I don't want to cause your daughter any grief and if you're upset that would upset *her* very much."

A vein pulsed in J.T.'s temple, a bad sign from such a usually laid-back guy. "Is there something going on with you and my baby girl?"

Baby girl?

Carson exhaled a long stream of cloudy air. He was definitely too old for this. But then he was dating a much younger woman, and hell, he wished his own parents had given a crap about his sister. He searched for the right words, the whole tongue-tied feeling completely alien for him, but then choosing the right words had never felt so important.

J.T. stepped closer, nose to nose and apparently more than a little miffed at Carson's extended silence. "*Sir,* I'm finding it hard to remember you're an officer. I'm finding it even tougher not to kick your ass off my porch."

"Go ahead. I was the one who peeled away the rank in there when I called you *sir.*"

"It's one thing if you're seriously dating, but if you're using her—"

Anger snapped. "Hold it right there." He didn't get outright mad often, but then nothing was logical in his head when it came to Nikki. "I respect your daughter and count myself one lucky bastard that she chooses to be with me."

J.T. pivoted on his boot heels away, chewing on a curse worthy of the saltiest of crewdogs.

Well damn. That was a little insulting.

A lot insulting.

He understood about the older man's wish for a nonmilitary life for his kids, but hell, he wasn't a total slouch.

J.T. cricked his neck from side to side before turning back around. "Is this serious? And don't tell me to ask her. I'm speaking with you."

Carson stepped alongside the old loadmaster and leaned his elbows on the porch railing while a rusted-out truck chugged past, exhaust mingling with the scent of mulchy leaves. He scrounged around for the right words to make this better for Nikki, for this man he'd flown combat with, a lasting bond. "I've heard you say for years no flyboys for your little girl. Was that bull?"

"I want an easier life for her than this—" he gestured back and forth to their uniforms "—a husband who's always gone, and getting shot at too often."

Husband. He didn't even bother denying the possibility existed. He tried a different tack. "You're speaking from a raw place right now because of the bombing and how close it hit."

"Could be." J.T. nodded a concession, ever fair. "Still, the military makes relationships tough enough, and I suspect you've got some extra stresses mixed in battling a drinking problem."

Ah. The real reason he disapproved. Somehow the seasoned chief master sergeant had figured it out when no one else had. "What makes you think that?"

"I don't talk much, but I'm always watching, and you go out of your way to avoid drinking, overly so."

"Plenty of people don't drink for any number of reasons."

"Are you telling me I'm wrong?"

When it came to Nikki, he needed to be honest every step of the way, because there wouldn't be another chance with her. J.T. wasn't the type to bandy the info around the squadron anyway. "You're not wrong. I wouldn't deny the problem if someone asked, but it's also not something I choose to advertise. I've been working at this for a couple of years, been completely dry and in a program for seven months."

Had he sealed his fate with Nikki's father? No hope for approval, ever? Entirely possible and totally more important than he'd expected.

J.T. sagged onto his elbows alongside Carson. "Thank you for being so open. I know that wasn't easy and it tells me you do care about my daughter."

Carson relaxed—for five whole seconds before he realized there was a *but* at the end of J.T.'s sentence. "And?"

"I respect like hell that you've fought this and seem to be holding your head above water. But you have to know this isn't something a father would wish for any child of his to live with."

"I agree." He had the same fears but staying away from Nikki had just about torn them apart. They needed to work through this insanity one way or another. "I've tried my damnedest to keep my distance."

"Tried." J.T.'s hands fisted before he continued, "Past tense?"

"Again, I'll say that I respect your daughter too much to discuss this further." The guy couldn't possibly want a blow-by-blow discussion. "Nikki's an adult. She deserves to be present so she can speak for herself."

"That earned you a couple more points."

Of course the conversation would have been a surprise for her if she had been here. "Nikki doesn't know about the drinking and I would appreciate it if you didn't say anything until I have a chance to tell her."

A slow growl echoed from the burly loadmaster's chest. "You've been seeing my daughter and you didn't tell her? I can't promise to keep quiet about that, and I'm actually re-considering that ass kicking."

Well deserved. No denying. "I don't mean for you to stay quiet forever. Just until tomorrow to give me a chance to tell her first. We're going sailing."

"Twenty-four hours?" J.T.'s fists unfurled against his legs. "That, I can do, but the clock starts ticking now."

Wind rustled through the trees, shaking a few more pine needles loose in a *tap, tap, tap* shower that filled the semi-comfortable silence. "Still want to hit me?"

"Yeah." A hint of a smile twitched the corner of his mouth. "But I always want to hit anyone who looks at my daughter."

They shared a laugh and Carson started to hope that maybe…

J.T.'s smile faded altogether. "Hurt her, though, and I *will* make you hurt back."

Carson stifled a wince over the inescapable reality that J.T.'s warning had come a few months too late.

"Hope it's not too late for me to be here."

Her eyes full of hot and brooding Carson, Nikki stepped out to join him on the small landing connected to the garage apartment. "I couldn't sleep."

She'd given up at midnight, digging her way into a pint of ice cream to eat away the disappointment when he left without speaking to her after his conversation with her father. Five spoonfuls into her double-fudge chocolate, she'd moved from disappointed to peeved. How could he leave her hanging like that?

Except here he was before morning and her anger eased.

"How did things go with my father? I hope he didn't give you a hard time."

Her father had scooped her mom up and off to bed, their need to be alone so transparent she'd slipped away without speaking to him. He was due his reunion, but it pissed her off that her dad had still found time to speak with Carson.

Hello? Last time she'd checked, twenty-three was a legal adult age.

"Your dad was rightfully concerned and surprisingly understanding. I didn't get my ass kicked, so I guess it's all good."

"Sounds too easy, but I'm not going to complain." Nikki rubbed her bare arms in the running tank, her thin cotton sleep pants not providing much of a barrier against the chilly breeze. And also not the sexiest lingerie, complete with flip-flops instead of the fantasy heels.

"I'd planned to wait until tomorrow's sailing trip to talk to you, but I had to see you." His hand pressed to the white wood slats behind her, his body shielding out the world. "I've been dying to touch you all day."

She totally agreed, arching into his kiss, into this moment she so needed and deserved after a stressful week of waiting, wondering as she resumed her life. He cupped the small of her back, tunneled under her T-shirt, his hand branding all the hotter in forty-degree air. Her tingling toes curled, toasty warm even in flip-flops. The searching sweep of his tongue ignited sparks along her nerves until she itched to shed her clothes, tug off his…

Not a wise idea outside, especially at her parents' house with late-night traffic whispering in the distance, closer, the sound growing until a truck rumbled down her street, a vehicle apparently in need of a new muffler.

Carson's mouth stilled on hers, broke contact, a tension bunching muscles along his shoulders. She opened her eyes and found him scowling—but not at her, his attention focused on something over her shoulder.

"Carson?" She ducked her head into his line of sight. "Are you okay?"

He tucked her aside, while keeping his gaze on the road. "I've seen that battered old pickup drive past at least three times tonight."

She looked around his broad shoulders. "Do you think it's someone assigned by Agent Reis to watch the house?"

He urged her back toward the apartment. "I don't know, but it looks damned familiar."

"You're right." She held her ground, squinting in the darkness, and realizing— No. She didn't want that to be true, but couldn't ignore the obvious. "That's my student. The one you called a thug. Billy Wade Watkins."

Without a word, Carson lifted her by the waist, deposited her in the apartment and thundered down half the wooden steps before vaulting over the banister to the lawn. He sprinted across the grass and over a hedge, toward the street. Good God, he was going to get run over. Her brain went off stun long enough to race after him, double-timing the stairs to the yard, her feet in flip-flops slipping along the damp grass, slowing her dash.

Carson reached the truck as it finished a three-point turn. He yanked the door open and hauled the driver out by the sweatshirt. Most definitely Billy Wade Watkins.

Even under the mellow nimbus of the streetlight she recognized her student well, baggy clothes, body piercings and black do-rag tied around his head. Her heart broke a little more to think she could have misjudged him.

Wait, she reminded herself. Hear his story. And get over there fast before the vein throbbing in Carson's neck exploded.

Her feet quickly turning Popsicle cold, she danced across the yard. "Carson," she called out. "Everybody calm down." She sidestepped the walkway hedge. "Billy Wade, what are you doing over here this time of night?"

Carson's grip on the boy's hooded sweatshirt stayed tight. "And don't even try to say you were just driving around or some other BS answer. I've seen you case this house three times in the last couple of hours."

"Billy Wade? Did you really do that?"

His eyes actually filled with tears below his pierced eyebrow. "I was only looking out for you, Miss Price. I swear. You've been having so much trouble. You've been really good to me. I wouldn't do anything to hurt you."

She studied his expression, beyond the tears that could well be of the crocodile variety. He was left-handed, but strong enough to have swung with either. Yet he seemed to be telling the truth. Still she couldn't miss the additional glint of something more.

A crush.

Her heart hurt for the kid, but she couldn't ignore what logic told her, as well. This child was as big as an adult, and while she knew she hadn't done a thing to encourage him... And ah damn, what a time to be standing outside in her pj's, albeit more modest than most sleepwear.

"I think, uh, I'm afraid my dad might have been trying to hurt you." He swallowed hard, blinking back the glint in his big thug eyes. "Because maybe he's the one who killed that pilot and my old man's afraid you'll remember."

Nikki crossed her arms, rubbing away the increasing chill. "Your dad?"

"Yeah, he was that guy Owens's sponsor and they talked on the phone that day, and then Dad was out really late."

Carson's hand fell away. "You're William Watkins's son."

"Yes, sir. How do you know my dad?"

Carson hesitated, then answered, "Our paths have crossed at the base."

Carson didn't expand on the statement and just as she'd read the undertones in Billy Wade's eyes, she couldn't miss that Carson was hiding something now. Something she didn't have time to analyze as the porch lamp snapped on.

A door creaked behind her, broadcasting her awake household a second before her father burst onto the porch in sweatpants, tugging a T-shirt over his head. Her mother followed, slower, cinching her satin robe at her swelling waist.

Great. She'd wrecked her parents' reunion.

J.T.'s eyes radar-locked on Carson, then Nikki in her low-slung sleep pants and tight running tank, then right back to Carson again with a furrowed disapproval.

Geez, she was an adult woman. Her father really couldn't expect she would enter the convent. And darn, she had more important things to worry about now.

She was too old to be living at home, even temporarily. Yet as much as she wanted to politely tell her father to tone it down a notch, she couldn't ruin his homecoming. Besides, the cop sirens sounding from around the corner made a big enough to-do for one evening. Please God, this would clear away the chaos once and for all. And after the chaos?

Even with the end possibly in sight, she wondered if she would ever have the normal life she craved back again.

Chapter 13

A day out on the ocean felt too normal with Nikki along.

Although Carson figured they were both due some peace after the chaos of the night before. His eyes on the distant cove where he planned to anchor soon, he gripped the wheel, sunburst nylon sail stretching tauter, the hull slicing faster through Charleston Harbor on a cloud-free winter afternoon. Nikki stood in front of him, equally as tense in the bracket of his arms.

At least they were finally away from the prying eyes of her father—who'd stayed out in the dark yard working on bogus-ass tasks until Carson gave up getting Nikki alone again. Apparently daytime outings with Nikki were cool by the old guy.

Sailing had been his solitary escape, alone on the boat even when there were boats bobbing or skimming in the distance. While he'd thrown a couple of fishing parties in the past, he'd never used his boat for dates, something private that would invade his sanctuary.

Now whenever he stepped on board, he would always think of Nikki with her face tipped to the sun or her swishing ponytail pulled through the ball cap. Chocolate hair swayed in time with the boat's rhythmic cuts through the waves. Wind plastered her clothes to her lithe body he now knew intimately well.

And with that knowledge came a possessiveness he couldn't deny. He wouldn't be Neanderthal enough to voice it, but he couldn't ignore the primal pump of rage that still charged through him every time he thought about that teenage kid stalking Nikki. A kid who happened to be the son of Will Watkins, Gary Owens's sponsor.

The fact was now public knowledge, thanks to Billy Wade's outpouring to the cops. The kid swore his old man owed Owens gambling money. They must have fought that night and Nikki saw the accidental death that resulted. The boy had confessed to the hang-up calls, using pay phones to keep from being traced. He swore he'd been trying to get the nerve to tell Nikki his fears about his father, thus the hang-ups. He adamantly denied having anything to do with slashed tires and a loose railing. And the Rohypnol? That must have been from Owens.

Carson's fingers gripped the wheel tighter. This was all getting too weird for his peace of mind, but he'd had no reason to guess the kid at Nikki's school was the son of someone in A.A.

Reis was looking into Will Watkins's alibi that night. The military retiree had started out the evening with Vic and Carson, going to a meeting, but that had wrapped up by ten. What about after?

Will had some hefty demons on his back, battling drinking and a gambling addiction. Or had it really been the son, a jealous kid lusting after his teacher and trying to throw off the investigators in desperation?

At least Reis had solid leads to follow and Carson figured he would keep Nikki occupied and in his sights at all times. He just hoped what he had to tell her today wouldn't send her overboard.

Talking about his alcoholism never ranked high on his list of favorite pastimes, but he was getting better at vocalizing the feelings and experiences. Discussing it helped others just starting on the road to recovery. However telling Nikki and seeing the disillusionment in her eyes would be tough.

Autopilot activated, Carson stepped away from the wheel, untying lines to slow the boat and ready to anchor. Would she notice he'd brought them to the cove by the small battlefield landmark where they'd made love for the first time? The trees looked like any other, and the two lopsided cannons could have been from a dozen other sites. But he knew otherwise.

Damn. He was turning into a romantic sap. He welcomed the exertion to work off excess tension and the protective need to keep Nikki close. Safe.

Nikki caught his gaze with hers. "I'm okay," she said as if reading his thoughts. "Nothing happened to me last night."

He was in over his head with this woman.

Carson sidestepped away from her to drop anchor. "When I think of what *could* have happened to you, all those times you were alone with that kid…"

Restless, edgy, he tossed the anchor into the harbor with extra force.

"I was never alone with Billy Wade for just that reason." Nikki stowed lines, already having picked up on his routine with a perception and ease that further closed his throat.

Her words did little to erase hellish scenarios of other horrific possibilities. He was definitely in over his head.

Carson closed the gap between them and pulled her to his chest, not as gentle as he should have been but his emotions were far from temperate. "I just want to keep you safe."

"There's nowhere totally safe. Ever. For now could you stop thinking?" She stepped from his arms, holding his hand and backing toward the hatch that led to the cabin below. "Just feel."

He followed her step for step along the slick deck, grateful for the reprieve from discussion she unwittingly offered. He was only too glad to put off the inevitable. "There's nothing I want more than to feel every inch of you."

"Then by all means—" her hand releasing his, she shrugged out of her windbreaker and hooked her fingers on the hem of her pullover and tugged upward, right there out in the open air and cold "—indulge yourself to your heart's content."

Heart?

He suspected the word wasn't too far off the mark when it came to this woman. Her windbreaker and sweater fell around her feet, leaving her in her jeans and mint-green silky T-shirt.

His hands shook as he hauled her back into his arms, only a few feet away from the solitude belowdeck calling to him.

With an empty bed.

Tangled sheets.

And Nikki.

They would get naked very shortly, no question about it, but first he had to taste her, fully, without interruptions from stalker teens or inquisitive investigators. Wind gathered speed over the stretch of ocean, encircling their locked bodies until Nikki shivered in his arms. From cold or desire? Either way, reason to take this party downstairs.

Slanting his mouth over hers, deeper, hotter, he hadn't been this nervous about having sex with a woman since *he'd* been the virgin. Maybe that was the whole point. This wasn't just about having sex. He was making love to her, and as tenuous as their relationship was, this could well be the only chance he would have to pour everything into loving her.

"Thank you," she whispered against his lips.

"For what?"

"For bringing me here, to this place where we found each other for the first time. For knowing the gesture would be sweet and special."

And suddenly coming here didn't seem so sappy after all if it made her happy. Three steps down into the galley, then they stumbled backward toward the sleeping quarters. The bed stretched from side to side, no room to walk around, the mattress the only real place to sit—or lie—together out of the biting wind. *Yes.*

As if she'd heard his thoughts, she moaned her agreement into his mouth. Minimal light filtered through the rectangular portals, slanting illumination over the brown linens in their cavelike haven.

Her frantic hands tore at his jacket, then yanked his long-sleeved polo shirt past his head, sending it sailing to the floor at the same time he finally managed to peel up her neon T-shirt and, heaven help him, her matching green bra.

Damn, he loved her bright colors and the way they echoed the brightness inside her.

The boat rocked under his feet with the gentle slap of each wave against the hull, but the soft swell of Nikki's breasts above the lacy cups rocked him even more. A chilly gust of salty air blasted through the hatch, beading tempting breasts against satin, luring him to touch more of her. All of her.

His mouth exploring her neck, he reached behind to close the door. Darker. Warmer.

Alone.

Lowering her, he extended an arm to brace on the edge of the mattress until they stretched side by side along the brown comforter. Shoes thudded—*one, two, three, four*—onto the waterproof flooring. "Do you want—?"

"Yes. Totally. Want you to stop talking."

"Roger." He could think of better ways to occupy his mouth, especially since she seemed so intent on getting them both in the buff ASAP. He clicked on the miniature lamp mounted to the wall, intent on recording every inch of her to memory.

On her back, she scrunched down her jeans with an enticing wriggle and kicked them free, revealing matching mint panties and oh-so-long legs. His pulse spiked, couldn't possibly jump higher.

And then she proved him wrong.

Nikki skimmed her foot up over his ankle, rucking up his

jeans to burrow her toes higher, rubbing back and forth, skin to skin contact all the more intense as the stakes rose for them.

He released the front clasp on her bra, desire pounding harder, pulling tauter. He grazed hot kisses down her neck, lower, so slow, tormenting until she splayed her fingers through his hair and guided him to…

Yes.

He blew warm air over the heart of her a second before he tasted her essence—hot and moist. And apparently just what she wanted if her gasps and sweet whimpers were anything to gauge by, her legs widening to give him more. All. Her release came hard and fast, her clawing grip on his shoulders sending a bolt of pleasure throbbing through him. He held her thighs and soothed her through the aftershocks.

Confined in the cramped hull, she grappled with his jeans, unbuttoning the fly one strained pop at a time. Her hand slid inside and…

Uh, what was he thinking about?

His mind blanked, thoughts washed away along with all his blood flooding south. Jeans flew off as fast as what remained of his restraint. Fishing a condom from his wallet, he sheathed himself and rolled on top of her soft scented body, lowering himself, seating deep inside her.

Her legs locked around his waist, urging him to move, move again, endlessly with an urgency echoed inside him. The boat undulated with waves that left her clinging tight to him for anchor. The surprise surges heightened the pleasure, deeper, harder, then shallow and faster.

Until her toned legs demanded he give all. He gritted his

teeth through the blinding drive to finish. But not before her…not before…

Her scream sliced through his restraint like the hull of a boat parting a wave, the wake crashing into a churning tumult that lasted and lasted, finally fading. Shuddering in the aftermath, he sagged on top of her, her sighs heating over his neck. Her hands glided along his sweaty shoulders in featherlight touches that slowed along with her breaths at the onset of her nap.

Shifting to his side, he pulled her closer, holding her while she slept. No more delaying. He would have to tell her about his alcoholism, something that could, and very likely should, send her running.

Why hadn't he done this back when the prospect of losing her didn't rock him even more than facing combat?

Resting on her side, Nikki watched Carson's perfectly sculpted face as he slept, not a peaceful nap, but restless, mixed with the occasional twitch as if he might wake at any second. The tiny digital clock blared three in the afternoon, plenty of time to let him relax a while longer. She stretched her arm from under the fluffy weight of the comforter and clicked off the tiny light, casting the cavelike cabin and Carson's features in shadows.

She'd sensed a tension in him while they made love, connecting in some way that scared her to her toenails. She hadn't known the emotions would come so fast, so thick, swamping her in more—deeper—feelings for Carson than she'd ever dreamed. She wasn't so naive that she couldn't recognize the explosiveness of how he made her feel in bed.

Four orgasms in one afternoon was nothing to sneeze at, although he seemed to tease them from her as easily as an achoo.

She'd thought their first time making love had been special, even their abruptly ended encounter months ago. Now she knew none of it had come close to what had been waiting for them.

Because they knew each other better? Or cared more? Could things grow stronger?

The caring part scared her. Really scared her. Because she didn't trust him not to break her heart again if they got closer. Her cold toes warming between his legs, she allowed her hands the unobserved pleasure of touching him, stroking along his muscled arms that had held her close, down his chest and lower still to his six-pack, tanned even in winter.

She couldn't avoid hearing whatever he'd wanted to say much longer. She'd chased off admissions with sex earlier. But whatever he was holding back, his reasons for leaving her that had nothing to do with work, would all come out soon.

Along with his connection in knowing Billy Wade's father, a man with a gambling problem.

Nikki flipped to her other side, away for distance, her toes already chilling just seconds after leaving the warmth of Carson's legs. Déjà-vu jiggled the vision in front of her as she fell asleep, taking her back to that strange night.

Strange room.

Strange bed…

How had she gotten here in this strange hotel-like place? And who was talking, their masculine voices so low she could barely distinguish the two from each other as she sprawled on the bedspread?

She couldn't remember anything after she'd climbed into Gary's car, sleepy. So sleepy. Her head pounded. Her stomach roiled. A couple of drinks shouldn't have done this to her. What was wrong with her?

Voices. In the hall or in the room? She struggled to focus, but her heart in her ears pounded louder than the whispers. She peeled her eyes open. Gary and another man stood at the foot of the bed. So close, she should be able to hear them but the world kept kaleidoscoping in and out.

She studied the back of the second man. He seemed familiar, even in jeans and a leather jacket, his hair trimmed military short.

His blond hair.

Panic clenched a vise grip around her throat.

The man in jeans and an aviator jacket turned in slow motion. No! built in her chest, crawling up her throat to stop him and what she didn't want to see but already foresaw. The denial lodged in her throat and he kept pivoting until she saw...

Carson.

Carson cranked the anchor up, prepping the boat to set sail back to Charleston. Before they reached shore, Nikki would know every dark secret from his past. Although he almost wished now he'd broached the subject with her earlier, when she'd been in a more receptive mood.

Nikki had gone silent since he woke from his catnap, refusing to meet his eyes and he didn't have a clue why. Now she sat back by the wheel, studying the other boaters in the distance, hugging her knees as she stared out over the stretch of murky water. No ponytail or ball cap, just wild windswept hair and the elegant curve of her neck he'd explored with kisses a couple of hours ago.

Before she'd shifted to deep freeze mode.

Women were tough enough to understand on a regular day and never had understanding a woman been more important. Stepping over lines and a loose life preserver, he made his way toward her. She flinched. Flinched?

Once under full sail power, autopilot set, he asked the question burning his brain. "Is something wrong?"

She dropped her forehead to rest on her knees. "I'm just confused, that's all." She turned her face to stare back at him, tears in her eyes. "I want to trust you, but it's difficult when I can't help but think you're not being straight with me."

Had her father already spoken to her? Regardless, the time had come to tell her what he'd only discussed with J.T.—and a room full of people sworn to uphold the anonymity of the program. "I'm an alcoholic."

"What?" Her head jerked up, confusion chasing away tears. "Wait. I heard you, I just don't understand. You hardly ever drink. Even with your flaming Dr Pepper call sign, I can only think of one time I've seen you with alcohol."

One time, the night they'd been together.

But if she hadn't been questioning his drinking with her initial comment, what had she thought he was keeping from her? They would get back to that shortly.

"Yes, I was drunk the night we slept together." Guilt hammered all over again, as strong and fresh as the morning he'd dragged his hungover butt to A.A. "I'd been working on staying sober for two years until then."

A wry smile kicked through the furrows of confusion. "Great. I was a drunken mistake."

He was making this worse, and that was quite an accomplishment since the situation had pretty much sucked from the start. "You could never be a mistake. You are the most amazing, tempting woman I've ever met. The only mistake was my selfishness that night, because I knew I would hurt you eventually."

Her chin jutted with a quiet stubbornness he'd seen often in her father. "You hurt me by walking away."

And in that stubbornness he could see that, regardless of her words to the contrary, she hadn't forgiven him, not really. So why was she sleeping with him?

He'd assumed being her first meant he was somehow special to her. Now he wasn't sure of anything and he didn't like that feeling one damn bit. "I joined A.A. after our night together. I'd had blackouts before, but not one that led me to hurt someone. It was a wake-up call."

She blinked fast, straightening. "You had a blackout that night?"

"We discussed this before—the reason I didn't remember we never had sex that night."

"A blackout? You didn't remember anything?"

Hadn't he already said that? "Not much, no."

He wasn't sure if that helped her come to grips with this or not, but it certainly sent her eyebrows trenching deeper until she softened and leaned ever so slightly toward him. Her deep freeze seemed to have ended. He could all but see the wheels churning in her brain as she sifted through his words. A promising sign and incentive to keep spilling his guts even if the talk grated all the way up his throat.

Carson rested an elbow on the silver railing, the waves below offering none of their usual comfort or answers. He shifted his attention to the speedboat in the distance. "I've always known I wouldn't get married. That's the reason I dated women with zero interest in commitment, until you came along and I started questioning what I knew, damn it, what I still believe, but am having trouble holding strong all over again."

"Why are you so sure you shouldn't get married?"

"My parents were drug addicts. Two of my grandparents had substance abuse problems, as well as an aunt and a couple of uncles. I've stopped counting the cousins with chemical dependency issues." He ticked off the dreary stat count on his fingers. "It's in my genes and I've seen what it can do to a family."

"Did any of them acknowledge the problem or get help?"

"My dad tried, along with one of my uncles, a couple of my cousins. But even with all the successes in A.A., I've seen failures, too. Hell, I was a selfish failure with you seven months ago."

She shifted to face him, her hands falling to rest on his thighs and searing through his jeans. "So you're doing this totally selfless thing in pushing me away, which proves you're actually a really good man. You've put us in a no-win situation, pal."

He gripped her fingers. "Jesus, Nikki, you just don't know how bad it was."

"Or maybe I know how good it *can* be."

Her optimism could be contagious, dangerously so. "I'm glad that you've had a life that leads you to trust that easily."

"So you're walking out again?"

"We're on a boat. I'm not walking anywhere." They were definitely stuck here until they hashed this out one way or another.

Her jaw shot out again. "That's not what I meant and you know it."

"Being with you scares the crap out of me, no question about it. That night I saw you at Beachcombers, it rocked me. Hard."

The mast creaked and groaned as an ominous silence stretched between them. "And you've been dry since last May? No more blackouts?"

He'd already answered that once. What was she driving at? Even as he understood he hadn't done squat to deserve her trust, he couldn't escape the sense of impending doom, thickening the late-afternoon air. "I'll admit, seeing you at Beachcombers that night was tough for me."

The boat pitched to the side, mast cracking, leaning.

Falling.

Seconds away from crashing into Nikki.

Chapter 14

Screaming, Nikki grappled for the boat rail. Anything stable in her abruptly tilting world as the mast leaned, held only by a couple of pathetically frayed metal lines.

"Carson!" she shouted, extending her arm toward him as she slid backward, toward the ocean.

"Jump!" he barked back. "Get clear of the lines before the boat pitches—"

A crack split the air as the mast careened out of control. The boat lurched to the side, catapulting Nikki airborne with only a few frozen seconds to gather her thoughts before…

Water gushed up her nose. Frigid and dark as she sank, not at all like the clear depths of a pool.

Up or down? Nikki couldn't determine which way since the bubbles swirled all around. All she'd learned in swimming classes said follow the bubbles but the underwater world churned and her senses shrieked conflicting messages.

She kicked. Against seaweed? No. Stronger. Slicing. Lines from the boat.

Ohmigod. Panic urged her to gasp, but she kept her lips pinched shut. She struggled to slide the metal lines—shrouds, Carson had called them—off her ankle and wrist. *Shrouds?* How horribly ominous that sounded.

And what an interesting word to tell her little student later. What an off-the-wall thought that stung her eyes with tears over the possibility she might not get to share in expanding his vocabulary any longer.

The watery world closed around her, wrapping like a blanket. Or a sail. The fabric sealed to her skin.

Her lungs burned, her skin numbing. Her brain even more so.

Panic gave way to terror that this might really be beyond her control. She could die.

How could she have been caught so unaware that she didn't notice the mast crashing toward her until too late? She'd been obsessed with the dream of Carson in the VOQ room the night Gary died.

Carson. Terror squeezed tighter. Where was he? If he'd been knocked unconscious, he could be drowning even now.

No. Hell no. She wouldn't let it happen.

She didn't care what he may have done the night Gary died. If Carson had been there, she was certain he didn't remember…none of which mattered if she couldn't find him now. She kicked against the restraints seeking to suck her deeper, ignoring the bite of metal through her skin.

The bubbles sparkled, brighter, her head lighter, her arms

and legs sluggish even as she continued to fight. Not much time left. Now that she was seconds away from checking out, too, she realized that the image of Carson had come in a dream, not in a memory flash like the recollections she'd recorded in her journal. Her confused and terrified mind could well have been playing tricks on her.

Something bumped against her. The boat? A shark? She shivered even though she'd long gone beyond numb.

Light pierced her cocoon. Death? No. The sail parted, sliced open, Carson's form looming as he split the water with sluicing sweeps of his arms, a knife in his hand.

He was alive. Relief threatened to steal precious seconds. She had to help or he would die trying to save her.

Kicking, he plunged down, unwinding the line encircling her ankle while she loosened the snaking vise around her arm. *Freedom.*

He clamped her to his side, surging up. She blinked back unconsciousness, but couldn't escape the stab of guilt over even thinking he could have lied about the night Gary died. Carson may have kept the alcoholism a secret, but this man would never have let her hang for his crimes. That much, she knew with a certainty as strong as the muscled arm banded around her.

The world righted as her equilibrium returned, up, up, blasting through the surface by the wounded boat. The massive keel along the bottom had righted the craft, even if the mast stretched a good thirty feet or more along the water, lines and sails such a tangled mess she wondered how he'd found her, much less freed her.

His feet trod water, brushing her with vital reassurance. Still he held her. "Are you all right? The mast didn't hit you?"

"I'm fine." She gasped, lungs aching, her feet pumping now as well since she didn't have to worry about dragging him down. "Thank you. Ohmigod thank you. And are you okay?"

"Fine." He didn't look fine. In fact he looked really pissed, his eyes stormy below a purpling bruise on his head.

Well, she was petrified to her toes. Only an idiot wouldn't be. They were in near-freezing waters, and while there were boats in the distance, they needed to book-it over before somebody lost a foot—or worse—to exposure.

"Somebody's head's gonna roll for this." Anger simmering, Carson paced in a back office at Beachcombers, while Special Agent Reis jotted notes. "I'm thinking it's going to start with you soon, Reis, if you don't figure out who the hell's trying to kill Nikki before she remembers what happened."

The horror threatened to crash over him again as heavy as that boom. The mast giving way, tipping the boat, launching both of them into the water. Then watching Nikki sink in a tangle of shrouds and sail.

His boots pounded hardwood floors in the antebellum building, intense, louder.

"Major, I understand you're frustrated." The agent sat on the corner of a desk, working a piece of gum while he typed notes in his PDA. "A freezing dip in the ocean will ruin a good mood."

"No." He stopped short, the window behind Reis providing too clear a nighttime view of the dock where someone intent on harming them had lurked in the past couple of days. "A deliberately broken mast will do that to a person."

"We can't know that for certain until your boat has been recovered and examined."

Carson wrenched his attention off the dock, back to the present and getting answers this man had the power to provide. "And I'm telling you, I keep that craft in tip-top shape."

"You weren't at all distracted today?" The agent tucked his PDA into an inside jacket pocket. "Couldn't you have screwed up locking the mast in place?"

For a second Carson wondered if maybe...then as quickly shoved aside the doubts. "I've been sailing by myself since I was ten." Which now that he thought about it didn't sound all that safe, but he'd been an expert in ditching his parents and nanny in those days. "And on the job, my life and the lives of others depend on following checklists. I do not 'screw up' in the air or on the water. Inspect those lines. I bet you'll find someone filed through the metal just enough to weaken one or two of the shrouds. Even a couple of small cuts would be imperceptible to the eye, while posing an insidious danger. Once the sails filled and pulled the lines taut, it would continue to fray until it snapped."

"An angle to investigate. I'll look into that once your boat has been impounded. I'll also ask around about activity at the dock."

Tension downgraded to half power. The guy was doing everything he asked, keeping him posted with all the facts.

Or was he? Had they all been wrong to assume Reis was top-notch at his job?

The door swung open, Nikki stepping through in a borrowed jean jumper from the proprietor, Claire McDermott, the dress a couple of inches short on Nikki, but dry.

And tempting with that extra stretch of exposed leg.

Reis straightened from the desk, his interrogator-perceptive eyes ping-ponging between the two of them. "Ms. Price, I assume you're all right."

She pulled up alongside Carson, fidgety, but understandable given their ordeal. "I'm running out of those nine lives, but otherwise okay." Her gaze skipped around the room full of spice plants. "And, uh, I think I remembered something on the boat right before all of this happened."

What? Carson's attention snapped as taut as the lines right before they'd popped.

"It wasn't a full-out memory like the other times, more of a mishmash dream. But I'm certain of one thing." Her restlessness settled into steely resignation. "There was another person in the room with Gary and me that night. A man. A blond man."

The implication sucker punched him. No wonder she'd gone tense after their nap and then asked him about blackouts. She thought he'd gotten drunk, gone after Owens and then forgotten.

His alibi only lasted until two in the morning with the emergency on the flight line that had called him away from his meeting. So he had no way of accounting for the in-between hours—except for a freaking zoo of origami animals he'd folded through the night to distract himself from thinking about seeing Nikki at Beachcombers, knowing she was dating another guy.

Reis pulled out his Palm Pilot again. "That Watkins kid has dark hair."

Nikki winced. "Which he colors according to his mood."

"His father has gray." Reis clicked away while Carson's

mind churned through this latest revelation. "Could the man you're remembering have had silver hair instead of blond?"

"It's possible, but I don't think so. And the clothes didn't seem right for Billy Wade. Jeans and a flight jacket."

Which gave her all the more reason to doubt Carson.

Reis shoved off the corner of the desk. "That could still be the father since retirees keep their leather jackets. But are you sure it was a man? Women have short hair, too."

One of Owens's old girlfriends on a jealous rampage?

Reis's talent for thinking beyond an obvious assumption was promising—and frustrating. How the hell could they rule anyone out? A military man or woman, active duty or retired, blond or gray, who happened to be right-handed. That could be half the flying community.

Nikki closed her eyes as if trying to recapture the image on the back of her lids. "If it's a woman, then she's really tall. It's all fuzzy, but I'm almost certain it's a man." Her lashes fluttered open as she shook her head. "I'm sorry. That's all there is."

Screw keeping his distance. Carson looped an arm around her waist, so grateful to have her warm and alive against him, he didn't bother to hide his feelings for her. "I think that's enough for one day, Reis. The medics wanted to admit her, but acquiesced if she would promise to rest."

The OSI agent pocketed his PDA again. "I hear ya." Halfway to the door, he stopped. "She's still staying with her parents, right?"

"Hello?" Nikki stiffened. "*She* is right here—"

"Major," Reis continued, "how about once you take her home we meet back on base and go over some personnel files to see what we can dig up?"

With the horror of Nikki almost dying still pounding through his skull, there was nothing he wanted more than to keep her in his sight. But with her stiff in his arms and her avoiding his eyes, he couldn't help wondering if she needed space, and God knows he wanted to dig in with Reis and find something, anything, to nail the bastard who'd done this to Nikki's life.

Besides, after hearing the truth about him she might well decide to steer clear of him and he would have to love her enough to let her go.

Love?

Damn.

What a helluva time to figure that out.

Her feet would never be warm again. Nikki wasn't so sure about her heart, either.

Sitting at her parents' kitchen table, she shook the can of whipped cream and squirted a hefty swirl into the steaming cup of hot cocoa her dad had made. What a crazy—confusing—afternoon. Finally, Carson was being open and honest with her, or at least he had been until the boat nearly killed them. He'd switched into protective mode again, dropping her off at her parents' with a toe-curling but too-brief kiss, before meeting up with Reis.

In her soul, she longed to grasp this new chance with Carson, but her emotions were all so surface level and exposed. She had to get this right—for both of them. She wanted to trust what he said about having his drinking under control, but he'd tossed so many negatives about the situation her way. She needed to be responsible enough at least to think through them.

Her lumbering father dropped into the chair across from her, silently drinking from his mug. Even more quiet than usual as he studied her across the wooden expanse, a new piece of furniture she'd helped her dad varnish after he'd bought it at the bare-wood store.

For an overprotective parent, these past days couldn't have been easy for him. She passed him the can of whipped topping. "Are you okay, Dad?"

"I should be asking you that, baby girl." His gaze rested on the raw ring around her wrist where the sail lines had immobilized her underwater.

"And I'm betting that because I'm your daughter, today was tougher on your ticker than it was on mine." She cupped her hands around the warm porcelain.

"You might be right." He set his World's Best Dad mug down slowly, his hand shaking ever so slightly but oh so tellingly. "I owe Scorch for saving your life."

"Are you okay with me seeing Carson?"

He nodded, suddenly overly preoccupied with how the can of whipped cream operated. "I'm not sure it would matter to you if I wasn't."

She sifted that around in her mind while sipping, chocolate and cream flooding her senses with childhood memories of other shared cocoa and late-night chats with her dad. She loved her father, no question, but she wasn't his little girl anymore. "It wouldn't change my mind, but it would matter."

"I know about his history." He rolled the can back across the table to her, his rugged teddy-bear face so compassionate she wanted to crawl in his lap and cry as she'd done during elementary school days.

Was it so wrong to seek his advice? Was that a step backward when more than ever she needed to add years in wisdom to her adult résumé? Still she couldn't stop the words. "Am I delusional to believe I can handle a relationship with a recovering alcoholic?"

"You're too old for me to tell you what to do."

Was she? At the moment it seemed less mature to assume arrogantly that she had all the answers. "I'm learning that you're never too old to ask your father for advice."

"Which proves you really don't need me after all." He patted her hand clutching the whipped cream can in a death grip. "You're more than ready to leave the nest."

Parental approval sure did feel nice no matter what her age. She flipped her hand to link fingers with her dad. "Does that mean I'm out on the sidewalk?"

"Not hardly, baby girl." He squeezed back with a familiar comfort that stung her eyes with tears at this landmark moment.

She really was crossing into a new era of her life. Would it include Carson?

Nikki slid her hand away and took another warming gulp from her mug. "What made you and Mom stick it out so long even though things were rocky?"

"But we did quit."

"After over twenty years of working at it." She hadn't been surprised when her parents announced they'd seen a divorce attorney, but it still hurt even as an adult.

A rare smile creased her father's craggy face. "Your mother and I are particularly hardheaded. It took us a while to get it right."

"That doesn't help me much."

"I assume this isn't a rhetorical question."

"I wish. He also worries about me being too young. And I think he puts too much stock in *your* certainty that I'm not equipped for the stresses of being an Air Force wife."

"Whoa. Wait." He held up both palms. "Of course I don't want you to go through the struggles. This is a tough life after all, but I've never doubted for a minute that you can handle anything that comes your way as long as you go in with your eyes open."

"Who are you, and what have you done with my quietly looming overprotective father?"

His smile cranked broader. "Your mother and I are working on better communication. Never thought I would buy into the notion of counseling, but it helps. What your mother and I have is worth fighting for."

She'd known they sought help to put their marriage back together. They'd even invited Chris and her along for a couple of family sessions. Why not apply that to her situation with Carson?

He assumed the alcoholism was more than she could handle. He might be correct—a possibility that closed her throat—but he might well be wrong. Either way, *he* had been making a decision that affected *both* of them. She should be a part of that equation, and to do that, she needed more information.

She'd been so set on protecting her heart, she'd let him shield her, as well, and that wasn't right. No one had ever fought for Carson. Sure he'd sought out A.A., but as far as she could tell, other than a lone English teacher, no one had offered help.

Yeah, she might get her heart pitched back in her face again, but she loved this man. Deep down loved him, flaws and all. Damn straight she wouldn't be like her mother waiting around for over twenty years.

Nikki was ready to fight for her man.

Chapter 15

"Do you want me?"

Carson lost total track of whatever Reis was saying to him on the other end of the phone, stunned instead by Nikki in his open office door.

From the determined look in her eyes, Carson suspected he had a fight on his hands. He just wished he knew which direction to check for the ambush.

He held up a hand indicating a one-second-wait while he finished his call to Reis about tapping the civilian police to do extra surveillance of the Price home. "Glad you're on top of this. I'll be in touch." He hung up the phone and redirected his attention to the hot-as-hell woman in front of him. "How did you get here? Please say you didn't drive alone."

"Dad's got leave since his return. He came in for some paperwork and I rode along." She lounged against the door frame, a seductress in khaki. "So? What's the answer to my question? Do you want me?"

"Before I answer, you should probably close the door."

Nikki stepped across the threshold, one long khaki-clad leg at a time—and holy crap, those were black heels to match her black silk shirt. Could her heels be the promised pair from their conversation a few days ago in this same room?

Tossing her lightweight jacket on the mariner's hook, she clicked the door closed and locked at the same time he instructed his secretary to hold his calls. Word was out about the two of them anyway, while he was still reeling from the whole concept of being in love for the first time.

They were already in over their heads, so he needed to grit back his concerns and forge ahead unless she said otherwise, because he wouldn't hurt her a second time.

He shoved aside the stack of files calling to him and wheeled his office chair back from the desk. "How about ask me that question again?"

Nikki narrowed the distance between them with hair-swishing strides. "Do you want me?"

That was a no-brainer. He took her wrist, careful of the raw ring from the lines, and pulled her into his lap. "So damn much."

Tunneling one hand into her hair and the other under her sweater, he kissed her until they both gasped for breath. He wouldn't be in any shape to get up from his chair for a long while, thanks to the sweet wriggle of her bottom against his crotch.

"Do you want to be with me? Not just tonight, but long term?"

He'd been prepared for her to walk, and now she was talking forever, something he couldn't deny that he wanted, too. With her. For a man with an extensive vocabulary, words were suddenly in short supply. He wouldn't run, but he couldn't blame her if *she* did.

"Damn it, Carson." She thumped his shoulder, then gentled her touch to skim tenderly over the bump on his head from pitching out of the Catalina. "Do you know how hard this is for me to say? I'm making myself totally vulnerable for you. The least you can do is give me an honest answer."

"Honestly?" There wasn't anything left for them but the truth. "I'm scared as hell of passing on my genes and I'm more afraid I'll ruin your life. You're not sure, either. Admit it, you thought I was the one who killed Owens."

That notion stung more than he would have expected even as she rested her head against his shoulder with total ease.

"If we're embracing this total honesty deal, then okay, I considered the possibility that you'd done it to protect me."

He struggled not to flinch. "You thought that, drunk, I would be capable of violence."

"I saw you in my dream." She tipped her head to glance up at him. Her silky dark hair grazed over his arm. "But I realize now it was a dream and not a memory, which means I've had to sift through to figure out which parts are real and which are distorted. The other times I remembered, I was awake so I could trust the full image."

"Are you sure?" He refused to have her fearing him. He'd lived that way for years as a kid and would *not* subject anyone to that hell.

"If you tell me, I will believe you."

Searching, he found trust in her eyes but couldn't bring himself to believe in what he saw. "So you do think I'm capable?"

"I know anyone is capable." Her fingers skimmed to the back of his neck, along his closely shaved nape. "I'm not sure I could kill someone coming at me. But I'm certain I could kill someone intent on hurting you."

He understood the feeling. "I did not kill Gary Owens. I was at an Al-Anon meeting that night with two other people," Will Watkins and Vic Jansen, "until I was called away to an emergency on the flight line. Then I went home and parked my sorry butt in front of the TV all night because I was missing you so much I was afraid if I went out I would end up on your doorstep."

Carson waited for her response, suddenly realizing that while he might not have a right to her unconditional trust, he sure as hell wanted it.

Finally, she nodded, rocked forward and pressed a long, close-mouthed but no less intense kiss to his mouth before settling to rest against his chest, arms still looped around his neck. "That's what I figured, but thank you for saying it for me anyway."

"Thank *you*." His arms slid around her and he stole a deeper kiss, needing to feel her warm alive body and banish the image of her wrapped in shrouds and a sail in a watery grave.

Her face tucked in his neck, she continued to tease his ear with feathery strokes that distracted. "Isn't Al-Anon a support group for family members?"

What had she just said and what did that have to do with

her other hand scratching through his flight suit along his pec? He replayed her words and—oh, uh, Al-Anon. Talk about a cold splash. "I help out there. The support group is open to helping families of people with other addictions. I feel like I have something to offer family members, as well, since my parents were addicts."

"So you belong to Al-Anon *and* A.A.?"

"Yes." Searching for words, he captured her hands in his, kissed her knuckles and kept them from distracting him into speaking without thinking, no doubt her intention. "Until I found A.A., nothing worked. It's still been tough. I truly believe that for alcoholics the booze affects them more or differently than other people. And through that extra effect it soothes something inside them, a pain or an emptiness or need. For a while you convince yourself the alcohol makes your life better. It's your friend because you live and cope at a higher level. Then the friend turns on you."

She linked her fingers with his so tightly he could imagine she might hold on forever.

"Those first few months without, there's this emptiness inside that begs to be filled. You also lose something in your way of life—the bar, the camaraderie of a beer and game of pool."

"I would imagine that's especially tough to give up in the flyer world."

"A.A. helps teach you how to fill that space, and of course there are over two million members."

"Two million?" Her eyes widened in surprise.

"And counting." He stroked the inside of her wrists with his thumbs. "I'm able to attend functions now that include alcohol without racing to phone my sponsor afterward— What are you thinking?"

She untangled her hand from his to tap his leather name tag. "How you said call signs come from a defining moment."

"I carry a heavy issue with me that's never going away." He rested his palm over hers tracing the word "Scorch." "This will always be there, and I know too well that it doesn't just affect the adults. While I appreciate that you're trying to be understanding, you need to comprehend how big a deal this is."

"I won't claim to know anything about the genetics involved in addictions running in families. Actually, I don't know much of anything about alcoholism. So maybe you're right. Maybe this is something I'm not equipped to handle."

His gut clenched. "I didn't say this is your—"

"Shhh. Listen. I'm saying I don't have enough information to make a decision, and it seems to me this affects both of us. So I should have a say in deciding something so huge."

He searched for a rebuttal…except what she said made sense, damn good sense. "What did you have in mind?"

"Let's go to an Al-Anon meeting together, let me see for myself what I'm in for. I'll go as a friend if the idea of thinking about forever totally freaks you out."

He fell even more in love with this amazing woman, wise beyond her years and deserving of the absolute best. "We've been naked together. I think we've gone past friendship."

"Can't we be both?"

At a crossroads, they would have to be both—or nothing at all. But then he'd pretty much already figured that one out for himself.

"There's a support meeting tomorrow night."

Make or break time. He'd seen plenty of families and marriages saved by Al-Anon, but most of those people had a foundation before the troubles hit. He and Nikki were starting out with the baggage. He couldn't dodge the dark-cloud feeling that the night would only accomplish one thing.

Helping her walk away for good.

As a trio of C-17s roared overhead for a night takeoff, Nikki stepped from Carson's truck into the parking lot outside the base chapel housing tonight's support group meeting. She hadn't expected the gathering to take place on base, and a smaller group promised less anonymity. Apparently Carson was cool with that.

They weaved around cars and other stragglers making their way toward the entrance, faces shadowy in the dim glow of the overhead halogen lamps. There was so much riding on this night and her nerves were wobblier than the funky heels she'd bought with the intent purpose of making Carson swallow his tongue.

Mission accomplished in that arena, at least.

He slid an arm around her waist as if he expected her to sprint before they reached the looming double doors of the social hall. "If you want to leave at any time, just say the word and we're out of here."

"You've said that twice already. Once when you picked me up, and again at dinner."

And dinner had been so sweet, a back corner table with candlelight and hand holding. He was trying so hard.

Or saying goodbye with a last supper.

"Nikki, I mean it. You don't have to do this."

Stopping by the front sign, she spun on her new heels with an old spunk that she refused to lose now. "Do you even want this to work? Or are you hoping walking in there will discourage me? You've talked about the genetics involved in patterns repeating themselves. Well you decided to break that cycle and sober up. Do you know how freaking outstanding that is? I think it's tough and heroic."

Shaking his head, he swiped aside her hair blowing in her face. "You're seeing things in me that don't exist."

She blocked his hand. "Stop that condescending BS. I'm seeing things in you that you've never allowed yourself to see. You even tried to hide them from me, but I said *heroic* and I meant it."

Was he subconsciously trying to sabotage this before they even made it through the door? And why? She touched his elbow. "Are you going to walk with me into that meeting, or do I go by myself? Because like it or not, I'm involved with an alcoholic."

"Believe me—" his jaw went tight "—I understand that well or we wouldn't be here. I just don't want you to get your hopes up for some magic pill answer tonight."

"There you go with the fatalism again." She couldn't stop the irritation from seeping into her voice when she knew this wasn't the time or place. Backing up the steps, she held up a hand. She refused to cry. "Hold on. I don't want to fight with you before we even get started. Just…just let me freshen up."

And pull herself together.

She spun away and shoved through the front double doors, head ducked as she made tracks past people to the restroom,

Carson's stark, resolved face imprinted in her mind, his oh-so-calm, logical—depressing—tone echoing. He almost sounded like Billy Wade Watkins, always expecting the worst.

Wait.

She gripped the edge of the sink, staring at her face paler than the white porcelain in her grip. Carson sounded like the child of an alcoholic, who'd numbed himself to expecting good things because then nobody could let him down.

Ohmigod. Why hadn't she seen the pattern before?

Because she hadn't been objective—like a teacher—when it came to Carson. Instead of picking a fight with him, she needed to hold firm and simply show him through her steadfast actions. He was right in saying she'd been unrealistic to expect everything to settle out because of one meeting.

A toilet flushed, announcing an end to her solitary haven. She smiled in the mirror at the stranger stepping from the stall. Resolute and ready to find Carson, Nikki yanked open the bathroom door and into the now-packed entryway.

So much for a small gathering. Where had all of these people come from? And why did so many of them look familiar?

Billy Wade—along with his father. She hadn't realized the teen's father was getting help for his drinking, and gambling, too, apparently. Vic Jansen stood at their side in what seemed like a supportive role when she hadn't even known Vic had a problem, either. Beyond them, more military acquaintances milled around.

Had each of them been told to put on their perfect face when on base, as well?

She'd been so judgmental of her home life problems growing up, never once realizing all the other military families in pain…drinking, gambling, even some parents supporting teenagers kicking a drug habit.

How many times had she told her students she wasn't looking for perfection, just their best effort? Something Carson needed to hear, as well, for both of them, because there would be no perfect reactions to all of this.

Just a very human, fallible best effort.

She retraced her steps through the lobby looking for him so they could enter the meeting together. She shouldered through, searching. She peeked into the gathering area, rows of folding chairs and a refreshments table, but no sign of Carson.

Maybe he'd gone outside to take a cell call. She stepped through the double doors into the parking lot, her heels crunching on gravel as she pivoted to look…

She bumped against someone, a hard-bodied guy. "Carson?"

A hand clamped on her arm, steadying her as she came face-to-face with…*Kevin Avery?* His cologne stung her nose, his blond hair glinting under the street lamp. "What are you doing here?"

Her question slammed around inside her brain, words spoken now and echoed in her mind from a night nearly three weeks ago.

His grip bit into her flesh. "I've been looking for you."

The ground spun under her feet, memories ricocheting around inside her head. Memories of *him,* a man she'd once dated because he resembled Carson.

She opened her mouth to scream, but he cut the shriek short

with a hand clamped against her lips. Hard. Unrelenting. And horrifyingly familiar. She struggled, wrenching to the side, kicking out.

Releasing her arm, his hand swung down. A dull pain crashed through the base of her skull, once, twice. The edges of the parking lot fuzzed, narrowing along with consciousness. Her dream-vision of the night Gary died now made total sense as she remembered…

Kevin Avery standing over Gary Owens's dead body.

Where was Nikki?

Carson peered over the crush in the corridor for the second time, having already checked the social hall. He'd only turned away for a minute to talk to Vic, and now he couldn't find her. He'd even sent someone into the restroom to look for her. She couldn't have left after she'd been so emphatic about staying.

Damn. Damn. Damn it all, he didn't like this one bit. Where was she and how could someone have plucked her from a group this large?

He didn't like the itchy premonition scratching along the back of his neck. They were in a public place, for God's sake. He pushed through the crowd, making his way toward the double doors.

Stuffiness and noise of the packed social hall gave way to the crisp night air and silence, no sounds other than the occasional whoosh of a passing car. Unease kinking tighter, he scanned the packed lot of empty vehicles all the way to his truck parked at the end with someone inside.

He exhaled a long stream of relief into the freezing night.

Through the back window, he could see Nikki's outline. A stab of disappointment followed.

She'd already given up?

As quickly as the thought slithered into his head, he nixed it, making his way across the dormant lawn toward his Ford. He'd always been the one to walk away, not her. She'd taken a lot of grief from him in the past and still she'd given him another chance. A chance he didn't deserve in any universe.

If she was in the car, then something must have happened to upset her or she wasn't feeling well. Either way, he needed to quit thinking about himself and get over there.

She was right. He'd given up on the two of them before giving them a decent chance. He'd thanked her for trusting him, but what about returning the emotion?

He'd been let down by his parents so many times, let down by adults who should have been there for a kid, somewhere along the way he had stopped putting faith in anyone when it came to relationships. Sure he was a delegation kind of guy at work, but there were tangible gauges of levels of success.

No score guides existed when it came to this whole love gig. He'd told himself he loved her, but hadn't done a thing right in committing. In order for this to work—and hell yes, he wanted Nikki, forever—then he needed to start giving one hundred percent.

He slid into the driver's side behind the wheel, but Nikki kept her face turned to look out. Damn. He had some major backpedaling to do.

"Nikki, listen, I'm sorry about earlier." He stroked up her arm to cup her neck. Was she asleep?

She sagged limply against the seat belt. Strangely slack, not even startling at his touch.

The premonition blasted into full scale alert a second before a looming form rose from the backseat of his extended cab. Carson jerked, ready to launch, attack.

A gun pressed to his forehead stopped him cold. Avery at the other end stopped him colder.

"Major, I'm really sorry it's come to this, but Nikki's enjoying a little nap from a tap on the head." The traitorous lieutenant shifted the gun ever so slightly until it pointed at unconscious Nikki. "Drive, or I'll be having a piece of her while you watch."

Chapter 16

No strange room or temporary amnesia this time. Even through the pounding in her head, Nikki recognized Carson's scent and the sound of his well-tuned truck.

And another cologne. Cloying. Hideously familiar.

The rest mushroomed back to life in her brain. Kevin. In the parking lot. Her mind blazed with thoughts of the night Gary died…then everything went dark.

Did Carson know? Had Kevin somehow stolen the truck?

She started to open her eyes—then rethought. For the moment she would stay limp against the shoulder harness anchoring her to the heated seats until she figured out what was going on.

"Avery—" Carson's voice rumbled from beside her on the driver's side "—you really don't want to do this."

Just the sound of him filled her with love—and dread that

he should be here at all. She'd prayed he was safe back at the church, searching for her, alerting the cops.

Anywhere but here.

"Nikki didn't leave me any choice," Kevin answered from behind her. "She kept digging for the memories."

"You killed Owens?" The shock in Carson's voice echoed within her. Kevin and Gary were friends. Kevin seemed so clean-cut and honorable. Except hadn't she just realized— how long since she'd been at the support meeting?—that military people had flaws and bad apples like anywhere else. Like the police force or other professions that as a whole pledged to protect.

But ohmigod, this went beyond a simple problem.

"Well, Major, I bet on a few games every once and a while to pay off my college loans. A top-notch education is important for getting ahead. You should understand that since your family could afford the best."

Kevin's hot breath blasted against her hair as he moved closer to her. Did he have a gun? He must, or Carson would have taken him out.

The truck shifted into a turn. "A Chief of Staff doesn't have a gambling addiction and bash in people's skulls."

Leather behind her creaked. "A Chief of Staff definitely doesn't have the taint of a gambling addiction on his record—" Kevin's words tumbled faster, angry "—and Owens was going to out me, just because he didn't like my little sideline of taking bets to pay my college loans faster."

"You were a bookie?"

It was all Nikki could do not to blurt her surprise, as well. Good God, how did he expect to keep that a secret? The guy really was an idiot—or so deep in his addiction he'd lost all sense of reason.

"Owens was going to rat me out, something about loyalty to the program. Jesus, all I did was help a few of his buddies in the program make a little extra at the racetrack."

Avery had targeted Gambler's Anonymous members? The guy truly was lower than slime. For money or his addiction or ambition, he'd sold his soul and bartered a few more along with it.

"I couldn't let that happen." His tenor tones pitched higher, faster. High-strung and nervous could be an advantage if they caught him unaware, or a liability if he got twitchy. "I had everything planned perfectly for Nikki to take the fall for an accidental death, self-defense during a rape attempt. Even drugged up, she fought a little when I took her clothes off after Owens was dead. But that just helped set the scene even better."

It took everything inside her to stifle down a shudder of revulsion at Kevin's hands on her while she was helpless. Her cheek even ached with the phantom memory of being slapped. Carson's low growl, however, vibrated the seat.

Kevin's forearm slid around her neck, against her throat. "The Rohypnol I put in her drink should have made her forget everything, but almost right away word spreads around the squadron that she was getting some of her memory back. She must not have drunk enough of the Rohypnol or she has some funky body chemistry. Regardless, I couldn't risk her remembering. I'd hoped the fall from her balcony would look like suicide from the stress."

"You tried to kill her?"

Nikki stifled her gasp of relief that Gary hadn't been untrustworthy after all, a fact she would savor later, but for now she needed to listen. And while she couldn't think of any logical reason for Kevin to spill all—beyond egotistical gloating before he killed them—she appreciated the bit of peace his words brought.

"I had the whole thing planned. I even sent her the fake e-mail from Gary to meet at Beachcombers. I sent one to Gary, too, with a half hour later arrival so I would have time to take care of her drink without him hovering over her like a lovesick nimrod. Thanks to that supersexy note, he really thought she wanted to get a VOQ room for a night together, and of course she was too drugged up to tell him otherwise. I'm so damn smart I even sent the e-mails from a base computer and the school library where Nikki tutors so they wouldn't be traceable back to me."

No wonder Reis had been checking out the high school.

Each of Carson's overly deliberate, controlled exhales filled the cab. "If you wanted her dead, why slash her tires?"

"That wasn't me. The way I hear it from Will, that kid of his really did have a crush on her. He would do anything to get her attention."

"Dude, you can't just shoot us."

Could Carson know she was awake and be filtering info? How could he know when she didn't dare give the least hint for fear Kevin would see?

Her heart squeezed at the notion that Carson was as in tune to her as she was to him. She'd longed for that connection and refused to lose it. They weren't dead yet, and damn it, she *did* intend to fight for her man. Whatever it took.

"Like I said, you haven't left me any choice but to kill you. But I'm more creative than that…. Pull over."

She peeked to orient herself and recognized the spot well—the small battlefield where they'd parked, talked. Made love. Water shooshed along the shore with none of its usual soothing tune. Why had Kevin chosen this location?

"Yeah, I followed you two here, and once I could tell you were nice and settled into the back of the truck for a romantic evening under stars, I headed over to your boat. Easy enough to file away at a couple of lines. Too bad you lived. But this time, my plan is foolproof. Brilliant in fact. Worthy of a guy on the fast track."

A rustle sounded from the back, like a paper bag.

"Just a little of this on the seat and even more in your system will explain why you drove the truck off the bridge while coming out to your favorite spot for a little romance."

A little of what?

The splash on her clothes hit an instant before the pungent fumes.

The unmistakable smell of alcohol.

The smell of alcohol saturated the air.

Soaked his senses.

Carson wiped his mind clear of everything but Avery's face and watched for the right time to move. He couldn't let himself think of Nikki slumped and faking unconscious next to him. He definitely couldn't think of the lush harbor side park beyond his windshield. The secluded locale was too full of distracting memories of being with Nikki and how much they had to lose at the hands of this unbalanced megalomaniac.

Megalomaniac. Another five-dollar word to share with Nikki's student, and by God, Carson intended to live long enough to do just that.

His 9mm shifting to kiss Nikki's temple again, Avery passed the bottle of tequila toward Carson, glass glinting in the hazy glow from the dash. "Take it. I even left the worm in the bottle for ya, Major."

Carson closed his fingers around the glass neck, all the while envisioning it was Avery's scrawny throat. Not at all tempted to do anything more than snap it in two and let the amber poison pour away. But he couldn't do that, not yet when he needed to play along for a while more. "Your plan doesn't sound foolproof to me. In fact I can already see a dozen holes."

Talk, you bastard. That would offer up more time to think.

Avery reached behind him again—Carson tensed—and came back with a big buckle belt, which he dropped on the seat. "Owens's. I'm so damn smart I saved this as a contingency in case I needed to set up someone else for the murder." The leather belt thudded to rest beside Nikki. "You never did have faith in my intelligence or ability to lead."

Good God, the kid was a second lieutenant, not the boss. "Then how about you explain your genius to a slower dude like me."

"It's quite simple actually. I'll knock you both out, drive the truck off the bridge and swim away while you drown. The bumps on your head will be attributed to the accident, another tragic DUI."

Well hell, the plan actually sounded as if it could work. His fist clenched tighter around the bottle as he fought off the possibility of losing this battle, ironically fought on a small, nearly forgotten historic field. The whispers of past wars rode the tide's ebb and flow. "Lieutenant—"

"Don't try ordering me around. Not now." Avery grasped a fistful of Nikki's hair and yanked.

She yelped.

Awake.

Damn, he'd thought she might be, but prayed she could simply sleep through this hell.

She blinked, not in the least groggy, apparently having listened to the whole exchange. "Carson, don't do it."

Avery tugged her hair tighter until the skin around her eyes pulled taut. "It's just a drink to save Nikki some pain and ease your own."

"He's going to kill us no matter what." Nikki's unwavering voice held a calm he wouldn't have expected from even a seasoned vet. "You don't have to do this for me."

He understood well what was going on here. There was no reasoning with this monster, only fighting to the death. Being captive had been bad enough with his crew, but seeing Nikki die and being unable to save her was beyond anything he could bear.

And even in the middle of the lowest point in his life, the heavy bottle in his hand didn't tempt him in the least. His mind was clear and focused on what mattered most. *Nikki.*

"I can make it painless for her. I really don't want to do this, but I can't sacrifice my whole future." Avery stared him in the eye without once shifting his weapon from Nikki, but Carson was ready to spring the second the man flinched. "Here's the deal. I'll knock you both out so she can drown while she's asleep. Simple. You just have to go along with my plan. But I can also beat the crap out of her and everyone will assume the injuries came from the wreck. What does it matter if you drink now? You're going to die. You might as well check out with one last taste on your tongue. You don't have to fight it anymore."

"Carson." Nikki's quivering voice drew his attention to her. "It's over."

The defeat in her tone pierced clean through him. He looked in her eyes, the neck of the bottle clenched in his hand with such easy familiarity. He expected to see anguish in her expression, even resignation.

Instead, he saw spunk, anger. Determination.

She hadn't given up at all. She was saying out loud what Avery expected to hear. Her eyes, however, were relaying something else entirely.

Carson glanced outside the windshield, no miraculous weapons to be found on the old battlefield, just the rickety bridge and water. He turned back to Nikki and realized they had everything they needed right here. Trust that flowed both ways.

He wasn't sure how, but she would get out of the line of fire long enough for him to take out Avery. If they died at least Avery couldn't hide a gunshot. There would be justice.

And they might well live. In fact, with Nikki by his side, the odds were damn good.

Eyes on hers, the connection between them hummed so tangibly strong he didn't need words. He raised the bottle, slow, as if torn, his hand shaking which kept Avery's rapt attention off Nikki for a few seconds.

Valuable seconds.

Avery's rabid gaze stayed locked, as if he got off on the control. The Lieutenant's ambition and need for power was all too clear.

Carson didn't dare look away from the bastard in the back, but in his peripheral vision, he could see Nikki's right hand sliding down. For the first time he cursed the luxury seats because the motorized controls wouldn't allow her to slam the sucker back quickly and ram Avery.

But her seat back would lower fast if she released the latch and pushed.

Carson could read her intent as clearly as apparently she read his. The move was risky since it might force Avery's gun arm down, but it *would* catch him unaware. Carson would just have to take advantage of that surprise to adjust the aim.

Even as he raised the bottle to his mouth, the fumes stinging his nose, glass kissing him like a familiar lover—a lover who'd betrayed him—never once did the faith in Nikki's eyes fade.

Time to act.

Simultaneously, she slipped down and slammed back the seat. Avery grunted in surprise. Carson swung the bottle at the copilot's face, jacking the gun arm up in reflexive defense. Glass and tequila sprayed the cab. A bullet pierced the roof, a second through the windshield before the weapon clattered to the floorboard. Nikki ducked, grappling for the gun and clearing the way for him to grip Avery's shirtfront.

Ears still ringing from the gunshots, Carson hauled him over the bench seat, slamming the younger man's face into the dash, once, twice, until he sagged. Unconscious. Thank God.

He couldn't waste a second on relief yet, not until he had Avery restrained and in jail. Convicted to a lifetime in Leavenworth would be damn nice, too.

Carson hauled Avery's limp body from the cab, face to the ground by a rusted cannon, hands behind his back in case the prone man regained consciousness. "Nikki, look in the floorboard for boat lines. Get them, please."

The need for vengeance for Nikki—for young Gary Owens, as well—fired hotter. The dead copilot had struggled valiantly to get his life together and this selfish ass had stolen Owens's second chance. Avery's actions could have subjected Nikki to a lifetime in prison. There wasn't a punishment harsh enough for that.

Nikki clambered over the seat, tugging free a length of boat line. She pitched the rope. Looping fast with a skill honed from years on the water, he trussed their down-for-the-count attacker, hands, ankles, securing him to the small cannon. In some distant part of his brain he heard Nikki placing a cell phone call to the cops. With an extra tug to his best sailor's knots, Carson stepped away from Avery and opened his arms to Nikki....

Damn certain he wasn't letting her go this time.

The next day, Nikki twisted the key in her apartment lock, tickled to her toes to have her life, her job, her home back. Her heart, however, was forever given to Carson.

And if she hurried, she would have time to change before he arrived to pick her up for whatever mystery outing he had planned.

How he'd found time to make preparations after the insane

night they'd had with Kevin Avery's arrest, she would never know. After her 911 call, Special Agent Reis had arrived, as well. The procedural intricacies were mind-boggling as the civilian cops debated with the military security police over who would get the first bite at Avery, one of his crimes off base, one on the government installation.

The SPs won. The kidnapping had begun on base after all, and the murder was the larger crime.

Nikki pushed inside her tiny apartment, no longer minding the bare walls she couldn't afford to fill yet. Instead, they represented all the time ahead of her and experiences to collect. Unlike Kevin Avery who would be locked up for life.

What a sad end for someone with so much potential. As a teacher, she couldn't help wondering where things had gone wrong for him. By the same token, she saw so many students with fewer advantages and opportunities who worked their butts off and made their own successes happen—without excuses.

After giving statements, she and Carson had swept away the glass from the cab of the truck and driven home with the windows open to air out the scent of alcohol and those hellish moments of abject fear. She'd called her parents with the details and to explain she was returning to her apartment. *Her* place and reclaimed life.

She slung her backpack up onto the kitchen bar with a hefty overloaded thump of work to accomplish. Hopefully with Carson at her side. Last night a shower together, making love, celebrating life until they both fell into an exhausted slumber had gone a long way toward settling her ravaged nerves.

Unloading her bag from a blessedly full day of teaching—
a wonderfully normal day with her students and a job she
loved—she knew now to cherish everyday life with her new-
found appreciation. She couldn't wait to show Carson her
blueprints for a miniature Viking ship she wanted to build
with her students for an upcoming unit.

She dropped to sit on the bar stool, her plans spread in front
of her. What a long way she'd come in a few short weeks. Her
crush-style visions of Carson had put him on a pedestal in a
way that would set anyone up for failure. Now she understood
the value of simple dreams and everyday life, the love of a
good, wonderfully human man to build a future with.

Love was a journey, not a destination.

Her doorbell chimed.

It seemed her trip was about to begin before she had a
chance to change from her work clothes into jeans. She raced
across the carpet, peeking through the peephole, blithe acceptance of safety having taken a serious hit lately.

Her eyes filled with Carson still in his flight suit. A smile
split her face and spread through her. Apparently he hadn't even
taken the time to change, either, instead rushing over to see her.

She swung the door wide. "Hey there, flyboy. I missed you
today."

He swept her into his arms for a kiss that sent that smile
singing further through her veins before he pulled away to
ask, "Would you like to go for a ride?"

She'd thought they were headed to her bedroom, but apparently he was sticking to his plan. "Do I need to change?"

Carson cupped her face, unmistakable love shining in his
crystal-clear blue eyes. "You're perfect as is."

"Not hardly." She arched up onto her toes to steal another kiss, a definite perk on this journey. "But thanks."

He extended his hand and she clasped it without hesitation, snagging her purse and locking her apartment before following him to his truck, a new windshield in place along with freshly cleaned seats. The horror of Kevin's attack would be tougher to erase. Thank God they'd made it through together. Her grip on Carson tightened.

Twenty minutes of easy silence and hand holding later, they reached…a marine repair yard? She squinted in the late-afternoon sun through the chain-link fence until she saw— yes—Carson's sailboat suspended in slings. "Wow, they were able to salvage your boat. That's awesome."

"It'll take time before she's seaworthy again, but the hull is intact." He put the vehicle in park and turned to face her. "That boat holds some irreplaceable memories."

A blush burned her cheeks. "Maybe we'll make more memories when it's afloat again."

"No *maybe* about it once we get her back in the water about a month from now." He winked.

She studied the landlocked craft, winging a prayer of thanksgiving the sturdy craft hadn't capsized altogether. "Thanks for bringing me here. Seeing this helped take the edge off what happened."

"Hell." He thumped his forehead. "I never considered you might not want to sail again. Hey, no sweat if this is a problem for you. I can put this puppy on the market before close of business today."

"You would do that for me?"

"It's just a thing," he answered without hesitation.

"I'm not so sure about that." Her mind filled with an image of Carson on his ship whether it was on the water or in the sky. "At the very least it's a piece of who you are, a way to center yourself."

"I've found a new center."

This moment had been so very much worth waiting for. "Carson, I don't have a problem with sailing. I'm not that faint of heart."

"I never thought you were. You're the strongest person I've ever met." He traced her jaw with callused fingers that rasped so gently against her skin before pointing outside again. "Actually I didn't bring you here just to see the boat. Look closer. I had the shop do one repair right away. See? There. She finally has a name."

Nikki searched, squinted, until she could decipher— "Isis. For my Egyptian project perhaps?"

How fun, Isis finding a flyboy, defying even the constraints of geography and history. A whimsical, romantic notion.

"Most definitely inspired by you and your teaching." He slid his arm along the back of the seat and cupped her shoulder.

"Of course a bit of the legend is backward." She sank against his arm and into spinning out the symbolism of his thoughtful gesture. "Isis saved Osiris from drowning, but you saved me that day in the harbor."

"Honey, you saved me from drowning in ways that have nothing to do with water." He hooked a knuckle on her chin to tip her face toward his. "Knowing you has turned my life around, grounded me, lets me fly, everything at once. The way I remember the story of Isis, she brought Osiris back twice."

"So this is our second chance?"

"If you want it to be." His forehead rested against hers. "I love you, Nikki. I know the words aren't fancy or impressively multisyllabic, but I mean it with everything inside me and look forward to showing you every day for the rest of my life, if you'll let me."

Her arms slid around his broad shoulders only to discover he was shaking as hard as she was. "God, Carson, I've been in love with you for almost three years."

"I'm sorry I wasn't the man I should be then, but I swear to try my damnedest to be worthy of your trust."

"I had some growing up to do myself." How strange to remember at this moment that she'd always told her students perfect wasn't required, only a best effort. Yet, she'd been expecting perfection from her parents, Carson, herself even, and because of that, she'd almost missed out on the purest perfection of all—true love.

His arms tightened. "I don't deserve you."

She arched back to stare him straight in the eyes. "Bull."

"What?

She flicked the zipper tab on his flight suit. "You deserve me and I totally deserve you. Although maybe you'd better not hold me to that when we have an argument, because I'm sure we will sometime since that's a part of loving and living, too." Perfect in its imperfection.

"As long as we get to make up and wake up in each other's arms." A passion she recognized well flamed to life in his blue eyes.

Nikki snuggled closer against his chest again, need sparking to life stronger, hinting it might be time to burn rubber back to her place. "Awaken to desire."

"Always," he whispered the promise against her lips.

Always.

Waking up in his arms.

She liked the sound of that very, very much….

* * * * *

We're thrilled to bring you four bestselling collections that we know you'll love…

Nights of Passion
Anne Mather

By Request

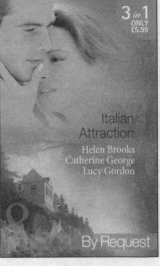

Italian Attraction

Helen Brooks
Catherine George
Lucy Gordon

By Request

featuring

by Anne Mather

MENDEZ'S MISTRESS

BEDDED FOR THE ITALIAN'S PLEASURE

THE PREGNANCY AFFAIR

featuring

THE ITALIAN TYCOON'S BRIDE
by Helen Brooks

AN ITALIAN ENGAGEMENT
by Catherine George

ONE SUMMER IN ITALY…
by Lucy Gordon

MILLS & BOON®

On sale from
15th April 2011

By Request

0411/05b

...Make sure you don't miss out on these fabulous stories!

The Elliotts: Secret Affairs
Susan Crosby
Heidi Betts
Charlene Sands

3 in 1
ONLY
£5.99

By Request

Blackhawk Desires
Barbara McCauley

ONLY
£5.99

By Request

featuring

THE FORBIDDEN TWIN
by Susan Crosby

MR AND MISTRESS
by Heidi Betts

HEIRESS BEWARE
by Charlene Sands

featuring

by Barbara McCauley

BLACKHAWK'S BETRAYAL

BLACKHAWK'S BOND

BLACKHAWK'S AFFAIR

On sale from 6th May 2011

*Available at WHSmith, Tesco, ASDA, Eason
and all good bookshops*

www.millsandboon.co.uk